A SAGA OF PASSION AND COURAGE SWEEPING OVER LAND AND SEA

Magnificent Oakhurst Manor—a plantation ruled now by the most violent of the Beauforts, where a beautiful freed black woman returned on a visit, and was trapped as a slave of hideous lust

Glittering New Orleans—where a beautiful heiress yielded to the sensual skill of a man old enough to be her father, and discovered she had committed the most horrifying sin of all

The most romantic capital of Europe—Vienna, where the true master of Oakhurst risked his life against fearful odds for his country's future and his own honor

The unmapped American Rockies—where a former Southern aristocrat became a legendary Mountain Man with killing skills to match any savage's and a burning hunger that no one woman could satisfy

All are part of the vast landscape of the latest, greatest novel in the mightiest epic ever to spring from the excitement and enthralling drama that was and is America.

LION OF OAKHURST

Big Bestsellers from SIGNET

To order these titles,
please use coupon on the
last page of this book.

Lion
of Oakhurst

(Third in the *Oakhurst* series)

By
Walter Reed Johnson

A SIGNET BOOK

NEW AMERICAN LIBRARY

TIMES MIRROR

COPYRIGHT © 1979 BY BOOK CREATIONS, INC.

Produced by Lyle Kenyon Engel

 SIGNET TRADEMARK REG. U.S. PAT. OFF. AND FOREIGN COUNTRIES
REGISTERED TRADEMARK—MARCA REGISTRADA
HECHO EN CHICAGO, U.S.A.

SIGNET, CLASSICS, MENTOR, PLUME AND MERIDIAN BOOKS
are published by The New American Library, Inc.,
1301 Avenue of the Americas, New York, New York 10019

FIRST SIGNET PRINTING, SEPTEMBER, 1979

1 2 3 4 5 6 7 8 9

PRINTED IN THE UNITED STATES OF AMERICA

LION
OF
OAKHURST

1

For years, more years than he could remember, Jerry Beaufort had nurtured his secret plan: his father and stepmother had to die. Then Oakhurst Manor, the most prized plantation in South Carolina, if not of the entire South, would be his.

Now, after scheming and temporizing, refining his plans and exercising a patience that was alien to him, he was ready to act.

Others, if they knew what he had in mind, might think him shortsighted and even stupid. If he waited long enough, he would inherit the magnificent estate, with its superb manor house and subsidiary buildings, its fine fields of cotton and tobacco, corn and vegetables, that required the labor of more than five hundred slaves. But Jerry lacked that patience. For many reasons.

His principal obstacle, as always, was his father. Jeremy Beaufort, now in his mid-forties, was one of those larger-than-life men whom no son could hope to emulate and who constantly made Jerry feel inferior. Papa's accomplishments were legion. A lawyer by training, he was one of the leading planters in the state, an authentic naval hero of the War of 1812, and, serving with the rank of commodore in the U.S. Navy, the man who had cleared the Caribbean Sea of notorious buccaneers who had preyed on the shipping of many nations. If that weren't enough, Papa owned one of the largest and most prosperous fleets of commercial ships in the country.

Even his attitudes were galling. Instead of ordering his overseer to whip the slaves in order to squeeze the last ounce of effort from them, he treated them with a compassion that was unique in the South. Ever since his own adventures in Africa he had adopted a humane attitude toward them that convinced Jerry his father was a nigger-lover.

Hell, he knew it. Look at Papa's long and close friendship with the Bantu prince, M'Bwana, who had risen to the rank of captain, distinguished himself in action against the buccaneers, and died in the final assault on their mountain stronghold in Santo Domingo. M'Bwana, his wife, Kai—who looked white and possibly was white, although she came from Algiers—and their son, Lance, had lived for years at Oakhurst Manor as the equals of the master and his family. Soon Jerry's thoughts would return to Lance, whom he also hated.

But someone else stood ahead of Lance on the list of those he loathed. His stepmother. Mrs. Jeremy Beaufort. Lisa. With her clipped English accent and her ravishing red-haired beauty. Even now, in her early forties, she was incomparably lovely. But Jerry despised her because she had taken the place of his late mother, the sainted Sarah.

Oh, Lisa made Papa happy, all right, but why shouldn't she? After all, she was the mistress of Oakhurst Manor, one of the first ladies of America, queen of her own domain. With a town house in Charleston, too, where she entertained people like Vice President John C. Calhoun, governors, and visiting dignitaries. Yes, and when she and Papa went up to Washington City they actually stayed at the White House as guests of President Andrew Jackson, who was Papa's good friend. It simply wasn't fair that some people seemed to enjoy every benefit life had to offer.

But Jerry knew the secret that Lisa and Papa had buried in their past. They had been lovers before Jeremy and Sarah married, and resumed the relationship after the marriage. To be sure, Mama had forgiven Papa before she died, telling him she had known of the relationship for years and that she realized their mutual attraction had been too great for them to resist. Jerry knew she had said it because he had eavesdropped outside the door. Well, if Mama had chosen to forgive them, that had been her business. Jerry intended to avenge her memory.

Not that Mama herself had been all that much of a saint. For years she had been sweet on Lester Howard, the Oakhurst Manor field overseer. He had shown the sort of person he was, after Mama's death, when he had married Dolores, a mulatto and former Santo Domingo prostitute, and had moved out west with her. The mere fact that Mama had even deigned to look at Howard proved how faulty her own character had been.

But the very worst of her sins had been her tendency to favor Lance over the son she had brought into the world.

Lance! Just thinking of him made Jerry's stomach turn. Lance, who was taller, stronger, and more agile. Lance, who had earned a *cum laude* degree at the College of New Jersey at Princeton, while he himself had been dismissed from William and Mary because of his drinking and gambling. Lance, whose horsemanship was second to none, whose aim with a pistol was deadly, and who handled a sword with the expertise of a born dragoon. As if that weren't enough, M'Bwana had taught Lance countless tricks of the African jungle, including the art of throwing a short, two-foot sword with lethal effect.

Perhaps the chief reason Jerry hated Papa was that Jeremy had actually sired Lance, making the younger man his own half brother. After M'Bwana's death he had legally recognized Lance's paternity, with Uncle Scott Emerson drawing up the papers, and Lance now called himself Lance Beaufort. In Jerry's opinion he was an unrefined barbarian, and disgraced an old and honorable name.

Not many people shared that opinion. Lance's mother, Kai, now Mrs. Scott Emerson and mistress of the adjoining plantation, doted on her darling paragon, as did Uncle Scott. As did Papa and Lisa. Well, the older generation was entitled to its warped opinions. His own time would come.

What hurt and confused Jerry was that Carolyn Emerson showed a distinct preference for Lance. Carrie, freckle-faced and scrawny while the three of them were growing up together, who had developed into a goddess with long honey-blond hair, delicate features, and a flawless figure. Carrie, for whose smiles every young blood in South Carolina willingly would sacrifice his soul.

But even Carrie wasn't as perfect as all that. Jerry knew things about her past of which even she was unaware, and he could thank his lifelong habit of listening outside closed doors for that. Carrie, who made her home with the Emersons, was the daughter of Scott's sister, Alicia, and believed her father was dead. Ha! Only Jerry knew that she was illegitimate and that her father was very much alive. Emile Duchamp was a New Orleans gambler and brothel owner, and Alicia had returned to him years ago, deserting her baby daughter. For all anybody knew, she was still living with him.

Fair enough. Jerry had plans for Lance, and for Carrie, too.

Refusing to admit, even to himself, that he was jealous of his half brother, Jerry was convinced his only reasons for disliking Lance were financial. Someday Lance would inherit Jeremy Beaufort's shipping interests and would become wealthy in his own right, which was outrageous. After disposing of Papa and Lisa, Jerry would take care of Lance, too, and would gain possession of the merchant fleet. It was no idle boast to tell himself that the day wasn't far distant when he would be the wealthiest and most powerful man in the state.

He was far too cunning to dwell on the possibility of killing Lance. The risk was too great, thanks to Lance's various skills. No, there was an infinitely better way.

That way involved Carrie, the Trelawney heiress, who was generously mentioned in Papa's will, too. Jerry wanted her. Not as his wife, under any circumstances! The purity of the Beaufort line had to be restored, and nothing would impel him to marry a bastard. All the same, he planned to bed her and pin the blame on Lance.

The scheme was so tidy that it elated Jerry. The authorities would send Lance to prison, and under state law he would lose his inheritance, which would go—automatically—to his half brother.

As for Carrie, she'd be thrown out by the highly moral Uncle Scott and Kai Emerson, and if she went the way of her mother, it would serve her right for her failure to appreciate the finer qualities of Jerry Beaufort. When properly played, retribution was the most wonderful of games.

Tonight, after years of planning and countless painstaking experiments, was the start. Jerry knew exactly what had to be done, precisely how to go about doing it.

The very age in which they lived was conducive to the taking of risks. The secure, snug world of the Eastern Seaboard states that had comprised the original United States of America was gone forever, largely because the effects of the Louisiana Purchase, made three decades earlier by President Thomas Jefferson, were just now being felt. America had expanded far beyond the Mississippi River, and the tide of immigration rolling westward soon would reach the Rocky Mountains.

President Andrew Jackson had a vision of a strong, united nation more than holding its place with the major powers of the world, but Jerry felt contempt for that point of view. He liked his bailiwick, intending to make it his own, and he agreed wholeheartedly with South Carolina's greatest citizen, John C. Calhoun, who insisted that the rights of the individual states were more important than those of the country as a whole, and who advocated the theory that an individual state had the basic right to nullify any law passed by the federal government that it disliked.

Calhoun lived up to his principles, no two ways about it, even resigning as vice president of the United States, thus thumbing his nose at President Jackson, and then having himself elected to the United States Senate, where he could torment the administration. Calhoun was Jerry's kind of man, and it went without saying that Papa and Lance were staunch admirers of Andrew Jackson.

Hell, Jackson was no gentleman, and he lacked class. The rabble he had allowed to inundate the White House after his inauguration on March 4, 1829, had set an example for all that had followed in the past few years. Jerry had heard it said that the boots of farmers and trappers had deposited mud in the corridors of every government building in Washington City, and he believed the stories.

The time had come when the rabble needed to be taught a lesson. Jackson had carried his experiment in democracy too far, even running the country with the aid of his so-called Kitchen Cabinet, cronies with whom he sat around the White House drinking raw frontier whiskey. Not even Calhoun, it appeared, was alert to the real dangers of the subversive influences that were corrupting the country.

If Jerry had his way, the nation would be governed by a handful of aristocrats, men born to rule. The way so many South Carolina plantations were run. Certainly not the way Papa, with Lance's encouragement, ran Oakhurst Manor, coddling slaves and even allowing those who wanted their freedom to migrate to the North. Back in Grandpa Beaufort's day tobacco and rice and various vegetables had been principal crops here, but any sensible man knew that Oakhurst Manor now depended exclusively on her cotton output. The place would show the right kind of profit only if the slaves were made to work as hard as they could. It was sickening just to hear people saying that Papa and those like him were "humanitarians." Like Andrew Jackson, they had to be eliminated for the country's good.

Jerry heard voices in the second-floor corridor, and opened his bedroom door a crack, just enough to see his father and stepmother emerging from the master suite.

Lisa Beaufort still looked like a girl rather than a mature matron. Her burnished copper hair was piled high on her head, no lines marred her lovely face, and her gown of yellow silk clung to her superb figure. As always, her face was animated as she looked up at her husband.

There was gray at Jeremy Beaufort's temples, and his powerfully built body was beginning to thicken, but his step was light, and he, too, looked far younger than his years. Squeezing his wife's hand, he grinned at her. "You're so beautiful I'm breathless," he said.

"If I am," Lisa replied, "it's because of your love."

They started down the broad staircase arm in arm, and

Jerry laughed without mirth as he closed his door soundlessly.

Two of his windows faced the front of the house, with its white-columned portico and long, tree-lined driveway. He stood there, concealed by heavy draperies, and made no move until he saw them leave in the lightweight carriage they used for short rides. It was typical of Jeremy to be doing his own driving, and his son heartily disapproved, thinking that a man of his stature should be attended by servants at all times.

When the sound of the horses' hooves and the creaking of the phaeton's wheels faded, Jerry's seeming lethargy vanished. He hurried to a clothes closet and unlocked a large metal strongbox that had been stored there. From it he removed its only contents, a long coil of thin rope that had been impregnated with tar. Attached to it and dangling from one end was an even longer coil of similarly treated thin string.

Forcing himself to walk at a sedate pace, Jerry went to the bedchamber occupied by his father and stepmother, and carefully placed the coiled rope under the thick mattress of the huge four-poster bed. Making sure the string was still attached to one end, he loosened the rest and dropped it out of the window. He had practiced that throw many times, and his aim was true: it landed just beyond the flower beds that his late mother had cultivated with such loving devotion.

Walking downstairs as though he had no care in the world, Jerry ordered a horse brought from the stables, and while he waited he wandered to the flower beds. There he stretched out the long string, fastening it to thorns on rosebushes to keep it off the ground. Finally he lighted the free end with a silver tinderbox and flint of the sort that gentlemen who smoked carried in their waistcoat pockets on social occasions.

The string burned very slowly with a faint, almost smokeless glow. The endless hours of experimenting with tar to determine precisely how much to use were paying priceless dividends.

The string would burn for five hours before it reached the bedroom of his father and stepmother. By that time they would have returned from the evening's gala at Trelawney, and if they followed their usual habits, they would retire immediately. As Jerry well knew, they almost invariably made love after a social evening.

Another full hour would pass before the fire reached the coil of rope beneath the mattress, and by that time Jeremy and Lisa would be asleep. The rope was far more heavily impregnated than the string, and within seconds the entire four-poster would be enveloped in flames. The couple would die without ever realizing what had happened.

As for Jerry, he would be much in evidence at the gala, ten miles away. Thirty or forty people would see him there when the fire broke out, and no one would connect him with it in any way. He would be appropriately devastated when he learned of the tragedy.

He sauntered to the portico, where a groom waited obediently with a saddled gelding. Jerry swished his riding crop because of the pleasure it gave him to see the sudden alarm in the slave's eyes. Then he mounted, and forcing himself not to glance in the direction of the flower beds, he started off on the ride to Trelawney.

Kai Emerson, matronly at forty, stood in the sitting room of the Trelawney master-bedroom suite and inspected her ward with great care, missing no detail. "Carrie," she said, "I was considered rather pretty in my day, and Lisa Beaufort was gorgeous. But neither of us compares with you."

Scott Emerson concurred as he beamed at his niece and ward. "That's true," he said. "I just wish your grandparents were here to see you, Carrie. How proud they'd be."

Carrie Emerson looked at her reflection in the long mirror set in the doorway, and knew they weren't exaggerating. Her long hair resembled spun gold, her blue eyes were enormous, and her full lips, delicately tinted, were a glowing pink. The low, square-cut neckline of her ivory satin gown revealed an expanse of unblemished skin above her décolletage. Her breasts were high and firm, her waist was tiny, her hips were gently rounded, and her long legs, among her best features, were concealed beneath layers of petticoats. She was slender and taller than most girls of nineteen, and her beauty was enhanced by an expression of high intelligence.

Carrie's glance did not linger on her reflection. The truth of the matter was that her appearance bored her, perhaps because she took her beauty for granted. Unlike the Sperling sisters and some of her other friends, she had no great interest in clothes and cosmetics. It was far more fun to canter across the fields or read either the novels of Sir Walter Scott or the essays of Washington Irving.

Besides, something else was uppermost in her mind at the moment. "I hope Lance arrives in time for the party," she said. "I just wish Uncle Jeremy hadn't picked today to send him off to Charleston on business."

Scott managed to keep a straight face. "Crises have a way of erupting by themselves in the shipping industry."

Lights of humor appeared in Kai's eyes. "Never fear," she said. "Lance is always on time."

Carrie glanced at the grandfather clock in the corner of the sitting room. "Then he'll have to hurry. The guests will be arriving soon."

A grinning young man tapped on the open sitting-room door, his hard-muscled bulk filling the frame. Lance had the Beaufort height and brawn, lacking only in Jerry, yet with it there were elements of Kai's sinewy grace. His dark brown hair was clubbed at the nape of the neck, and, as always he was modestly if expensively dressed in a dark, unobtrusive suit. His teeth gleamed in his tanned, strong face, and his hazel eyes were tender as he looked at Carrie. "When I make a promise," he declared, "I always keep my word."

Advancing into the room, he kissed his mother lightly, then shook his stepfather's hand. "Your servant, Mama. And yours, Papa Emerson." Turning again to Carrie, he bowed low. "I'm shocked by your lack of faith in me, ma'am."

Carrie flushed, but held her ground. It was odd how her relationship with the twenty-two-year-old Lance had changed after he had come home from college. Throughout their childhood they had enjoyed an easy camaraderie, but now a new element had been added, one that constantly excited and challenged both of them. "I find your impudence dismaying, sir," she replied.

"Impudent, am I?"

"I suggest you wipe off your boots before the guests arrive," Carrie told him, maintaining her advantage.

Lance chuckled. "If you have eyes in your head, ma'am—and you do, as any man who has been haunted by them well knows—you'll see my boots are already wiped. Now, as I hear carriages in the driveway, may I escort you to the door?"

It was typical that no one else had yet heard the sounds of approaching guests. Lance's hearing, like his other senses, was extraordinary.

Carrie's sigh was exaggerated. "I'll think about it. Don't rush me."

"There's no time to think." Lance slipped her hand through his arm, and inclining his head to his mother and stepfather, led her off down the stairs.

The older couple followed at a more sedate pace.

"I wonder," Kai said with a smile, "whether they realize yet that they're in love. It's so difficult to remember what one thinks and feels at their age."

"They're moving toward recognition, I believe, but they haven't quite reached that point yet," Scott said. "Once Lance is aware of it," he added, "he'll lose no time sitting Jeremy and me down for a long talk in depth. In which he'll explore every facet of the present and the future."

"Lisa and I have been planning the wedding for months," Kai said demurely.

Her husband looked startled for a moment, then chuckled.

"We've also been debating where they should live. I want them here, and Lisa wants them at Oakhurst Manor."

"Neither is appropriate," Scott said. "Jeremy and I are agreed they should have a home of their own, and we're seriously thinking of buying a house for them in Charleston."

"In the city? Both of them love the outdoors. They go for a canter together every morning, regardless of whether Lance is sleeping here or at Oakhurst Manor. Carrie never stops experimenting with flowers and vegetables. And you know how much Lance loves to hunt and fish. That's his most important legacy from M'Bwana."

"They can always come to the country on weekends," Scott said. "But Jeremy is gradually giving Lance more and more control of the shipping interests he's going to inherit one day, so he'll soon be spending most of his working days in Charleston. Besides, it will be good discipline for him. And for Carrie, too."

"I've never known two young people less in need of new disciplines," Kai replied. "Both of them exercise so much self-control they sometimes frighten me."

"They're wise," Scott said. "There are deep, wild feelings seething inside both of them, and if those emotions are ever unleashed, may the Lord have mercy on anyone who stands in their path. There's an element of Alicia in Carrie that the girl doesn't recognize, and Lance takes after you and Jeremy. Not the way you are now, but as you once were."

Kai halted and looked up at her husband in mock anger. "Are you accusing me of being staid, Mr. Emerson?"

Scott ignored the knock at the front door that heralded the arrival of the first guests and hugged her. "Never, Mrs. Emerson. But I try to keep it secret that I'm married to a spitfire."

Recovering their aplomb, they advanced with great dignity to the front door.

By the standards of 1830 the gala was a small, informal party, a meeting of friends and neighbors from other plantations. Such a gathering gave the men an opportunity to talk business and politics in groups, while the ladies discussed church affairs, styles, and recipes, as well as exchanging the latest gossip.

According to an unwritten but rigidly observed code, the older couples gathered indoors, with the men preferring whiskey to the punch that servants were ladling out of cut-glass bowls in the yard. The young people, after paying their respects to their host and hostess, promptly adjourned to the lawn, where the scene was lighted by lanterns and where supper eventually would be served.

No fiddlers or other musicians had been hired, as the occasion didn't warrant such ostentation, but youth was not to be denied music. Two of the young men and one of the girls had brought their violins, another youth removed a fife from his saddlebag, and Lance produced a small

West Indian drum, which M'Bwana had brought him from the Caribbean many years earlier, for a friend to play.

So youth had its music, and it escaped the attention of few that Carrie and Lance danced together most of the time. Many other couples joined them on the lawn, but Jerry Beaufort stood alone in the shadows, taking little part in the festivities.

He had promised himself that this was one evening he should stay sober, but the punch, which contained brandywine, rum, and fruit juices, was delicious as well as warming, and gradually his resolve weakened. This was the night for which he had been waiting, the most important night of his life. The night his hated father and stepmother would die. So he had real cause for celebration.

When the amateur musicians rested and sipped cups of punch, Carrie and Lance made certain that the needs of the various guests were attended to, and then wandered together to the far end of the lawn, beyond the perimeter of the lights. They strolled together without quite realizing what they were doing, both of them unconsciously seeking a few moments of privacy, and it was a natural gesture for the girl to take her companion's arm.

Lance broke the silence. "Riding into Charleston this morning, I found myself doing a great deal of serious thinking," he said, "and I did the same coming home."

"Is that good or bad?" she asked, using the bantering tone of their childhood.

Lance halted abruptly and turned to her, his face suddenly solemn. "That, I believe, will depend on you."

Carrie's smile faded, and she returned his gaze.

"For the past six months," he said, "I've been earning a very solid salary at the shipping company. At supper last night Papa gave me a whopping increase, along with a share of the profits. It's been no secret that someday those interests will be mine. But right now—for the first time—I'm financially independent."

"I . . . I'm glad for you," Carrie murmured.

"He also hinted rather strongly that he thinks I ought to establish residence in the city, and I agree with him. I've been busier and busier there, and I'm fortunate that I'll be able to come to Oakhurst Manor and Trelawney on week-ends."

"I'll miss you," she said.

All at once Lance became uncomfortable, shifting his weight from one foot to the other. "That," he said, "is what I wanted to talk to you about."

Carrie knew now what he had in mind, and waited.

His embarrassment increased. "You and I have been to-gether all of our lives. We were brought up as brother and sister. You see what I mean."

She looked wide-eyed. "I'm afraid I don't."

"It occurred to me to wonder if you might be interested in moving into town, too."

It was difficult for Carrie to conceal a smile. "You and I are no longer children, you know, and we aren't actually blood relatives."

"My whole point exactly," Lance said, and stammered. "The truth is that I've become very attached to you. That is to say, my feelings aren't what they were when we were younger. I've been realizing it more and more since I came home from college."

"What is it you realize?" she asked, gently prodding him.

"Damnation, Carrie, how can you be so stupid? I'm try-ing to tell you I love you!"

"Stop shouting. There's nothing wrong with my hear-ing."

Lance grasped her by the shoulders. "Will you or won't you marry me?"

Carrie's humor faded, and she looked up at him with moist eyes. "Of course I will. I've known for a long time that you love me. And although you haven't asked, I hap-pen to love you, too."

He stared at her for a moment, his expression incredu-lous. Then, conscious of his great strength and not wanting to hurt her, he tenderly took her in his arms.

The world seemed to spin faster as they kissed, and both were breathless when they drew apart.

Carrie was shaken. "We'd best go back to the party," she said.

Lance nodded. "I'll talk to Papa and to Papa Emerson

this very night," he said as they started back toward the circle of light.

"It would be wiser to wait until tomorrow, I think," she told him.

As always, her judgment was better than his, and he agreed. "I'll wager they'll be surprised."

The girl made no comment, but knew better. Unless she was badly mistaken, the older Beauforts and Emersons had been anticipating a declaration of their love for a long time. Only Lance himself had been unaware of feelings that were obvious to everyone else.

Soon after they rejoined the party, an "informal" supper was laid out on wooden tables on the lawn. Because of the nature of the affair, the repast was regarded as simple.

One of the staples, served at every party in the area, was a Charleston favorite, she-crab soup, a thick chowder that included roe as well as crabmeat. A lighter alternative, for those who preferred it, was a gumbo made with a chicken base. Carrie made no mention of the fact that the okra, onions, celery, baby green beans, and other vegetables in the gumbo had been grown in her own garden.

Roasted turkeys, complete with dressing, had already been sliced. So had a number of smoked hams, their delicate flavor immediately indicating to everyone present that they had come from Oakhurst Manor; Jeremy Beaufort's smokehouse was said to be the best in the state. There was steaming barbecued beef, too, cooked to a turn so the meat flaked, and served with a hot sauce that was one of Kai's culinary secrets.

Lisa Beaufort's contribution was a recipe for meat pasties that she had learned in Jamaica. Beef and pork were ground finely and mixed with herbs and peppers, with each portion then wrapped completely in dough and baked over a slow fire. The juices were sealed inside the meat pies, and the guests washed them down with mugs of mead, a honey-based beer.

There were varieties of cold meats and hot breads, too, as well as heaping bowls of lettuce, cucumbers, and radishes, the dish being known as "Italian salad greens."

For dessert there were pecan pies made from an old Georgia recipe that had been in the Emerson family for generations, as well as fruit pies made with locally grown peaches, blueberries, and strawberries.

A mild wine punch was served with the meal, and for the few who preferred something stronger there was whiskey from Pennsylvania, rum from New England, and gin imported from Holland. But only Jerry Beaufort and a few of his cronies drank to excess.

Soon after the meal ended and the younger people returned to their dancing, the members of the older generation began to take their leave.

Jeremy Beaufort couldn't stop yawning, and a smiling Lisa said to Kai and Scott, "I think our time has come. If we stay much longer, he'll fall asleep and I'll have to drive the phaeton home."

Jerry stood in the shadows and watched them with glittering eyes as they drove off. Good-bye, Papa, he thought. Good-bye, Lisa. I'll see both of you in hell.

The merrymaking continued for the better part of another hour, but eventually the younger crowd grew tired, too. Kai and Scott were relieved; they had stayed up to act as chaperons for the unmarried, but their vigil was drawing to an end.

It occurred to Scott that social life on a plantation had changed since his own youth, when the frontier mentality had still prevailed in the Carolinas and Georgia, and the memories of General Francis Marion playing hide-and-seek with the British in the War of Independence had been strong.

Men like Scott Emerson and Jeremy Beaufort had fought in the War of 1812, so they had gained a lively appreciation of the freedom they had struggled to preserve. Today's younger generation was softer, perhaps because no dangers threatened them. Even the Indian menace had been ended, when today's young men had been children, in General Andrew Jackson's whirlwind campaigns in Alabama and Florida.

Maybe Scott did youth an injustice, and he hoped the young would rally to the colors, as his generation had done, in time of need. Changes in the nation's economy were making people soft, and they were taking for granted what their elders had worked so hard to attain. The great plantations were prospering, and so were the businessmen of Charleston and other cities. Yet any man of vision knew it was the farms of the West that were responsible, and that it was the produce carried down the Ohio and Mississippi rivers that was making America buoyant.

Free land was the real answer, of course. Any dirt farmer or big-city artisan who failed could pull up stakes, go West, and make a fresh start on a tract of one hundred and sixty acres that the federal government gave him free of charge. Various interests were nipping away at the president, trying to persuade or force him to change the policies he and his predecessors had followed, but they weren't making much headway. Andy Jackson wasn't the sort who gave in to pressure.

Scott grinned when Lance and Carrie joined him and Kai on the portico to bid farewell to the departing company. Lance gave an older man hope. He would get along anywhere, under any circumstances.

Suddenly a young man pointed a finger and raised his voice in a hoarse shout. "Fire!"

Far off across the open fields of cotton and tobacco they saw flames leaping toward the night sky from the direction of Oakhurst Manor.

Most of the company were so stunned they were unable to move.

But Lance Beaufort reacted instantly. Not wasting a second, he ran to the stable behind the main house, and there he went directly to the stall of Bantu, his favorite stallion. Rather than lose precious moments saddling the horse, he leaped onto the animal's bare back and galloped off at full tilt toward the home of his father and stepmother.

He was almost out of sight before the others recovered from their astonishment and prepared to follow him.

It was said that when Jeremy Beaufort had been a young man he had ridden from Trelawney to Oakhurst Manor on one notable occasion in eight minutes. Tonight his son covered the distance in no more than five.

As Lance drew near, he saw that the fire was coming from the second-floor master-bedroom suite and that the rooms directly above it were engulfed, too. A number of servants were milling around in the yard, but with no one to direct them, they were helpless.

"Form a bucket brigade and bring up water from the pond!" Lance shouted as he dismounted. Not pausing to see whether his instructions were followed, he mounted the stairs three at a time, then put his shoulder to the door at the entrance to the suite and crashed through it into the sitting room.

Thick clouds of smoke enveloped him, causing him to choke and filling his eyes with tears.

He dropped to his hands and knees and fought his way to the bedroom.

There he found an inferno, and by the light of the flames he saw a sight that made his blood run cold. Lisa was lying on the floor, sprawled grotesquely, and it was impossible to determine whether she was still alive.

Jeremy was wandering around the room, and appeared crazed, lacking any sense of direction. His swallow-tailed coat was on fire, but he did not appear to know it.

"Papa!" Lance shouted, and instantly bore him to the floor, rolling him over and over until the flames were extinguished.

"Can't see," Jeremy gasped. "But never mind me. Help Lisa. I . . . I pulled her to the floor. But something happened to my eyes. Can't find her now."

Lance picked up Lisa as easily as though he were lifting a doll, and slinging her over one shoulder, he put his free arm around his father. "I have Lisa," he said. "Hold on tight, and I'll get both of you out of here."

Inch by inch, foot by foot, he fought his way to the sitting room, where the furniture was already in flames. Inch by inch, foot by foot, he struggled toward the central corridor beyond.

Lisa moaned.

At least she was still alive, Lance thought, and redoubled his efforts.

Only his physical strength and his equally great determination enabled him to reach safety. Then, still carrying Lisa, still guiding his blinded father, he made his way down the broad staircase to the fresh air of the lawn.

By the time the company from Trelawney arrived at Oakhurst Manor, Lance had the situation under control. House servants and field hands had formed an efficient bucket brigade, and the flames were dying down. As a subsequent investigation would prove, only the master-bedroom suite and three smaller rooms above it had been destroyed.

A servant had been sent for a physician, but as luck would have it, Dr. Pickens had spent the evening at Trelawney and was part of the arriving group.

Under his ministrations Lisa soon regained consciousness, and aside from a few superficial burns, was none the worse for her terrible experience.

Jeremy's condition was far more serious. One side of his face and a portion of his body had been seared, and cocoa butter was smeared on his burns. Worst of all, he had lost his eyesight.

The last to reach Oakhurst Manor was Jerry, prepared to accept the condolences of relatives and friends.

"The damage can be repaired without any trouble," he heard someone say as he approached the group on the lawn.

Then he saw Lisa, standing on her own feet and bending over Jeremy.

He heard his father speak in a lucid voice, even though it was obvious he was in great pain.

"You can thank Lance," an emotional Scott Emerson said to Jerry. "He saved the lives of your father and Lisa, God be praised."

Jerry moistened his dry lips and forced himself to say the right things to the right people, but he was seething. His efforts had been in vain, his long years of planning and working toward one goal had been wasted.

"Thanks" to Lance.

Very well, he would begin again. Nothing would prevent him from achieving his ends. But he would learn from his experience, and this time he would first dispose of Lance before getting rid of his father and Lisa.

2

It had to be true that politics made strange bedfellows. The austere Senator Daniel Webster of Massachusetts and the convivial, equally brilliant Senator Henry Clay of Kentucky had despised each other for years, and as rivals for the leadership of the Whig party they remained wary of each other. But it was their mutual opposition to President Jackson that brought them together.

They sat together in the living room of Webster's modest boardinghouse suite in Washington City. The host offered a bottle to his guest, who declined it, then poured himself a stiff shot of rum. His colleagues knew, as his constituents did not, that he enjoyed his liquor. "Henry," he said in the deep, resonant voice that made him America's greatest living orator, "I support Jackson without qualification in his defense of a strong Union, but that's where I draw the line. Most of his policies are crazy."

"Well, he's wrong to fight for the abolition of the United States Bank," Clay replied, enumerating on his fingers. "He's wrong to be handing out free land to anybody who wants it. He's opening the West faster than the country can absorb the expansion."

19

"And he's dead wrong to be paying subsidies to American shipping companies. I believe in a strong American merchant marine, but not at the expense of the American taxpayer."

"Precisely," Clay said. "Take the case of Commodore Jeremy Beaufort in South Carolina. Now, I have no brief against Beaufort. He served the country well when he rid the Caribbean Sea of the pirates who were causing great damage to the shipping of the whole civilized world, and I like him."

"I happen to admire Beaufort myself," Webster said. "I'm afraid you've picked a poor example, Henry."

"Not at all. He set up his merchant fleet with Jackson's help, and now he's a firm supporter of the president. When you figure there are literally hundreds, even thousands of men around the country whom Andy Jackson has enlisted in his cause that way, I don't see how in the devil we can fight him."

Webster's grin was weary. "Well, we certainly can't beat him at his own game. He gives every good government job that comes along to deserving Democrats, while the Whigs starve. He has the jobs to give, and we're powerless to stop him."

"Like it or not, and I don't," Senator Henry Clay said, "we're in for a long, dry spell while Andy Jackson continues to run the country his own way. On second thought, Dan, I think I'll have a drop of that splendid rum."

Lance looked up at the Beaufort crest on a carved plaque above the library fireplace, and silently read the family motto: *Aspera ad virtutem est via.* "It is a difficult road that leads to virtue."

No man better knew the truth of that saying than Jeremy Beaufort, who had endured many tribulations but had triumphed over all of them. Now he was engaged in his greatest struggle, a battle for his eyesight, and the outcome was in doubt.

His younger son, who had just arrived at Oakhurst Manor after spending several days in Charleston, began to pace. He had learned nothing about his father's condition since going off to the city, and now that he had come home again, a feeling of anxiety threatened to overwhelm him.

His extraordinary sense of hearing told him that someone—a woman—had left the bedchamber that Jeremy was using while the master suite was being repaired, and was moving down the central staircase. A moment later he recognized Carrie's footsteps, and in spite of his worries, he was smiling when she entered the library.

They embraced and kissed silently, and not until they drew apart did Lance see there were deep, dark smudges of fatigue beneath her eyes.

Without preamble Carrie replied to his unspoken question. "Lisa and I are following the doctor's orders and keeping poultices moistened with a sassafras solution on Papa Beaufort's eyes," she said. "We've been taking turns, working around the clock, and we're under instructions not to stop until the doctor gives us the word."

"Then you don't know whether he'll recover his eyesight?"

"Not yet," she said, sinking wearily onto a leather couch. "The doctor says he can't make any predictions, not until the burns and smoke damage are completely healed."

"I see. How are his spirits?"

"You and Papa Beaufort are remarkably alike, Lance. He hasn't uttered one word of complaint, and he keeps insisting that Lisa and I stop fussing over him. It bothers him that one or the other of us is attending him day and night, even though he knows the poultices must be kept damp at all times."

"You look tired," Lance said.

"I am, a bit," Carrie admitted.

"Then you must let me substitute for you."

"Neither you nor anyone else. Lisa and I won't allow it. Your mother offered to come over from Trelawney to help out. But we insist on doing this job ourselves. He's eager to see you, so we'll go upstairs as soon as Lisa finishes feeding him his supper. At least he's beginning to regain his appetite, so that's a good sign. If you can, persuade Lisa to go over to Trelawney for her own supper. Your mother and Papa Emerson very much want her to come, and the change will do her good. She needs the diversion."

"I'll do what I can," he replied, sitting beside her and taking her hand. "What's Jerry contributing these days?"

Carrie's lovely face darkened. "Nothing," she said. "In fact, he isn't even here. He's gone off to visit some friends up in Greenville, and both Lisa and I were happy to see him go. Jerry has changed since we were children, Lance. Or maybe I see him now through different eyes. There's something about him I can't analyze. I only know he makes my skin crawl."

Lance smiled. "Oh, Jerry may be lazy and inclined to shirk his responsibilities, but he's harmless enough."

"I don't agree. I've seen him looking at you or at Papa Beaufort when he doesn't realize anyone is watching him, and I swear, there's murder in his eyes."

He chuckled indulgently. "He doesn't have the courage to shoot a rabbit or catch a fish. But never mind Jerry. We have something far more important to discuss. Us."

"What about us?"

"I've been doing a lot of thinking off in Charleston this week," Lance said. "And it strikes me we'd be selfish if we say anything right now about wanting to be married."

"That's precisely the way I feel," she replied. "I'm so relieved. I think we ought to wait until we know more about Papa Beaufort's eyes. At the very least, we should keep our plans to ourselves until he regains his strength."

"That much is settled. It places a greater burden on us, but we owe it to him—Lisa, too—to be considerate. Even though it won't be easy."

"I know," she murmured.

His grip on her hand tightened. "Carrie, I want you more than even you know. But I love you too much to compromise you before we're married. Somehow we'll manage to wait."

"Of course we will." Suddenly she straightened and became brisk. "Let's go upstairs."

Aware of the dangers of intimacy, they did not touch again as they went to Jeremy's sickroom.

The master of Oakhurst Manor was propped up in a four-poster bed, his back supported by a mound of pillows, his eyes covered with a thick, damp poultice.

Lisa, who sat beside him, was bone-weary, but smiled gamely at her stepson. "I'm so glad you're here, Lance," she said. "Your father has been fretting for hours, wondering when you'd arrive."

"Is that you, son?" Jeremy asked in a loud voice.

"I'm here, Papa." Lance bent down to kiss him on the cheek.

"Good! Did you get the Boston contract? Has the *Elizabeth* put into port from Santo Domingo yet? And what's the status of that molasses cargo—?"

"One thing at a time, Papa," Lance said gently as he interrupted. "I'll give you a full report. First, though, Carrie and I want Lisa to go over to Trelawney for supper."

"Oh, no. My place is right here," Lisa said.

"I insist," Lance said, "and so does Papa."

Jeremy was somewhat bewildered, but heard the authority in his son's voice and went along with him. "He's right, my dear, I do insist."

Lisa shook her head. "The men of this family are too much for me," she said with a helpless laugh. "I can handle you separately, but when you band together, I run up the white flag."

Lance helped her to her feet.

"I'll take charge now," Carrie told her.

Lisa bent over her husband and kissed him. "I'll be back in time to tuck you in for the night," she told him.

"Lance," Jeremy said after she had gone, "I'm damned if I'm an invalid, even if these women treat me like one."

"Of course you aren't, Papa." Lance spoke carefully, concealing his feelings. His father, the most resourceful and energetic of men, truly was an invalid now, and the knowledge was almost too much to bear.

Carrie prepared another sassafras poultice, and while she applied it Lance began to tell his father the details of new developments in the shipping business.

Jeremy heard the huskiness in his voice and tried to ignore it. He couldn't see his son's face, to be sure, but it was easy enough to guess that he was undergoing a strain. Under no circumstances, however, could Jeremy allow himself to dwell on his infirmity. If willpower could restore his sight, he would see again, and he forced himself to concentrate on his shipping business.

Suddenly, after his questions had been answered and Lance finished his recital, the presence of the young people irked him. He wanted to be alone to organize his thoughts, a luxury that had been denied him since the fire. "The breeze coming in through the window is warm," he said, "so it must be a lovely evening. Why don't you young people take a stroll down to the pond? That's what I'd do if the idiotic doctors didn't make an issue out of keeping me in bed."

"We'll stay right here with you, Papa Beaufort," Carrie said, her expression indicating to Lance that they had to be firm.

"I appreciate all you've done for me, Carrie," Jeremy said, "but it can't give you and Lance any pleasure to play nursemaid to me."

She made no reply, instead dipping a fresh poultice in a pail of lukewarm sassafras water, wringing it out, and placing it over his eyes.

"Damn it, go away for an hour, both of you, and don't come back until I send for you." Jeremy had no idea how irritable he had become.

Lance, in spite of his own strength and spirit of independence, had never disobeyed his father, and automatically rose to his feet.

Carrie's quiet nod indicated that she expected him to sit down again. "We're staying," she said sweetly.

"Boy," Jeremy said, "if this stubborn wench won't leave of her own accord, I order you to throw her over your shoulder and take her away!"

Carrie's laugh was a blend of good-humored indulgence and stubborn determination. "He wouldn't dare," she said.

Here was the escape Lance was seeking. "She's right, Papa, I wouldn't dare."

"I've seen you face crocodiles in the Everglades and kill poisonous snakes with a spear at a distance of only a few feet. Do you mean to tell me you're afraid of this slip of a girl?"

Lance grinned. "Well, not afraid, exactly, any more than you're afraid of Lisa. But I'm sure you know even better than I, Papa, that some women exercise a kind of moral authority that makes them dangerous when you cross them."

"I'm betrayed," Jeremy said, and sank back against the pillows.

Carrie was gracious in victory. "Lance will go down to the kitchen and bring you a dish of custard with crushed fresh raspberries, Papa Beaufort."

Jeremy laughed in spite of his annoyance. "You know I have a weakness for custard with raspberries. Is this my reward for surrendering?"

"I hadn't thought of it that way," she said, her voice bland.

"May the Lord help the man who marries you, girl! I feel sorry for the poor devil!"

Lance's expression, as he looked across the bed at Carrie, strongly indicated that he didn't share his father's opinion.

A physician who specialized in diseases of the eye came to Oakhurst Manor all the way from Richmond, and approved of the treatment prescribed by the local doctors. "In my profession we're expected to work miracles, Mrs. Beaufort," he told Lisa, "but my hands are tied. Even the most powerful magnifying glass isn't strong enough for me to make an accurate assessment of the damage your husband has suffered. So one guess is as good as another, and I hesitate to make a prognosis. Continue with the same treatment, and pray that it will be effective. I'd be a charlatan if I made you any promises."

The days passed and became weeks. Lisa and Carrie doggedly maintained their vigil, allowing no one else to share it with them.

"Jeremy is my husband, and I love him," Lisa told Kai and Scott Emerson when they urged her to accept help. "It's more than my duty to look after him. It's my one desire, and I won't leave his side unless and until he's cured, even if I must nurse him for the rest of our lives."

Carrie was equally adamant. "I was just an infant when my mother deserted me," she said. "Papa Beaufort gave me a home and security and love. I'm doing more than thanking him by sharing Lisa's task. It's my way of telling him that I'm returning his love in full measure."

Lance worked harder than ever, dividing his time between the shipping business in Charleston and the plantation, whose affairs he now supervised. He and Carrie had little time to themselves, and privately agreed it was just as well. Their desire for each other was so great they might have found it impossible to resist temptation had there been more opportunities to be alone.

Jerry continued to absent himself from Oakhurst Manor. He wrote a brief note to the effect that he was leaving Greenville to visit other friends in North Carolina and would return home "soon," but no more was heard from him.

Jeremy's spirits lagged, and only the constant optimism and good cheer that Lisa and Carrie exhibited sustained him.

The repair work on the master suite and third-floor rooms was completed, so the invalid was moved back to his own permanent quarters. He was strong enough now to leave his bed for several hours each day, and was conducted to an easy chair in the sitting room. There, as in the bedchamber, Lisa and Carrie took turns attending him, never leaving him alone to brood on his fate.

One afternoon, in the sitting room, Carrie was reading to him from the essays of Washington Irving, whose writing he enjoyed, and occasionally she paused long enough to apply another in the unending stream of poultices. Lisa was taking a nap in the adjoining bedchamber, and Lance, who had come back to Oakhurst Manor the previous night, was somewhere on the plantation checking on the work of the field hands.

Jeremy was increasingly restless, and, his physical vigor having been restored, he refused to sit quietly. Instead, after the application of each poultice, he held it over his eyes and paced up and down in front of the windows, Carrie having made certain that no furniture obstructed his path.

The girl refused to be distracted by the sound of his footsteps on the floorboards beyond the edge of the rug, and her voice remained steady as she continued to read.

The footsteps halted, but she did not falter.

Jeremy spoke in a strained voice, scarcely above a whisper. "Nobody told me the live oak in the front yard was cut down," he said. "But we've got to dig out the stump. It's ugly and ruins the lawn."

The astonished Carrie lowered her book and stared at him.

Jeremy was standing in front of a window, the poultice having fallen to the floor beside him.

"Papa Beaufort!" The girl leaped to her feet and ran to him.

He turned to her, his expression one of awed wonder. "My God, Carrie, I can see again!"

She hugged him impulsively.

His exuberant shout brought a tousled Lisa hurrying into the room.

Jeremy went straight to her and kissed her.

All three laughed and wept simultaneously, and Carrie sent a servant to fetch Lance without delay.

He arrived a short time later, his boots dusty and his shirt soaked with sweat.

"Our prayers have been answered, son," Jeremy said as he came into the room. "The Lord has seen fit to restore my sight."

Lance embraced him, and tears came to the younger man's eyes, too.

A messenger was sent to Trelawney, and soon a breathless Scott and Kai galloped across the fields.

Jeremy read prayers of thanks from the book of Psalms, and then the two closely knit families held an impromptu celebration. Lance went down to the wine cellar for a large bottle of champagne, and everyone marveled at the near-miracle. There were scars at the corners of Jeremy's eyes and on his lids that he would bear for the rest of his days, but his vision was unimpaired.

"I just wish Jerry were here to share in our happiness," he said. "Then our joy would be complete."

No one replied, and Carrie averted her face so he wouldn't see her expression of distaste. A strange thought occurred to her, and she couldn't put it out of her mind: Jerry was an outsider, and his presence would inhibit the pleasure that all the others felt. It was fortunate that he wasn't here.

Somewhat ashamed of herself, she blurted the first thing that came to her mind. "Now," she said, "we don't have to keep our secret any longer."

The four older people looked at her in surprise.

Lance immediately came to her rescue, even though the method of breaking their news wasn't appropriate. "Papa," he said, "I'll discuss this in private with you and Papa Emerson, according to protocol. But, as Carrie says, there's no reason to keep our secret any longer. We want to be married."

Kai burst into tears, Lisa wept, too, and everyone started to talk at once.

"This is the biggest and most important day of my life," Jeremy said when the hubbub subsided. "I've not only regained my sight, but Carrie is going to be my daughter-in-law. My happiness is complete."

Unexpectedly and with no advance notice, Jerry Beaufort returned to Oakhurst Manor after an absence of more than two months. Offering no explanation of his whereabouts during that time, he resumed his normal routines as though nothing out of the ordinary had happened. His comments on his father's remarkable recovery were brief, and the congratulations he extended to Carrie and Lance on their betrothal were perfunctory.

Lisa, who usually exercised caution in her criticism of the family's elder son when speaking to Jeremy, nevertheless felt compelled to express her feelings to him. "I hate to say this," she told him, "but he acts as though he really doesn't care what becomes of any of us. He seems to live in a world of his own. He's so bloated that I'm certain he was drinking heavily while he was away."

Her husband's smile was indulgent. "Don't worry about Jerry," he said. "He'll straighten out. My brother, Tom, was pretty wild when he was young, but he settled down and made something of himself. He was a successful planter before he went into the diplomatic service, and he's been doing a fine job at our legation in Paris. I'm sure Jerry will soon buckle down to work, too."

Lisa looked at him across the breakfast table and decided to say no more. If Jerry was ambitious, no one had seen that side of his nature. Even more important, she knew enough about men to realize that the heir to Oakhurst Manor had strange, inexplicable quirks in his nature. She had seen him looking at Carrie with an only partly concealed lascivious expression in his eyes. She had seen pure hatred when he glanced at his father and at Lance. And when he sometimes gazed at her, she felt a chill run up her spine. It was absurd, however, to tell Jeremy that his son was dangerous. He would refuse to believe the charge, and she could offer no real proof to substantiate such an accusation. So it was best to hold her tongue, although she intended to keep her stepson under observation. If she was right about him—and she was seldom mistaken in her impressions—he would err someday, overstepping the mark and revealing his true nature.

She served Jeremy another dish of steaming grits, then looked up when a servant came into the dining room with the morning's mail.

Lisa sorted the letters, and looked with interest at a heavy parchment envelope which bore the legend "Office of the President, Washington City." She gave it to her husband without comment.

Jeremy read it immediately. "Well," he said, and gave it back to her.

The communication was brief:

> My dear Jeremy,
>   I am eager to see you on a matter in the national interest.
>   Bring your good wife here with you, and extend my felicitations to her.
>   Yr. obdt. svt.,
>   Andrew Jackson

"I wonder why President Jackson wants to see you," she said.

Jeremy shrugged. "We'll soon find out. A request like this is a summons that can't be ignored, so we'll go up to Washington City. Can you be ready to leave in a day or two?"

"Of course." Lisa hesitated, then expressed her innermost fears. "I just hope he doesn't want you to go to sea again as the commander of a navy squadron."

He reached across the table and took her hand. "I promised you when we were married that I'd never be separated from you again, and I aim to keep my word. I love my country as much as any man, but I love my wife more. I've done my duty at sea, and if the president wants to reactivate my commission as commodore, I'll have to refuse."

"That's all right, then," she said, and her relief was infinite. Now that she was middle-aged, she could no longer tolerate the anxiety engendered by a long separation, and the truth of the matter was that she felt secure only when she and Jeremy were together.

They departed early the following morning in a carriage drawn by a team of bays, with Jeremy handling the reins himself, as usual. During his absence Jerry would be in charge at Oakhurst Manor, and Lance, already deeply involved in the shipping business, would be in sole control of affairs in Charleston.

When possible, as was the custom, they made overnight stops with friends who owned plantations and farms in the Carolinas and Virginia. Only when necessary did they stay at inns, and after spending twelve days on the road they reached the nation's capital, which former President John Quincy Adams accurately described as "the most miserable little town in America."

Government was Washington City's only business, and although a building boom had been under way since Andrew Jackson had first taken office in 1829, the facilities were still woefully inadequate. New government office buildings were springing up to accommodate the expanding bureaucracy, but there were still relatively few taverns and inns in town, and housing was in short supply. There were only a handful of private homes, many located in nearby Georgetown, and most of these were occupied by Cabinet members, Supreme Court justices, and other high-ranking officials.

An overwhelming majority of senators and representatives, along with most other officials, were required to live in boardinghouses, ramshackle dwellings so crowded that legislators were required to share sleeping quarters with their colleagues. Washington City was a community of men for the simple reason that most officials were compelled to leave their wives and families at home and to put up as best they could with housing conditions.

Almost without exception the streets were rutted dirt roads, and even Pennsylvania Avenue, the link that connected the president's mansion and the Capitol, had not

yet been paved with cobblestones. So, when it rained—
which it often did in the Potomac River basin—streets
were reduced to seas of sticky mud. Newcomers were horrified to discover that there was not one sidewalk in the
town. Rents were exorbitant, the meals served in most inns
were inferior, and the heads of foreign legations received
extra pay from their governments for serving at what was
regarded as a hardship post.

Perhaps the most comfortable dwelling in Washington
City was the White House, as the president's mansion had
been known since its repainting after the British had set it
on fire during the War of 1812. The staff was large and
well-trained, guest quarters were ample, and the president's
cook served hearty, simple Tennessee fare.

The atmosphere was informal, in keeping with Andrew
Jackson's concept of democracy. Two Marine Corps sen-
tries stood duty at the main gate, and were stationed there
solely for purposes of demonstrating the dignity of the
presidency. The staff consisted of the president's principal
secretary, his nephew Andrew Donelson, and three as-
sistants, all of whom worked in their shirtsleeves. As the
president was a widower, his official hostess was Donelson's wife, Emily, who was helped by a housekeeper, a
cook, three chambermaids, a laundress, a gardener, and a
handyman. President Adams had utilized a staff of twelve,
but one of Jackson's first acts had been to reduce the number of servants.

The housekeeper conducted Jeremy and Lisa Beaufort
to a large bedroom at the rear of the White House, where
a vase filled with fresh-cut flowers greeted them. Emily
Donelson sent word that she hoped Lisa would join her
for tea, and Jeremy was conducted to the president's office.

The grizzled Andrew Jackson, his hairline receding rapidly and his face more hawklike than ever in spite of his
futile attempts to gain weight, sat behind a cluttered desk
piled high with documents. Mementos of his military campaigns were everywhere, and although the day was fairly
warm, a small fire was burning in the hearth to dispel the
dampness that was a perennial Washington City problem.

Like the members of his staff, the president worked in
his shirtsleeves and had loosened his stock for the sake of

comfort. Limping slightly from an old wound he had acquired in a duel, he crossed the room to greet his guest, a gnarled hand extended. "By the Eternal," he boomed, "you're a sight for sore eyes!"

Jeremy, who had not seen him since his election, grinned at him. "You're looking well, Mr. President."

"If I am, it's no thanks ot this place. This job is like being condemned to a term in prison," he grumbled. "I manage to get out for a canter before breakfast every morning, usually down to Rock Creek and back, but it's the only exercise I get. The rest of the day I'm stuck in this room, and blame near everybody who comes to see me wants something. Have a chair, boy, and tell me how you're progressing at Oakhurst Manor."

Jeremy knew he wasn't making small talk, and replied honestly, saying that the plantation had never been in better shape and that profits had never been greater.

"One of your sons is running the place now?"

"I haven't completely given him his head, but he's learning."

"Your other son is doing well with your shipping interests, I hear. I saw a Treasury report just the other day that indicated he's almost doubled your West Indian trade in the past year."

"Lance is very competent, Mr. President. I'm proud of him."

"As well you should be. So you'd say your sons could look after your affairs if you were to take a leave of absence, so to speak." The president's expression was calculating.

"I might be able to leave them in charge," Jeremy replied cautiously. "Do I gather you want me to come to work for you, Mr. President?"

"That's a fair guess." Andrew Jackson chuckled, and leaning back in his chair, spilled tobacco crumbs on his shirt front as he stuffed a pipe.

"I must be honest with you, sir. I've promised Lisa we won't be separated. She's had a dread of it ever since she was held captive by the Santo Domingo buccaneers for a year. So, if you want me to return to navy duty, I must respectfully refuse, Mr. President."

Again Jackson laughed. "We'll leave the fighting to the

young fellows, and I wouldn't try to separate you and
your wife for anything in the world. What I have in mind
is rather different. Secretary of State Van Buren tells me
your brother is doing a first-rate job as our chargé
d'affaires in Paris, so maybe a talent for diplomacy runs in
the family. We have a need for someone who is forceful
but can handle relations delicately. In Vienna. As U.S.
minister, head of the legation there. I realize you don't
need the money, but the Congress has approved extra pay
for the rental of a house there. And I'd sweeten the pot by
transferring your brother to Vienna to act as your chargé
d'affaires."

"I'm flattered, Mr. President, and I'm sure Lisa would
enjoy living in Vienna for a time."

"She'd be the perfect minister's wife. All those Austrian
and Hungarian princes and dukes would be charmed by
her."

"There's no doubt of that," Jeremy said. "But there's
one drawback, sir. I've not only never served as a member
of the diplomatic corps, but also I knew next to nothing
about the affairs of the Austrian Empire. I wouldn't want to
let you or the country down."

The president became tart. "If I didn't think you were
competent, I wouldn't offer you the post. You and the
Emperor Franz the First have a great deal in common,
which is what made me think of you for the position. He's
made an expanding sea trade a keystone of his nation's
prosperity, and in his wars against the Turks, which they've
been fighting for a century and a half, he's been successful
because he's employed the same techniques you used against
the Caribbean buccaneers. And Van Buren is convinced
you'll get along with the foreign minister, Count Metternich, the old rogue."

"I'm inclined to accept, sir, so I can justify your faith in
me," Jeremy said. "But I'd like to discuss this with Lisa
first."

"By the Eternal, I'd have no respect for you if you
didn't. When my Rachel was alive, I never made an important decision without first getting her approval." A
fleeting, wan smile revealed the loneliness of the man who
held America's highest office. "Van Buren will join us for
dinner tonight, and tomorrow he can start to brief you on

what you'll need to know in Vienna. His people are already at work collecting documents for you, and you'll have enough reading matter to keep you busy on the voyage. I'll expect you and your wife to join me in my sitting room for a drink before dinner."

Jeremy was dismissed, and took his leave. Lisa hadn't yet returned to their bedchamber, and he weighed the offer carefully as he waited for her.

Anxiety wreathed her face when she rejoined him. "Emily Donelson is a lovely girl, but I couldn't enjoy myself. I've been wondering what the president said to you."

He told her about the request.

"Vienna! How long would we be there?"

"Assuming I can handle the assignment, at least a year or two. Few Americans have ever visited that part of the world, so this is a rare opportunity."

"Could we see other parts of Europe as well?"

"Of course. Another factor in favor is that my brother would be helping me. The president is very shrewd."

"It will be wonderful to see Tom and Margot for more than a brief visit, I must say. The only problem is leaving affairs here in the hands of the boys."

"I have no worries about the shipping business," Jeremy said. "For all practical purposes, Lance has already taken charge. He's as competent as he's trustworthy."

Lisa forced herself to ask a necessary question. "And Oakhurst Manor?"

He hesitated for a moment. "Jerry is old enough to accept responsibility. I'll grant he's been slow to take hold, but my absence will force him to take charge. He'll be pushed into a make-or-break situation."

"Suppose he falls down on the job?" Lisa wanted to know.

Jeremy was uncomfortable. "To an extent," he said, "Oakhurst Manor runs itself. Even if Jerry shows no profit while he's learning, we won't be too badly hurt. The experiment is worth making, and I hope he'll surprise us by making good. Besides, Scott Emerson will be close at hand, and as my lawyer he'll be in a position to intervene if Jerry makes a botch of things."

She was inclined to agree. Even if Jerry failed to mend his ways, she could see him doing no permanent damage.

But something else was preying on her mind. "I'd urge you to accept," she said, "if it weren't for the engagement of Lance and Carrie. Am I right in thinking the president will want you to go to Austria fairly soon?"

"Immediately, I imagine."

"Then there's no opportunity for Kai and me to arrange the wedding before we go."

"I've had some ideas about that, too," Jeremy said. "I'm sure Scott and Kai would love to join us in Austria for Christmas. They could bring Lance and Carrie with them, and we could hold the wedding in Vienna. I'd much prefer a small family group to the huge mobs we'd have to invite to a wedding at Trelawney."

"What a bright notion," Lisa said. "Carrie told me the other day that she and Lance dread the very thought of a big wedding. They're not extroverts, either of them, and I'm certain the prospect of a small family wedding thousands of miles from home will appeal to both of them. I know them well enough to predict they'll just leap at the plan."

"I can think of only one drawback," Jeremy said. "It wouldn't be wise for the whole family to be out of the country at the same time. Someone will have to stay behind to make any necessary decisions that arise, as they do regularly. And that means Jerry wouldn't be able to join us for the wedding and family reunion."

"If that's your only worry," Lisa said with a wry smile, "you can dismiss it from your mind. I can assure you that Jerry won't be heartbroken."

Jerry Beaufort was admitted to the inner sanctum of Senator John C. Calhoun's Charleston office after only a short wait, and he felt completely at home in the presence of South Carolina's first citizen. After all, their families were friends, and Senator and Mrs. Calhoun had attended a number of parties at Oakhurst Manor.

Certainly no man in the United States was more distinguished than Calhoun, who had served as vice president under both Jackson and John Quincy Adams, as secretary of war, and as a member of the House of Representatives. His alert, intense eyes made him look young, even though his generously long hair was turning gray and his waistline was thickening.

Always courtly, he stood and shook his young visitor's hand. "Well, Jerry," he said, "don't tell me you're becoming interested in politics!"

"Yes, and no, Senator."

"You've heard about your father's appointment, no doubt."

Jerry shook his head. "No, sir. He's in Washington City, but he hasn't written."

"There's no love lost between the president and me," Calhoun said, "but protocol forces him to notify me of any jobs he gives to South Carolinians. Your father is going to be the new U.S. minister to Austria."

Jerry's pulse quickened, and he averted his face so the senator couldn't see his eyes. "I'm very pleased, sir," he said. "I reckon I'll have Oakhurst Manor to run, so that makes this visit doubly important. Senator, some of my friends and I admire your stand on states' rights so much we're eager to put teeth into your position."

"Oh?" Calhoun, the consummate political veteran, became cautious.

"My friends and I agree with you, Senator, that we've got to start looking after our own rights because nobody else is going to do it for us. Your position got me to thinking. I've read that in some of the territories in the West, citizens are banding together on their own to make sure that folks do things their way. Well, we could do the same kind of thing here."

Calhoun looked at him in astonishment. "Are you suggesting the formation of a vigilante organization?"

Jerry was proud of himself. "Yes, sir!"

"Then you miss the entire thrust of my philosophy, young man." The senator was firm. "I've taken the stand that a state, through its legally elected legislature, with confirmation by its legally elected governor, has the right to nullify a federal law harmful to its best interests. What you're suggesting is a form of armed insurrection."

Jerry became aware of his stern disapproval and became uneasy. "It amounts to the same thing."

"Indeed it does not!" Calhoun was emphatic. "Your method would reduce the whole of the United States to a reign of terror conducted by gangs of armed men seeking to serve their own interests at the expense of the public good. I shall do everything in my power to prevent the formation of any such bands in South Carolina!"

As Jerry left the office, he told himself that John C. Calhoun, like everyone else in a position of authority, was afraid of his own shadow. There were times when a man had to protect his interests by taking the law into his own hands.

3

Neither the Democrats nor the Whigs objected to President Jackson's appointment of Jeremy Beaufort, and the Senate confirmed him as United States minister to the Austrian Empire by unanimous vote. A navy frigate, the *Constellation*, was under orders to join the Mediterranean fleet, so it was directed to pick up Minister and Mrs. Beaufort in Charleston, cross the Atlantic and Mediterranean with them, and drop them off at Trieste, where they would be met by a delegation of imperial hussars and escorted to Vienna.

Couriers from Washington City delivered stacks of documents to Jeremy, who was already rushed, putting his business affairs in order and giving instructions to his sons that covered every possible contingency. Fittings for Lisa's new wardrobe kept her busy, and in addition she supervised the packing of her favorite china, silverware, books, and bric-a-brac, which she was taking with her. They were so occupied that they refused the offer of Kai and Scott, who wanted to give them a farewell party.

Instead the two couples spent several days prior to the sailing in Charleston, the Emersons bringing Carrie into the city with them. Lance, who was already there, discreetly moved out of his room so he wouldn't be too near to Carrie, and took quarters in the most remote wing of the town house.

Someday, Carrie knew, she would become the mistress of the elegant dwelling, but she refused to allow herself to think about such matters. It was enough that she and Lance loved each other and would be married in Vienna at Christmas.

The delay in their marriage plans had been inevitable, and both were sufficiently adult to struggle against a sense of disappointment. They realized that a major wedding could not be organized in South Carolina in a period of a few weeks, so they reconciled themselves to the delay. Jeremy was making a sacrifice of his personal interests by accepting the appointment as minister to Austria, so the least his son and future daughter-in-law could do was to make a minor adjustment in their own plans. They insisted that Jeremy and Lisa had to be present for the ceremony, and it was only a few months until Christmas.

Jerry stayed behind at Oakhurst Manor until the last possible moment, joining the others in Charleston just in time for dinner on the evening prior to the sailing. He took little part in the festivities, and, as both Carrie and Lisa noted, he seemed totally indifferent to the pending departure of his father and stepmother. He appeared to be in an uncommonly jovial mood, however, even deigning to join in the conversation over a meal of shrimp with pungent sauce, gumbo, broiled crabs, and a roast of beef coated in brandywine-flavored pâté.

Much to Carrie's relief, Jerry vanished immediately after dinner to attend to business of his own. For reasons she couldn't explain, much less analyze, his very presence caused her almost physical discomfort.

The following morning everyone accompanied Jeremy and Lisa to the dock. The latter wore a long cape of watered yellow silk over a gown of the same material, topping her ensemble with a broad-brimmed velvet hat that sported an enormous yellow feather. State Department representatives and navy officers gaped at her when she alighted from her carriage.

"You'll have to be careful," a joking Scott said to

Jeremy, "or the Emperor Franz himself will fall in love with her."

"If he doesn't," was the reply, "he'll be unique."

The farewells were brief, with both Jeremy and Lisa bestowing most of their affection on Carrie. "We'll be counting the days until Christmas," Lisa told the girl.

The warships in the harbor fired a farewell salute of fifteen guns as the gig of the commodore commanding the *Constellation* carried the new minister to Austria and his wife to the waiting frigate. A fife-and-drum corps on board played a medley of military airs.

Tears came to Kai's eyes, and Scott, knowing how she would react, had a handkerchief ready for her. Carrie clung to Lance's arm, and neither spoke for a time.

"For Papa's sake and for Lisa's," he murmured, "I'm glad we're waiting."

"So am I," the girl replied. "It isn't easy for either of us, but we owe it to Lisa and Papa Beaufort to be married in their presence."

He squeezed her hand. "I reckon you and I will be counting the days until Christmas, too."

Jerry stood apart, saying nothing, his joviality of the previous evening having given way to what appeared to be a moody silence. None of the others realized it, but he was actually rejoicing inwardly.

His attempt to do away with his father and stepmother had failed, to be sure, but he entertained no regrets. Thanks to Andrew Jackson, they would be living five thousand miles from South Carolina for several years, and that suited his purposes splendidly. He had ample time to make new plans for them before they came home again.

Meantime he had revised his priorities, and had placed Carrie and Lance at the top of his list. He was outraged by their betrothal, finding it beyond credence that Carrie preferred his half brother to him. Not that he himself had proposed to her, of course, or ever would.

Aware of her past, he had no intention of marrying such a person. Unlike his half brother, he had impeccable standards. He was proud of the Beaufort name, and under no circumstances would he sully it by taking a bastard as his wife.

On the other hand, Carrie was exceptionally attractive,

by far the loveliest girl he had ever known. And the most
desirable. Which meant that he wanted her and intended
to have her.

Lance stood in his path, but that was all to the good,
too. He knew better than to tangle directly with a giant
whose strength was prodigious, but there were ways—
subtle and indirect but sure-fire—to immobilize him, perhaps to be rid of him for all time. Only a very clever
person would dream up a scheme that would serve two
ends at the same time.

Scott and Kai stood in his way, too, but Jerry was not
concerned about them. When his plan unfolded, they
would be powerless to oppose it, and would have no opportunity to block it. By the time they became aware of
what was happening, it would be too late.

The *Constellation* weighed anchor, the band played
again, and Kai wept fresh tears. Carrie waved a handkerchief; Lance and Scott drew their dress swords and flour-
ished them over their heads. Jerry raised an arm for a
moment in a weary, token gesture, then let it fall to his
side again. He had no intention of wasting his energy on
people who would be living five thousand miles away from
the world that mattered to him.

The frigate's sails filled slowly as she headed out of the
harbor, and the group on the dock prepared to leave.
"We'll have a bite to eat at the house before we drive out
to the country," Scott said.

"Good," Lance replied. "I'm ravenous."

Carrie laughed. "You're always hungry."

Jerry lagged behind as they walked to the waiting carriage.

"Are you coming with us?" Scott asked him.

He shook his head. "Sorry, but I have business here in
town before I ride back to Oakhurst Manor."

The others couldn't imagine what "business" might be
occupying him, but they were too polite to pry.

Jerry waited until their carriage disappeared from sight,
then walked quickly up the waterfront street, which was
lined with taverns, bordellos, and small shops that catered
to the sailors of many lands whose ships came to Charleston. He was overdressed in a cream-colored silk suit that
called attention to him, but he ignored the stares of pas-

sersby as he made his way to a three-story building of yellow brick, which was more substantial than the other waterfront houses.

A black man with a long scar down one side of his face, wearing a brace of pistols in his belt, opened the door a crack, then admitted him. "You're expected, Mr. Beaufort," he said.

"Thanks, Taffy." Jerry flipped him a coin, and familiar with the establishment, sauntered into a small parlor and mixed himself a drink of whiskey and water at a tiny bar in the corner.

While he drank it, a girl came into the room, tall, slender, and heavily made-up, the shade of her unblemished skin indicating that she was probably an octoroon. Her gown of sleazy satin was slashed almost to the waist in front, and she tossed back her long hair when she saw the new arrival.

"So it's you," she said.

"Good afternoon, Nellie." He raised his glass to her.

The girl approached him, the swaying of her hips exaggerated. "I was wondering if you'd show up today."

Jerry plunged a hand inside her gown and began to fondle her bare breasts. "You missed me, eh?"

"I always miss you," Nellie said, nestling closer to him.

Suddenly he released her. "We'll have to wait," he told her. "I'm seeing Oscar."

"Let Oscar wait," she pouted.

"Oscar never waits for anyone," said a deep basso voice in the doorway.

The man who stood there was middle-aged and totally bald. No more than five feet tall, he weighed more than two hundred and fifty pounds, but in spite of his freakish appearance he was the most feared figure on the waterfront. Tavern owners and pickpockets, prostitutes and thieves, took care not to cross him, and even the wealthy customers who were cheated in his gaming rooms never complained to the authorities. The Charleston constabulary, who knew him well, were unable to find witnesses willing to send him to prison.

"Out, Nellie," he said.

The girl stamped her foot. "Jerry is my best customer!"

Oscar snapped his fingers.

Nellie reluctantly moved toward the door.

"Later," Jerry called in an attempt to mollify her, "after Oscar and I have had a little talk."

The short, heavyset man said nothing, but stared at him with hard, cold eyes.

Jerry always felt nervous in his presence. Gulping his drink, he poured himself another.

"Well, Beaufort?"

"Don't worry, I always keep my word."

"That's fortunate for you," Oscar said. "You have the initial payment?"

Jerry reached into an inner pocket, withdrew a leather pouch, and handed it to him.

Oscar spilled the contents on the bar, then counted slowly. "One thousand dollars, with another thousand to be paid the day of the operation."

"I . . . I'd like to renegotiate the terms," Jerry said. "One thousand dollars is a very large sum of money, enough to support a bank clerk or a greengrocer and his family for at least a year."

"My terms are firm and not subject to renegotiation," the fat man said, his voice grating. "And remember, if something goes wrong or you change your mind, no matter what your reason, I keep this first thousand."

"That's pretty harsh." Jerry swallowed hard.

"In fact, this is now mine." Heavy fingers returned the money to the pouch, which vanished into a pocket. "People who do business with me know I never quibble over fees. Pay my price and you get results. That's Oscar Griffin's motto."

"I'm not quibbling or quarreling, Oscar," Jerry said. "I've never once objected when I've lost money at your poker table—"

"Why the hell should you object? Are you hinting I run a crooked poker game?"

"Certainly not!" Jerry resisted the desire to wipe a film of sweat from his upper lip. He was deathly afraid of this grotesque, beady-eyed man, but had come to him because it was necessary for the achievement of his goals. He didn't have to like Oscar to get the job done.

"When do we go to work? Tomorrow? The next day?"

"Not that soon. I don't want Scott Emerson and his wife around when we move."

"For once I agree," Oscar said. "Emerson is a smart lawyer, and tough. He's one of the few men in the state with the courage and ability to send me to jail." Suddenly a hamlike hand shot out and grasped the front of the younger man's ruffled shirt. "Let's understand one thing, Beaufort. If you talk out of turn and cause trouble for me, you won't survive long enough to go to jail!"

He released his victim so suddenly that Jerry staggered backward and hit the wall.

"I'm showing faith in you, Oscar," Jerry said, trying in vain to recover his shattered dignity. "You've got to trust me, too."

"I trust nobody. That's why I'm successful."

"It's in my own best interest for me to keep my mouth shut. I condemn myself if I give you away."

"I'm glad you realize it. See that you don't forget it."

"I won't." Jerry wished himself elsewhere. "I'll give you as much advance notice as I can. As much as a couple of days, and no less than twenty-four hours."

"Suit yourself, but my lads are disciplined, and won't need that much time." All at once Oscar became amiable, only his eyes still hard and unyielding. He poured himself a small drink of Dutch gin, then downed it in a gulp. "We're going to have a long partnership, you and me."

It occurred to Jerry that he had opened a door he might not be able to close. The payment of fees aside, Oscar would be in a position to demand and receive both money and favors for years to come. Well, it was too late to think about that now, and Jerry realized he'd have to make the best of a ticklish situation.

Oscar splashed more whiskey into the younger man's glass. "Stop fretting, Beaufort. You take care of your end of the operation, which should be simple enough, and we'll do the rest."

Jerry's craving for liquor increased, and he took a deep swallow of his fresh drink.

"Start relaxing right now. Seeing we're partners, you can have Nellie for the afternoon at no charge."

"I . . . I'm afraid I've already had too much to drink."

"Hellfire," Oscar said, "you don't have to bed the wench

yourself. The way I hear it, you'd much rather watch a girl perform with other men."

Jerry flushed. Apparently nothing in a man's private life was too delicate to be hidden from this overweight monster.

"Here." Oscar thrust an unopened bottle of whiskey into his hand. "Take this with you. Taffy will start sending customers up to Nellie, and you can spend the whole afternoon watching them through a peephole in the door. Enjoy yourself."

Jerry hesitated for a moment, but the temptation was too great. Seizing the bottle, he left the room.

Oscar Griffin watched him with narrowed, contempt-filled eyes. Yet he was grateful to this weakling. It was people like Jerry Beaufort who enabled him to earn a very comfortable living.

A complex case involving a large inheritance on which Scott Emerson had been working for several years had been appealed to the Supreme Court of the United States, and one day, about a month after the departure of Jeremy and Lisa for Europe, Scott was summoned to Washington City for the long-awaited hearing. For the next week he spent long hours at his desk preparing for his appearance. Then he left, taking Kai with him and telling Carrie they would return in three to four weeks.

"We won't spend any more time in Washington City than we must," he said. "It'll take no more than a morning for the case to be heard, and with luck the court will hand down its decision the next day. So we're sure to be home by the first of the month."

Jerry was elated when he heard the news, and he knew his luck was riding high. Scott and Kai departed on a Thursday morning. Lance was in Charleston, and if he followed his customary routines, would return to Oakhurst Manor for the weekend late on Friday evening. His arrival, including its timing, was vital to Jerry's scheme, but there was nothing he could do to change Lance's schedule in any way. With continuing luck, all the pieces would fall into place. The risk was great, but there was no alternative, and he was determined to push ahead. This was the opportunity for which he had been waiting, and he had to take the chance.

At noon on Thursday Jerry made a hurried trip to the yellow brick house on the Charleston waterfront, and his stay there was brief. He met with Oscar Griffin just long enough to hand him a pouch containing a second payment of one thousand dollars, and with a tight smile he put his plan into operation.

"Tomorrow night," he said.

On Friday evening Jerry ate an early supper, and a short time later a number of shadowy figures arrived at Oakhurst Manor, each of them traveling alone so the house servants wouldn't think that the young master was giving a party.

At ten P.M. Jerry left the mansion, saddling his own horse and riding to Trelawney across the fields so he wouldn't be seen on the road. He tethered his mount in a grove of trees a quarter of a mile from the Trelawney manor house and went the rest of the way on foot. So far, so good.

No lights were burning in the parlor or any of the other ground-floor rooms, and Jerry's heart beat faster. His luck was holding.

He looked up at the second-floor windows above the portico, and they were dark, too. Carrie had retired for the night, going to bed early, as she always did on Fridays so she and Lance could see each other at breakfast on Saturdays. Perfect!

Careful planning, including meticulous attention to detail, was paying off handsomely.

The one physical activity in which Jerry had excelled as a child was the climbing of trees, so it was an easy matter for him to shinny up one of the white columns of the portico to its roof. There, lying down so he wouldn't be seen by a passing servant, he donned a mask fashioned from a cotton stocking. It completely covered his head and face, with tiny holes cut for his eyes, nose, and mouth.

Taking his time in spite of a desire to hurry, he unwound several lengths of thin but strong rope from his middle. Holding them in one hand, he rose and silently climbed into the house through an open window.

Carrie was sound asleep, her blond hair tousled.

For a long moment Jerry stood over the bed staring down at her.

He wished he had brought a bottle of rum with him to bolster his courage, but it was too late to think of that now.

He hauled down the covers, breaking into a cold sweat when he saw how appealing the sleeping girl looked in her thin nightgown. Working quickly, he tied her ankles to the bedposts, spread-eagling the lower part of her body.

Carrie awakened slowly, then saw the masked man looming over her. Instantly awake, she sat up and clawed at him.

Jerry punched her brutally in the mouth, and she fell back on the bed, a trickle of blood oozing from her lower lip. He managed to catch hold of one of her hands, and as he secured it to the bedpost above her, she fought him with all her strength, her nails raking him, her teeth sinking into his shoulder.

He grunted, but took care not to speak so she wouldn't recognize his voice. There was still too much fight in her, so he struck her a second time, then a third.

Carrie was no match for him, but, still struggling, she opened her mouth, intending to scream for help.

He shoved a gag into her mouth.

She managed to bite his finger, and the taste of his salty blood mingled with her own.

Silently cursing her, he shoved the gag deeper into her mouth. Now only her remaining arm still had to be secured.

Fear gave Carrie greater strength, and she freed herself from his grasp.

Jerry was becoming desperate, and almost wrenched her arm from its socket as he finally managed to tie it to the bedpost.

The girl was helpless now, and looked up at the madman with horror and loathing. The portion of his mask that covered his mouth was soaked with saliva.

He ripped away her silk nightgown, and the sound of the cloth tearing seemed to fill the room.

Then, unable to resist the impulse, he caught hold of her bare breasts and squeezed them.

Carrie's fear gave way to agonizing pain.

Clumsily, hurriedly, Jerry lowered his breeches. Already aroused, he climbed onto the bed and mounted his victim.

She writhed and strained in an attempt to free herself, but there was no escape.

Forcing his penis into her vagina, he assaulted her brutally, ripping her maidenhead.

Tears of rage, fear, and disgust ran down her face.

A spreading pool of blood turned the sheets crimson.

Carrie vaguely thought she recognized her attacker, but her fear and loathing were so great that she couldn't actually identify him.

His rape completed, he climbed off the bed, dressed, and leaving his victim trussed and gagged, departed the same way he had entered her chamber. The whole incident had taken only a few minutes.

Returning to the portico roof, Jerry made certain that no servants were abroad. Then he jumped to the ground, forced himself to walk rather than run to the grove of trees, and hauled himself into the saddle.

A few minutes later he was back at Oakhurst Manor. There he unsaddled his horse, returning the animal to its stall.

At ten-forty-five P.M., a scant three-quarters of an hour after his departure, he walked into the library, where a group of silent men awaited him.

"It's done," he told them. "On your way!"

They left immediately, mounting their own horses and cantering off in various directions. An keen observer would have noted that one headed north, another south, a third east, and the fourth west. Spurring their horses, they were losing no time.

Until now Jerry had not touched liquor all evening, but he felt he deserved a drink. He poured himself a liberal quantity of whiskey, then raised his glass in a silent toast. What he had failed to accomplish months earlier in the fire, he was achieving now. There was no way he could lose.

Lance was tired after a long, hard day's work in Charleston, but he relaxed on the ride home. His spirited chestnut stallion, Bantu, knew they were going home, and cantered smartly, effortlessly, down the road.

Trelawney was off to the left now, and Lance half-stood in the saddle. No lights were burning in the manor house, so he assumed that Carrie was asleep. He felt a familiar glow as he thought of her, and estimated it would be another eight hours before he saw her. She was expecting him for an early breakfast, and he would be on time.

A party of three men, all heavily armed, galloped past him, scarcely bothering to glance at him.

Lance was puzzled. Ordinarily there was little or no traffic on the country road that led to Oakhurst Manor, certainly not at this time of night.

Apparently something was amiss. At the very least, something out of the ordinary was taking place.

His never-failing sixth sense did not desert him now. He headed his horse off the road, pointing him toward a patch of woods, and the huge beast picked a surprisingly delicate path for himself through the maze of trees.

At virtually the same instant, Bantu and his master sensed the presence of men a few yards ahead. The stallion raised his ears, and Lance's light touch on his neck caused him to halt and stand motionless, his breathing inaudible.

Lance made out the sound of the voices of three different men.

"I'm sure it was Beaufort," one of them said in a deep baritone. "They told us he's big, and the fellow we saw on the road was huge."

"Besides," a second declared, "nobody else would be riding on this isolated road at this time of night. He couldn't be anybody except Lance Beaufort."

"We'd better notify the posse," the deep baritone said.

"No!" The third man, apparently in charge, spoke with sharp authority. "He can't be stupid, and he might take alarm if the whole posse starts bearing down on him. He was riding a mighty fine horse, and there's always a chance he might get away."

Posse? Take alarm? Lance became taut. It was obvious he was in trouble of some sort, but he couldn't imagine the reason, and felt bewildered.

"Then we'll have to take him ourselves," the deep baritone said.

"Right!" The man in charge was emphatic. "It won't be long before the entire county is alerted, but we want the credit for taking him—dead or alive."

Dead or alive? This was serious. Lance carried no weapon other than his dress smallsword, which would be virtually useless in a confrontation with three foes. But why it should be necessary for him to defend himself was beyond his imagination.

"We want the reward, too," the deep baritone said with a laugh.

"How much is it?" The speaker sounded younger than his companions.

"The fee is always the same for a rapist. One hundred dollars in gold."

A rapist? There had to be a mistake, a horrible mistake. Lance wanted to protest his innocence, but caution compelled him to remain silent and continue to listen.

"Does the girl have to identify him first, Johnny?"

"It ain't likely," the leader replied, "that Carolyn Emerson is in any condition to talk to anyone. A woman who has just had that experience is inclined to be mighty hysterical, you know."

Lance froze. Carrie had been raped! He felt as though the earth was rocking beneath Bantu's sturdy feet.

Not only had his beloved been assaulted, but he was being accused of the crime!

Suddenly a primitive force exploded within Lance. Reason deserted him, and he felt as though he was being enveloped in a sheet of searing flame.

Scarcely aware of what he was doing, and not caring, he touched Bantu's flanks with his toes.

The stallion surged forward, and in a moment man and beast burst into the clearing where three riders were sitting on their geldings.

It didn't matter to Lance that the odds against him were three to one or that his opponents were armed. His darling Carrie had been attacked. He was being held accountable.

Before the trio could recover from their initial surprise, Lance leaned forward in his saddle and lashed out at the nearest of the posse. Knuckles crashed against bone as he caught the man full in the face, knocking him to the ground, where he sprawled unconscious.

The leader, a burly man in his late thirties, turned to the newcomer, snatching his pistol from his belt.

Before he could use it, however, Lance leaped to the ground and hauled him from his saddle. Fighting with demonic fury, the younger of the Beaufort sons struck the man repeatedly, bore him to the ground, and smashed his head against a rock.

The third of the trio had drawn his own pistol but was afraid to use it until the infuriated Lance moved away from the man he was mauling. Now the posse member had his chance and raised his weapon.

Before he had the opportunity to fire, however, Bantu came to his master's rescue. The great stallion reared and snorted. His front feet flailed furiously, then descended on man and gelding. The rider toppled to the ground, and Bantu's front hooves descended on him, stamping him.

The frightened gelding bolted and took off, crashing through the woods.

Lance's head cleared slightly, and he straightened. The carnage that had been wreaked in a matter of a few moments was almost beyond belief. The man he had hauled to the ground was dead. So was the one whom Bantu had trampled. The third was still unconscious.

Aware of what had to be done, Lance collected the pistols of the dead men and a long sword carried by the third.

Then he mounted Bantu and quickly left the clearing.

What he had just done did not yet matter. Only Carrie was on his mind, and he had to see her.

He backtracked through the woods, then rode in the direction of Trelawney. His mind was still spinning and his heart felt like a lead lump within him, but his instinct for survival remained strong, and he still had the sense to make his way through the fields rather than take the road.

He crossed the boundary that separated Oakhurst Manor and Trelawney, and when he drew nearer to his destination, the sound of many voices caused him to slow his pace. At last the manor house came in sight, and he realized that oil lamps and candles had been lighted in all of the rooms on the ground floor and the second floor.

Someone was standing inside the window of Carrie's

bedroom, directly above the portico, and Lance recognized the local physician.

Then suddenly he became aware of his own danger. At least a dozen armed men were standing on the lawn in front of the Trelawney manor house. A full posse had indeed been aroused. Although he didn't know it, Oscar Girffin's men had done a thorough job, and the entire county was being alerted.

Lance knew it would be worth his life if he tried now to go to Carrie. The moment he was recognized, all twelve of the men on the lawn would start shooting at him. The reason he was being accused of the dreadful crime was irrelevant: they would kill him, and it didn't matter that they might later discover they had been mistaken.

All at once it dawned on him, too, that he had left two dead men behind in the woods. He and Bantu were killers, and when the bodies were found, which might happen at any moment, the posse would double its efforts to capture him. Dead or alive, probably the former.

Never in his life had Lance avoided a battle, but the odds against him were overwhelming.

If he wanted to live, he had to flee. There was no choice, no alternative. Only later, in some manner he couldn't yet fathom, could he try to establish his innocence.

It didn't matter that the very thought of doing harm to Carrie made him ill. It didn't matter that he thirsted for vengeance against the perpetrator of the outrage. It didn't even matter that, by running away, he seemed to be confirming his guilt.

Above all, there was no way he could see Carrie now. And from a realistic point of view he knew that aside from offering her what small comfort he could, there was literally nothing he could do to help her. He could imagine the travail she was suffering at this very moment, but her anguish would be worse if he were killed making an attempt to reach her side.

He had his health, his stallion, the arms he had taken from the posse members, and enough money in his purse to last him for a week or two on the road.

After he put enough distance between him and his pursuers, he would write to Carrie, and would send a letter to Papa Beaufort and Lisa in Vienna, too.

At this moment, however, his one paramount consideration had to be the saving of his own neck.

He turned away from Trelawney, and tears came to his eyes. He wasn't deserting Carrie, he told himself, but by leaving he was making it possible for him to fight her battles later.

Bantu walked quietly. At his master's gentle touch the stallion quickened his pace.

Both of his captured pistols ready for immediate use, Lance headed for the swamps at the far end of Oakhurst Manor. He knew every inch of that difficult, seemingly impassable terrain, and when he reached the tangled bushes at the edge of the swamp, some of them nine and ten feet high, he breathed a sigh of temporary relief. At least he had the chance now to plan his escape.

It would be too dangerous to seek refuge in Georgia, Alabama, or North Carolina. When a rapist or murderer—and there was no doubt that he was the latter—was being hunted, it was customary to notify the authorities of neighboring states. So he would be sought there, too.

That meant he had to cross the mountains into Tennessee, at the very least. And he could waste no time. It was urgent that he cover as much ground as possible tonight, so he could leave the county, and he would have to ride all day tomorrow, too, so he could maintain a head start over messengers taking word of his crimes, both real and imagined, to other places.

There was no time like the present to begin. He looked off in the direction of Trelawney, even though he couldn't see it, and for the first time since his ordeal had started, he spoke aloud. "Good-bye, my love," he murmured.

Then he spurred Bantu, and began the long journey toward the northwest.

In less than a decade the myth-makers of the Whig party would create an image of General William Henry Harrison that would win him election as the ninth president of the United States. They would trumpet that he had been born in a log cabin and still lived in one. It didn't matter in the least that his father had been a wealthy Virginia plantation owner, that he himself had never known financial hardship in a long and distinguished career, and that his home in the little town of North Bend, Ohio, although not quite a mansion, was very comfortable.

What did count was that General Harrison knew as much about Indians as any man in the United States. The conqueror of the great chieftain Tecumseh at Tippecanoe during the War of 1812, he had served with distinction as governor of the Indiana Territory, then as a congressman and senator from Ohio. He had negotiated more treaties with Indian nations than any other man alive, including President Jackson, so it was only natural that the delegation from Missouri should stop off at North Bend after visiting Washington City in order to seek his advice.

Now in his late fifties, with a long, lean face and graying hair, Harrison greeted his guests with great courtesy. Serving them mugs of hard cider made from Ohio apples, he displayed his usual modesty. "Gentlemen," he said, "I doubt if I can tell you anything you haven't already learned in Washington."

The delegation leader, a fur buyer from the frontier town of St. Louis, shook his head. "They don't know much of anything back there, General," he said. "Mention Indians at the War Department, and they don't know what you mean. Our settlements are pushing clear across Missouri now, all the way to Independence, and we have a strong hankering to know how much trouble the tribes are going to give us."

"The patterns haven't changed much since the first colonists settled in Virginia and Massachusetts," Harrison replied. "The Indians are resentful—just as you'd be—when outsiders move into their territory, destroy their hunting grounds by cutting down forests and creating farms in the wilderness. Push them just so hard, just so far, and they'll fight like hell to preserve their rights. I don't believe the Indians of the Plains country, or those of the Rocky Mountains, either, are different. I doubt if they'll move out of their own free will just to accommodate new settlers."

"Then we're in for a long spell of trouble," the delegation leader said.

Harrison's smile was thin. "Yes, as long as the administration continues to offer free land to anyone who wants it. I tried hard in the Senate to institute a policy of offering hard cash and new territories to the Indians who are currently being displaced. But Andy Jackson doesn't see the problem my way, and I lost."

"What should we do, General?"

"Keep your powder dry," Harrison said. "And hope that a new generation of leaders will arise in this country who will treat the Indians the way we'd like to be treated if we wore their moccasins. Unfortunately, it takes a special breed of man who can win the trust of the tribes, and there aren't many of them around."

4

Pushing himself and his stallion to their limits, Lance spent sixteen to eighteen hours in the saddle each day as he rode to the northwest. Avoiding large towns like Greenville, he bought fodder for Bantu and meat and bread for himself in small country stores, even though he knew the presence of a stranger would cause comment and, perhaps, be remembered. He slept for no more than a few hours at a time, usually in deep woods, and he felt reasonably certain he was staying ahead of posses trying to capture him.

He breathed a trifle more easily when he crossed the state border into North Carolina, but he was still taking no chances and continued to follow the same tactics, avoiding the larger population centers and, whenever possible, traveling by night. He made certain never to be seen on roads where traffic was relatively heavy, and he took care to speak to no one. Riding at a rapid clip with his broad-brimmed hat pulled low over his forehead, he was a solitary figure, and other travelers who might have been inclined to be sociable avoided the scowling young giant.

Still traveling toward the northwest, Lance was forced to slow his pace somewhat when he came to the rolling foothills of the Great Smoky Mountains. He had no maps and preferred to ask no directions in the stores at which he paused or the villages he skirted. Instead he relied on his instincts, his own ability to judge, and at last he found passes through the mountains.

He knew he was in Tennessee when he saw a weather-beaten sign that told him he was in Sevier County. His clothes were travel-stained, so he bought rugged trousers, shirts, and a heavy pair of boots at a crossroads store. Now, at least at first glance, he resembled the farmers and artisans of eastern Tennessee, thus further reducing the chances that he would be recognized and captured.

In any event, he reasoned, it was unlikely that his pursuers would have sent an alarm as far as Tennessee. So he was in a far more relaxed frame of mind as he headed north toward the French Broad River. His immediate destination was the town of Knoxville, where he hoped he could find work of some sort to replenish the funds in his shrinking purse.

As his danger receded, Lance had more time to think and brood, and the turn of events that had resulted in his flight sickened him. Due to no fault of his own, he was a fugitive, and if he dared to return to Oakhurst Manor or Charleston, he would be in peril of losing his life before being given the opportunity to prove his innocence. He had no idea how such a terrible mistake had been made, how justice had been subverted. For the present, however, the cause of the error was irrelevant to his situation. It was enough that he was believed to have committed a crime and that scores of men were intent on shooting or hanging him.

Even worse than his own plight was the tragedy of what had happened to Carrie. Now he loved her even more than he had deemed possible, and his heart ached for her. He could imagine what she must be suffering. In the depth of his soul he felt certain that Carrie herself knew it had not been he who had raped her, but that belief was small consolation. What mattered was that her grief had to be overwhelming, yet there was nothing he could do to comfort or help her in her time of anguish.

Carrie was ever-present in his waking thoughts, and when he slept for brief periods he invariably dreamed about her. In these dreams she was holding out her arms to him, appealing to him to come to her. He was frustrated beyond measure because he could not, and a feeling of guilt pervaded him. He could only counsel himself to be patient, to cling to the hope that someday the true cause of justice would triumph. When that time came, he would be able to return to Carrie, and he swore he would more than compensate for his absence now, at a time when she needed him.

Someday, too, he would learn the identity of the man who had raped her, and would choke the life out of the filthy wretch with his bare hands. Any other form of killing would be too merciful; the bastard deserved to suffer all the torments of hell that could be devised for him.

Better able to travel at a somewhat more leisurely pace now, Lance allowed himself the luxury of a longer night's rest when he saw the banks of the French Broad River ahead. Having bought a razor and a small container of homemade yellow soap, he shaved for the first time since he had fled from Oakhurst Manor. Then he bathed in the river and washed his clothes. Having selected a small clearing in a heavily wooded area as his stopping place for the night, he draped his clothes on the branches of evergreens to dry, then dropped off to sleep with a pistol and sword close at hand. Others might have thought the night too chilly to sleep unclad, but Lance was as impervious to the elements as he had been as a child, when Papa M'Bwana had taught him to cope with outdoor living.

He was more tired than he had realized, and slept soundly. In fact, his sleep was so deep that sunlight was filtering into the clearing through the oaks and evergreens when he awakened. He opened his eyes, saw that Bantu was grazing peacefully nearby, and he stretched lazily.

All at once his infallible sixth sense told him he was not alone in the clearing, and he snatched his pistol as he sat upright.

A woman in her late twenties, perhaps five or six years his senior, was staring at him. Her homespun dress could not conceal her attractive figure, and as she gaped she ran a hand lightly through her reddish-blond hair.

"Do you always sleep naked on other people's private property?" she demanded.

Lance felt the blood rush to his face as he reached for his smallclothes and hastily donned them.

A light of ironic humor appeared in the woman's pale eyes. "Maybe you just like to show off your build," she said. "The only man I ever knew who was in your class was my late husband."

Apologizing and stammering, Lance climbed into his pants, drew on his shirt and stockings, then stamped into his boots. "I . . . I didn't know this was private property, ma'am."

"Well, it is. I live yonder, beyond the edge of the woods." She pointed off to the left. "My husband was clearing it to enlarge our farming area when he dropped dead. Two years ago last week. Who are you?"

"I'm Buck Collins, ma'am, and I'm sorry—"

"No need to be. It's been a long time since I set eyes on a man with your build. Come along, and I'll give you breakfast."

Lance gathered his other belongings, which he stuffed into his saddlebag, and leading Bantu, walked meekly beside the woman.

She was the Widow McBain, she told him, Elsa McBain.

Her house was an unpainted one-story building, obviously in need of repair. In fact, the whole property reeked of neglect. Someone had piled logs behind the house, but they had yet to be split for firewood.

Two of the windows had been boarded up because the glass in them had been broken. A makeshift gate was in place at the entrance to the pigpen, and there was a hole in a corner of the roof of the barn directly in back.

Elsa McBain saw Lance absorbing the ramshackle state of her property. "There's just so much a woman who lives alone can do," she said tartly. "It's hard enough to tend the chickens and pigs and grow the crops I need to survive."

He followed into her kitchen, which, in contrast with the disrepair he saw outside, was spotless. "It can't be easy for a lady who lives by herself. I'm surprised you'd even ask a stranger to come back here with you."

"Rubbish! My husband was a giant, too, and you big

men are always the most gentle. It's the little weasels who cause problems for a woman. You're harmless, Buck Collins. I wouldn't want you to get riled up at me, but you'd do no harm to anyone so long as your feathers don't be ruffled. Sit!"

He obeyed meekly and took a chair at the table of scrubbed pine.

Paying no further attention to him, the young woman busied herself at the wood stove.

"Here," she said, handing him a large wooden bowl. "This is some of last night's leftover soup. It'll put a damper on your appetite while I fix a proper meal."

The soup, filled with chunks of meat and vegetables, was delicious. It was the first hot food Lance had eaten in the better part of two weeks, and he discovered he was ravenous.

The next course was a huge bowl of porridge, and Elsa McBain gestured toward a pitcher. "Help yourself to as much milk as you like. I have five cows, and they produce so much that I barter what I don't use for salt, sugar, and flour."

Lance ate heartily, and there appeared to be no end to his appetite.

The main course was a half-dozen eggs, which she fried with slabs of country bacon, and with it she served him a half-loaf of homemade bread and a container of sweet butter.

She herself ate little, but watched him over the rim of her mug of steaming coffee. "I like to see a man enjoy himself at table," she said.

He was uncertain whether she was speaking to him or to herself. "Mrs. McBain," he said as he carefully wiped up egg yolk with a chunk of bread, "I don't like to accept charity from anyone. There must be a few dozen jobs around here that a man can do for you, and I hope you'll let me repay you by working off my debt to you."

Elsa's smile was tight, but a hint of genuine pleasure appeared in her eyes. "You took the thought right out of my head," she said.

Lance went to work with a vengeance, first repairing the pigpen gate. Then he attacked the logs, and his unreleased fury, combined with his prodigious strength, enabled him to cut the better part of a cord in a remarkably short time.

Then he fashioned some new planks for the barn roof, finding a saw and plane, along with other tools, in a portion of the barn that looked as though it had been neglected for a long time. He hammered the new planks into place, and was so intent on what he was doing that he lost all track of time until he saw Elsa McBain standing below, beckoning to him.

"How many times does a body have to call to you before you hear her?" she demanded. "Dinner will be cold if you don't wash up in a hurry!"

As she retreated toward the house, it occurred to him that her walk was surprisingly provocative. Certainly she had a lithe figure, but he tried to put her out of his mind.

That proved difficult. Dinner consisted of steak, mashed potatoes, lima beans, and a loaf of fresh baked bread, served with another large container of butter. For dessert there were sweet melons, the best Lance had ever tasted.

"The more I eat," he told her, "the more I'm indebted to you, ma'am. At this rate I'll never pay you back properly."

"That suits me just fine," she replied, her manner suddenly complacent. "Now, before you finish the roof, be sure you feed and water your horse. Then, after you're done with the roof, the chicken house needs fixing. After you're done there, I want you to look at this stove before you put the new glass in the windows. The panes are at the far side of the barn."

Lance grinned for the first time in many days. "What's wrong with your stove?"

Elsa looked at him in exasperation. "If I knew, I'd have fixed it long ago. All I can tell you is, it don't draw proper."

He returned to his labors, and again became so absorbed that it was dusk before he realized how quickly time had passed.

By now, he reasoned as he returned to the farmhouse, he had more than paid for the two large meals he had eaten. He would thank Elsa for her hospitality and be on his way again. By tomorrow night at this time he would reach Knoxville without difficulty.

His hostess, however, had other ideas. She had prepared a supper of cold meats and salad greens, and giving him no opportunity to protest, directed him to sit down.

They ate by candlelight, drinking a bottle of dandelion wine that Elsa had made.

"I like this arrangement," she said as they finished their supper. "The Almighty knows I need a man to help me around this place, and judging from your appetite, you were half-starved when you got here. I ain't nosy, so I'm not asking where you're from or where you were heading. Stay here and help me for as long as you like. You'll have room and board, and I'll share whatever profits we make, fifty-fifty. What do you say?"

Lance was surprised by her offer, and hesitated before committing himself.

"That's settled, then," Elsa said decisively.

Lance smiled and shook his head. Maybe he had been trapped, but the situation did have advantages he couldn't afford to ignore. He was being offered a refuge, where his material needs would be met, in a rural area far from his enemies in South Carolina. If he stayed here for a time, there was a chance that the man who had really assaulted Carrie would be caught and it would be safe for him to return home. So there was a great deal to gain and nothing to lose by staying.

Elsa was irritated by his continuing silence. "I already told you there's no strings attached," she said. "Anytime you get persnickety, I can throw you out. Anytime you don't like the meals I cook or decide you're working too hard, you can get out."

"I reckon I'll hang around for a spell," he said.

She stood and went to the sink. "You can bring me a bucket of water from the well," she said, "and it won't hurt you none to dry the dishes after I wash them."

As he drew a bucket of water at the well outside the kitchen door, he wondered how her late husband had tolerated her bossiness. On the other hand, as he was discovering, it was difficult to disobey Elsa McBain's orders, and he suspected she was capable of staging a tantrum when she was crossed.

He filled the bucket, as she had directed, and they cleaned up by candlelight. At night the faint lines in her forehead and at the corners of her eyes that showed so plainly in broad daylight were muted, and Lance realized she was actually rather pretty. She had led a rough life that was aging her before her time, but he guessed that before her husband's death, she had been very attractive.

As soon as the work was done, Elsa vanished into the little house's only bedroom, closing the door behind her.

Lance's night vision was extraordinary, so he needed no candle to light his way as he went out to the barn to make certain that Bantu was comfortable for the night. Then, before returning to the house, he used the privy, and realized the temperature was much lower than it had been the previous night.

When he reached the little parlor, it occurred to him that he had a problem. The largest piece of furniture in the room was a homemade settee, complete with two small pillows, that was scarcely big enough to hold two people sitting side by side. He would have to drape his legs over one of the wooden arms if he tried to stretch out on it, and it would be impossible to sleep there.

Since he had no real choice, he made a small fire in the parlor hearth to take away the chill, then lay down on the wooden floor. His discomfort was great, so he removed his boots, otherwise remaining fully clad, and placed the two settee pillows beneath his head. The floor was hard and unyielding, but he was tired after his day's work and became drowsy.

Suddenly the bedroom door opened. Elsa, wearing a voluminous linsey-woolsey nightgown, stood in the frame, holding a lighted candle on a plate.

"If that ain't the limit," she said. "A man can't do a day's real work if he don't get a proper rest. You march yourself in here, Collins!"

Lance reluctantly hauled himself to his feet and joined her.

Elsa pointed to her oversized feather bed, by far the largest single item of furniture in the house. "There's space aplenty for two to sleep there. We've had as many as four when my cousins come to visit. If you're feeling more modest than you were when I found you in the clearing this morning, you'll find my late husband's nightshirts in the second drawer of the chest yonder. But you don't need one for my sake."

She turned, went back to the bed, and blew out the candle.

Lance noted that she took care to stay on one side, near the edge.

Again Lance hesitated, not wanting to cause fresh complications. But he was weary and the soft bed looked inviting, particularly as he had slept only on the ground in the last fortnight. So he weakened and undressed, but balked at the idea of wearing one of the late McBain's nightshirts. He had slept in the raw ever since he had been an adolescent, and hated to be encumbered.

The feather bed was soft beyond his dreams, and relishing its warmth, he snuggled beneath the comforter, taking care to remain as far from his hostess as possible.

All at once Elsa McBain turned to him, her voice strident in spite of her apparent attempt to speak softly. "When I saw you out yonder in the woods, as naked as a jaybird," she said, "it came into my mind how long it's been since I had me a man with the proper equipment to tend to my needs."

Lance told himself he should have known she would make advances to him. It was too much to hope she would leave him alone.

"What's the matter, Collins?" she demanded. "Don't tell me you're bashful."

"Well," he said, temporizing as he thought fleetingly of Carrie, whom he loved with his whole heart, "my life is complicated."

"Not right now it ain't," Elsa said with conviction. "What you and me do in the nighttime is no part of our bargain." She paused, then added, "This is special."

Obviously, he thought, the woman would be insulted if he rejected her.

She gave him no opportunity to find an excuse, however. A hand snaked toward Lance under the covers, and unerringly found its target. "I got you now!" she said in triumph, and began to play with him.

He was a young, vigorous male in the physical prime of life, and he couldn't help responding. It was impossible to resist the expertise of this determined woman.

Elsa swarmed over him, smothering him with kisses, then teasing him by biting his shoulders and chest. "I tell you true," she muttered, "a man like you ain't easy to find."

Lance tried in vain to take the lead, but she gave him no chance, and even though he was becoming aroused, he had to swallow a laugh that welled up within him.

Elsa was so starved for love that she kept the initiative, and the only way he could have assumed it would have been by using his superior strength to overpower her. But she was so frenzied she kept him off balance, her arms and legs, hands and mouth furiously busy.

The astonished Lance found it difficult to believe he was being used as a love object.

Elsa mounted him, then commanded, "Show a little life now! Don't you play dead!"

He responded with full vigor, and through the haze of his growing desire he realized she was taking him. Incisively. Joyously.

She screamed aloud, raking his shoulders and chest with her nails as they reached a climax.

When their ardor subsided, Elsa moved away as rapidly as she had approached him. Turning to the far wall and inching to her own side of the bed, she spoke with succinct clarity. "Get plenty of sleep, Collins, you hear? Because we'll do it again in the morning before we start in on the day's chores."

Carolyn Emerson was convinced that her life had been shattered. Not only had she been robbed of her virginity by a crude rapist, but everyone in the county knew of her unhappy situation. She cringed whenever she thought of the posse that had spent twenty-four hours scouring the neighborhood, or the physician who had examined her.

As if her own situation were not bad enough, it was inconceivable to her that Lance had been accused of the crime. She had protested, telling the doctor and a dozen others that she was positive Lance had not been her attacker. Not only did she know him too well, realizing he would never commit such an act, but the man who had assaulted her, although tall, was no giant. There was only one Lance Beaufort.

Besides, as she had tried to explain, she and Lance were betrothed, and planned to marry in a few months. So there had been no reason for him to attack her.

No one had listened to her. A warrant had been issued for his arrest. And a substantial sum, to which many planters had contributed, had been offered for his capture, alive or dead.

Carrie was living in a horrible, warped dream that had no end. At night she dreamed of the masked intruder who had assaulted her with such callous brutality. During the day she was suffused with shame, unable to face friends or acquaintances.

Even when Lance's innocence was established, as she felt certain it would be, he would no longer want her. Nor would any other young gentleman of standing or substance. She had been disgraced, and for the rest of her days would bear the stigma of her dreadful experience.

As a direct result of what had happened to her, Lance was a fugitive, certain to be killed if he dared to return to Oakhurst Manor. How he must hate her!

It was a small relief that Uncle Scott and Mama Emerson were away from home on their business trip. Uncle Scott, who had always been so proud of her, would be crushed. And Kai, who had not only given her a mother's love but was actually Lance's mother, would be doubly hurt and bewildered.

No one except the clergyman and the physician came to call on Carrie. The friends she had known since earliest childhood were conspicuous by their absence. But members of the posse continued to keep watch on Trelawney so they could nab Lance if he returned, and Carrie felt as though she were living in a filthy jail.

Life at Trelawney was unbearable.

She was convinced she had no future here, and there was no future she wanted anywhere without Lance. Even by herself, however, it would be impossible to make a fresh start. For years to come, any visitors to Trelawney would whisper about her. She could never again shop in Charleston or walk down the city's streets without having fingers pointed at her. People would regard her with the same scornful contempt they reserved for the bordello girls. And every man she met would be certain to think of her as an easy mark.

She tried not to think about the masked man who had assaulted her, but he crept repeatedly into her consciousness. She would know him if he came near her again. Never would she forget the sound of his rasping breath, the touch of his clammy hands. Not only would she know him, but she would plunge a knife into his heart.

Indulgence in daydreams served no useful purpose, however. Carrie surveyed the shambles that had destroyed her life, and saw no escape.

For a week she was listless, struggling to recover from her shock. Then, gradually, she gained fresh strength, and at the end of a second week she knew Uncle Scott and Mama Emerson would be returning home in a few days, so she could delay no longer. She had to act now, immediately, before they got back to Trelawney.

Her ability to reason logically and intelligently temporarily warped by her experience, she believed there would be less burden on Scott and Kai if she vanished before they arrived. They would grieve for her, of course, but in the long run she would be doing them the greater kindness by relieving them of the burden she had become.

It would be far better for her, too, to take herself elsewhere. She would be a marked woman for the rest of her days in the Charleston area.

She had no vocation, no way to support herself, even though she had no immediate financial problems. So it was difficult to decide where to go.

Only one possible solution crossed her mind, and it occurred to her repeatedly.

Her own mother, Alicia Emerson, whom Carrie scarcely remembered from early childhood, had run off to New Orleans. All that the girl had ever learned of the incident was that her mother had gone off to the South's largest city to join a man named Emile Duchamp. Neither Uncle Scott nor Papa Beaufort would discuss him, and it was obvious they had little respect for him.

But he must have had some qualities that had made him attractive to her mother, Carrie thought. Perhaps they were still living together. After all these years, it was even possible they were married.

So the girl made up her mind to go to New Orleans, and there would make an attempt to find her real mother and Emile Duchamp. Surely they would give her at least a temporary refuge until she could find honorable employment.

She had no choice, she told herself. The Emersons would not be forced to share the burden of her shame. And in New Orleans, a city of almost fifty thousand people, she would be unknown, just another newcomer in search of a living. She could hide in anonymity there, and wouldn't be forced to endure the gossip and half-suppressed laughter of friends and strangers.

Thanks to birthday and Christmas gifts, Carrie had accumulated a cash nest egg of slightly more than five hundred dollars, an ample sum to take her to New Orleans and, if necessary, rent a small place to live there. She filled only one leather box with clothes, leaving most of her wardrobe behind. In a new existence she wouldn't need as many gowns as she would have required had she become Lance Beaufort's wife.

She put her few items of significant jewelry in a small purse which she wore on a chain around her neck, and she left only one important item behind.

Arising at dawn one morning, she wept as she wrote a note to Uncle Scott and Mama Emerson:

As soon as you come home you'll learn of my awful catastrophe. But don't weep for me, I beg of you. What's done is done, and cannot be repaired. I love you too much to force you to share the burdens of my plight. You deserve to be free of all filth for all of your remaining days. I must assure you, with my whole heart, that Lance is not guilty of the crime against me. I don't care how many accuse him, he didn't do it. One day his name will be cleared. When he comes back to Oakhurst Manor, as I am sure he will, please give him my engagement ring, which I leave with this brief note. I cannot, in good conscience, keep it. Tell him, too, that I love him and will never stop loving him, as long as I live. I love both of you, too, more than I can

ever tell you. It is because of this love that I am
leaving. Please don't try to find me. I'm no longer a child, but am a woman now, and am stronger than you think. May God watch over you
and spare you further hurt.

She could not bring herself to sign the letter.

Before sunrise two of the servants carried the leather
box to a small waiting carriage. Carrie took the reins,
turned for a last lingering look at Trelawney, and drove
off. She wished she could pay a final visit to Oakhurst
Manor, too, so she could see it for the last time. But that
would mean seeing Jerry again and perhaps answering his
questions about her intentions. For reasons she couldn't
fathom, Jerry made her very uncomfortable and she had
no desire to set eyes on him again.

Carrie drove southwest toward Mobile, where she would
engage passage for herself and space for her horses and
carriage on a Gulf ferry that would take her to New Orleans. She had concealed a small knife in the folds of her
dress and was prepared to use it if trouble developed on
the road, but she anticipated no problems. She looked and
acted like a lady, even though she alone knew she had
been defiled, and South Carolina was a civilized state in
which ladies traveling by themselves were safe on the
roads, provided they took elementary precautions.

Remembering conversations between Lisa and Kai, she
drove until late afternoon, stopping well before nightfall at
a small inn, where she negotiated the overnight price of a
room and meals before she consented to stay.

She followed the same routine in the days that followed,
and her journey was uneventful. Driving straight to the
waterfront when she reached Mobile, she engaged passage
on a ferry that was departing that same afternoon, and she
made certain she had a private cabin for the voyage,
which would last three nights.

A stroll through the ship's saloon and other public
rooms quickly convinced Carrie that she should avoid
these quarters, which were crowded with salesmen, traders,
Mississippi River barge workers, and a variety of other
men, most of them rough and all of them bold. A woman,

especially one who was young and beautiful, was regarded as fair game.

So she retired to her own cabin, arranged to have her meals served there, and kept her door bolted at all times. She did not emerge again until the ferry sailed up the Mississippi delta and docked at the busy New Orleans waterfront.

Carrie went ashore quickly, and found her horses and carriage waiting for her at the foot of the pier. She stood for a few moments, bewildered by the sights and sounds of the city. Men were everywhere, some in the handsome attire of the gentry, others in the rough buckskins of the frontier. They spoke English with a variety of accents, and she heard French, too, as well as Spanish. Most of the dock workers were blacks, but here and there in the throngs the girl saw her first Indians, most of them wearing ponchos of crudely woven cloth, with feathers stuck in their matted hair.

There was no other woman in sight. Feeling very alien and fearful, Carrie wondered if she had been wrong to come to this strange place. Perhaps she should have stayed at Trelawney, no matter how hopeless her future would have been there.

Then she saw a constable in a short cloak, and was reassured when he approached her.

"This is no part of town for a lady to loiter in, ma'am," he told her. "Can I be of help to you?"

"I hope so," Carrie replied. "I'm looking for a lady named Alicia Emerson."

"Do you know her address?"

She shook her head.

"Well, you might see the chief clerk at City Hall, but I don't know whether he could help you. There's been talk of making up a city directory of addresses, but the town has been growing too fast for that, I'm afraid."

Carrie drew a deep breath. "I wonder if you could tell me where I might locate a gentleman named Emile Duchamp?"

The constable peered at her sharply. "So you want to see Duchamp, do you?"

She could have sworn the constable was leering at her, but that wasn't important. He seemed to know the name she had mentioned, and that was all that mattered. "You ... you've heard of him?"

"I guess everybody in town knows Emile Duchamp," he said, and looked her up and down with slow insolence.

Carrie couldn't understand the constable's attitude. "Be good enough to tell me where I can find him, sir," she said haughtily.

He raised his hand to his helmet in a mock salute, then gave her specific directions. "Maybe I'll be seeing you again," he told her as she climbed into her carriage.

The traffic was too congested for her to ponder on the meaning of the constable's remark, and the number of coaches and horsemen on the streets increased as she drove to the heart of the city.

There she lost her way twice, but was determined to reach her destination, and finally came to a magnificent four-story brick house, set back from the road, with a long semicircular driveway. Emile Duchamp had to be very prosperous indeed to own such a house, and the girl felt somewhat relieved.

A black groom in livery appeared on the front steps as Carrie drove up to the entrance, and she told him she was seeking Duchamp.

"He ain't here at the moment," the man said, "but Maria will look after you. I'll take your carriage and animals to the stables out back."

Carrie thanked him, dismounted, and was met at the door by a woman in a serving maid's uniform who led her to a small parlor. There, as she sat down, she was conscious of the richness of her surroundings. The rug on the floor came from the Ottoman Empire, the ornate furniture upholstered in velvet could have been made only in France, and the many items of bric-a-brac that dotted the chamber, including a charming porcelain clock that was chiming the hour of twelve noon, had to be imported, too. The room reeked of wealth.

While Carrie was drinking in her surroundings, a handsome middle-aged woman who might have been a quadroon came into the room, her gown of maroon taffeta rustling. Her smile was disarming. "I am known as Maria," she said. "May I be of help to you?"

Carrie started to rise, but the woman waved her back to

her seat. "I'd very much like to see Mr. Emile Duchamp," the girl said. "My name is Carrie." She preferred not to mention her last name to anyone but Duchamp himself.

Maria was in no way disturbed, and nodded blandly. "May I ask why you want to see him?"

"It's . . . a very personal matter."

"Of course, my dear." Maria's smile broadened. "I imagine he'll be here in about an hour and a half. That's the time he usually arrives. May I offer you the chance to freshen yourself before he gets here?"

"Oh, that's kind of you. I've been traveling for days, and I feel filthy. In fact, since there's time, I might even change into one of the dresses in my leather box. Your porter took my carriage around to the stables, and—"

"There's no need to bother," Maria assured her. "Your figure is perfect, and I'm certain we'll find something here that will be the right fit for you. Emile loves elegance, and I'm quite sure he'll be delighted to see you."

Giving the visitor no chance to reply, Maria led her up a broad staircase that reminded Carrie of Oakhurst Manor.

Two young women were chatting on the first-floor landing, but broke off their conversation to stare at the passing new arrival. They scrutinized her with care, but there was only curiosity in their glances, and neither showed any hostility.

Carrie was surprised to note that both were wearing filmy negligees, which seemed slightly odd at noon, but she assumed they were house guests who had slept late. Both were heavily made up, too, and for a moment they bore a fleeting resemblance to the bordello inmates whom Carrie had seen on shopping expeditions in Charleston. But the notion was absurd, and she put it out of her mind.

Maria climbed another flight of stairs, then opened the front door of a handsome suite that consisted of a sitting room and a bedchamber, both furnished in the elaborate style that the Empress Josephine of France had favored. There was too much gilt and velvet, too many tassels, and too much carved furniture for Carrie's personal taste, but she was nevertheless impressed. Emile Duchamp had to be very wealthy to own such an imposing residence.

The servants were remarkably well trained. Two black

maids and a porter, all carrying buckets of steaming water, followed Maria and Carrie into the sitting room, where they poured the water into a gold-rimmed porcelain tub. The porter bowed himself out and closed the door behind him.

"Let the maids bathe you, my dear," Maria said. "They're experts at the art." She herself sat down, making it plain she had no intention of leaving.

Carrie hesitated, her natural shyness making it difficult for her to disrobe in front of strangers. But she told herself not to be a prude. The maids at Trelawney often had bathed her, and she certainly didn't want this city woman to think she was totally lacking in sophistication. She inhaled sharply, then removed her clothes.

"A truly glorious figure," Maria said, "and I don't believe I've ever seen a lovelier face. You resemble a statue of a Greek goddess, my dear."

Unaccustomed to such explicitly candid flattery, the embarrassed Carrie submerged herself in the tub.

Before the maids washed her with a scented soap, they poured a vial of pungent perfume in the water, and the odor of musk filled the room.

Carrie submitted to their ministrations, then allowed them to dry her and brush her long, honey-blond hair. One of them handed her an undergarment of thin silk that clung to her waist and extended to the upper part of her thighs.

"I hope," said Maria, who had been observing the girl in approving silence, "that you'll allow me to make you up. I'm told I'm rather clever with cosmetics."

Relaxed by her bath, Carrie thought that the hospitality here was overwhelming. Slightly amused by the offer, she shrugged. "If it's no imposition," she said, "I don't mind."

The woman decorated her lids with a blue substance that emphasized the deep color of her eyes, which were then rimmed with a subtle black kohl. Color was applied to her cheeks, a brilliant shade of rouge brought her full lips to life, and a tiny but effective beauty mark was pasted on a cheekbone. Then another was put in place just above one of her breasts.

Never had Carrie herself used cosmetics so freely, and she felt slightly uneasy.

As a final touch Maria applied rouge to her nipples.

The girl started to protest.

"Please, my dear." The woman was firm. "I know what I'm doing."

The maids produced a gown of black lace.

Carrie found her voice. "You've forgotten stockings and a breastband," she said.

"You won't need them. The gown is more effective without them, believe me." Maria slipped sandals with very high heels onto her feet.

The girl allowed the maids to drape her in the gown, in spite of her misgivings. The neckline was shockingly low and wide, half-exposing her breasts, which the rouge emphasized.

As a last touch Maria added long, dangling earrings of silver and a thin black band around the newcomer's throat. "Now," she said, pointing to a full-length pier glass, "look at yourself."

Carrie stared at her reflection, and had to admit the result of their ministrations was startling. There was no doubt that her beauty was emphasized, but the combination of the heavily applied cosmetics and the daring gown struck her as overly bold. "You . . . you don't think I look like a trollop?" she asked uncertainly.

"Hardly," Maria assured her. "You're spectacularly lovely, and there's no reason for you to hide behind a screen of false modesty."

The porter was summoned to take away the porcelain tub, and came into the suite carrying a bottle of cooled French champagne and several glasses on a tray. Before departing, he stopped short and gaped at the girl.

Maria was amused, and laughed as she dismissed the porter and maids. "Amos has seen a great many attractive girls," she said, "but you stunned him." She opened the bottle and poured two glasses of the wine.

"Isn't it early in the day for this?" Carrie asked as she was handed a glass.

"Emile believes champagne is appropriate at any hour," Maria said, and raised her glass in a toast. "We'll drink to the success I know you'll enjoy."

The wine was the finest Carrie had ever tasted. Oakhurst Manor and Trelawney were known for their cellars, but neither boasted a champagne this light and dry. "I wonder if Mr. Duchamp will be willing to help me find a position," she said.

Maria stroked her bare shoulder, then ran a hand lightly across her breasts. "You need have no worries, my dear. I'm sure he'll be utterly enchanted by you."

The intimate gesture was surprising, but the woman's words bolstered Carrie. The wine was strong, too, and for the first time since her nightmare at Trelawney she felt a surge of optimism and hope. Perhaps, in this city where she was totally unknown, her future wouldn't be as bleak as she had envisioned it.

Maria finished her own champagne and stood. "I have some things I must do," she said. "Help yourself to the rest of the wine, and I'm sure Emile will be joining you at any moment." She leaned down and kissed the girl on the mouth. "Welcome to New Orleans," she added, and left the suite.

Carrie, alone now, decided the woman meant nothing untoward by her gestures, but was just naturally affectionate and friendly. The champagne really was delicious and was helping her overcome the sense of depression that had gripped her for so long, so she poured herself another glass, then downed it a little too quickly.

Never mind, it was too good to waste, and she decided to finish it before it stopped bubbling.

Again she stood, and inspecting herself anew, she couldn't help giggling. It was true that she bore something of a resemblance to the bordello girls of Charleston, but she could not deny, either, that her dress and makeup enhanced her beauty. Certainly no one looking at her would guess that she had been the helpless victim of a sexual attack. If bold clothes and the lavish use of cosmetics provided her with a shell that would help conceal her secret, she would not hesitate to use them.

She drained the last of the wine, saluting herself in the mirror. It occurred to her that she was somewhat intoxicated, but at the moment she didn't care. New Orleans would bring her good luck. At the appropriate moment in her conversation with Mr. Duchamp, she would reveal that she was Alicia Emerson's daughter and would inquire after her mother's whereabouts, but she would not speak up too quickly. It was possible that, after all these years, her mother and Duchamp were no longer on good terms, and if the man could help her find gainful employment, she didn't want to antagonize him.

A tap sounded at the door, and it opened before the girl could answer. A slender man with silver-white hair, elegant in a suit of pale silk, with lace at his collar and cuffs, came into the sitting room and bowed as he kissed her hand.

"I am Emile Duchamp," he said, "and I can't tell you how pleased I am that you've come to me. Maria has just been raving to me about you, so I hope you'll allow me the privilege of looking at you myself."

He was so charming, so sincere, that Carrie didn't mind allowing him to look her up and down at length.

"Positively ravishing," he said. "I'm an expert on beauty, and I must admit to you that you stand in a class by yourself."

This sophisticated man of the world seemed to mean every word of the compliment, and she glowed.

The porter returned with another bottle of champagne, then departed hastily.

Emile Duchamp waved the girl to a velvet-covered divan, joining her there after he opened the wine and filled two glasses.

"I've already had more than I usually drink," Carrie told him. "I'm not sure I should have any more."

"It can't possibly hurt you, take my word for it." He handed her a glass, and his smile was charming. "Maria says you're called Carrie."

She nodded, and was on the verge of telling him her last name, but decided to wait, as she had planned.

"Your accent tells me you're a Southerner."

"I'm from South Carolina."

For a moment a cloud passed across his face. "I've only visited the state briefly, and my memories of it are none too happy. But you more than make up for the past, Carrie. Hereafter I shall always think of South Carolina as an enchanted state."

She was so embarrassed that she took refuge in her wine, drinking the better part of the contents of her glass.

Duchamp instantly refilled it. "And now you've come to New Orleans."

"I . . . I'd rather not talk about my reasons for leaving home," she said.

"I have no intention of prying," he told her as he took her hand. "Your past if your own, and I only hope you'll allow me to share in your future."

The room was beginning to spin, but the sensation was anything but unpleasant. "You're so kind, I must be honest with you, Mr. Duchamp—"

"Emile. I refuse to stand on formality with you."

"Emile, then." She realized he was stroking her hand, but thought it would be rude to withdraw. "My funds are limited, so I've got to find work."

"If you'll trust me, Carrie, I give you my pledge that you won't have a care in the world." He waited until she finished her drink, then placed his hands on her shoulders. "Will you put your faith in me, dear Carrie?"

Again she was overwhelmed by the combination of his charm and sincerity. His gaze was almost hypnotic, and it comforted her to know that here was someone who was genuinely interested in her future. "I will trust you," she said, "even though I scarcely know you."

"That's something we can rectify," he said, and kissed her.

Carrie was startled by the rapidity of his approach, but he was so gentle, so soothing, that she made no attempt to push him away. Perhaps the large quantities of wine she had consumed were making her careless, causing her to behave as she wouldn't have done had she been sober. But after feeling unclean since being assaulted, it made her feel good to know she was desirable.

Emile took her in his arms, his embrace light, and tenderly forced her lips apart.

Carrie found herself replying to his kiss.

He began to caress her, his touch as soft as a whisper.

Neither then nor later was she able to figure out how it happened, but the next thing she knew she was stretched out on the divan. The upper part of her gown had been pulled down, and now Emile was kissing and caressing her breasts.

It was too late for her to protest. She was a guest in his

house, with no way to defend herself from his advances, even if she called out for help. But it would be too mortifying to make a scene. Possibly her very appearance had encouraged him, and if she had wanted to halt him, she should have said something when he had first taken her hand.

Besides, it didn't matter. She discovered she was actually enjoying his ministrations, and was becoming sexually aroused. She thought fleetingly of Lance, then put him out of her mind. She loved him, but she couldn't dwell on him now, not when this man's hands and mouth were becoming increasingly insistent.

Certainly Emile knew precisely what he was doing, and completely disrobed the girl without effort.

His lovemaking became demanding.

The room was spinning violently now, and all Carrie knew was that her own desire was growing. She didn't quite know what the man was doing to her, but it didn't matter. The experience was new to her, and she felt as though warm waves were washing over her, then carrying her on the surface of an endless sea.

Emile took her, still deft and gentle and considerate.

She found release, and clung to him for a time. Then, when he moved away from her and stood, she looked up at him with misty eyes and a half-smile.

"You're not only beautiful," Emile told her, "but you're a marvelous lover." Inwardly he rejoiced. This girl was worth her weight in pure gold, and for a time, at least, until she became more experienced and demanded the lion's share, he would be able to keep fifty percent of her earnings.

Within six months she would bring him enough income to pay for the emerald ring that Alicia had pestered him into buying for her.

Before he departed, he bent down and kissed her again.

"Welcome to New Orleans," he said, repeating Maria's words, and then the door closed behind him.

Carrie remained stretched out on the divan, indifferent to her nudity and too intoxicated to drag herself into the adjoining bedchamber.

Only a few thoughts managed to penetrate the density

of her befuddled state. First she had been raped, and now she had been seduced.

Emile Duchamp didn't know her identity, and knew her only by her first name.

She wanted to weep for the Carrie Emerson who had been, the Carrie Emerson who had loved Lance Beaufort with all her heart and all her soul and all her mind. But that girl was dead.

A new Carrie Emerson had come into being, a wench so provocative and bold that a strange man had been impelled to make love to her within moments of meeting her.

That, it appeared, was her true destiny.

5

———••◆••———

Life on the farm near the French Broad River in Tennessee was anything but easy. Lance had never shirked, but here he labored in the fields from sunup to sundown, uprooting tree stumps to increase the arable land, plowing and planting, weeding and removing rocks from the soil. He did innumerable chores around the place, making repairs that had been ignored since the death of Elsa McBain's husband, and even on Sundays he worked, adding a new room to the house at her insistence.

She drove a hard bargain, continually nagging him to work harder and faster, finding two new jobs for him before he finished one. She was equally demanding as a mistress, insisting that he make love to her every night and invariably taking the initiative on those occasions when his own interest flagged.

Elsa's attitudes made Lance increasingly uneasy. He was grateful to her for the refuge she had inadvertently given a refugee, but he did not feel he was beholden to her. He more than earned the roof over his head, even the ample well-cooked meals she served him. A hired hand who accomplished only a fraction of what he achieved would be paid wages in addition to his room and board, but Elsa had not given him a penny of the vastly increased income he had generated. She was taking advantage of him, as though she sensed that he was hiding from the authorities.

Even their intimacies created no sense of guilt within him. It was true that she gave him a measure of sexual satisfaction, but he was no more enamored of her than she was of him. He was still deeply in love with Carrie, although circumstances forced him to be unfaithful to her. Elsa was the aggressor in their relationship, setting the pace, making demands, giving neither sentiment nor a feeling of romantic attachment in return for the physical gratification that she seemed to regard as her due.

What bothered Lance more than anything else was the notion that Elsa was beginning to think of their relationship in long-range terms, that she wanted to make it permanent. She owned her land, her house, and her livestock, and now she had found an employee who perfectly suited her vocational and personal needs. Lance did the work of two or more hired hands, he suited her in bed, and he made no unreasonable demands.

Sometimes, when he awakened early in the morning and found her studying him, her expression thoughtful, he was afraid she intended to suggest that he marry her. For the present he found the arrangement comfortable as well as convenient, but he had no intention of spending the rest of his life with this selfish, dominating woman. If the situation became intolerable, he was prepared to move on.

Suddenly and inexplicably Elsa's manner changed. Each Monday she went into the nearby village of Blueberry Hollow to buy flour, sugar, and other staples, and one Monday, returning from her errands just in time to prepare a large noon dinner, she seemed subdued and thoughtful. Usually inclined to chat, she was quiet, somewhat withdrawn all through the meal.

Lance thought nothing of her new attitude until that night. For the first time since his arrival she refrained from demanding that he make love to her. The following morning, when he awakened, he found her sitting up in bed, regarding him with a grave, speculative expression.

That stare followed him for days. Sometimes Elsa accompanied him out to the field and watched him. At meals she was silent, but her eyes seemed to bore into him. And at night she stayed at the far side of the bed, pretending she was asleep.

Lance began to piece together the reasons for her new approach when, for the first time, she began to question him about his past. Where was his home? Why was he in Tennessee, and what had his destination been when she had stumbled on him in the clearing beside the river?

Increasingly uneasy, he couldn't fathom the cause of her changed attitude, but made up his mind to find out. The chicken coop needed repairs, and one afternoon, immediately after dinner, he told her he was going to Blueberry Hollow to buy the necessary wire.

Elsa's only reply was a raised eyebrow.

"In all the weeks I've been here," Lance said, "I haven't once left this property. I can't fix the coop until I get the wire, and I figure the outing will do me good."

She shrugged. "Mr. Enders at the general store knows you're living here," she said, "so you can charge the wire and whatever else you need."

Not quite understanding his reasons for taking such precautions, he packed his spare clothes and other belongings in his saddlebag, then armed himself with his sword and brace of pistols before he saddled Bantu. So far, nothing confirmed his suspicion that Elsa McBain had turned against him.

The ride into the village on a rutted dirt road was uneventful. He saw a scattering of small homes, passed the one-room schoolhouse, and headed straight for the largest building, the general store, which resembled a barn.

Barrels of sugar and salt, flour and pickled beef lined one wall. Bolts of calico, linen, and woolen cloth were piled onto shelves, and the counters were jumbles of farm tools, patent medicines, and rusting iron frying pans. Several other customers were ahead of Lance, and as he awaited his turn, he wandered around the establishment looking at the merchandise.

A wizened man behind the counter, presumably Mr. Enders, was watching him, the man's expression remarkably like that of Elsa in recent days.

The United States Post Office facilities occupied one

corner of the store, and pinned to a wall was a large printed poster that made Lance's blood run cold:

WANTED!

for

MURDER

and

RAPE!

Below was his name, a brief physical description, and the information that one thousand dollars in cash would be paid for information leading to his apprehension.

All at once Lance realized that Elsa McBain had seen the poster and was weighing his worth. He was valuable to her, both as an unpaid hired hand and as a lover, but one thousand dollars was a small fortune, representing a greater profit than she could show under the best of circumstances in three or four years.

Lance knew without looking again behind the counter that Mr. Enders was still watching him.

Pretending he hadn't seen the poster and demonstrating what he hoped was a lack of concern, Lance snapped his fingers as though he had forgotten something. Still behaving casually, he sauntered to the door and left the store.

Afraid he was still under observation, he took his time unhitching his stallion, but his manner changed the moment he was in the saddle.

"Go, Bantu," he whispered, and the great beast started off down the road, quickly increasing his speed to a full gallop.

"To hell with Mr. Enders, Elsa McBain, and anybody else who wants my head on a platter," Lance said aloud as he headed due west on the road that, halfway across the state, would bring him to the capital, Nashville. It would take time before Elsa and Mr. Enders consulted each other and a new posse was formed, but he was taking no chances and pressed his mount to the limit. Bantu responded as he always did, accepting the challenge, and they left a thick cloud of dust on the road behind them.

Had Lance stayed at the McBain farm for a few more days, he realized, he would have been captured and returned to South Carolina in chains. Instead he was still free. Free of Elsa and her incessant demands, too, and he laughed aloud.

Again he was a fugitive, but there were compensations. He had no ties to hold him down, and thanks to his labors on the farm, he was in superb physical condition. It would take the combined efforts of a half-dozen husky men to subdue him.

What bothered him most, as Lance thought about it, was the size of the reward offered for his capture. It was obvious to him that someone of means had put up the vast sum of one thousand dollars, someone who was anxious to have him caught and hanged. Offhand he could think of no one who might hate him that much, no one who stood to gain by his death.

Not that it mattered. His one task now was to escape from the net that was being spread for him. He realized, with almost startling clarity, that his situation made it necessary for him to leave the United States. If the alarm had spread as far as Tennessee, it would be broadcast elsewhere, and nowhere on the soil of the country he loved would he be safe from prosecution.

He continued to ride west, pausing just long enough to buy fodder for his stallion and jerked meat and a loaf of bread for himself. Not until long after midnight did he pause in a small, uninhabited valley beside a stream for a few hours of rest.

In the days that followed, Lance dared to take a great risk by riding on the roads rather than making his way across fields and through wooded areas. The chances of his capture were greater, but he made far better time and relied on his own strength and that of his mount if he should find himself in danger. As he had done previously, however, he made detours around major population centers, and at no time did he stop for more than a few hours.

By the time he reached the western part of Tennessee he knew what had to be done. He changed his course, riding up into western Kentucky. Then, rather than pay the price demanded by bargemen, he saved the cost of a ferry and instead encouraged his stallion to swim the better part of a mile across the Mississippi River.

Now they were in the new state of Missouri, and again Lance headed westward, this time toward the town of Independence, which was located only three miles south of the Missouri River. The largest and fastest-growing community in Missouri, it was the last outpost on American soil, even though it had been founded only three years earlier, in 1827. Beyond it lay unorganized, unsettled land. Far to the west lay the "disputed lands" claimed by Spain, Mexico, the United States, and Great Britain. Only there, where no authority of any kind existed, would he be truly safe.

Each mile he traveled took Lance farther from his beloved Carrie, but that couldn't be helped. He had no choice, and could only vow that someday he would give her the full measure of his love and protection in return for the unavoidable anguish he was causing her now. No matter what happened, he would cherish her for the rest of his days. Perhaps, before he pushed off into the unknown, he could send her a brief note from Independence that would assuage her worries.

After spending interminable days and nights on the road, Lance approached the western border of Missouri, beyond which lay the domain of the Kansas Indians, and only now did he ask specific directions. Many years earlier, Lester Howard, the Oakhurst Manor overseer who had helped supervise Lance's upbringing, had moved out here. With him had come his mulatto wife, Dolores, whose life Papa M'Bwana had saved in Santo Domingo and who in turn had befriended him.

The color barrier in the older portions of the South had made it impossible for the Howards to remain in South Carolina, and they had created new lives for themselves on the frontier.

As Lance reached the Howard property, he estimated that their farm consisted of at least one thousand fertile acres, where corn, wheat, and vegetables were growing in abundance. He noted, too, that a number of hired hands were at work in the fields. The Howard home was a substantial two-story frame house, neatly whitewashed, and behind it stood a cluster of barns, stables, silos, and other outbuildings.

The still-handsome Dolores herself answered the new arrival's tap at the front door. She stared at him for a long moment, then wept as she hugged and kissed him. There were tears in Lance's eyes, too.

Dolores summoned her husband from the fields by blowing on a conch-shell horn, a souvenir of her Caribbean days that she used only in emergencies. Lester Howard hurried to the house, and he, too, embraced the young giant who, as a child, had been his protégé.

The Howards stopped all work for the day, and as they sat in their bright, cheerful kitchen over mugs of steaming tea, Lance brought them up-to-date on developments of recent years. They plied him with numerous questions about the family, which he answered in detail.

Then, when he told them of recent happenings, they became grim, and there was a silence when he completed his recital.

Lester was the first to speak, running a hand through his gray, thinning hair. "Who do you suppose attacked Carrie?"

Lance shrugged. "I have no idea."

"And who do you imagine posted that huge reward for your capture?"

"I don't know."

"It had to be Jerry," Lester said.

Dolores nodded. "You're right, dear. Jerry has always hated Lance. He's been consumed by jealousy ever since you were very small boys."

Lance was stunned. "But, my God! He's my half brother."

"All the more reason he hates you. You're smarter and stronger," Lester said. "You outshine him in every way."

"It wouldn't surprise me," Dolores said, sipping her tea, "if it was Jerry who assaulted Carrie."

Lance's eyes narrowed. "What makes you say that? If you're right, I'll go back to Oakhurst Manor and kill him in cold blood."

She shook her head. "No, don't. It's just a woman's feeling that I can't prove. I spent a great deal of time with all three of you when you were children and I was acting as your governess, and it strikes me as typical of the way Jerry would react to your engagement to Carrie. He'd want her for himself—for the moment—while spoiling your life and hers."

Lance compressed his lips until they became pale.

"Pay no attention to me," Dolores told him. "You could cause yourself even more harm if you tried to obtain revenge against him. Be patient, Lance, and the truth will all come into the open eventually."

"Have you been in touch with Jeremy about all this?" Lester wanted to know.

"I can't possibly write to Papa," Lance said. "He's five thousand miles from Oakhurst Manor, trying to do a good job in a new type of work for President Jackson. There's nothing he can do to help me. Or Carrie. And I see no point in creating new burdens for him."

His unselfishness was typical of him, Lester thought. "What are your plans?"

"I aim to make a new life for myself in the Rocky Mountains," Lance said, "and if I can earn some money in the fur trade, I'll write to Carrie and ask her if she's willing to join me."

Dolores started to protest, but her husband shook his head and she subsided. Lester was right. Lance had staggering problems, but he was a man now, not a boy, and it was his privilege to work them out in his own way. "We hope you'll stay with us for a time," she said.

"There's nothing I'd like better," Lance replied. "I'd also appreciate the opportunity to earn some money so I can buy myself a rifle and ammunition. Also some bits of steel and scrap iron."

Lester grinned at him. "Bits of iron and steel, eh? You're planning to make some of those short Bantu spears that M'Bwana taught you to use."

"I figure they may come in handy in mountain living."

"The Lord has been good to us," Lester said, "and if it hadn't been for the generosity of Jeremy and Lisa we wouldn't be here in the first place. It so happens I have a spare rifle in first-class condition and all the ammunition and gunpowder you need. Yes, and I'm sure you'll find all the scrap metal you'll want in my workshop out back. Seasoned oak makes the best spears, as I recall, and we've recently cut down a couple that we haven't even trimmed yet. So there's ample raw material for several quivers full of spears."

"More important than all that," Dolores said as she rose from the table, "is the special steak I'm going to broil for supper. And the cherry-and-custard pie that was always Lance's favorite when he was a boy."

As Lance hugged her again he had the feeling that he had come home. If Carrie were here, too, he would be happy.

Kai Emerson collapsed and had to be put to bed when she and her husband returned to Trelawney from Washington City, found Carrie's note awaiting them, and learned of the tragic events that had taken place during their absence.

Her husband, meanwhile, lost no time trying to trace Carrie. He also made a thorough investigation of the assault on Carrie and the circumstances of Lance's flight. He paid a visit to Oakhurst Manor, conferred with the county sheriff, and had a long, candid talk with the physician who had attended Carrie.

These activities kept him busy for several days, and by the time he had gleaned as much as he could, Kai had recovered sufficiently from her initial shock to discuss the entire matter with him.

"God only knows where Carrie has gone or what's become of Lance," he said as they sat down to a light supper. "They disappeared separately, and there's been no trace of either of them. Our only hope is that they'll both show up somewhere one of these days."

Kai's sigh was tremulous. It was almost impossible for her to believe she had lost both her son and future daughter-in-law.

"Looking at the overall situation as dispassionately as I can through a lawyer's eyes," Scott said, "there's no proof whatever that it was Lance who assaulted Carrie."

"He couldn't have done it! I don't say that because I'm his mother. But I know he loved and respected her too much."

"I'm certain you're right, dear," Scott said. "Unfortunately, we have no proof. It may take me a little time to have the rape charge against Lance nullified, but I believe I can do it eventually. However, there's no doubt at all that Lance was directly responsible for the deaths of two members of the posse that had been formed to capture him. So the murder charge against him will have to stand, even though the two men he killed were Charleston water-front scum who belonged to Oscar Griffin's gang."

She fought back her tears. "How is it possible that Griffin's people were involved in all this horrible mess?"

"I just don't know," Scott said, "and it's one of the mysteries I intend to explore. No one is shedding any tears for bullies who were involved in many crimes, but there's nothing specific I can do to clear Lance's name until we learn more."

"Oh, dear."

"I'll do it, never fear," he told her, then hesitated for a moment. "I hate to say this, but while I was visiting Jerry at Oakhurst Manor today, I gained the distinct impression that he knows more than he told me." Jerry, he refrained from adding, had changed for the worse. Not only was he intoxicated when Scott went to Oakhurst Manor, but it was obvious that he had reversed his father's policies and was encouraging his overseers to whip the slaves in order to force them to work harder and longer.

"What's happening to the shipping company?"

"Jerry has taken charge there, too, even though he knows little about its affairs."

"I'm afraid you'll have to send Jeremy the bad news," Kai said as she fought for self-control.

"I intend to write him a long letter tonight. I hate to upset him and Lisa, but they have a right to know what's happening here."

"I'll add something to the letter," she said, "although, to be truthful, I honestly don't know what I can say that will ease the burden for them, any more than it can be eased for us."

The girl who was known only as Carrie was the new star of Emile Duchamp's exclusive New Orleans bordello, the undisputed queen of all she surveyed. No other inmate wore clothes as daring or used as many cosmetics; no other girl was as willing to drink with the customers, and her reckless attitude inflamed the men who came to the establishment.

Her independence was unique in the history of the place, but no one objected, no one reprimanded her. In fact, both Duchamp and the madam of the house, Maria, encouraged her to do as she pleased. Their reasons were simple: no girl, ever, had earned as much money. The more attractive inmates charged their customers ten dollars, but Carrie commanded fees as high as one hundred dollars, and New Orleans bankers, Louisiana plantation owners, and wealthy merchants visiting the city from other parts of the country vied for her favors.

She herself selected those whom she permitted to accompany her to the largest suite in the house. Her standards were high, and she rejected boors, men who were drunk, and anyone else whose appearance, manners, and personality did not appeal to her. Soon after her arrival she established a routine that was unvarying. Instead of allowing customers to indicate that they wanted her to go upstairs with them, it was she who granted the privilege after interviewing them in a downstairs parlor.

She was friendly with the other girls, put on no airs with them, and willingly went with them on shopping expeditions. Her beauty was so superior that few of them envied her, and they appreciated her generosity with her large, ever-growing wardrobe. She freely lent her colleagues demure dresses for their shopping excursions and provocative gowns for occasions when they were entertaining special customers. They could borrow her hats and jewelry whenever they pleased, too. As one of them remarked, she seemed to have no interest in material possessions. She seemed to buy expensive dresses for the sheer sake of owning them, and then forgot about them.

The girls were amused by her attitude toward Emile Duchamp. It was common knowledge in the house that he had followed his usual practice with new arrivals and had seduced her on the day she had first come to see him. But thereafter she hadn't permitted him to come near her again, and on the one occasion when he had tried to insist, she had threatened to walk out. He had subsided immediately, unwilling to risk losing the biggest money-maker he had ever employed.

Carrie had tamed Maria, too. Every girl in the place was expected to submit to the woman's advances from time to time in order to curry favor with her. But Carrie refused. Such relations revolted her, she said, and she informed Maria she was willing to be her friend, provided the woman behaved herself. From that time forward Maria was careful to keep her hands to herself.

The most intriguing aspect of Carrie's personality was her ability to keep a distance between herself and everyone else, even the men who went to bed with her. She laughed with her clients, teased them, and behaved with abandon when alone with a man behind closed doors, yet no one felt he really knew her after he left the establishment. The other girls reacted in the same way. In spite of her friendliness, Carrie never discussed her past.

One of the shrewder girls summed up the situation neatly. "You'd almost think," she said, "that Carrie sprang out of nowhere the day she came here. She threw away the clothes she brought with her, and she sold her horses and carriage. She's never said a word to anyone about her family, her own home, or anything that's ever happened to her. You'd think she had been born the day she came to Emile's."

The analysis was truer than Carrie's colleagues knew.

She was two people now. One was the gaudy and gorgeous harlot, the most sought after wench in New Orleans, who selected her own clients and set her own terms, already the most celebrated and notorious girl in the city. The other was the calm and sensible Carolyn Emerson of Trelawney, betrothed to Lance Beaufort and loving him with her whole being.

There was no conflict between these two sides of her personality. The harlot was rampant, to be sure, but when Carrie was alone, in the privacy of her own suite, she quietly longed for the day when she and Lance would be reunited and her world would turn right side up once again. She had to admit the possibility, however, that the day she wanted so badly would never come.

In the meantime she had to live each twenty-four-hour period for its own sake, and she tried to make the best of her new world. Late one morning, shortly after she awakened, she said to Maria, "Tell Emile I want to see him as soon as he gets here. It's important."

An hour or two later the dapper Duchamp arrived, after first visiting New Orleans' largest gaming house, which he also owned. Profits on card games had been better than usual the preceding night, so he was in an amiable mood when he joined Carrie in her sitting room.

She was wearing a spectacular new gown of red satin with a breathtakingly low, square-cut neckline and a slit high on one side of her skirt that revealed her long, lovely thigh. Duchamp studied her with lively appreciation, then fixed his gaze on a new bracelet of solid gold, more than three inches wide, that graced a slender wrist.

"I see that you didn't lose much last night," he said.

"I didn't do badly," she replied with a shrug. "But our arrangement doesn't make me very happy."

"Oh?" He was instantly alert.

"There are a dozen girls here," Carrie replied, the hard and calculating expression in her eyes belying her beguiling smile, "and I earn more than any six of them together. If they choose to give you half of their earnings, that's their business. But I want to keep more of what I bring in."

"Not so fast," Emile protested. "If it weren't for me—"

"I refuse to listen," she said, her voice metallic. "I came to you voluntarily, and I've built my own clientele. No one can claim any part of my success, and I want a larger share of the rewards. Beginning immediately."

"I'd be stupid to deny your popularity, but if I increase your share, I'll be setting a dangerous precedent. We couldn't keep a new arrangement quiet. The other girls will learn about it, and they'll start demanding more, too."

Carrie shrugged prettily. "That isn't my problem," she told him.

Emile was known for his violent temper, which he found it difficult to control, and it began to soar. "I think you're an ungrateful bitch!" he shouted as he jumped to his feet and loomed over her.

She neither rose to her own feet nor shrank from him. "My demands," she said icily, "are not subject to negotiation. You may take them or leave them."

He raised a hand, obviously intending to strike her.

Carrie fixed him with a level gaze. "If you touch me," she said, "I'll leave at once and I won't come back. I mean that."

His face a deep red, he forced his hand back to his side.

"There are certain advantages to making this place my headquarters," she told him. "It's convenient to be here, and I don't have to hire my own servants or attend to my own housekeeping. But there are other houses in New Orleans that would be delighted to have me. On my own terms. Or I could even set up my own place, and you can be sure that all of my clients would follow me there."

She was far shrewder and tougher than Emile had realized, and he capitulated to her. "I'll give you an additional ten percent," he said.

Her smile broadened, indicating that she knew she had won. "I want a full two-thirds, no less," she said flatly. "And you'll still earn more from me than you do from anyone else here. Take it or leave it, Emile."

"You give me no choice," he said. "What are you going to do with all your money, Carrie?"

"I really don't know," she said, "and that's the truth. Not that it matters. There's a principle involved, and that's what matters to me."

Emile knew she meant what she said, and told himself she was the most unusual, extraordinary trollop he had ever encountered. Someday he'd have to find out why she was so different from all the rest.

Lisa Beaufort was the rage of Vienna. As her sister-in-law, Margot, remarked, "Every nobleman, every general, every member of the court is in love with you, Lisa. I think the emperor himself would give you a duchy if you asked him for it."

Jeremy, who was pleased with his wife's popularity, plunged into his new position with his customary vigor. He opened complicated negotiations for the first Austro-American trade treaty, he arranged for American cavalry officers to come to Austria for a year of special training, and he engaged in the delicate task of working out a new agreement permitting subjects of the Austrian Empire who wanted to leave the country to migrate to the United

States. The Hapsburg rulers of Austria, like royalty everywhere, were shaken by the revolutions of 1830 that swept
across Europe, and never before had the position of an
American minister been as important or significant.

One evening each week the members of the diplomatic
corps were expected to attend a special reception given by
the emperor and attended by Count Metternich, the powerful foreign minister. Lisa, seated at her dressing table in
the large master bedroom of the comfortable town house
that was located only a short distance from the imperial
palace, was preparing, with her usual scrupulous attention
to detail, for the event.

Her husband came into the room, having just returned
from his office at the legation, and, ever sensitive to his
moods, she knew instantly that something was amiss.

"What's wrong?" she asked, putting her jar of kohl on
the table.

Making no comment, Jeremy handed her the letter he
had just received from Scott and Kai Emerson.

Lisa grew pale beneath her makeup as she read of the
catastrophic events that had taken place at home.

"This is so awful," she said, "that I can't grasp it all."

"I've been in a daze for the past hour," he told her. "I
showed the letter to my brother, and for the first time in
his life he was speechless."

"What can we do?" Lisa was always practical.

"Scott appears to have taken every possible step. He's
certain the absurd rape charge against Lance will be
dropped, but it will take longer to nullify the murder
charges." Jeremy began to pace the length of their bedchamber. "I feel so helpless. We're so incredibly far from
home."

Lisa rose, put her arms around him, and kissed him.
"We'll work this out, darling."

He clung to her for a long moment. "I hate to let
President Jackson and the United States down when I'm
needed here. But I feel like going back to Oakhurst Manor
and taking charge myself."

"Whatever you want to do is what I want, too," she
said.

"All that holds me back right now," he said, "is that by
this time it may be that Lance and Carrie have been lo-

cated and the problems have been solved. As Tom finally pointed out to me, Scott wrote this letter two months ago. That's a long time, and a great many things may have happened in the past eight weeks."

"I suggest we sleep on this and not make up our minds until tomorrow. If worse comes to worst, Tom can handle your various negotiations with the Austrians until a new minister comes here."

"Not really. By the time the president appoints someone else, has him confirmed by the Senate, and sends him here, it will be a full six months, and by that time the favorable initiatives will have been lost. However, you're right. We'll make no final decisions until tomorrow."

"Would you rather we don't go to court tonight?"

"We're expected, and I've got to have some private words with Count Metternich. These imperial assemblies are perfect for the purpose. It's my duty to go, so we'll do it. I've never yet failed to do my duty, and I don't intend to begin now."

Those who attended the royal court that night noted that the wife of the American minister was far less animated than usual.

Jeremy and Lisa spent a restless night, and it was dawn before they dropped off to sleep, so they stayed in bed somewhat later than usual. A small breakfast was served in their bedroom, and they were eating listlessly when their butler came in with a letter that had just arrived.

It proved to be from Jerry, and after his father quickly broke the seal, they read it together.

By now, Jerry said, they would have learned the tragic news from Scott Emerson. He himself had refrained from writing until he could report positive developments. Unfortunately, there were none.

"But let me assure you, dear Papa and Lisa," he wrote, "that I am acting in your stead during your absence. Rest assured that I will do everything possible for both Lance and Carrie. Acting as your deputy, I shall do all that you would do if you were here."

An expression of great relief appeared on Jeremy's face, and he sank back in his chair with a deep sigh. "Thank God for Jerry," he said. "As long as he's taken charge,

there's no immediate need for me to resign my post and
go home."

Lisa averted her face so he wouldn't see the shocked
disbelief in her eyes. He wouldn't believe that his faith in
Jerry was unfounded, and they would only quarrel if she
tried to point out his error. Yet she knew, as he apparently
could not, that Jerry would not lift a finger to assist either
Lance or Carrie. On the contrary, she was positive, he
would do everything in his considerable power to harm
both of them.

6

"Lance, I don't quite know how to tell you this," Lester Howard said, "but there's a notice on the wall of the Independence post office, offering a reward for your capture. We'll gladly hide you here, as best we can, but our hired hands know you're here, and I'm afraid some of them will find a thousand dollars too large a sum to resist."

"There's no way I'd place you and Dolores in jeopardy," Lance said. "What's more, I've never hidden anywhere, and I don't aim to start now. I'll leave first thing in the morning."

Dolores wept, but realized there was no real choice.

Refusing a cash gift or loan, even though his purse was almost empty, Lance took his leave early the next day. The rifle, ammunition, and gunpowder Howard had given him made him feel secure, and he knew he had to make his own way.

Bantu swam across the broad Missouri River, then man and stallion began the long trek across the virtually uninhabited plains of Kansas. The journey was lonely, but there were few difficulties. The terrain was flat, the land covered with knee-high prairie grass and patches of wild corn that provided ample fodder for the horse. Lance shot rabbits, prairie dogs, and weasels for his own sustenance, cooking them in a small iron pot that Dolores had insisted he take, and there were many small clear streams where the water was pure and cool.

One morning Bantu whinnied, then sidestepped with agility, and Lance saw a snake, more than three inches in diameter and at least five feet long. He shot the reptile without delay, then regretted his haste and vowed he would not make the same mistake a second time.

A few days later his horse again demonstrated uneasiness, and this time Lance was prepared. Curled up beside a large rock in the tall grass, its tailbones sounding a warning, was a diamondback rattlesnake. Its head was raised and it was ready to strike.

Lance drew one of the short spears he had made at the Howard farm, took quick but careful aim, and threw it. The sharp point landed between the snake's eyes, and after writhing convulsively the reptile stiffened and died.

Where there was one rattler there had to be another, Lance knew, and began a careful search, dismounting and stirring the grass with the butt of his rifle, which he held at arm's length. He did not have long to wait.

An ominous rattle sounded behind him, and he whirled just in time to take another spear from its quiver and fling it. The reptile had actually begun its strike after rearing its head high, and this time the point penetrated its throat, landing with such force that it came out at the back of its head. This rattler was the male, and wriggled for a far longer time before it died.

Conquering his distaste, Lance milked the venom from both snakes' sacs, then spread the sticky, foul-smelling substance on the tips of all his spears. Now he felt truly safe, and was ready for any eventuality.

In the next week he caught a glimpse of a small party of Indian warriors in the distance, men of medium height who were naked to the waist. They were on foot and he was mounted, so they made no attempt to molest him, and he soon lost sight of them. That night he took no risks, however, and slept lightly.

A few days thereafter, as he was heading northward into the Nebraska country, Lance suddenly halted his mount. The grass was shorter here, and directly ahead, stretched out on a patch of bare ground, was an Indian who looked as though he was either dead or asleep. On the ground beside him were a knife, a drinking gourd, a long spear, and a length of plaited vines that, apparently, had been used as a rope.

The brave made no move, so Lance dismounted and, a pistol cocked and ready for instant use, approached him with great caution. The brave was alive, he discovered, but was either asleep or unconscious. Filling the gourd with water from a brook only a few feet away, Lance raised his head and roused him sufficiently to give him a few sips.

The Indian opened his eyes wide, realized that a white man was helping him, and, to Lance's astonishment, spoke to him in English. "You help me, so I thank you," he said.

Taking strips of dried meat and a small handful of parched corn from his pouch, Lance fed it to him.

Little by little the Indian gained strength, and by night-fall was sufficiently recovered to tell his story. His name was Ponca, he said, and he had learned the tongue of the white man from a missionary who had visited his village when he had been a child. He was member of the Kiowa nation, which lived far to the east. Buffalo, deer, and other wildlife had vanished suddenly and unexpectedly from his people's hunting grounds, so he had been a member of a party that had traveled west in search of meat.

He had fallen ill, and had been so severely afflicted with a high fever that he had no longer been able to move. So his fellow warriors had left him to die on the prairie, and taking his horse with them, had gone off. Ponca had no idea how many days had passed since their departure.

Lance gave him more to eat that night, then fed him again early the next morning. Drinking large quantities of water from the brook, too, Ponca showed a marked improvement but was still too weak to travel.

Promising he would return, Lance rode off in search of game.

In midmorning he heard a rumble that sounded like a sustained roar of thunder, even though the sky overhead was clear. The noise grew louder, and when a smudge on the horizon grew larger, then became identifiable, he smiled at his own naiveté. A herd of buffalo was approaching, running at a full clip.

Never had he seen buffalo, but his instinct told him to make no move, and he steadied his jittery mount. There were several hundred of the shaggy beasts in the herd, he guessed, with gigantic bulls in the lead, cows and calves in the center, and another group of bulls acting as a rear guard.

Forcing Bantu to hold still, Lance felt his heart beating faster as the whole herd bore down on him, threatening to trample him and his horse. Just before they reached him, however, the herd split and began to move past him on either side. The thunder of the creatures' hooves was deafening, their stench and the thick cloud of dust they raised choked him, and some passed so close he could almost reach out and touch them.

Bantu showed his mettle by refusing to panic, and continued to stand motionless.

The stallion's reaction steadied Lance, and he knew now what needed to be done. He drew his rifle from its sling, waited until the rear guard approached and then fired at a young bull.

His shot caused the beast to stumble and fall to its knees, then roll onto its side. The rest of the herd, frightened by the sound of gunfire, raced away at an even greater speed.

The bull was still alive, and Lance had to fire two more shots before dispatching him.

Then, rather than try to drag the carcass to the place where Ponca awaited him, he returned there for the Indian in order to bring him to the buffalo. Bantu objected to the presence of another rider on his back and started to buck, but Lance spoke to him sternly and he subsided. Less than an hour later they reached the dead buffalo.

That night they ate steaks, and Lance skinned the beast, then butchered the carcass.

For the next week, while Ponca slowly recovered his strength, Lance was busy. He smoked almost innumerable strips of meat over a fire made from wood that Ponca gathered, and he cured the hide, too, then fashioned cloaks and boots that would be useful in winter. Ponca fashioned knives and made a shield from the bones, so almost no part of the carcass was wasted.

Ponca's gratitude to the man who had saved his life was boundless. "I will go with you," he said.

"I'm heading toward the high mountains, where I can find furs."

The Kiowa's resolve did not waver, even though Plains Indians rarely ventured into the Rockies. "Then I will go to the high mountains also," he said.

Even after Ponca was well enough to travel, however, they stayed in the plains of Nebraska because their problem of finding suitable transportation puzzled them. Two men could not ride for long distances on one horse, not even a mount as strong as Bantu.

One morning, as they were eating grilled buffalo meat for breakfast in front of their fire, they found what promised to be a solution. Ponca raised his head, listened intently, then jumped to his feet and pointed toward the north.

Squinting and shading his eyes, Lance saw a small herd of wild horses grazing on the prairie, and knew what had to be done. "I'll cut one out, and if I can, I'll drive him toward you. Do you reckon you can lasso him with that vine rope?"

If the Kiowa felt any doubts, he did not show them. "I will do it," he said.

Not wanting to take the time to saddle Bantu, Lance decided to ride bareback, and armed only with his pistols, he started off toward the north, then made a wide loop so he could approach the horses from the far side and drive them south.

When he drew nearer he counted three mature stallions, the largest of them far smaller than Bantu, five mares, and a number of their offspring. Studying the herd, Lance selected a young stallion whose age he estimated at about two years. That beast was the best of the lot, the horse he wanted for his companion.

Bantu was thoroughly enjoying the game, and seemed to know what to do before he was given instructions. He galloped swiftly, then slowed his pace and trod more quietly.

One of the older stallions, presumably the leader of the herd, turned to do battle with the intruder, but quickly changed his mind. He was no match for the huge beast bearing down on him, and he knew it. So he sounded an alarm, whinnying softly, then started off toward the south.

The entire herd followed obediently.

Lance saw that the young stallion he wanted was riding on the right flank, so he edged forward to drive a wedge between the horse and the rest of the herd. Bantu responded instantly, and again his hooves pounded on the ground.

Gradually Lance drew closer. He was only two hundred yards from the herd, then one hundred. He touched Bantu's sides with his knees, and the great stallion surged forward, still gaining on the herd.

Lance waited as long as he dared, then drew a pistol and fired it into the air.

The herd panicked and veered to the left.

The young stallion tried to follow, but Bantu cut him off, and his loud snort warned the two-year-old not to tamper with him. The cutoff maneuver was complete: the young stallion was isolated now, and the rest of the herd hastily withdrew.

Unable to follow, the young stallion plunged straight ahead, and soon approached the spot where Ponca was standing motionless, his lasso in his hand.

Bantu remained close behind the quarry, and Lance was ready to intervene if the young stallion tried to change course toward either the right or left.

Almost unaware of where he was going, the wild horse remained on a collision course with the Kiowa. Only at the last moment did he sense the man's presence, and by then it was too late. The lasso flew into the air, then dropped over his head.

The animal bolted, dragging Ponca on the ground behind him. Lance was close enough now to come to the Indian's aid. Both men grasped the end of the rope, then managed to throw it over the sturdy shoulders of Bantu, who stood rock-still.

The flight of the wild horse ended abruptly, and he sprawled on the ground.

Ponca approached him cautiously, holding the end of the lasso, and when the beast regained his feet, the Indian quickly mounted him.

The horse was outraged, and demonstrated his feelings

by rearing and bucking in an attempt to throw the man who dared to sit on his back. But Ponca refused to be thrown, even though the animal reared and bucked repeatedly, moving in viciously angry circles as his hooves flailed and flashed.

Twice it appeared as though Ponca would be hurled to the ground, but somehow he managed to retain his seat.

Lance, who knew he could not interfere now because only the man who mastered the wild stallion would be able to ride him, watched the Indian with growing admiration. Ponca was in his own class, an expert rider.

At last the young stallion realized he had been defeated and stood still, his flanks heaving as he fought for breath.

Ponca patted his neck and spoke to him soothingly, then loosened the lasso, for which there was no longer a need. At last the animal became completely calm, and Ponca jumped to the ground, moved off a short distance, and dug up some roots.

When he brushed them they appeared to be a dull reddish color, and Lance guessed they were wild beets.

Ponce fed some to the young stallion, then gave the rest to Bantu. "Horses like these," he said with a tired grin. "They have a taste as sweet as the white man's sugar."

Not only had he acquired a first-rate mount, Lance thought, but the animal was fortunate, too, because he had a master who knew and understood horses.

Now they were ready, at last, to travel on to the Rocky Mountains.

The young black couple in Boston, brother and sister, called themselves Beaufort because they had no other surname. Their grandmother had been the late Cleo, for many years housekeeper at Oakhurst Manor. Her son, Willie, an expert cabinetmaker, had been released from slavery by Jeremy Beaufort, his childhood companion, and, marrying a free woman, Amanda, had gone with her to Boston to live.

There Paul, their son, and Cleo, their daughter, had been born. After their parents had died in a fire, Paul and Cleo had made their home for many years with the late Sarah Beaufort's father and stepmother. Now they were adults, on their own in the world, and both had successful professional careers. Paul was a physician and surgeon, and was so talented, so deft, that his many patients ignored the color prejudices of the period. Cleo, who had inherited her mother's slender beauty, was a teacher in the Boston elementary schools.

They made it their practice to dine together one night each week, sometimes going to an inn near the hospital where Paul served, but more often eating at Cleo's small apartment, where they had greater privacy. One evening Cleo prepared her brother's favorite meal, clam chowder and a beef stew with wild onions and mushrooms. Then, knowing he would be tardy, she moved the pots to the side of her stove.

Paul arrived an hour late, and was so out of sorts that not even a glass of mulled cider mollified him. "Sometimes I think I went into the wrong profession," he said. "I should have been a simple cabinetmaker, like our father."

"A very good cabinetmaker," Cleo said emphatically.

"Sure, but it was an uncomplicated existence. I performed surgery on three patients today, and I can still hear their screams. No man in his right mind should become a doctor until science finds some way to kill a sick man's pain during an operation. Laudanum helps after surgery, but all the poor patient can do is bite the wooden block while he's on the table."

"You'll feel better about it tomorrow," Cleo said.

Her brother shook his head. "No, there have been too many yesterdays, and my nerves are ragged."

She laughed, and as always when she was animated, her face became exceptionally pretty. "Don't tell me. You still want to go out to the Rocky Mountains to hunt for fox and lynx and bear—or whatever the pelts are that bring such a huge price here!"

"What's wrong with that?" he demanded, becoming indignant.

"You're a doctor, Paul, not a hunter and trapper."

Paul Beaufort assumed a dignified pose. "For the past ten years I haven't taken a single day's holiday. I worked my way through medical school, and since that time I've been so busy in my practice that I don't even take time off on Sundays and holidays. I'm supposed to be an expert rifle shot, a marksman, but I have no chance to hunt, and I refuse to kill little squirrels on the Boston Common."

His sister laughed again as they moved to the dining table.

"I don't share your sense of humor," Paul said. "When I was a boy at Oakhurst Manor, M'Bwana took me hunting when he and Lance went out, and later I went with Uncle Jeremy, too. It's part of me. I don't intend to give up my practice. Medicine is my life. But—just for a year or two—I want to fulfill a dream I've had ever since I was small. Just the other day I was reading a magazine article about the wonderful, wild lives the mountain men lead—"

"You're an incurable romantic," Cleo told him.

"Maybe so," Paul replied, "but I owe myself a sabbatical. This is good chowder."

"Thank you. If you want a break from work, I wish you'd come with me to South Carolina."

Paul put down his spoon and glared at her. "Now you're the one who is mad!"

"Hardly. I have wonderful childhood memories of Oakhurst Manor, too. And I want to put flowers on Grandma Cleo's grave. I think about her all the time."

"South Carolina is not for the likes of you, Cleo," her brother said emphatically.

"Why not?"

"You're the wrong color, and you're too good-looking. There is no such thing as a free black down there, and you'd be exposing yourself to the insults and advances of every white man you see."

"Rubbish. Now you sound like the abolitionist newspapers. I'm taking a ship to Charleston, and from there it's just a short trip to Oakhurst Manor. I'll come home on a brig, too, so what possible harm could come to me?"

"In case you've forgotten or don't read newspapers anymore, Uncle Jeremy is in Vienna. He's the U.S. minister to Austria."

"I know, but his sons are bound to be there, and I know they had tremendous affection for Grandma Cleo, too."

"You'll be far better off if you stay here, marry the right man, and settle down." He was on dangerous ground now, and knew it.

Cleo glowered at him, her dark eyes smoldering. She

had engaged in two serious romances and had indulged in affairs with both men, much to her brother's annoyance. But she had no regrets; perhaps she had been giving in to a wild streak in her own nature. "Someday I'll meet the right man for me," she said.

He was aware of her problem. Not many blacks in Boston could match her education, and prejudices on both sides made it difficult for her to establish an enduring relationship with a white man. "You've got to persevere," he said.

Cleo couldn't resist taunting him. "You insist on freezing out West in the mountains—"

"Right! I've already arranged for a two-year leave of absence, and I'm going next month!"

"Well," she said, "maybe I'll be ready to settle down after I come back here from Oakhurst Manor. I have as much right to indulge in daydreams as you do."

They had reached an impasse, which was not unusual, both of them being so stubborn, so Paul concentrated on his beef stew, which was excellent.

They dined together three more times, and on the last occasion Paul brought his sister a bottle of wine and a bouquet of flowers. "These are in the nature of farewell gifts," he said. "I'm taking a coach day after tomorrow and will go to Cincinnati. From there I'll go by boat down the Ohio to the Mississippi, and at a trading-post town called St. Louis I'll buy myself a horse."

"Now you're just showing off how much you know about geography," Cleo said, then softened. "I hope we'll see each other again."

He grinned at her. "I'm indestructible," he said. "If I could survive medical school and the hell of the years I've spent in the surgery, I can survive anything."

Cleo refrained from telling him that she had booked her own passage to Charleston the following week. She knew he would deliver another lecture, and she was already familiar with every word he would say to her. It was preferable, by far, to keep her plans to herself.

She saw Paul off on the morning his coach left for Albany, the first stage of his long journey, and then she busied herself with her own preparations. She needed few new clothes, but there were several last-minute purchases to make. Being frugal, she had rented her apartment to a friend for a period of two months. Perhaps she was an incurable sentimentalist. Perhaps, like her brother, she was merely restless and wanted a change in scenery. Whatever her real reasons, she was on her way.

The voyage on the merchantman, which carried only two other passengers, was uneventful. Cleo slept late, walked on deck, and spent most of her time reading. Thoroughly rested after eight days at sea, she arrived in Charleston and immediately went about the business of renting a horse and small carriage to take her on the two-hour journey to Oakhurst Manor.

All at once she learned what it meant to be a black woman in a slave-owning state. There was a delay in completing the transaction at the livery stable, and suddenly she was confronted by a burly deputy sheriff armed with a pistol.

"If you have any identification papers, girl, show them to me," he said, his manner threatening.

"Of course." Cleo displayed great dignity as she reached into her purse and handed him several documents.

He scrutinized them with care. "Well, you aren't a runaway, it seems."

"Hardly," she sniffed.

She was handsome, so he jumped to conclusions. "What are you doing in Charleston?"

Her plans were none of the sheriff's business, but Cleo was conscious of the authority he represented and took care to reply politely. "I'm visiting a plantation called Oakhurst Manor. I spent a lot of time there with my grandmother when I was small."

"I've heard of the place, of course. Who hasn't?" The man scowled at her. "How long a time do you intend to stay there?"

Cleo couldn't help becoming huffy. "Several weeks."

"I'm asking for your own good, girl. Maybe you don't know the laws of this state, but you'd better clear out in less than two months. Or get a special court order that establishes your position as a freewoman. Otherwise you'll automatically become a slave, and will be the property of the owners of Oakhurst Manor."

Cleo was shocked, and for the first time wondered if her

brother had been right. Perhaps she had been foolish to make this trip, but she had come this far and had no intention of turning back now. "I won't forget," she said.

Only when the deputy sheriff gave his approval would the proprietor of the livery stable rent her a horse and carriage.

By this time night had fallen and Cleo was hungry, but it occurred to her that she might create further embarrassment for herself if she went to an inn or even a simple tavern for supper. Since no members of her race were freemen here, it was possible she might be refused service. She would have to wait until she reached Oakhurst Manor to eat, and again she realized it might have been wiser not to come here.

There were few travelers on the country road, and she made the journey without incident. She smiled as she turned into the long, familiar driveway. Oakhurst Manor had not changed, and was precisely as she remembered it.

The groom who appeared to take her horse and carriage stared at her. "Hey, now," he said. "You're pretty fancy. Who do you belong to?"

Cleo was irritated. "Nobody," she said.

He looked at her without comprehension.

The majordomo who came to the front door and admitted her to the house was puzzled, too, even when she identified herself.

"I lived here for a number of years when I was a child," she told him. "Cleo, the housekeeper, was my grandmother."

It was apparent he had never heard of the old woman.

The girl couldn't help wishing she had stayed in Boston. "Please tell Jerry and Lance I've come for a visit."

The man stiffened. "Lance don't live here anymore," he said, his face wooden, "but I'll tell Master Jerry." He left her standing while he mounted the stairs.

Cleo felt a surge of excitement as she looked around and saw that little in the house was changed, but she was uncomfortable, too. It disturbed her that Lance was no longer here. Jerry, whom she also recalled vividly, had been a thoroughly unpleasant child, blaming others for his own misdeeds and whining when he was caught.

The majordomo returned and beckoned, his expression sly. "You're ordered to come upstairs."

Cleo was annoyed by his choice of words.

He conducted her to the master-bedroom suite, into which Jerry had moved after the departure of his father and stepmother for Europe, and tapped timidly at the door.

"Send her in," Jerry called.

He was sprawled in an easy chair, a glass in one hand, and he looked Cleo up and down slowly, insolently, as she walked into the sitting room.

"Well," he said. "You really are Cleo. You've become so pretty I hardly knew you."

"Thank you, Jerry," she said, feeling awkward.

He put his glass on the table beside him, stood, and unexpectedly embraced her.

Cleo was surprised, but realized she was in no position to protest. She was a guest in his house, and was here on his sufferance.

To her astonishment his grip tightened and he kissed her.

She wanted to pull away from him, but again she refrained. It was evident that he had been drinking, so perhaps it was best to humor him.

He began to fondle her.

She realized he was becoming aroused, so she eased away from him.

Jerry grinned at her. "It's good to see you after all these years," he said. "Have a drink." Giving her no chance to reply, he splashed a generous quantity of whiskey into a glass, thrust it into her hand, and waved her to a chair.

She didn't want to offend him, so she took the glass and sat. "I'd love something to eat," she told him. "I've had no supper."

He tugged at a bell rope, and a frightened house slave appeared. "Bring some meat, bread, and a bottle of wine, and be damn quick about it," he said, jabbing a finger at the woman. "Anything else you want?"

"Meat and bread will be just fine," Cleo said, and felt sorry for the woman. Apparently the warm, easy relationship between the masters of Oakhurst Manor and their servants no longer existed.

While they waited for the food, Jerry asked her a number of questions about herself and her brother, but paid little attention to her answers. He refilled his glass, then insisted that she accept another drink, too.

Cleo didn't care for the strong taste of the whiskey, but nevertheless complied.

The slave returned with a tray of food.

"You took long enough," Jerry said, and raised a hand to strike her.

She cringed and mumbled an apology.

Cleo was horrified.

The woman glanced at her, her expression making it obvious that she believed a black girl would visit Jerry Beaufort for only one purpose.

Jerry seemed to have something of the same idea, and scrutinized Cleo closely as she ate.

The meat and bread were delicious, but she had lost her appetite.

"You haven't touched your wine," he said.

She took a small sip.

"Drink it!" he ordered, raising his voice, and was satisfied only when she took a large swallow. "I'll send your horse and carriage back to Charleston first thing in the morning," he said. "They charge by the day, you know."

She thanked him, but realized that without her own means of transportation she was isolated here.

There was a tap at the door, and the majordomo entered with Cleo's valise. "Where do you want me to put this luggage, Master Jerry?" he asked.

"Just leave it, and I'll attend to it myself."

The girl's uneasiness increased. She knew she wouldn't feel so uncomfortable if Lance were here, but he wasn't, so she had to make the best of her situation. Paul had been right. It had been an error to come to Oakhurst Manor.

Jerry drained his glass, stood, and, taking her hands, pulled her to her feet. "Now we'll find out how grown-up you've become since the last time we saw each other," he said.

It was impossible to mistake his purpose, and Cleo froze. She had maneuvered herself into an impossible position. If she called for help, no member of the household staff would dare to come to her assistance. If she stalked out, she had nowhere to go, no place to find refuge. The unpleasant boy had become an even more unpleasant man, and in a slave-owning society she couldn't appeal to the authorities, either.

She had already seen signs that convinced her Jerry hadn't outgrown his vicious temper, and there was no telling how he might react if she resisted his advances. She knew she was afraid of him, and with good cause. Remembering what the deputy sheriff had said to her, she realized that if Jerry destroyed her documents she had no way of proving she had been born free. Dear Lord, it would be a simple matter for him to trick her into slavery, and no sheriff or constable in this part of the country would listen to her, no court would even bother to hear her story. She had made the worst mistake of her life by coming here.

Jerry began to tug at her dress.

His breath smelled of alcohol, he wove unsteadily on his feet, and the girl knew he was even more intoxicated than she had realized, so he wasn't responsible for his actions. And it would be useless to appeal to his reason.

Rather than allow her expensive clothes to be torn, she removed them. Obviously she had no choice and was being compelled to surrender to him, so she decided to make the best of her predicament. The prospect was loathsome, but at least she would get it over and done.

"That's more like it," Jerry said thickly, his face flushed and his eyes glowing. "Give me what I want and you won't regret it. I'll get you all sorts of pretty things."

He was treating her like a cheap prostitute, but there was nothing Cleo could do about it. She had allowed herself to be maneuvered, and now it was too late. Casting aside the last of her dignity, she removed her underclothes and stood before this lurching, drunken creature in the nude. Later tonight she would find her rented horse and carriage in the stables and would return to Charleston, then book passage north on the first ship that put into port.

Jerry began to fondle her breasts, his hands fumbling. "You'll be glad you came here," he muttered. "I won't disappoint you."

Cleo closed her eyes and allowed him to do what he pleased with her. Humiliated and heartsick, she could only hope that time passed swiftly. It was even possible, with luck, that he might lose consciousness at any moment.

Thinking he was being playful, perhaps, he pinched her breasts, then slapped her hard across the buttocks.

The physical pain Cleo suffered was considerable, but that was the least of her injury, and tears came to her eyes.

Jerry laughed manically, picked her up, and carried her into the adjoining chamber, where he dropped her onto the four-poster bed.

She averted her face as he undressed, afraid she would be sick to her stomach.

Jerry surprised her by slapping her with even greater force. Hauling her close, his hands rough, he bit her lower lip until blood spurted from it. Now he laughed longer and harder.

He was not only drunk, Cleo thought, but he was truly insane.

"Now we'll find out what kind of games you learned up North," he muttered. "Ours are better, and what you don't already know, I'll teach you, even if it takes us a year. But what a year that will be!" His laugh ended in a cackle.

Terror and misery enveloped Cleo. He was far too shrewd to permit her to escape: he was making her his slave as well as his mistress.

7

The flatlands of Colorado stretched westward, seemingly toward infinity, the unrelieved topography of the plains giving no hint of the mountain grandeur that lay ahead. The area was uninhabited by humans, and when Lance and Ponca reached the area, the former found it difficult to understand why there were no settlements here. There were rivers everywhere, including the mighty Arkansas, which they used as a guide on their journey, and the soil was rich. But rainfall was scarce, and there was almost no vegetation except the short pale grass that reached out toward the horizon. Occasionally the monotony of the landscape was relieved by a stunted, spindly tree or a patch of wildflowers, some red, some yellow, and some blue, but otherwise there was nothing.

The day would come, Lance reflected, when irrigation canals would be dug and the plentiful water supplied by the many rivers would be utilized. Ultimately eastern Colorado would produce as many crops as Oakhurst Manor.

For the present, however, no nation bothered. The United States included the region within its boundaries un-

der the terms of the Louisiana Purchase of 1803, but
Mexico disputed the claim and Great Britain questioned it.
No country wanted to fight over the territory, although it
had many attractive features.

The most obvious of them was the presence of wild animals in large numbers, and Ponca said that many Indian
tribes regarded the area as the finest of hunting grounds.
Huge herds of buffalo roamed the region, attracted by the
grass and water, and Lance saw deer and antelope, packs
of wolves, and vast numbers of prairie dogs and rabbits.
No man ever went hungry here.

On the fourth day of their journey across the Colorado
plains, the calm was broken when Ponca, shading his eyes,
suddenly pointed. "Hunters," he said.

In the far distance Lance made out a group of mounted
men.

The two groups drew closer, heading toward each other,
and it soon became evident that there were at least a
dozen men, mounted on ponies, in the hunting party.

Ponca studied the paint markings smeared on the Indians' faces and torsos. "They are Sioux," he said. "They are
far from their home. They are here to find food."

A few of the warriors carried ancient muskets, Lance
saw, but the majority were armed with spears and bows
and arrows.

As the two parties drew still closer, the Sioux notched
arrows in their bows.

Ponca became apprehensive. "They want your
firesticks," he said. "They will kill to get them. The Sioux
are greedy, and show no mercy."

Lance continued to ride forward.

The Kiowa's nervousness increased. He didn't want to
display cowardice, a trait his tribe regarded as the most
shameful of crimes, but at the same time he knew they
were heavily outnumbered. "Our horses are much swifter
than their small horses. It would be easy to escape from
them."

Lance remained on the same course.

"You wish to fight them?" Ponca wanted to know.

"Only if we must." Lance had no intention of running
away. There were many hunting parties in the region, and
if he and his companion bolted, the word of their flight

would spread. So sooner or later they would be cornered and slaughtered. Consequently, he reasoned, it was far better to put up a bold and uncompromising front now.

Ponca, who had never used firearms, removed his lasso from his belt and hoped they would get close enough to the braves to use it.

When no more than one hundred and fifty feet separated the two groups, the leaders of the Sioux gripped their muskets. One who rode in the front rank, whose feathered headdress indicated he was a personage of consequence, raised a hand, and the entire party halted. Their faces impassive, their arms ready for instant use, they waited to see what the approaching pair would do.

Lance knew he was being challenged, and deliberately moved forward another fifty feet before he halted, too.

Ponca sucked in his breath.

Instinct told Lance that the situation required deeds rather than words. Although Indians loved conversation, as he gleaned from his companion, talk would not relieve the predicament.

He looked around, and off to his left, about forty feet away, he saw a lone dwarf pine that was no more than four feet tall and approximately two and a half inches in diameter. It suited his purposes admirably, and he knew what had to be done.

Acting with such speed that he was able to accomplish his purpose before the Sioux quite realized what was happening, he reached into his quiver and with full force hurled one of his short spears at the little tree.

The metal point cut through the soft wood, splitting the trunk and causing half of the tree above the spot to waver and fall.

Ponca's gasp of admiration was barely audible.

The Sioux were stunned, and their pose of impassivity forgotten, they gaped at the tree like children who had just seen an act of inexplicable magic performed.

Their leader was the first to react. Dropping his musket to the ground as an indication of his nonbelligerent intentions, he dismounted and walked forward slowly, his left hand raised, palm outstretched and heel thrust forward in a sign of peace.

Lance responded with equal dignity. He, too, dismount-

ed, but before approaching the Indian he took care to re-
trieve his short spear, thrusting it back into its quiver.
Then he gave the peace sign, too, and approached the Indian.

The Sioux said something unintelligible.

Ponca materialized beside his friend and interpreted for
him. "The sachem of the Sioux calls Lance his brother,"
he said.

"Tell him he is my brother." Lance found it difficult to
refrain from smiling.

Again the sachem spoke, this time at greater length.

"He offers his brother a share of buffalo meat and
corn," Ponca said.

"What do you think?" Lance demanded. "Is it safe?"

"No harm will come to Lance and Ponca now," the
Kiowa assured him. "The Sioux know that only a great
chieftain could break a tree in two with a throwing stick."

"Then we accept."

Two of the warriors scoured the area for buffalo chips
and mounds of dried grass to make a fire, and soon large
chunks of bison meat were cooking. Following the example of the braves, who formed a circle around the fire,
Lance sat cross-legged on the ground.

The Sioux were curious, wanting to see the short spears,
so Lance passed around the one he had used, first telling
Ponca to warn them not to cut their fingers on the point
because of the rattlesnake venom he had smeared on it.

The warriors were doubly awed, and honored him by
insisting that he eat the first piece of meat they took from
the fire. It was too rare for his taste, but he nevertheless
ate it.

In the next hour the Sioux provided him with valuable
information. Game abounded between the plains and the
mountains, they said, and never had they known such good
hunting anywhere. But they warned him that a large party
of Apache from the Wyoming country was in the area, attracted by the presence of game. Members of this tribe
hated all white men as well as members of other tribes
with whom they had no alliances, and they would be certain to kill him and his companion if their paths crossed.
Not even his marvelous spears could save them, and the
Apache, indifferent to any casualties they themselves might

suffer, were renowned for their relentless pursuit of those whom they regarded as foes.

After the meal the two groups went their separate ways, with Lance and Ponca maintaining a vigilant watch for the Apache. Lance had learned much from the encounter, and gaining a true understanding of Indians and their ways was essential, he knew, if he hoped to survive in the wilderness.

Forty-eight hours later he had an opportunity to further his education. He and Ponca came to the foothills of the Rocky Mountains, where they climbed steadily onto higher ground. There were even more rivers here, many of them fast-flowing, and forests of pine, cedar, and hemlock appeared. In many of the rivers were dams built by beavers, which Lance regarded as a hopeful sign. Once he became acclimated to the surroundings, he would begin trapping operations. As he well knew, beaver pelts sold for high prices in the major cities of the Eastern Seaboard.

They climbed a steep hill, making frequent detours around boulders that littered it, then paused at the crest to rest their horses for a few moments.

Ponca, whose eyesight was as keen as his companion's, spotted a movement in the little valley that stretched out ahead of him, and alarm registered on his face when he recognized the distinctive red and yellow paint of the Wyoming Apache.

"There are a half-hundred of them," he whispered, "and they have seen us, too."

Like the Sioux, the Apache were mounted on ponies, and Lance noted immediately that a number of them carried ancient muskets or old rifles that traders had sold them in return for animal skins. Flight was futile, because not even a horse as swift as Bantu could make good time across this rugged terrain, and the Indians would be sure to catch up with him.

He made certain that his own long rifle and pistols were primed, loaded, and ready for use. Then, as the Apache moved toward him and his companion, he calmly showed Ponca how to reload the weapons, giving him ammunition and powder. "Fill the firesticks for me, as rapidly as you can," he directed. "Hand them back to me as I use them, and keep them coming."

Ponca understood, and nodded.

Even though the odds against them were great, Lance knew they held a number of advantages. By far the greatest of them was his own marksmanship, in which he had complete confidence. M'Bwana and Jeremy had taught him the use of firearms from the time he had started to walk, and no Apache could match his skill and experience. Then, too, the rifle Lester Howard had given him was a superior weapon, infinitely better than the old guns the Indians were carrying. His pistols were ordinary, to be sure, but he knew their peculiarities, and that could help considerably. Finally, he was on high ground and was forcing the enemy to come to him. That could make a difference in the outcome, too, and he refused to think of the consequences if he failed.

The Apache were bold, as usual, making no effort at concealment on the wooded slope as they left the valley below and spurred their ponies up the hill. In the lead was a grizzled warrior who wore a beaded buffalo-skin cloak. He carried a battered musket that might have seen service in the American Revolution a half-century earlier, and the mere sight of that weapon raised Lance's spirits. From all that Papa Beaufort had ever told him, such guns were notoriously inaccurate.

He raised his own rifle, took aim at a yellow mark between the chief's eyes, and gently squeezed the trigger.

The crack of the shot echoed across the foothills, and the Apache leader toppled from his pony's back to the ground.

Lance handed the rifle to Ponca for reloading, and before his foes could recover from their surprise, raised one of his pistols. The shot was tricky at this distance with the smaller weapon, but his arm was steady, his eye sharp, and his aim true.

A second Apache fell to the ground, dead before he landed there.

Lance fired his second pistol, and felt a twinge of disappointment because, this time, his aim was less than perfect. He merely wounded and incapacitated a brave, but did not kill him.

Ponca grinned as he handed his friend the reloaded rifle.

By now the Apache were recovering from their surprise and began to return the fire. As Lance had suspected, however, they lacked experience, their weapons were untrustworthy, and most of their shots went wild, passing far on either side of their targets or whistling harmlessly overhead.

Lance maintained his own steady, deadly fire, and soon the side of the hill was littered with the bodies of Apache killed and wounded. Riderless ponies milled around, some whinnying in terror, and impeded the progress of the braves who continued to advance.

The Apache were renowned for their courage, and lived up to their reputations. In spite of the casualties they were suffering, they came up the hill in waves, even though many knew they would die. Had someone stepped forward to take the place of their fallen leader, they might have enjoyed greater success, but they continued to rely exclusively on the weight of their numbers, and their casualties soared. They kept up a lively fire, too, but they took careless aim, sometimes shooting blindly, and not one of their bullets endangered the pair at the crest of the hill.

At last the survivors could tolerate no more. At least twenty of their comrades had been killed or wounded, and the man at the hilltop seemed invincible. The Apache fled in sudden panic, scattering in all directions. As was their custom, they made no attempt to take their dishonored wounded and dead with them.

Lance remained motionless in his saddle, alert and ready to resume his fire if the Indians formed new ranks and attacked again. But the Apache had no stomach for further battle, and vanished into the evergreen forest.

Ponca's high-pitched laugh of triumph replaced the sound of gunfire, and he was elated when his friend promised to teach him marksmanship.

They resumed their ride toward the mountains, and were not molested again.

The first of the legends about the man who would become known as the "giant white devil" had sprung into being.

Alicia Emerson Duchamp was bored. For years she had wanted to be Emile's wife, and for the past decade, ever since the death of his invalided first wife, she had held that dubious distinction. Oh, she was comfortable enough; his gaming house and his bordello saw to that. But she lived outside the pale of polite society, the ladies of New Orleans looking through her as though she didn't exist. It didn't matter that she had a bigger house, more expensive clothes, or more servants.

She slept late because she had nothing better to occupy her time, and she ate too large a meal at breakfast for the same reason. It no longer mattered that she had lost her figure and was far too fat. She dawdled away her afternoons on shopping expeditions, frequently buying objects for which she had no use. For a time she had enjoyed being driven around the nicer residential districts of the city in an open carriage, but that pleasure had been spoiled for her because no one who saw her acknowledged her existence, so she gave up the practice.

Alicia came to life only at night. Emile liked to eat his principal meal of the day at home rather than in inns or taverns, where he was interrupted by gaming-house habitués or men who visited his bordello. So Alicia dined alone with him, and if he was in a good mood, she sometimes accompanied him to the gaming house after dinner, her fingers covered with rings, her ample figure swathed in rustling taffeta.

Occasionally, although she hated to admit it to herself, she thought about her girlhood at Trelawney, or the later period when she had lived at Oakhurst Manor with her baby. That life was buried in the past, but she couldn't help envying the handsome, confident young woman who had lived it.

Well, what had happened couldn't be altered, she thought as she sat in the overly ornate parlor absently eating chocolate candies as she waited for Emile to come home. He was good to her, at least by his own standards, and she had achieved the financial security she had craved so desperately. For all the good it did her.

The front door slammed, and Alicia knew from the stamping of heavy footsteps that Emile was in a foul mood. Nevertheless she lifted her face for his token kiss when he joined her, but was not surprised when he stormed past her to the sideboard and poured himself a drink.

"Problems today, my dear?" she asked dutifully.

"That damn girl held me up, practically at gunpoint," he said, fuming.

"What damn girl?" Alicia wasn't really interested.

"The new one at the House on the Avenue, who charges—and gets—the highest prices in history. I've told you about her, but you don't listen!"

His charge was true, and with good reason. Alicia was aware—all too painfully aware—of his custom of bedding newcomers to the place and it had hurt her all the more in recent years because he hadn't made love to her. So to protect her peace of mind, she had formed a habit of her own, that of literally blocking out the sound of his voice whenever he mentioned the House on the Avenue.

But tonight a sense of malicious amusement pervaded her as she realized that one of the inmates had won a financial advantage over him, so she broke her self-imposed rule. "What did this girl do?"

"We have a standard arrangement. They keep half of what they earn, and I pay their expenses out of the other half. It's never been any other way, for anyone. But she's demanded two-thirds of her earnings, and I had to give in because she threatened to walk out and take all her clients with her."

Alicia couldn't help laughing aloud.

"You're as bad as Carrie," Emile said. "She laughed at me, too."

She grew tense and spoke carefully. "What did you say her name is?"

"Carrie."

"I mean her last name."

He shrugged. "I have no idea. Some of the girls prefer to use only their first names, and I never pry into their personal lives. As long as they do their jobs, that's good enough for me."

Alicia tried to conceal her agitation and adopt a casual tone. "I assume she's from the South."

"Of course." He was somewhat surprised by her sudden show of interest. "We rarely have girls from any other part of the country. Women who go into that line of work usually find places closer to their own homes."

"I was just wondering," Alicia said, and wiped the perspiring palms of her hands on the divan.

Emile pondered for a moment. "Let me think. As I recall it, when she first showed up at the House on the Avenue I believe she mentioned something about coming from South Carolina."

There was a long, deep silence. "She's pretty, I suppose."

"Gorgeous!" He was emphatic. "She has blond hair that hangs to her waist, and she has a face and figure to go with it."

Alicia's skin crawled. "I'd like to see this Carrie." Her throat was so dry she rasped.

Emile raised an eyebrow. "You would? I don't believe you've visited the House on the Avenue in at least fifteen years."

She clenched her fists, then forced herself to relax. He would become suspicious if she showed her feelings too plainly. "Oh, I'd like to see this paragon who can not only charge enormous fees but also force you to accept her terms."

"Her popularity will fade," he said. "It always does."

"When may I go?"

"Not tonight, Alicia. This is her busy time. She's always with a client, and another is always waiting. Some of them wait for hours." He guessed he had to indulge his wife's curiosity. "Go around noon, when they get up for the day. Maria will point her out to you, but I hope you won't stare or ask Carrie too many questions. The girls are inclined to become resentful when people treat them like animals in a zoo."

"I wouldn't dream of being rude," Alicia said, "and I certainly have no intention of speaking to her. I wouldn't know what to say to such a person."

Her reply was precisely what Emile wanted to hear, so he gave his approval. "I can see you doing no harm, so I'll send word to Maria that you'll be dropping in."

The next seventeen hours were the longest Alicia had ever spent. She could eat almost no dinner, and that night she remained wide-eyed. She finally dropped off to sleep

just before dawn, but a nightmare jarred her awake again.
At breakfast she astonished her household staff by refusing
more than token portions.

At last noon came.

No customers showed up that early in the day, but the
place hummed with life. It was the gossip hour, and the
inmates drifted to the largest of the ground-floor parlors,
where they exchanged stories about their previous night's
experiences. Many of them regarded this period as the
most pleasant of the day.

One of the last to come downstairs was Carrie, who was
clad in a semitransparent nightgown and matching peign-
oir that one of her clients had just given her. She wore
her hair loose, and it tumbled down her back. She had not
yet bothered with cosmetics for the day, and her scrubbed
face looked remarkably young and appealing.

As she helped herself to coffee, the others exclaimed
over her new outfit.

The youngest member of the group, a redheaded seven-
teen-year-old named Melanie, who had just arrived from
Virginia, was the most admiring. Carrie had taken the girl
under her wing because of her extreme youth, selecting
her customers for her and not permitting her to have anything to do with those who might be rough with her or display perverted tendencies.

"I've never seen anything so charming," Melanie said.

"If you like it so much, come to my suite later, when I
dress for the day, and I'll give it to you."

The ecstatic Melanie was speechless for a moment, then
stammered her thanks and finally said, "Has Maria seen it
yet?"

Carrie shrugged.

"Show it to her, Carrie. You really must. She's in the
little parlor right now with a visitor. Some old lady."

It was easier to comply than listen to the girl's nagging.
She saw Maria sitting in the small parlor with a guest, a
middle-aged woman who was enormously fat, wore too
much makeup, and was overdressed. They stopped talking
as she approached.

Then Maria spoke to her. "I was just boasting about
you, Carrie," she said, emphasizing the girl's name.

Carrie had no desire to be drawn into their talk. "I

won't keep you a minute," she said. "Melanie insisted I show you this new outfit. I got it as a gift last night."

"It becomes you marvelously, my dear," Maria told her.

Carrie was on the verge of making a banal reply before leaving, but cut her answer short when she saw the fat woman gaping at her, with eyes protruding and her jaw hanging down. The woman seemed to be ill: she was trembling violently as she clutched the arms of her chair, and rivers of perspiration streamed down her face, spoiling her makeup and making her look grotesque.

Not wanting to be near if the visitor had a heart attack, Carrie quickly rejoined the other girls.

Maria hurriedly brought the guest some smelling salts and a glass of brandywine.

After a time Alicia grew calmer. "I'm so sorry," she said. "I must have eaten something last night that disagreed with me."

"Are you all right now?"

"Much better." Alicia patted her face, smudging her makeup even more. "And thank you for showing Carrie to me. She's every bit as beautiful as both you and Emile said."

"Yes, she's unique." Maria accompanied the visitor to her carriage, and was relieved when she departed. Emile would be upset and angry if his wife became ill here.

Alicia ordered her driver to take her home, and when she arrived there she retired immediately to her bedroom. Opening a locket that contained a snippet of a child's blond hair, she held it in her hand and stared at it, not moving for hours.

At last she stirred. Wearily hauling herself to her feet, she gathered all of her more expensive jewelry, which included rings, brooches, earrings, bracelets, and necklaces. Some had belonged to her mother and grandmother, while others had been gifts that Emile had given her over the years.

She placed them in a box, and inside the lid placed a brief unsigned note, which she printed rather than wrote in longhand: "From an Admirer."

Summoning her driver, she handed him the box and told him to take it without delay to Carrie at the House on the Avenue. Under no circumstances was he to reveal the identity of the donor of the gift.

Then she rummaged in the chest of drawers that stood in Emile's dressing room. Finding what she wanted, she carried it to the parlor and sat again. She had several hours to wait, but the time passed more quickly now, far more rapidly than she would have imagined possible.

When he at last arrived, she gave him no opportunity to speak. "I went to the House on the Avenue today," she said, "and I saw the girl called Carrie."

Ordinarily Alicia was quiet, almost meek, displaying an indifference to anything that took place outside her home. Now, however, even though she spoke softly, her face reflected an intense fury that was extraordinary, and Emile assumed she was jealous. He nodded, but took care to make no comment.

"You had an affair with her, didn't you?" she demanded.

He cleared his throat. "We've had a tacit agreement over the years not to discuss certain matters. I think it would be wise not to change our ways."

"That means you did sleep with her." Alicia's eyes burned with a strange intensity.

Her husband shrugged. He had no desire to hurt her, but she seemed insistent on creating an issue.

"Apparently you didn't know her."

He was puzzled.

"I recognized her instantly," Alicia said. "I'd have known her anywhere. I guess you've forgotten how I looked when I was young. Except for her hair color, she looks exactly as I did—many years ago."

Emile couldn't understand the point she was trying to make.

"She was born in this house," Alicia said, speaking slowly and distinctly. "She had to take my name because you and I weren't married at the time, so she was known as Carolyn Emerson."

Color drained from his face, and he began to tremble.

"Yes, Emile," she said, "that girl is my daughter."

He covered his face with his hands.

"She is also your daughter. You've committed incest with your daughter, Emile."

"For God's sake, stop!" he cried, and swayed on his feet.

"This is my punishment for deserting her and leaving her at Oakhurst Manor. This is your punishment for refusing to acknowledge her all these years."

Emile sank into a chair before he fell, and closed his eyes again. The enormity of all that had happened overwhelmed him. Not only was he guilty of incest, but the star inmate at the House on the Avenue was his only child.

Alicia reached beneath a cushion and removed the box she had taken from his chest of drawers when she had returned home early in the afternoon.

He heard a clicking sound, opened his eyes again, and saw that she had removed his dueling pistols from the box. They were superb weapons, with hair-spring triggers, and he always kept them loaded, ready for use. He knew what Alicia intended as she stood, a pistol in each hand, and slowly approached him. She had never touched firearms in her life, and it would have been easy enough to knock the weapons from her hands, but he made no move, no attempt to use force or to dissuade her.

Alicia drew closer to him, step by step. This was their fate, and neither made any attempt to avoid it. Her face was creased in a wild grimace, her eyes were crazed.

She placed the muzzle of one pistol against Emile's chest and pulled the trigger.

He died without making a sound, slumping in his chair as a crimson stain spread across the front of his white shirt.

She placed the muzzle of the other pistol against her temple, took a deep breath, and fired. For an instant she continued to stand, then crumpled to the floor at her husband's feet, the hideous grin still on her face, her sightless eyes staring vacantly into space.

The authorities who were summoned by the frightened members of the household staff did not reveal the true cause of death, but merely announced that Emile Duchamp and his wife had died in an accident. They suspected some connection with the gaming establishment he owned, and consequently, for their own reasons, wanted time to investigate that possibility.

They knew, as did few other people, that his silent partners in both of his business enterprises included several of New Orleans' more prominent citizens. The investigation revealed nothing of importance, however. Duchamp's partners took over active control of both the gaming establishment and the bordello, hiring a manager for the former and placing Maria in complete charge of the latter.

Only a few people attended the brief joint funeral services. Maria was there, but the inmates of the House on the Avenue were conspicuous by their absence. None had any fondness for Duchamp, and none had been acquainted with his wife.

Carrie was indifferent to his passing. She had despised him because of what he had done to her, but she had insulated herself in a cloak of callousness, virtually anesthetizing herself and making it impossible to feel anything. So, she discovered, she bore him no ill will.

It was far more important to confirm her new profit-sharing arrangement with Maria, and this she did without delay. Maria tried, as Duchamp had done, to dissuade her from taking an increased percentage of what she earned, but she merely repeated her threat to leave, and the new director of the bordello promptly gave in to her wishes.

Duchamp was gone, and that was that. Carrie found her own mind occupied with the unexpected gift of the box filled with handsome and expensive jewelry. The rings were worth thousands of dollars, one of the brooches was worth a small fortune, and a diamond bracelet was exquisite.

Several pairs of earrings, some of gold and some of silver, didn't suit Carrie's fancy, so she gave them to the young newcomer, Melanie, who was as excited and pleased as a child.

Carrie tried to guess the identity of the donor, and when that effort failed, she discreetly questioned several of her wealthier clients. It soon became evident to her that none of them had been her benefactor, so she gave up the attempt.

It was enough that she had acquired the jewelry, and she really didn't care who had given her the lavish gift.

8

---◦━◦━◦---

The Arapaho village was located high in the Rocky Mountains, nestling in a tiny valley that was surrounded by snow-covered peaks. Lance knew the mountains as well as he had once known the lands in the vicinity of Oakhurst Manor; he and Ponca had crisscrossed the Great Divide many times, and were thoroughly familiar with every pass, every trail. Their hunting and trapping operations were flourishing, and every few months they returned to the village laden with pelts, which they sold at premium prices to the traders who regularly visited there.

Unlike other, nomadic Arapaho, who were ferocious, the villagers were a quiet people who subsisted on meat they obtained on hunting expeditions, and augmented their diet by bartering meat for grain, with various Plains Indians. They lived in caves, as their ancestors had done for centuries, and one of these dwellings was set aside for Lance and Ponca, who stored their beaver, lynx, fox, and other furs there. The pair were always welcome, particularly because they shared their abundant supplies of meat with the Indians, and they had gradually come to regard the village as their headquarters and home.

128

As a rule, when they returned to the Arapaho community from an expedition, the children of the village turned out to greet them, and were rewarded with gifts of meat. Now, after spending ten weeks in the wilderness, Lance and Ponca returned to a different reception as they led their horses and pack mules into the compound.

The village was silent, and its residents remained in their own caves.

Lance and Ponca unloaded their furs and meat, then hurried to the cave of the sachem, carrying quantities of elk meat as a special gift.

The old man sat cross-legged beside a fire near the entrance, and scarcely raised his head as they entered.

They exchanged glances, both of the new arrivals wondering if they had inadvertently offended the Arapaho. Lance, who had made it his business to learn their language, as well as that of the Sioux, which was the principal means of communication between members of different tribes, acted as spokesman. "Is our father unhappy with his friends?"

"He is unhappy," the old man replied dolefully. "But his friends have done no wrong."

Lance had learned enough of Indian manners to ask no further questions, but to wait for an explanation.

It was not long in coming. The village had enjoyed peace and prosperity for many years, the sachem said, but now it lay under a curse of the gods. A vicious mountain lion, larger and more ferocious than any puma ever seen in the area, was preying on the village. Bold as well as cunning, it seemed to be everywhere, one day lurking near the trail into the heights that the warriors used when they went hunting, the next skulking in the vicinity of the swift-flowing stream where the women went for water.

During the past moon the cougar had mauled a squaw who had survived but would bear the marks for the rest of her days, then had torn off the arm of a young brave. Only yesterday it had killed and partly devoured the body of a boy of seven summers.

Parties of warriors had been organized and had gone in search of the beast, but the lion had been too shrewd. When outnumbered, it either vanished into the pine forests or disappeared above the timberline, its reddish-brown coat affording it perfect camouflage because its color blended with that of the rocky terrain.

"Animals are sometimes wiser than men," Lance said gravely after he and Ponca heard the recital. "They know when they are outnumbered and will attack only when the odds are in their favor."

The sachem was grim. "The squaws bring water only when braves go with them to protect them," he said. "No warrior dares to hunt alone. The children must hide in the caves with their mothers. The Arapaho suffer great shame, but there is nothing we can do to end this curse."

Lance knew what needed to be done. "The lion must be killed by one man who goes out alone to meet and conquer him," he said. "If more than one man goes, the beast will run away and wait for another day."

The old man nodded. "These things I know," he said. "But there is no Arapaho who has the courage and the strength to meet this terrible creature alone."

Lance did not hesitate. "I will meet the lion and will kill him for you. Then there will be no need for the people to be afraid anymore."

The sachem shook his head. "You are strong," he said. "You have courage. But no man is stronger or has more spirit than the young brave who lost an arm. The lion will do to you what he has done to others who walk alone. You will surely die."

"I think not," Lance said quietly. "My firestick will speak, and that will be the end of the terror."

The word of his decision spread, and that night the entire village gathered in his honor. Meat was roasted, grain was mixed with water and pulverized, and the medicine man, his face and torso streaked with paint, did a ceremonial dance around the white man to protect him.

Lance placed greater reliance on his rifle than he did on the powers of the medicine man.

The next morning, after an early breakfast of dried elk meat, he left the village. As a matter of course he carried his skinning knife in his belt and slung his quiver of short spears over his shoulder, but it was his long rifle, already primed and loaded, that would dispose of the lion. He carried extra ammunition and powder, although he thought it likely that he would be obliged to kill the creature with a single shot. There was no beast wilier or more resilient than the mountain lion, so he regarded it as unlikely that he would have an opportunity to reload and fire a second time.

In order to attract the puma, he also carried a chunk of raw meat to use as bait.

He headed into higher ground, starting toward the boulders that stood above the timberline on rising ground. Walking easily but warily, he made good time, and paused occasionally to stand very still. Cougars left no tracks, so he would have to rely on his own skill in locating the beast.

Slowly he made his way to the field of shale, a vast expanse of flat pebblelike rocks that lay below the snow of the upper peaks. The area was littered with boulders, some the size of a man's fist, others as high as the Oakhurst Manor portico. There was no sign of the puma anywhere, but after a lifetime of hunting experience Lance did not lose heart. For all he knew, the puma already had him under observation.

He climbed for another half-mile, then saw a large boulder, roughly the size of a trapper's cabin, that seemed ideal for his purposes. An opening at one side would serve perfectly as a peephole, so he decided this was the place to set his trap.

He placed the chunk of meat on the rocks in front of the boulder, then moved behind it. If his plan was effective, the cougar would be attracted by the meat, but could be watched through the hole in the stone. In fact, it might even be possible to fire at the creature through that hole, using the thick rock of the boulder as a shield.

Lance moved behind the boulder and waited.

The sun rose over the plains of Colorado far to the east of the mountains. The sky was overcast, but nevertheless grew somewhat brighter. A stiff, steady wind was blowing down from the peaks to the west, and that was all to the good, Lance decided, because the odor of the raw meat would be carried to the pine forests below. All the signs were favorable.

He heard no sound, but his almost infallible sixth sense caused him to look over his shoulder.

There, no more than one hundred feet from him, was a mountain lion, and he knew this had to be the killer of whom the Arapaho were afraid. The beast, a tawny reddish-brown in color, was the size of a pony, with a large head, powerful body, and strong legs. It was creeping toward him with the subtle stealth of a cat, its yellow teeth bared, its long tail switching menacingly from side to side.

Lance knew that his own living flesh rather than the chunk of raw meat was the bait.

He turned, his motions smooth and fluid so the great beast wouldn't be alarmed, and raised his rifle to his shoulder.

The mountain lion moved still closer, ready to pounce.

Lance steadied himself, took careful aim, and fired.

There was a heart-plunging click, and nothing else happened. The rifle failed to discharge.

The mountain lion gathered itself for the fatal leap at its victim.

There was no opportunity to check the weapon for its malfunction, much less reload. Lance cast the useless rifle aside, braced himself, and reached for one of the short spears in the quiver at his shoulder.

At that instant the lion sprang, its claws extended, its open mouth revealing its sharp, saberlike fangs.

Lance threw the spear, praying that his aim was true.

The shaft sang through the air and met the cougar in mid-flight. The beast fell short of its quarry, dropping to the shale and skidding several feet before it could halt. So great was its strength that, even though the shaft of the spear protruded from its throat, it was able to pounce again.

A second spear buried itself deep in the animal's flesh before the lion could jump again. It was so close that Lance could see the gleam in its yellow-green eyes, so close he could feel the hot breath of the puma on his skin.

Now the rattlesnake venom in which the tips had been smeared took effect. The great cat shuddered convulsively and dropped dead at the hunter's feet, one reaching claw actually grazing the man's leg before it died.

Lance looked down at the cougar, and as he calmed himself, he knew he had enjoyed the narrowest of escapes. Had the beast come another eighteen inches closer, he would have died, too.

But there was nothing to be gained by dwelling on what

might have been. He had accomplished his mission, killing the puma, and nothing else mattered.

He removed the spears, cleaning them and returning them to the quiver. Then he drew his knife and expertly skinned the lion, noting that a half-dozen buzzards were already circling overhead. As soon as he left the scene, the vultures would descend, and would be followed by hyenas that would appear out of nowhere. In a short time only the skeleton of the puma would be left.

Carrying the head and skin, Lance returned to the Indian village.

Scores of eyes watched him from the caves, and within moments the Arapaho poured into the open. Children leaped and shouted in ecstasy, squaws wept, and even the normally taciturn warriors grinned broadly as they saluted the man who had destroyed the killer beast.

Ponca appeared and clapped his friend on the shoulder, his manner indicating that he had been certain of the outcome of the battle.

A fire was lighted, and soon one of the senior braves sent up smoke signals that told other Arapaho communities over a distance of many miles the good news: the killer lion was dead.

Lance presented the animal's head to the sachem, and two of the squaws carefully removed the skin so they could begin the delicate drying process that would fashion a cape. That garment would become Lance's proudest possession.

Drums began to throb, and soon all the people of the village joined the medicine man in a celebratory ceremony, chanting and dancing around the man who had restored their safety and honor.

Lance wanted no fuss made over him, and was embarrassed by the acclaim. He had done his duty, and that was sufficient glory.

At the climax of the ceremony the drums fell silent, and the old sachem spoke for all his people when he intoned, "The Arapaho give a new name to their friend who has saved them. From this day he will be called the Lion."

Cleo was beyond despair. She was confined in a small chamber on the top floor of Oakhurst Manor, behind a locked door, and there she was served her meals. The days passed, then the weeks, and there was no escape.

It suited Jerry's fancy to keep her stark naked, and although she was provided with cosmetics, she was permitted to wear no clothes. When the young master of Oakhurst Manor sent for her, she was conducted into his presence, and she lived only for his entertainment and sexual gratification.

She was compelled to drink whiskey with him until she became ill. When he cracked a whip at her feet, she danced for him, sometimes being compelled to work herself into a frenzy. Occasionally it amused him to dress her in silk stockings, perhaps a tiny apron or a corselet, but even these scraps of clothing were removed before she was returned to her own room, where she collapsed in exhaustion and shame.

It did not matter that she had been born free, that she had acquired a sufficient education to have earned her living teaching school. Her documents had vanished along with her clothes, and she was Jerry Beaufort's creature, his personal slave, his wench. His satisfaction had become her only reason for being, the only reason she was still alive.

No member of the household staff even bothered to listen to her explanation that she was the granddaughter of the long-dead Cleo, for so many years the beloved housekeeper of Oakhurst Manor. No member of the present staff had even known the old woman. Few of the servants felt sorry for the girl. They knew she had come to the plantation of her own volition, and in their opinion she was a prostitute who had earned her fate. A handful, perhaps, felt sorry for her, but they exercised care not to reveal their opinions. Jerry was a harsh and unforgiving master, and had they dared to express their thoughts, they would have been severely punished for their temerity.

Early in her captivity Cleo had summoned the courage to protest bitterly. Jerry had beaten her, slashing her across her bare back and buttocks until his arm had grown weary, then leaving her unconscious in pools of her own blood.

That experience had broken her spirit. Now she lived only to please him, emptying her mind and indulging in any antics he demanded. He owned her body, and her soul had withered.

Jerry placed no limit on the food and drink Cleo was served, and she began to rely more and more heavily on whiskey to ease her mortification. When he forgot her existence for days at a time, she drank to relieve her boredom. When he called her to his suite, she poured whiskey down her throat to anesthetize herself sufficiently to tolerate the ordeal. And sometimes she drank, too, so she wouldn't hear the voice of her brother warning her not to make the journey to Oakhurst Manor.

Cleo lost track of time. It was enough that more than two months had passed since her arrival, that under the law she was now a slave, and that Jerry Beaufort had every right to deal with her as he pleased. Even if she escaped, she had no recourse, nowhere to go, and would be returned to the plantation in chains when she was captured.

She lived from day to day, relieved when he seemingly forgot her existence for a time, and dreading the next summons into his presence. She was convinced he was mentally unbalanced, but that knowledge in no way made her situation any easier. Sometimes, when he gave parties, she could hear the sound of music and the voices of guests below, but she knew it would do her no good to cry out for help. She was black, a slave, and a female, so no one would listen to her.

Only the spark to stay alive that burned more strongly within her than she knew prevented Cleo from throwing herself out of her prison window.

Late each day she daubed cosmetics on her face, knowing that Jerry would whip her if she appeared before him without makeup. The act became second nature to her, and she performed it without thinking.

At sundown one dreary evening a middle-aged serving woman unlocked the door, glared at the girl in obvious disapproval, and announced "You're wanted."

Cleo gulped a quantity of whiskey before following the woman to the master suite on the second floor. As always, she was oblivious of the staff members who stared at her nude body.

Jerry was sprawled in an easy chair in his sitting room, a glass in his hand.

Seated opposite him on a divan was a short, heavyset man, totally bald, with gimlet eyes.

"Here she is, Oscar," Jerry said as the shrinking Cleo came into the room. "What do you think?"

Oscar Griffin studied the girl, inspecting her as he would have looked at a prize cow. "A splendid body," he said at last, "and a pretty enough face. You didn't exaggerate, Beaufort."

"I told you the truth, Oscar," Jerry said. "She's marvelously hot-blooded, which is why I'm willing to rent her to you whenever you want to stage exhibitions for your Georgia friends."

"I'll make up my own mind about that," Oscar Griffin replied, a touch of asperity in his voice. Then he turned to Cleo again, a faint smile at the corners of his thin lips, and crooked a finger.

She didn't dare disobey, and took several hesitant steps toward him.

"Closer," he commanded. "We'll soon see if Beaufort's boasts about your hot-blooded nature are justified or just talk."

Jerry giggled. "You'll let me watch, Oscar?"

The fat man glanced at him with contempt. "Do what you please. If it will make you happy to hear her screaming and begging for more of what I give her, stay around."

Reaching up suddenly, Oscar caught the girl off balance as he hauled her to the divan and spread her out there.

Cleo was compliant because she had no choice, but this new humiliation was too much.

Oscar began to toy with her, his hands strong and unexpectedly knowing.

In spite of her disgust, Cleo responded to his ministrations and felt herself becoming erotically aroused. She couldn't hold still and began to wriggle.

Oscar became busier.

Jerry watched every move, his eyes bright.

A low moan welled up within Cleo, and its sound broke the silence.

Oscar Griffin laughed coarsely. "A good beginning," he said. "Now I'll really go to work."

Even as Cleo writhed, tossed, and gasped for breath, her mind was active. This degradation was the last straw, and she could not tolerate another. The mere thought of being "rented" to this creature for display in "exhibitions" was more than she could bear, and she knew she had reached the limit of her endurance.

She had to kill Jerry Beaufort, even if the effort cost her own life.

There were many in Vienna who were envious of the dynamic American minister and his lovely wife, but the life led by Jeremy and Lisa Beaufort was anything but serene.

Scott and Kai Emerson wrote regularly from Trelawney, but had no news to report. Repeated inquiries were being made all over the United States, but there was still no sign of Lance or Carrie, no indication of where either might be located. Both had vanished, and it was impossible to determine whether either was alive or dead.

Scott rarely visited Oakhurst Manor, where Jerry was in charge. Reading between the lines, Jeremy couldn't help wondering if Scott was hinting that his presence was no longer wanted at Oakhurst Manor. The very idea seemed outlandish, but Jeremy couldn't imagine why else he went there so infrequently.

It was proving difficult, too, to determine the state of affairs at the Beaufort shipping company. Jerry had taken charge there, too, but paid no attention to his father's requests for an accounting. Jeremy asked Scott for information on the subject, but the replies were vague.

"Perhaps Scott can't find out," Lisa suggested.

"How could that be?" Jeremy was indignant. "I'm sure Jerry has nothing to hide. Besides, he knows Scott has been my attorney for many years, and a request from him is the same as one from me."

Lisa thought otherwise, but kept quiet.

"One of these days," her husband said, "if various situations over there aren't clarified, I'll have to submit my resignation to President Jackson and go home. The lack of information about my business affairs is maddening, and the continuing disappearance of Lance and Carrie is even worse!"

Lisa had to agree, but knowing he felt it was his duty to stay at his post, she said nothing.

She had troubles of her own, but aware of his worries, kept them from him. She confided in her sister-in-law, Margot, who felt as she did. Lisa could cope with her situation, even though it was difficult and embarrassing to do so, and what Jeremy didn't know wouldn't hurt him.

Then, unexpectedly, the problem came into the open.

The Beaufort brothers and their wives attended a reception at the Hochburg, the imperial palace, and Lisa, attired in a gown that looked like liquid silver, created her usual sensation. Even the emperor complimented her, and she was besieged with requests from gentlemen who wanted to dance with her.

Jeremy caught a glimpse of her waltzing with a colonel of hussars before he and the British minister adjourned to a small anteroom for a serious discussion of current diplomacy with Count Metternich, the distinguished Austrian foreign minister.

After the talk Jeremy went in search of Lisa, but didn't see her on the dance floor, and neither his brother nor his sister-in-law knew where she had gone.

The party had spread out over twenty or thirty rooms in the huge palace, so Jeremy, a cup of mild punch in hand, wandered from one to another.

As he headed down a long corridor a door opened and Lisa emerged. He knew her well enough to realize she was both disturbed and angry as she stalked off in the opposite direction, holding her long skirt above her ankles so she could move more rapidly.

A few moments later she was followed into the corridor by Baron Klaus von Emmerlich, a forty-year-old member of the Austrian aristocracy and a landowner. Attired in a resplendent dress uniform, he was bemused, and it was his confident, smug expression that gave Jeremy pause. Something out of the ordinary was happening.

A short time later Jeremy rejoined his wife, who had recovered her aplomb and was her usual charming self. He waited until they left the reception and returned to their rented house before he mentioned the matter.

Lisa, who was removing her jewelry, obviously didn't want to discuss the matter. "It was nothing," she said. "Really, dear."

He raised an eyebrow and waited.

She knew concealment was no longer possible, and sighed. "I haven't wanted to upset you," she said, "and I can assure you I can take care of the situation."

Jeremy continued to wait.

Lisa unhooked her gown, stepped out of it, and donned a dressing robe. "One day about a month ago," she said, "I went for a canter in the Prater with Klaus, and then I had tea with him. That was my mistake. I learned that a lady doesn't encourage an Austrian nobleman that way, no matter how innocent she might be. Ever since that day, Klaus has been pestering me to have an affair with him, and hasn't listened to my refusals."

Jeremy stiffened.

"But I believe I made it very plain to him tonight that I intend to have no affair with him or anyone else! Just dismiss the whole matter from your mind, dear."

"My wife has been insulted," he said in a low voice.

"Oh, dear. The last thing on earth that I want is a fuss. There has been no harm done, and—"

"No man can make advances to my wife with impunity," Jeremy said.

"Now you know why I didn't tell you," the perturbed Lisa said. "You're a diplomat accredited to the imperial court, and a scandal might cause complications. President Jackson would be furious if you got into a fight because of me."

"On the contrary, he'd be the first to applaud," Jeremy replied. "In case you don't know it, Lisa, Andrew Jackson killed one man and wounded another in duels that he fought to protect the good name of his wife!"

Her worst fears were being realized. "Klaus is a deadly swordsman and an equally expert pistol shot."

"I reckon I can look after myself," he said, "and even if I can't, I'll have to take the chance. The honor of my wife is at stake!"

The following morning Jeremy had a brief talk with his brother, and Tom Beaufort immediately paid a visit to Baron von Emmerlich at his town house.

The baron appointed a second, who conferred with Tom, and as the challenged party, von Emmerlich had the choice of weapons. He elected that the duel be fought with pistols, and the weapons were duly supplied by a colonel of the imperial guard.

The British chargé d'affaires, Sir Harold Northrop, reluctantly consented to serve as referee, and a royal physician, Dr. Walther Hummellmann, agreed to be in attendance.

Jeremy didn't want Lisa to become unduly concerned, so he made no mention of the arrangements to her. But two days later, when he stealthily slipped out of bed more than an hour before dawn, dressed in black, and crept out of the house, she knew for certain what was happening.

She wished she had managed to keep quiet about Klaus von Emmerlich. She had put him firmly in his place, and he wouldn't have annoyed her again. Men were absurdly adolescent when questions of what they called honor were at stake, and now the fat was in the fire. Under the code of dueling, she knew, neither participant would be satisfied until blood had been shed.

Wide-awake and shivering, Lisa drew on her robe and went downstairs to the kitchen, frustrated by her own inability to prevent a senseless duel. None of the servants were up and about yet, so she brewed a pot of strong Turkish coffee, a specialty in Vienna, and retired to her bedroom.

Not even Lance could have prevented his father from fighting this duel, she thought. It occurred to her, too, as it had in the past, that perhaps she and Jeremy loved each other too much for their mutual good. Because both had suffered for each other's sake in the past, he was fiercely protective of her, trying to shield her from harm or abuse of any kind, and sometimes he was too zealous.

She had misjudged Klaus von Emmerlich, she knew, and in retrospect she realized she would have been wise to reject his invitation to ride with him in the Prater. In spite of his subsequent attempts to seduce her, however, no harm had come to her. She had restrained the baron, keeping him within bounds, and had not been harmed.

Now, however, Jeremy was risking his life for her sake, and she knew she wouldn't want to live if anything untoward happened to him.

Lisa huddled in her bedroom, enveloped in dread.

Meanwhile, Jeremy, escorted by his brother, was riding

in a light carriage to the Vienna woods outside the city. He didn't feel talkative as the coach rumbled on the cobblestones of the still-empty streets, but there were things that needed to be said.

"Tom, I wrote a new will last night, naming you and Scott Emerson as executors. Here it is." He handed the document to his brother.

"Nothing will happen to you," Tom told him. "Von Emmerlich has no idea how handy you are with firearms."

"I hope you're right," Jeremy said, "but if the worst should happen, I want you to promise you'll take care of Lisa for me."

"Of course."

"I'll even ask that you take a leave from the State Department long enough to locate Lance and Carrie, and bring them home to Oakhurst Manor. Only the Lord knows what's become of them, and they're in my thoughts constantly."

"You know you can rely on me," Tom said.

"There's one more thing that bothers me," Jeremy said, and hesitated. "I mention it only because this is no time for me to hold back, although I can't quite put my finger on what's wrong. Tom, I'm uneasy about Jerry, even though I can't pinpoint the reason. Maybe it's simply because Lisa doesn't trust him, so she may have put doubts in my head. Or there may be more to it than that. He's my firstborn son, so I want to be fair to him. Whatever my feelings and the reasons for them, if I don't live I'd very much appreciate it if you'd go home to Oakhurst Manor and look thoroughly into his affairs."

"Of course. I haven't seen Jerry since he was a child, so I scarcely know him these days," Tom said. "But to be honest with you, Margot and I were always uneasy about him when he was a little boy. He wasn't like other children."

"Well, he isn't like you or me, that's for certain. Or like Lance, either. But—as I keep reminding myself—he is my son, and I do my best to accept him as he is. He may be doing nothing wrong, in which case you'd have no worries. But if there are problems, I'd expect you to find them and root them out."

Tom gripped his brother's shoulder. "Depend on me," he said.

"I do." Jeremy sat back against the cushions of the carriage and lapsed into silence again.

The sky was growing brighter by the time they reached the Vienna Woods, an extensive tract of many acres that, until recently, had been used as an imperial hunting preserve. The driver knew their destination, which neither of the American brothers would have been able to find with ease, and took a path that led to the edge of a small grassy clearing.

Sir Harold Northrop and Dr. Hummellmann had already arrived. Jeremy and Tom shook hands with them, then retired to one side of the clearing, and while they awaited the arrival of the other principal, the referee carefully inspected and loaded the brace of pistols that the duelists would use.

A few moments later another carriage arrived, and Baron Klaus von Emmerlich came into the clearing, accompanied by his second. Both wore the scarlet-and-gold uniforms of imperial guard officers, and the baron carefully removed his plumed helmet before bowing to the referee and the physician.

He and Jeremy studiously avoided looking at each other.

Sir Harold moved to the center of the clearing, and summoning the seconds, requested them to inspect the weapons. This they did, at length.

"The guns are beauties," Tom told his brother. "They're perfectly balanced, with hair triggers. You can knock a fly off a wall with either of them."

Jeremy nodded, smiling slightly. As always in a time of crisis, he remained remarkably cool, suppressing his fears and thinking with clarity. He knew he was facing a man thoroughly familiar with firearms, and he was confident that his skills were equal to those of the baron. His cause was right, so he was willing to take his chances in fair fight.

Now Sir Harold summoned the principals, who continued to avoid each other's gaze. "Gentlemen," the referee said, "I am required under the code of the duel to inquire whether you are willing to reconcile your differences without resort to bloodshed. Mr. Beaufort, are you, as the challenger, so willing?"

"Certainly," Jeremy replied, "on the single condition that my opponent apologizes to my wife for his undue attentions to her."

"What is your reply, Baron?"

Von Emmerlich smiled sardonically. "After I dispose of this Yankee," he said, "I shall be free to pursue the lady as I please."

It was obvious to Jeremy that the man's deliberately shocking insult was intended to anger him so much that his aim would be spoiled. He had no intention of falling into such a trap, however, and refrained from making an additional comment.

Sir Harold was slightly flustered by the unorthodox remark, but his diplomatic training stood him in good stead and he quickly recovered his aplomb. "The duel will be fought," he said. "You will take your weapons from this case, gentlemen, and then you will each walk twenty paces to opposite sides of the clearing. At that time you will turn and hold your arms at your sides until I give you the signal to fire. At that time you may fire at will. After discharging your weapon you will be good enough to drop it on the ground. If either of you draws blood, he will be adjudged the winner. If neither draws blood, the honor of both participants will nevertheless be regarded as avenged, and no repetition of this engagement will be permitted. I trust I have made my instructions clear."

Both opponents inclined their heads.

Sir Harold opened the weapons case and extended it before him.

Jeremy deliberately allowed von Emmerlich to choose first, then took the remaining pistol and held it at his side. What his brother had told him was accurate. It was of French make, as were most superior dueling pistols, and its balance was superb. The butt fitted into the palm of his hand, and he felt a surge of confidence.

"Be good enough to walk twenty paces, gentlemen," Sir Harold said.

Jeremy counted off the appropriate distance, then turned, standing erect.

For the first time his eyes met those of von Emmerlich,

and he suddenly realized that the gratuitous insult had been a great deal more than that. He saw sheer hatred in the man's eyes, and knew beyond any doubt that the baron intended to destroy him.

Ordinarily, in a duel, a participant tried to inflict a flesh wound on his foe, but this occasion was different. Jeremy realized he had to kill or would be killed.

He steadied himself as he awaited the signal.

"Gentlemen," Sir Harold said in a low, steady voice that carried across the clearing, "you may fire at will."

Neither hurrying nor dawdling, Jeremy raised his pistol, took careful aim, and squeezed the trigger.

Two shots rang out simultaneously.

Baron Klaus von Emmerlich dropped dead, his opponent's bullet between his eyes.

At the same instant Jeremy crumpled to the ground. A searing pain enveloped him.

Tom rushed to his side and dropped to one knee beside him. "Where did he hit you?"

"In the hip, I think," Jeremy gasped. "I'll be all right."

Dr. Hummellmann saw that nothing could be done for the baron, so he came to Jeremy and examined him. "The bullet appears to be lodged in your hipbone," he said, and was concerned because there was so little bleeding. "We'll take you home, and I'll be able to examine you more thoroughly there."

Baron von Emmerlich's second and carriage driver carried his body to the waiting coach.

Jeremy was unable to stand, much less walk, so it took the combined efforts of Tom, Sir Harold, and the physician to place him in his carriage. He refused the laudanum offered to him to make him more comfortable, wanting no opiate until he learned the extent of his injury.

Only now did it occur to him that he had killed the baron, and he was satisfied. Lisa's honor had been duly avenged.

The drive back to the city seemed endless.

Jeremy was in agony, but his mind continued to function clearly. "Tom," he said, "when we get to the house I'll be grateful if you'll go in ahead of us and assure Lisa that I've survived. I don't want her overly upset when she sees me being carried in."

As it happened, Lisa was looking out of a ground-floor window, watching for her husband's return. When she saw him lying on the seat of the coach, her hand flew to her throat, but she remained dry-eyed and did not give in to hysteria.

Servants helped carry Jeremy to his own bed, and on the walk up the stairs Tom told Lisa the outcome of the duel.

She wasted no grief on Klaus von Emmerlich. Her husband was her only concern.

Dr. Hummellmann sent a runner to the imperial court to fetch two of his colleagues, and they hurried to the house, then assisted him in making a prolonged examination of the patient.

Jeremy's pain was still intense, and he looked forward to the dose of laudanum that would give him relief, but first he had to hear the verdict.

"My initial diagnosis was correct," Dr. Hummellmann said to him and Lisa. "The bullet has embedded itself in the hipbone."

"Can you remove it, Doctor?" Lisa asked.

"I deeply regret that I can't," he said. "I imagine that someday the art of medicine will be sufficiently advanced for a surgeon to perform such an operation. But if I were to make the attempt now—and my colleagues are in complete agreement with me—Mr. Beaufort would be a hopeless cripple for the rest of his life."

Jeremy grimaced. "What's my alternative?"

"In many instances the bullet works itself out of the human system, and the body then heals completely," Dr. Hummellmann replied. "There are many cases on record where this happened to men who were wounded in the Napoleonic wars. If you're careful, Mr. Beaufort, and if you don't aggravate your wound, your chance of achieving a total recovery is excellent."

"What is my husband's alternative?" Lisa asked as she steeled herself for the reply.

"He will walk with a limp until the bullet leaves his body," Dr. Hummellmann said. "So I recommend that he stay off his feet as much as possible. This won't be easy, because he'll feel like walking again in another two weeks. If he takes my advice, he'll perform his duties sitting in a wheelchair that I'll have made for him, and at no time will he actually walk."

Jeremy refused to give in to the pain that felt as though a knife blade were pressing into his hip. "Maybe I ought to resign my position as minister and go home," he said.

The physician shook his head. "In my opinion that would be the worst thing you could do, sir," he said. "In a short time you'll be able to resume your duties here. If, as I've indicated, you confine yourself to a wheelchair. If you leave, however, a journey of five thousand miles to the United States stretches ahead of you. You'll travel by coach, even by horseback. You'll spend weeks on board a ship that will be at the mercy of the elements, and I can almost guarantee that you'll never walk properly again. I can't promise that you'll recover totally if you follow the regimen I've prescribed for you, but at least you'll be able to do your duty as a diplomat, and there's a strong possibility you'll recover."

No matter what he did, Jeremy thought, the outlook was bleak.

Dr. Hummellmann carefully measured a quantity of laudanum into a glass, then added water to it. "There's no need for an immediate decision. Drink this, and by tomorrow you'll be feeling sufficiently well to discuss the matter with Mrs. Beaufort." He thrust the glass into Jeremy's hand.

Taking a deep breath, Jeremy downed the bitter brew. He knew from his experience when he had been wounded as an officer in the navy that the opiate would begin to take effect soon and that he would be sound asleep in less than a half-hour.

"I'll return for your decision tomorrow morning," Dr. Hummellmann said, and bowed himself out.

"I know you're anxious to go home, dear," Lisa said, "but the advice makes sense. Stay here, continue to serve President Jackson, and there's at least the possibility that you'll recover."

In spite of his pain he grinned at her. "I find it odd that Andrew Jackson carried a bullet in his body for years after he fought a duel for his wife's honor. He told me himself that it didn't pull out until some months after he moved into the White House."

"You and President Jackson are more alike than any two men I have ever known," Lisa said. "You needn't have challenged Klaus von Emmerlich, but you insisted. Now, as a result, you may never walk easily or without pain again. Was the duel worth that?"

"Of course," Jeremy replied without hesitation. "The baron died because of his rudeness to you, and I've served notice on the world that no man can insult or degrade the woman I love without paying the consequences."

Lisa was ever conscious of his love, and that knowledge made it easier to tolerate his injury. At least he was alive, and for that much she was infinitely grateful.

Perhaps it was her lot to take care of him for the rest of her days; if that happened, she would have no complaint. She remembered all too vividly that her first husband, Rear Admiral Saunders of the Royal Navy, had been an invalid for years, and she had devoted herself to him. She had never loved Dickie Saunders; Jeremy was the one man she had ever known for whom she would willingly die.

Therefore she would do everything in her power for him. Lisa realized he was upset by the continuing disappearance of Lance and Carrie, and that, for the first time, he was opening his eyes to the machinations of Jerry, too. Consequently he was eager to return to Oakhurst Manor.

Not if she could help it, she promised herself. As long as there was a chance he would walk again if he stayed off his feet, she would see to it that he spent the coming months—years, if need be—in a wheelchair.

Like most powerful, strong-willed men, Jeremy didn't quite understand that he was actually ruled by his wife. And like most clever, loving wives, Lisa had gone to great pains to conceal that knowledge from him.

That day was ended now. If necessary she would have to demonstrate to him that, for the sake of his lifelong health, she was in charge. She was worried about Lance and Carrie, too, and she hoped that someday Jerry would be exposed as a pious fraud. But these concerns were secondary.

The one thing that mattered to her was that her vigorous, athletic husband be restored to full health. He would fret and be miserable as a cripple, and she would go to any lengths to prevent him from taking the risk that he wouldn't be able to walk again, much less to go hunting or stand on the quarterdeck of a ship, ride across the fields of Oakhurst Manor, or compete with Lance in trials of skill and prowess.

The laudanum was taking effect now. The creases of pain gradually vanished from Jeremy's face, and he dropped into a deep, dreamless sleep.

Lisa stood and looked at him, then bent down and kissed him. "God bless you, dear," she murmured. "I shall do everything I can to help and protect you, even from yourself."

9

The largest Indian settlement in the Rocky Mountains was a town of the Jicarilla Apache nation, which had a population of about two thousand. It was a remote place, located at a height of five thousand feet in a broad valley completely surrounded by snow-capped mountain peaks. There the squaws grew corn, sugar beets, and other crops that augmented the hunting and fishing of the warriors.

The Jicarilla were as ferocious as their Apache cousins who lived farther to the north, so other tribes left them to their own devices, even though their town was a tempting target. Few outsiders ventured into the valley, and even the American, British, and French-Canadian mountain men ordinarily gave it a wide berth. Any stranger who aroused the ire of the Jicarilla Apache was risking his life and his scalp.

There were several mountain men, however, who didn't know the meaning of fear. One was Jim Bridger, who had spent an entire winter with the Jicarilla. Another was the fabled Kit Carson, who had been a frequent visitor and was said to have taken a Jicarilla maiden as his wife.

The third was paying his first visit there. The bearded

giant known as the Lion rode out of one of the high
passes, accompanied by his Indian friend, Ponca, and leading a caravan of pack mules. Lance sat easily in his
saddle, seemingly relaxed but alert. It was no accident that
brought him to the community of the Jicarilla. His "nose
for weather," as Ponca called it, told him that an unsea-
sonably early winter blizzard would strike before the next
day, and he didn't want to be caught on the mountain
heights when the snow fell and the winds roaring down
from the icy glaciers began to howl. There was no other
refuge within hundreds of miles, so the town of the Jicarilla Apache would have to extend its hospitality to him
and his companion.

The pair were under observation from the time they
emerged from the pass, a party of senior Jicarilla Apache
watching them from behind the shelter of towering boulders. The braves took no unnecessary chance, as was their
custom. Those armed with muskets trained them on the
approaching strangers, and the rest held their bows and arrows ready for instant use.

Lance seemed unaware of the presence of others anywhere in the vicinity. Then one of the warriors moved
slightly, dislodging a few pebbles beneath one of his
rawhide-clad feet. Only someone whose hearing was extraordinary would have heard the sound, but Lance's sen-
sitivity was such that he heeded the warning.

Automatically, instinctively, he reached for one of the
short spears in the quiver at his shoulder.

The Jicarilla exchanged puzzled, uncertain glances.
Here was a white man carrying one of the most powerful,
accurate firesticks ever made, but he preferred a spear far
shorter than any the Indians had ever seen. Why?

All at once the truth struck the leader of the party like
a thunderclap. "The Lion!" he whispered.

Now the other braves understood. This was the legendary Lion, a man endowed with superhuman strength whose
short spears were magically lethal.

A national tradition and lifelong training had made the
Jicarilla courageous, but they were not foolhardy. No warriors in their right minds would attack a giant who could
not be harmed by firesticks or arrows, but who could kill
with the slightest touch of a short spear.

Taking care to lower their weapons, the braves came into the open, and their leader raised a hand, palm upward, in greeting. "Hail to the Lion," he called.

Lance returned the salute, holding his spear in his other hand. "Hail to the Jicarilla Apache," he replied in the language of the Sioux. Once he would have felt he was taking part in a silly charade, but the mountains were in his blood now, and their customs had become second nature to him. The gestures he was receiving and returning were no game, but were the very essence of life itself.

The braves surrounded him and Ponca, then escorted them into the town. Lance did not return his spear to its quiver until he assured himself that the reception would be friendly.

He knew he and Ponca would be safe when the sachem of the community emerged from his house, a stone hut reinforced with clay, and offered a welcome. The chief was a husky middle-aged man whose head was shaved except for a center strip of long, plaited hair stiffened with bear grease. He walked with the aid of a stick, and Lance noted that there was a row of neat stitches on the outside of his sore ankle.

That was curious, because as far he knew, the mountain Indians had no knowledge of modern surgical techniques. A scar on the ankle indicated that a swelling of some kind had been cut, and that the long incision subsequently had been sewn.

The sachem indicated he was delighted to offer his hospitality to the Lion and his companion.

Lance explained he sought refuge because a heavy snow would start to fall at any time.

The warriors looked at each other without expression. The sky overhead was clear, the faint breeze that blew from the southwest was balmy, and mountain flowers still grew in crevices. Winter would not come for many weeks, and their attitude indicated that although they respected the Lion as a fighting man, they didn't think much of him as a prophet.

Squaws began to prepare a meal for the new arrivals in a stone-lined pit outside the hut of the sachem. There was venison steak, which had been soaked in fermented juice of dandelions to make it tender, fresh-caught mountain trout taken from a small rushing river that marked the boundary at one side of the town, and the usual pulverized parched corn mixed with water. Lance had forgotten the taste of roasted corn, but had grown so accustomed to the pulverized version that he accepted it as natural.

He, Ponca, and their host sat cross-legged before the fire, and as they ate, the sky overhead became black, even though it was only midday. Then, suddenly, snow began to fall, gently at first, and gradually becoming thicker.

The prophecy of the Lion was fulfilled, and word of his remarkable talent spread quickly through the town. Braves, squaws, and children appeared from huts, drums began to sound, and soon the Jicarilla were engaging in a ceremonial dance honoring the Lion, whose gifts were not shared by lesser mortals.

The wind became chilly and Lance drew his tawny lion-skin cape around his shoulders, further impressing his hosts.

The Indians continued to cavort, the parade and dance led by a painted medicine man who seemed somewhat awkward as he rattled a gourd filled with animal bones.

Lance glanced at the man, and was puzzled. He was no Jicarilla. In fact, he wasn't even an Indian, but was black.

The medicine man was looking at him, too, staring at him with a strange expression. Suddenly he stopped dancing, moved closer, and gaped.

"Dear Lord!" he shouted in English. "I'll be damned if you aren't Lance Beaufort!"

All at once Lance knew him and leaped to his feet. "Paul Beaufort!" he roared.

They embraced, pounding each other on the back and laughing exuberantly. The last Lance had known, Paul was practicing medicine in Boston, and it was almost inconceivable that he should be in this primitive Indian community taking part in the superstitious rubbish that marked the activities of the Jicarilla Apache medicine men.

It was equally odd to Paul that this buckskin-clad, bearded giant, famed as the Lion, could be the wealthy Lance Beaufort, heir to an Oakhurst Manor fortune and head of a major American shipping enterprise.

For the moment there was no opportunity for either to

offer an explanation. The Jicarilla were pleased that the Lion and their medicine man obviously knew each other, and only Ponca looked incredulous. At the sachem's invitation Paul joined them in the meal, and not until it ended was the former Massachusetts doctor able to take the guests off to his own hut.

Snow was falling heavily now, precisely as Lance had predicted, and the wind was growing stronger. But squaws had built a fire in the crude hearth at one side of the hut, clay chinking prevented outside air from coming in, and when a thick buffalo-hide flap was lowered over the entrance, it was warm inside.

Lance, Ponca, and Paul sat down around the fire, the Kiowa still marveling.

Lance had to agree. It was extraordinary that a boyhood companion who used the Beaufort name should appear out of nowhere in this wilderness.

Paul told his story first. For a long time he had wanted to come to the Rockies and live the life of a mountain man, so he had taken a two-year leave of absence from his practice for the purpose. Once he had learned the terrain and how to survive here, he had prospered as a hunter and trapper, but bad luck had overtaken him when the Jicarilla had captured him.

For weeks he had felt certain they intended to kill him, sacrificing him to their gods at their annual harvest festival, but fate had intervened when he had seen a serious infection on the ankle of the sachem. He had persuaded the chief to let him perform an operation, which he had done with primitive instruments.

Paul's luck had changed. The sachem had survived and was gradually recovering the use of his leg. In gratitude he had "promoted" his savior to medicine man.

"What my story proves, I guess," Paul said with a grin, "is that a man can't really get away from his profession. Between us, I'm mighty sick of this mumbo-jumbo, though, and I'd like to get back to hunting."

"I reckon we can arrange to take you with us when we leave," Lance said.

"There's nothing I'd like better than to throw in my lot with you," Paul said, shaking his head, "but the sachem depends on me now, and I'm sure he won't let me go. I may have to stay here for life."

Ponca smiled as he entered the conversation for the first time. "You are wrong," he said. "Lance is the Lion. All the tribes of the mountains know him. None will deny his wishes."

They decided they would learn soon enough whether the attempt would succeed.

Now it was Lance's turn to tell what had happened to him, and his voice thickened as he spoke of Carrie's rape and the false charge that had almost led to his own capture and execution. He had not spoken aloud about Carrie in many months, but just mentioning her name made his separation from her almost unbearable.

It was true that he had created a whole new life for himself. Not only was he alive in the mountains, well able to look after himself, and creating legends, but his success as a hunter and trapper was earning him enough money to make him financially independent. But nothing he had done, nothing that had happened to him, caused him to love Carrie any the less.

She was still the only woman he had ever wanted, the only one he would ever love. He knew it deep down, and someday he would have to take the risk of going back to South Carolina to find her. Ultimately, he would be able to establish his innocence and would be reunited with his beloved.

Paul was deeply touched by his recital. "I believe in the cause of justice," he said, "but sometimes it isn't easy to hold on to one's convictions. Frankly, I'm worried about my sister." He told how Cleo had insisted on going to South Carolina in order to visit their grandmother's grave.

Lance made no immediate comment, but stared thoughtfully into the fire.

"To be honest with you," Paul said, "if you or your father were at Oakhurst Manor, I know no harm would come to Cleo. But with Jerry in charge . . . Well, I don't know."

"Neither do I," Lance said.

"Maybe I'm being unfair to him, but I sure didn't like him as a boy."

"He hasn't improved with age."

"I hate to say this," Paul declared, "but I can't help wondering if he was responsible for what happened to Carrie."

"The same thought has occurred to me," Lance said, and clenched a huge fist. "I'll tell you this much. If he was, and I can prove it, I don't care if we share the same blood. I'll follow him to the ends of the earth and throttle him with my bare hands."

He spoke with such deadly earnestness that even though it was very warm in the hut, Paul shuddered.

Even Ponca, who knew nothing of the people they were discussing, saw what he called "the Lion look" in Lance's eyes, and told himself that the days of his friend's enemy were numbered.

The snowstorm lasted for seventy-two hours, leaving high drifts in the valley of the Jicarilla Apache, but at last it subsided. The sun came out, the wind blew from the southwest again, and the snows began to melt.

It was time for Lance and Ponca to be on their way.

"I have my horse," Paul said, "but I doubt if the natives will let me use it."

"We'll soon find out," Lance told him. "Come with me, and let me do the talking."

They went to the hut of the sachem, and Lance exchanged elaborate courtesies with him before coming to the point.

"The Lion and Ponca go now," he said. "The medicine man of the Jicarilla is the brother of the Lion. So he will go, too."

The sachem shook his head vigorously. Then he pointed to his ankle.

Here was the key to the situation, and Lance was quick to take advantage of it. "The medicine man has lost his magic," he said. "Only if he spends the time of the snows with the Lion will he become strong in magic again."

The sachem looked shaken.

"When the time of flowers comes again," Lance continued, "the medicine man will return to the town of the Jicarilla Apache. Then he will tend the leg of the sachem. If the sachem permits this, his leg will become whole again. If he refuses, his leg will rot and fall off." He told the lie with a straight face.

The leader of the tribe needed no further urging. "The medicine man will go," he agreed. "The Lion will make him strong in magic again."

Not until the trio and their pack mules were safely beyond the borders of the town did Paul Beaufort laugh aloud. "I swear, Lance, there's no one like you. Listening to you back there, I'd have thought you had spent your whole life with these tribes."

"Maybe I'll have to stay out here for the rest of my days," Lance replied. "If it weren't for missing Carrie so much that she haunts me constantly, I wouldn't mind."

Business at the House on the Avenue was slack during the holiday season, and relatively few men came to the establishment. Only Carrie did not suffer. Her clients continued to visit her, and she had no complaints.

She was secretly relieved. When she had nothing to occupy her she was inclined to brood, and at such times she thought so long and hard about Lance Beaufort that she wanted to scream. Perhaps if he knew what she was doing now he would no longer want her, but she couldn't allow herself to dwell on that aspect of her situation.

It was enough that she still loved him and knew beyond any doubt that he loved her, too. If and when they were reunited—and she was convinced that day would come— she knew he would believe her when she told him that the many men who had made love to her meant nothing to her. She was still Lance's. She still belonged to him, just as he belonged to her. These were the verities that made her life worth living, that gave her hope for the future.

One evening she made up and dressed with her usual care in a sleek gown that matched her hair, then went down to the dining room to join the other girls for a light meal before the customers began to come in. Her colleagues complimented her, as they always did, and Melanie, who accompanied her into a small sitting room when they finished eating, was ecstatic.

"I'd give anything to be like you," she said without envy. "You have just about everything that anybody could want."

It was impossible to explain to one so young, and Carrie simply shook her head and smiled.

"I mean it," Melanie insisted. "The new owners let you do anything you please. You could go off on a long holiday if you wanted one—"

"I have no wish to go anywhere." Carrie didn't mean to be curt, but it was impossible for someone like Melanie to understand that she wanted no time alone, no lulls in her life when she would be forced to think about what might have been.

"When you don't like a client, you just refuse him," Melanie continued.

"That's my privilege. It's also yours and that of everyone else here."

"I wouldn't dare, Carrie. You're the only one who can get away with it!"

They were interrupted by a smiling Maria, who came quietly into the room. "There's a visitor here from South Carolina who has asked for you, Carrie. He says he heard of you, and he's willing to spend several hundred dollars for the privilege of a few hours with you."

South Carolinians always made Carrie nervous because she was afraid that someday she would encounter a man she had known in her previous life. If the visitor had merely heard of her, however, it meant that she wasn't acquainted with him. "Send him in, Maria, and I'll have a few words with him."

The director of the establishment was pained by her independent attitude. Even the queen of New Orleans couldn't afford to turn down clients who offered fees of several hundred dollars. But it was useless to argue with a girl who knew her powers and was adamant in her exercise of them.

Melanie stood, intending to leave.

Carrie airily waved her back to her seat. "Don't go," she said. "If this man doesn't suit me, we can continue our chat."

The younger girl sat again and rearranged her slit skirt so it concealed her legs. It wasn't often that she or anyone else had the chance to "interview a client," as the inmates called Carrie's system.

Maria sighed as she went off to fetch the customer. Carrie felt almost as though she owned the place, and for all practical purposes she was beyond control, making her own rules. Anyone else who behaved as she did would be disciplined, perhaps even dismissed, but profits would plunge if Maria got rid of her, and the new owners, who never came near the house, might even be impelled to seek a new madam.

Bringing the man with her, she presented him to Carrie and Melanie, then departed.

Oscar Griffin helped himself to a pinch of snuff as he sat. "I'm told there's no one quite like you," he said to Carrie.

She took an instant dislike to the bald, beady-eyed man, and merely shrugged.

"We'll soon find out," he said.

Her smile was cryptic.

Oscar leaned forward in his chair. "I'm no ordinary customer," he told her.

She was cynically amused, but withheld comment.

"I own a place like this in Charleston," he said. "Not as elegant yet, but I intend to expand it. If I like you, I'll take you there with me."

Under no circumstances would she work in a Charleston house. Not only would she run the risk of seeing Scott and Kai Emerson on the street or in a shop, but the clientele well might include young men who had been lifelong friends. "What makes you think I'd even be interested?" she demanded.

"I'd make it well worth your while," Oscar said.

"No, thank you." Carrie smiled, but her tone was firm.

He smiled in return, obviously confident of his own ability to change her mind.

His arrogance annoyed her. "To tell you the truth," she said, "I don't care to go upstairs with you, either." Her dismissal was flat, uncompromising.

Oscar was outraged. "Why not?"

"For one thing, I doubt if you can afford my fee. One thousand dollars."

The sum was absurdly high, and even Melanie was astonished by her friend's high-handed attitude.

The stunned Oscar Griffin peered at Carrie, unwilling to believe she was serious. When he saw that she meant what she said, however, he turned to inspect her companion. The redhead was very pretty, and was young enough to be malleable. With training she could be taught to serve the needs of customers who demanded something different to whet their appetites.

"I'll take you instead," he said.

Melanie was startled by his brusqueness. She, too, disliked this hard-eyed little man, and found something menacing in his attitude. Reacting instinctively, she shrank back in her chair.

"My friend doesn't care to go with you, either," Carrie said, immediately protecting the younger girl.

"Since when do you wenches decide these things?" Oscar asked, his voice rising.

It was evident that he intended to create a scene, and Carrie had no patience with him. "I advise you to leave," she told him.

Oscar stood, feet planted apart, and glared at her.

"If I must," she said pleasantly, "I'll have you thrown out."

He made no move.

She reached for a bell rope.

Oscar hesitated for an instant, then stormed out, cursing wildly.

The unpleasant incident had ended, so Carrie promptly put the man out of her mind.

Although neither she nor Oscar realized it, she had struck a sharp blow at the vanity of a man who had played a major role in the events that had led her to come to New Orleans and enter the life she was now leading.

Jerry Beaufort had to die. There was no alternative, Cleo decided, no other way to end the misery of her existence. No matter what happened to her, she had to kill him. Her captivity and degradation were beyond endurance, and her torment would end only when she murdered the man who had ruined her life.

She had two problems: obtaining a weapon and concealing it.

The second unexpectedly solved itself. In return for providing the loathsome Oscar Griffin with what he called "entertainment" on several horribly unpleasant occasions, Jerry had "rewarded" her by giving her a dressing robe that he permitted her to wear when she went back and forth between her own quarters and the master-bedroom suite. Cleo's pride had been so shattered that she no longer minded being paraded in the nude when she went through the corridors, but the robe was an answer to her most pressing need. Best of all, it had a pocket in which she could hide a weapon.

Each night she was given a knife and fork to use at her meal, and she found it relatively easy, one evening, to steal the knife on her tray. If the serving maid who brought her meals to her room noticed that she had taken the knife, the woman had the compassion not to mention it to anyone.

Thereafter, for a week, Cleo spent hours each day carefully honing the knife on the stone window ledge. When it was as sharp as a razor, she finally desisted, deciding it was ready now.

Her courage almost deserted her when she had to wait for many days before being summoned into Jerry's presence again. The knife already reposed in the pocket of her robe, but she wondered if she had the strength and determination to kill with it. Never had she used any weapon against a fellow human.

Late one afternoon, however, her door was unlocked and the house servant called to her in the usual words: "You're wanted."

Cleo slipped into the robe, then took a larger-than-usual gulp of whiskey to steady herself.

The serving woman looked at her in disgust, but made no comment as they made their way down to the second floor.

Jerry was in an amiable mood. "My friend Oscar has just come home from New Orleans," he said, "and I've rented you to him for the day tomorrow. I'll be taking you into the city in the morning. Be prepared for a long day." He chuckled and rubbed his hands together, enjoying the prospect of what lay in store.

Cleo's stomach turned over, and she realized that the revelation was precisely what she needed to strengthen her resolve.

All at once Jerry's mood changed, and he became petulant. "I gave you that dressing gown on the distinct understanding that you wouldn't wear it in my presence. Remove it!"

She had no choice.

Now!

Instinct impelled her to open the robe, then approach him slowly. She forced herself to smile, and tried to distract him by wriggling her hips as she advanced slowly.

"Well, you're learning, my girl," Jerry said as he waited for her.

Cleo's hand crept into the pocket and closed over the handle of the knife.

As Jerry reached for her, she struck, slashing at him wildly with the knife.

But her terror was so great that she closed her eyes and missed his face by a fraction of an inch.

Before she could strike again, he wrenched the knife from her hand, and it fell to the floor beyond her reach.

She had failed, and there wouldn't be another chance.

Jerry was hysterical, and throwing open the door, he bellowed for help.

His shouts brought a half-dozen servants hurrying to the sitting room, and their faces became grave when they learned what had happened. There was only one punishment for a slave who tried to murder a master.

Jerry went racing down the stairs and ran out of the house, still shouting.

Cleo was left in the charge of the majordomo and another butler, both of whom took care not to speak to her or look at her. Their own lives were in great danger now, and they well knew it.

The overseer and his assistant were summoned, and Jerry became a trifle calmer when he had spoken to them, but he was still agitated and paced up and down on the lawn.

All work stopped at Oakhurst Manor. The field hands were brought in and herded into an area behind the barn. Then the house servants were summoned, and the mood was established by the overseer and his helper, both of whom were now carrying braces of pistols in their belts.

Then several of the male slaves were forced to erect a gibbet. Those who had lived and worked at Oakhurst Manor for years had never been subjected to such a sight.

The entire group, more than five hundred in all, watched in stony silence as Cleo was led behind the barn. She was completely naked, but held her head high.

She had failed miserably, it was true, but she had stopped being a craven coward, and she would not die in vain.

Jerry stood near the gibbet, his face ashen.

As Cleo was led past him, she paused for an instant, then deliberately spat in his face.

Now it was he who was the coward. Afraid to demonstrate his temper in the presence of the hundreds of slaves who might riot and kill him, he wiped the spittle from his face but made no other move.

The overseer pointed to a box beneath the gibbet.

The girl needed no help in mounting the box, and stood looking out at the servants and field hands.

They returned her stare in silence, their faces drained of all expression.

The loose end of the rope was thrown over the crossbar, and a frightened male slave was ordered to climb to the top, fasten the rope, and make it secure. He obeyed with alacrity.

"Do you want to let the wench hear a reading from the Bible, Mr. Beaufort?" the overseer asked.

Jerry shook his head.

The overseer cleared his throat. "Is there anything you want to say, girl?"

"Yes." Cleo's voice was firm and strong, ringing out across the assemblage, and even those who huddled at the rear of the crowd could hear every word plainly. "I was born free, and I lived as a freewoman until I came here to visit the grave of my grandmother. I was tricked into a life of shame, but I'm ashamed no longer. I'm proud of what I did today because it sets me truly free. I'm only sorry that I failed, but I say to you, Jerry Beaufort, that I'll be avenged."

She turned to him, a smile of terrible scorn on her face.

Jerry gestured impatiently.

The overseer kicked away the box from beneath the girl's feet.

The noose tightened and held.

Cleo's expression did not change, and she was still smiling as she died.

The hundreds who saw her hanged would never forget her smile.

Her last conscious thought was that she was of some use after all: as she died she could read pity in the eyes of the slaves at last, and mingled with it was strong admiration for her courage. She would not be forgotten at Oakhurst Manor, and her spirit would survive for generations to come.

The overseer cut down her dead body, and it crumpled to the ground.

The heavy silence was broken by Jerry's high-pitched, maniacal laugh.

10

---•◦•◀▶•◦•---

"We're blame near invincible," Paul said, his voice registering both surprise and pleasure as he and his partners sat around their campfire eating a steak of fresh elk meat.

Ponca grinned. He had predicted months earlier that no Indians would show hostility to the formidable trio, that even renegade mountain men would keep their distance, and his prophecy had been borne out.

Only Lance remained silent, staring into the fire as he leaned toward it, his sinewy fingers interlaced.

Paul and Ponca understood his mood, and respected it. Spring, like the winter that had preceded it, had come early to the Rockies, and whenever the seasons changed, Lance seemed to retreat into himself. It didn't matter, at least for the moment, that he and his partners had sold a very large quantity of furs to traders who were traveling to the United States, and that his purse was heavy. He didn't care, either, that he had earned the admiration of white man and red man alike, and was regarded as the most formidable and skilled of the loosely knit confederation of explorers and hunters known as mountain men.

Whenever the seasons changed, his thoughts turned

more forcibly than ever to Carolyn Emerson. To the life they might have been living together as husband and wife at Oakhurst Manor and in Charleston had not an unfair and cruel fate decreed otherwise. To others the arrival of spring meant that game abounded again, plants grew in the valleys, and tiny flowers came to life in mile-high crevices. To Lance spring meant that he was losing yet more time in his ever-present desire to be reunited with Carrie.

He was so restless that an inner voice urging him to return to Oakhurst Manor, regardless of the consequences, almost drowned out all sounds. Fortunately his common sense intervened. Perhaps he was still being sought by the authorities on the absurd charge that he had assaulted Carrie. It was probable, too, that he was wanted for the murder of the two members of the posse he had killed. If he went home it was likely he would be arrested and imprisoned.

That, however, was not what deterred him from making the long journey to South Carolina. He feared no man, and it would take the combined efforts of a small army to capture and subdue him.

What gave him pause was the realization that after all this time it was probable that Carrie had married someone else. By now she—and his family—undoubtedly assumed that he was dead. She would be foolish to wait, to save herself for a ghost, for a man who no longer existed.

Lance realized that a kind of moral cowardice was preventing him from going back to Oakhurst Manor. He, who shrank from no man or wild creature, was afraid to face a long-range future in which Carrie didn't play the pivotal role. It was the hope of being reunited with her that sustained him, that enabled him to withstand the rigors of mountain life, to overcome the harsh weather, to face potential enemies with equanimity. Deprived of that hope, he was afraid that he would crumble and be revealed as a weakling.

He confided his fears in no one, knowing that even Paul and Ponca would scoff. As Paul had just said, they were almost invincible, and it was he who formed the unyielding hard core of that strength. His partners would laugh if they knew that his inner existence was centered on the fervent wish to make Carrie his wife and spend the rest of his days with her.

Suddenly the heat of the campfire became unbearable. Lance cast aside his lion-skin cloak, but he still felt uncomfortable. Saying nothing to his companions, he rose abruptly and wandered off into the evergreen forest that adjoined the campsite.

Paul and Ponca made no comment as he left. Knowing his mood, they were not surprised, and they realized that after he wrestled alone with the inner torments that were torturing him, he would return to the fire and thereafter would be at peace within himself for several months. They were his brothers, but they respected his need for privacy.

The sun was moving lower toward the snow-covered peaks that lay to the west, its light filtering through the pines and hemlocks and junipers. There was no sound except the faint rustling noise made by a small animal that caught the scent of the man and crept away. Paying scant attention to where he was going, Lance walked for a time, then sat on a flat rock. A clump of tiny scarlet flowers grew close to his hand, and he admired them but did not pick them. It was wrong, he believed, to destroy any product of nature that man didn't need for his survival.

He had to get a grip on his emotions, Lance told himself. He was behaving like a sentimental adolescent. After all this time it was likely that Carrie had forgotten his existence. He would be wise to put her out of his own mind for all time, even though he knew he was asking himself to do the impossible.

All at once he realized he was not alone in the forest. Looking up, he saw a mammoth shaggy grizzly bear standing on its hind legs only a few feet from him. He had been so lost in thought that he hadn't even heard the beast approach, and now he would pay for his carelessness.

He had left his rifle behind, and hadn't even brought his pistols or his quiver of short arrows with him. His only weapon was the skinning knife he carried in his belt, and it could scarcely equalize the odds in an encounter with an animal that weighed at least three hundred and fifty pounds.

Escape was impossible. A thick snarl of bramble bushes lay directly behind Lance, and not only would the thorns tear at him, but the bear undoubtedly would follow him into the tangle.

There was no way he could use his superior intelligence in the struggle that lay ahead, either. Cunning was of no avail, and he believed he was doomed. Certainly his own strength was no match for that of the gigantic beast, which achieved a height of seven and a half feet.

The bear snarled, revealing two rows of yellow teeth, and its huge front paws swept back and forth in a sawing motion. One blow from a heavy paw would be enough to knock a man unconscious. The beast was not a carnivore, the man realized, but nevertheless would kill its victims.

The only hope, remote at best, was to strike first and, with great luck, incapacitate the animal sufficiently to get away. Grizzlies were slow, Lance knew, so his own sole advantage was that of whatever speed he could utilize.

The bear lumbered forward, its small dark eyes measuring the distance to the two-legged creature it was challenging.

Utilizing the few odds he possessed, Lance drew his skinning knife and struck first, plunging the blade deep into the bear's chest.

The wounded animal's roar of pain and anger echoed through the forest, sending a flock of birds into hasty flight and causing small animals in the vicinity to scamper away.

Before Lance could withdraw his knife and strike again, the bear enveloped him in a deadly embrace, crushing him. Thick claws pressed into the man's flesh, and he could smell the foul odor of the animal's breath.

Using all the strength he could muster, Lance pulled the knife free, then plunged it into the bear's body a second time.

The animal's rage compensated for the injuries he had sustained, and he hugged the man harder, trying to squeeze him to death.

Lance struck again and again with his knife, but the bear refused to go down. It was just a matter of time now before the beast would prevail, even though badly injured. No mere man had the strength or stamina to sustain such a struggle for more than a few minutes. Aiming as best he could for the bear's heart, Lance drove his knife in all the way to the hilt. The blow seemingly had no effect.

A rifle shot reverberated through the forest.

The bear continued to hold the man in its deadly grip for a few moments, then toppled back onto the ground.

The dazed Lance almost fell on top of him, but staggered back and began to weave in a circle.

Ponca raced up to him, a smoking rifle still in his hands, and shouted, "You teach me to shoot good!"

Lance grinned at him weakly.

Paul was close behind. "We heard the bear roar back at the fire," he said, "so we knew you were in trouble. We headed for the spot where the birds went up into the air, and then we found you."

He made a cursory examination.

"I'm all right," Lance muttered.

"You're in better shape than I expected," Paul told him. "I must admit you're the only man on earth who could fight a grizzly to a complete standstill. I'll patch you up after we get back to the campsite. Lean on me."

Lance refused, proudly insisting on walking alone.

"The only damage I can see so far is a claw mark on your face."

Lance raised a hand, and was surprised to discover that his cheek was bleeding.

"You'll have a scar as a souvenir for the rest of your days," Paul said with a chuckle. "But you're lucky you're still alive."

"I go back and skin bear," Ponca announced. "Not good to waste pelt."

He turned back into the forest while the others went on to the fire.

There Paul made a thorough medical examination, then shook his head. "Astonishing," he said. "I can find nothing wrong with you except the claw mark on your face." He splashed brandywine onto the cut.

Lance winced slightly, but made no sound, even though the pain was intense.

"After your face heals," Paul said, "you're going to look like a real tough. You'll have a scar four or five inches long."

Lance shrugged. With Carrie so far away and the chance of being reunited with her so remote, he cared nothing about his appearance. At the moment he was glad to be alive.

Later that night Ponca made a necklace of the bear's teeth for him as a memento, and Lance vowed he would wear it until he could present it to Carrie.

"I've got to ride over to Oakhurst Manor," Scott Emerson told Kai at breakfast, "and I'm not looking forward to it."

"I know," she replied. "Any meeting with Jerry these days is so unpleasant."

"You saw in Jeremy's last letter that he indicated he'd appreciate a report on the affairs of his shipping company, so I spent yesterday and the day before there, looking over the books and talking to various staff members. I'm afraid I have some questions to ask Jerry."

"That doesn't surprise me. Isn't it awful to feel that way about the son of Jeremy and Sarah?"

"I have no proof as yet that Jerry is mishandling any funds, but I do have several large question marks. I just hope he can give me answers that will satisfy me—and ultimately his father."

"How much is involved—or shouldn't I ask?"

"Strictly between us, dear, I can't account for about fifteen thousand dollars."

Kai was shocked. The amount was enormous, and she doubted that even the most prominent and influential men in the state earned that much in a year. Certainly it was far higher than the salary paid to President Jackson.

"I'm not saying—yet—that Jerry has taken that money out of shipping-company funds and falsified the books," Scott declared, frowning as he spoke. "But I'm afraid it looks that way to me. Naturally, I won't make any specific charges against him, and I know I can't write that kind of accusation to his father unless I can pinpoint this whole mess."

"That's wise," Kai said. "Jeremy is still very partial to Jerry."

"Less than he was before he was hurt in that duel," Scott replied. "Lisa has always felt the way we do about Jerry, and I wouldn't be surprised if her influence is beginning to bear fruit."

"I just hope all of us are wrong," Kai said as she poured him a cup of strong Caribbean coffee.

"So do I—for Jeremy's sake rather than his son's."

She was lost in thought for a moment. "I can't imagine what Jerry might be doing with all that money. He buys himself no new clothes or horses. Oakhurst Manor far more than earns its own way, and I don't think that even Jerry could spend thousands of dollars on his liquor."

Scott's smile was pained. "Don't mention this to a soul, but I've heard rumors in Charleston that when Jerry goes into the city he spends a great deal of his time at a place owned by a notorious onetime convict named Oscar Griffin."

The name meant nothing to Kai.

"Apparently he runs a gaming house, with a small bordello on the side."

"How disgusting."

"I doubt that Jerry is throwing away large sums of money on women." Scott stirred sugar into his coffee.

Kai sipped her own coffee, which she drank black for the sake of keeping her weight down. "Don't be too sure of that. If it's true that he kept some poor slave girl locked up in the manor house—the one he supposedly hanged when she tried to kill him—he well might be squandering a fortune on women."

"We haven't verified that story, so it may be nothing but loose gossip," Scott said. "And in any event, one could buy a couple of dozen attractive slave girls for the kind of money we're discussing. Jerry has never shown that kind of interest in women, and I doubt if he could handle a harem."

"Then you think he's losing money on gambling?"

"It could be. The chief of the Charleston constabulary tells me that Griffin runs a card game every night and that the stakes are high. If I must, I'll ask for a private report from the police spies who check Griffin's place from time to time. That's one sure way of finding out whether Jerry goes there. I've hesitated to ask because police informers frequently talk out of turn. So, for Jeremy's and Lisa's sake, I don't want to create any more talk about Jerry than there is already."

"It's all so unsavory," Kai said.

"That it is." He stood, then bent down to kiss her. "I don't intend to stay at Oakhurst Manor any longer than I must. Wish me luck."

The ride from Trelawney took only a short time, and a groom with a livid welt on his face took the attorney's horse. The man looked as though he had been slashed, perhaps with a riding crop, but Scott thought it discreet to ask him no questions.

Instead he allowed the majordomo to escort him into the house, and he waited in the library. He had loved this room since his boyhood, when old Paul Wellington Beaufort, then the master of Oakhurst Manor, had worked on his accounts here. After his untimely death the task had been assumed by the late Sarah, and in more recent years Jeremy had accepted the burden. Now dust was thick on the plantation's ledgers, Scott noted, and it was obvious that no one had touched the account books in a long time. Jerry was in sole charge of Oakhurst Manor these days, but it appeared he was negligent, to say the least, in the performance of his duties.

Scott had to cool his heels for almost a half-hour before the young acting master of the place came down the stairs. Jerry was wearing an old bathrobe and carpet slippers, his eyes were puffy, and even though the sun was not yet high overhead, there was the smell of liquor on his breath.

At least he had the grace to apologize for his tardiness. "I'm sorry it took me so long, Uncle Scott," he said. "But I had a little celebration with some friends last night, and I needed a couple of drinks just now so I could start functioning again."

It wasn't Scott's place to tell him he was drinking more than was good for him, so it was preferable to ignore the subject. "I won't keep you long, Jerry," he said. "I just want to talk to you for a few minutes about the shipping company. I've spent the past couple of days there, you see."

Jerry stiffened. "You have?"

"Yes, your father asked me to look at the records and talk with the staff."

When Jerry was placed on the defensive, there was a nasty edge to his voice. "He did? I find it strange that Papa didn't mention anything of the sort to me."

Scott realized his own integrity was being questioned, but he remained civil. "I have his letter in my study desk at Trelawney," he said quietly. "Ride over later in the day, if you wish, and I'll gladly show it to you."

Jerry disposed of the idea with a limp wave of his hand. "I'll take your word for it, Uncle Scott," he said, his tone as well as his words still insulting.

Scott had to struggle to control his temper. Jerry had become a complete boor, but because of a lifelong friendship with his father it was best not to become embroiled in a quarrel with him. "I went through the ledgers at the shipping company with the bookkeeper, and I also had separate talks with all of the senior staff members. None of them could give me a satisfactory answer to several questions."

Jerry had recovered his self-confidence, and smiled.

Scott removed a sheaf of papers from his pocket and spread them on the library desk. "The list on the left side shows the expenses of operating the company in the past year. The figures in the middle column indicate the income derived from each voyage made by a Beaufort merchantman during that time. And the column on the right denotes the profits."

The younger man took the sheet of paper and scanned it briefly, his manner indicating that he had little interest in the subject.

"Keep that final figure in the lower-right-hand corner in mind," Scott said, and picked up another sheet of paper. "Here are the various amounts used to buy new cargo. And here are the sums currently deposited in three Charleston banks. The only banks that your father—and Lance after him—ever used."

Jerry glanced at the second sheet, then yawned.

"Now," the lawyer told him, "a process of simple arithmetic will show you that these two sets of figures simply don't balance. There's a discrepancy of slightly more than fifteen thousand dollars." He tapped the figure with a quill pen to emphasize it. "In other words, that sum seems to be missing."

Jerry made no reply.

"Do you have any idea how to account for the loss?"

"This is the first I've heard of it."

Scott knew he was lying. The bookkeeper, who had been with the company for almost twenty years, ever since Jeremy had founded it, had stated only yesterday that he had called the matter to Jerry's attention several times. The bookkeeper was scrupulously honest, but in a situation like this his word would carry less weight than Jerry's.

Scott decided to take a different approach. "I was wondering if the fifteen thousand could have been deposited in a new account somewhere. Perhaps without the knowledge of the company officials. That would be legitimate, and not too unusual."

"Who could have removed the money and deposited it in a new account?" Jerry was wide-eyed.

"You," Scott said, coming to the point.

The younger man looked pained. "I already told you, Uncle Scott," he said, "that this is the first I've heard of the situation. So I couldn't be responsible for moving the money elsewhere. And I'd have no reason for doing it."

Scott merely shrugged. In interrogations he used the technique of saying as little as possible, allowing suspects to dig their own verbal graves.

"Maybe Lance took it before he ran away," Jerry suggested. "It could be that he absconded with the money and is using it to start a new life for himself somewhere under an assumed name."

The viciousness beneath the seemingly glib comment was almost more than Scott Emerson could tolerate. "I've looked thoroughly into that possibility," he said. "At the time that Lance disappeared, the shipping-company ledgers balanced. To the penny. In fact, the accounts were in perfect shape. As nearly as I can figure it, money began to vanish about six months after he went away, and the drain since that time has been steady."

"I hate to make unfair accusations, Uncle Scott," Jerry said, "but it could be that some of the company's employees are dishonest and have been robbing the till."

"I think it unlikely, because none of them have the right to withdraw funds from any account except the one reserved for expenses, and that account balances. Besides, under the cross-checking system I helped your father to establish many years ago, it wouldn't be possible for them to steal."

Jerry heaved himself to his feet, went to a sideboard, and poured a stiff shot of whiskey, which he drank neat. He shuddered slightly, coughed, and turned back to the older man, a hint of defiance in his attitude. "Then I'm afraid I don't know what to tell you. This is as much of a mystery to me as it is to you."

It was necessary to put a halt to his evasiveness, but Scott remained polite. "If you don't mind, I want to examine the only sets of figures that haven't been available to me. Your own lists of withdrawals from all three accounts." Here was the crux of the matter, and it would be easy enough to discover the younger man's guilt if he had siphoned off fifteen thousand dollars from the bank accounts.

"That's very personal," Jerry said. "It seems to me that my private records are strictly my own business."

"In this instance they're also your father's, since he owns the shipping company." Scott was firm, but his manner was still calmly judicial.

Jerry hated being pushed into a corner, and black rage surged within him, but he managed to control himself. "Are you indicating that you suspect me of stealing?"

"Not necessarily. You might have many valid reasons for helping yourself to shipping-company funds. I simply seek the facts, and in your father's absence you're in total charge of all his interests, both here at Oakhurst Manor and in Charleston."

"Ah, that's my whole point." Jerry found the loophole he had been seeking. "Ordinarily I wouldn't mind showing you all of my records and accounts, Uncle Scott, but there's a matter of principle involved. Since I have absolutely nothing to hide, however, I'll tell you what I'll do. I'll send off a letter to my father myself, explaining the situation to him and asking him what he wants me to do. If he writes back to me that he wants me to open all of my personal files to you, I'll be happy to oblige."

The maneuver was very clever, Scott realized. Jerry would take his time sending off a letter to Vienna, and might delay for many weeks. When he did write, ultimately, he could color his position in such a way that Jeremy well might agree with him that he could refrain from revealing his financial transactions.

The worst of the situation was that it was delicate and difficult to come between father and son. Scott had been Jeremy's lifelong friend and adviser, but even their closeness might not stand up under the test of interference with the rights of a son whose faults he had so rarely seen.

This way, since it took a long time for mail to travel between the United States and Austria, many more months would pass before Jeremy's letter outlining his wishes in the matter would be received. And during that time Jerry could continue to help himself to the shipping-company profits. No one would be able to halt him.

"If you insist," Scott said, "that's the way we'll have to handle this problem."

Jerry knew he had won, and celebrated by helping himself to another drink.

Scott stood, frowning and shaking his head before he departed. "I've known you since the day you were born, Jerry, and I've always felt close to you. So don't take it amiss when I say that you're drinking more than is good for you."

"I can judge my own capacities." Jerry's mood changed instantly, and he became surly.

"I hope so. Because all sorts of stories are being told these days, and I'm sure none of them would make your father and stepmother very happy."

"What kind of stories?"

"Well, the most unsavory of them is that you kept a slave girl locked up in the house, and that recently you had her put to death."

"What I do with my slaves—and how I treat them—is nobody's business but my own. You can tell anybody who's talking about me to mind his own goddamn business. With my compliments."

His bristling hostilities were so great that Scott lost no time taking his leave.

Jerry went to a window and, eyes narrowing, watched him as he rode off. Scott had no right to be nosing around in his financial affairs, much less subjecting him to implied criticism. If he wanted to take funds from the shipping company, that was his own concern. And if a wench like Cleo had to be hanged after making an unwarranted attack on his life, just because she had resented the innocent pleasures he had enjoyed without doing her any real harm, it had been his prerogative to deal with her as he had seen fit.

One thing was sure. Scott Emerson would be wise to attend to his own affairs at Trelawney and stay away from Oakhurst Manor. Or, Jerry decided, he would attend to Emerson and his wife as he had tried to do away with his father and Lisa.

The afternoon visitors had departed, and the House on the Avenue was enjoying an early-evening lull. Carrie, still making her own rules, had spent several hours on a shopping expedition, and stopped off in Melanie's room to show the younger girl her purchases. As always, Melanie approved of everything she had done.

Her enthusiasms were so great, so innocent, that Carrie couldn't help saying, "You know, you ought to get out of this line of work. It isn't good for you, and at seventeen you're certainly young enough to make a wholesome new life for yourself."

Melanie giggled.

"I mean it," Carrie told her, raising an eyebrow. "Nobody can stay in a place like this for more than a limited time without being influenced and changed."

"What about you?"

"Oh, I can take care of myself," Carrie replied. "And I guess I'm just greedy. I'm putting aside large sums of money, and when I have enough for financial security, I'll quit. But I'm somewhat different, Melanie. I don't drink with the men who come here, and I can pick and choose. So it's easier on me than it is on any of the rest of you."

"I want to be just like you, Carrie."

"I've had good luck. More than my share of it. Get out before you're too old."

"May I tell you a secret that nobody else knows?" Melanie's green eyes looked enormous.

"Of course."

"I lied about my age when I came here. I'm just sixteen. I won't be seventeen for another couple of months."

"Then go back to Virginia at once!" Carrie lost patience with her. "You've told me you're still on reasonably good terms with your family and that they don't know how you've been earning your living here—"

"Right. They think I'm a governess." Again Melanie giggled.

"Then go home. Forget all about this place. Find the right man and marry him."

"You don't understand, Carrie." The girl pouted. "Life at home was so dull. I like excitement. And as for men, I'm sure I'll meet somebody right here who'll give me more thrills—and travel and expensive clothes—than I could ever find in the Virginia farm country."

Carrie didn't know quite how to counter her arguments.

Before she had a chance, however, they were interrupted by a deep basso roar that rolled up the central staircase. The sound was followed by the tinkle of feminine laughter.

"You tell her I'm here," the man shouted, himself exploding in laughter, "or I'll go upstairs and find her myself!"

"It's Pierre!" Carrie exclaimed, and jumped to her feet. He would not only charge up the stairs if she didn't appear at once, but if he had been drinking and felt in a playful mood, he was capable of making a shambles of the place.

She hurried down the stairs, and couldn't help laughing as she ran. Of all her clients, Pierre Gautier was unique.

A stranger who passed him on the street wouldn't be able to guess that he was one of the wealthiest and most powerful men in the American West. A French Canadian by birth and a professional bateau operator who had brought furs to Quebec, he had come to the United States as the owner of one small barge, which he himself had poled down the Mississippi River. Today a naturalized United States citizen, he owned a large fleet of barges, and it was his boast that he carried more grain, more furs, and more timber, vegetables, and other merchandise from the Mississippi headwaters to New Orleans than his two largest competitors combined.

Carrie saw him at once as she entered the main parlor, where he was surrounded by Maria and a half-dozen of the girls. A huge bull of a man, he was dressed, as always, in the simple rough shirt and pants of a Mississippi boatman. His boots were shabby, and the battered hat he wore on the back of his head had been crushed out of recognition. He had a stubble on his face, his hair was badly in need of trimming, and his callused hands hadn't been washed that day. Obviously he had just arrived in town and hadn't taken the time to improve his appearance before coming here.

"There she be!" Pierre roared. "There's my girl!" He lifted Carrie into the air as easily as though she were a small doll, then kissed her with a display of his customary exuberance.

"Put me down, sir," she told him. "And don't come near me again until your appearance is respectable!"

Pierre was remarkably gentle as he returned her to the floor. "How do you like that?" he demanded of the others in mock indignation. "I don't see her for three, four, five months, but right away she gives me a big lecture."

"Your whiskers are rough," Carrie told him, "and your hands are filthy."

His smile was uncertain until he assured himself that she was teasing him. "Pretty soon Pierre will be so damn fancy you won't see straight," he said fervently.

Maria and the inmates knew he meant it. He had been coming to the place for years, but after seeing Carrie for the first time he hadn't looked at anyone else. It was common knowledge that he was madly in love with her, and it was taken for granted that he would monopolize her time during his entire visit to the city.

Clients were not encouraged to stay overnight at the House on the Avenue, but Pierre Gautier was the exception. A groom was sent for his luggage, and Maria personally escorted him to the room that, nominally, he would occupy during his stay.

Carrie went off to her own suite to dress for the evening.

The better part of an hour later, Pierre presented himself for her inspection. She tried not to wince when she saw his scarlet breeches, gold waistcoat, and swallow-tailed coat of black-and-white-striped satin. His hair, plastered close to his head, was redolent of bear grease, and even his pearl-handled pistols were in bad taste. But he had given himself such a close shave that he had nicked his face in two places, and had scrubbed so hard in his bath that his face glowed.

"You look . . . very striking, Pierre," Carrie told him.

She was genuinely fond of him, and made no attempt to hide her feelings. He was a tender, considerate lover, a generous client, and a true friend eager to fight her battles for her. He was always anxious to please her, and in spite of the gaudy costumes he wore in a vain attempt to impress her, she recognized his worth. Of all the men she knew, only Pierre would come to her aid in an emergency.

The thought often occurred to Carrie that perhaps the principal reason she liked Pierre so much was that he reminded her of Lance Beaufort. Like Lance, he was loyal, completely devoted to her. And because he, too, was a hulking giant, there was a physical similarity.

Pierre insisted on taking her to the most expensive and fashionable inn in New Orleans for dinner. Carrie knew they created something of a spectacle. Her heavy makeup and flashy dress advertised her profession, and Pierre's appearance was bizarre. She saw several of her regular clients, the ladies with them presumably their wives, but she looked through them and knew they were relieved. But it didn't matter what anyone thought. Pierre was real and honest, and she preferred him to all the rest.

His table manners were abominable. He ate with his knife, cramming food into his mouth, and with no visible effect he polished off two large bottles of wine. Then, after scrubbing his mouth and hands with a napkin, he looked somberly across the candlelit table.

"Now we make important talk," he announced.

Carrie didn't know what he had in mind, and watched as he fumbled in an inner pocket.

He removed a small box and thrust it at her. "Pierre bring you present."

Inside the box were a pair of long diamond earrings worth a duke's ransom, and Carrie was touched. "I can't let you spend this much on me," she said, and meant it.

He glowered at her. "I earn plenty much money," he said, "and I wanted to get you a nice present. You keep it, or I'll break your damn neck."

She smiled at him, wanting to weep because of his sincerity, and knowing he would be pleased, donned the earrings at once.

"No lady is more beautiful," he said, catching her hand. "I want to marry you."

The startled Carrie disengaged herself. "You can't mean that," she told him. "You know how I earn my living."

"I don't care," he replied fiercely. "You marry me and other men will stay away."

Certainly that much was true. If she placed herself under his protection, no one else would dare come near her.

All at once he softened, and when he addressed her again, his voice was wistful. "You're the most lovely lady in the whole world," he said.

Carrie was moved. He truly wanted to marry her, and was willing to ignore her unsavory past. She knew no one else able to demonstrate that generous a spirit.

There were complications, however, that he didn't and couldn't understand. "Thank you for your proposal, Pierre," she said. "I treasure it. I can't accept just yet, and I don't want to reject you, either. I . . . I can't explain my reasons, but I'll need time to think before I give you an answer."

"Take all the time you want," he said, relieved that she hadn't turned him down.

They returned to her suite at the House on the Avenue, and there Pierre made love to her. Later, after he had fallen asleep, Carrie was still wide-awake. Slipping into a negligee, she went softly into her sitting room, and standing at an open window, made an attempt to sort out her thoughts.

In many ways his proposal was attractive. Paramount among them was that she would be able to abandon the life of a harlot for all time.

Pierre's wealth would give her the financial security she needed, the peace of mind she craved. If she didn't want to live in New Orleans, she knew, Pierre would be delighted to build a mansion for her in Natchez, Memphis, or some other city convenient for his business, where she wasn't known.

She didn't love him, and he knew it, but that was no drawback, either. It was enough for him that she thoroughly enjoyed his company, and he was confident that his own love someday would cause her to respond.

What she couldn't tell him because she didn't want to hurt him was that it was impossible for her to learn to love him. She had given her heart to Lance, and it was his as long as she lived. She had tried hard to conquer her feelings toward him, but had failed, and she knew further attempts were useless.

So, it seemed, it would be wrong to marry Pierre. Carrie had no fear of being able to take her marriage vows seriously. If she did marry Pierre, she would give him absolute, unqualified fidelity, which would be his due.

But she would be mentally unfaithful to him. It would be agony to be married to him while yearning for Lance.

The hope that someday, in some way she couldn't even imagine, she and Lance would be reunited was the ever-present dream that nourished and sustained her. Carrie wasn't yet able to give up that hope.

If she could have Lance, she wanted no one else, nothing else, not even the financial security that otherwise was so vital to her. In spite of Pierre's kindness and gentleness, she realized, she wouldn't be considering marriage to him if he were poor. On the other hand, she would go to the ends of the earth with Lance, even if he didn't have a single copper in his pocket. So it was obvious to her that her demand for security was only a substitute for the love that she and Lance were unable to share.

Looking at a star shining in the sky above the rooftops of New Orleans, Carrie stared at it for a long time. Why was she procrastinating, forcing Pierre to wait for an answer to his proposal? Simply because she was wishing a miracle would take place, that Lance would appear and take her in his arms.

"Dear Lord," she murmured, "bring my Lance back to me."

11

—••◄►••—

For all practical purposes the hunting and trapping season came to a close as the end of summer drew near. Scarcely able to handle all the pelts they had accumulated, Lance and his associates made their final preparations for the long journey that would enable them to sell directly to merchants, thereby enabling them to earn maximum profits.

They packed their furs in tight bales, then loaded them onto the backs of twenty sturdy pack mules and started eastward out of the mountains. By common consent Lance rode in the lead, with Ponca bringing up the rear, and Paul moving up and down the caravan making certain that no mule strayed.

The partners were pleased by their success, and Paul was looking forward to a visit to civilization, even though he was already planning an extension of his leave of absence from his medical practice. And Ponca was looking forward to his first trip to towns larger than the Indian communities he knew.

Lance, however, was indifferent to the joys of the cities they would see, and was secretly afraid his yearning for

Carrie and his desire to return to Oakhurst Manor would become unmanageable. He had left the mountains for the sole purpose of obtaining the best price possible for the furs that were the result of a year's hard work.

What he was really anticipating was the annual rendezvous of mountain men, which he had never before attended and which would take place later in the autumn at the headwaters of the Mississippi River. There his colleagues would gather for a week of eating, drinking, and comradeship. They would buy supplies and new weapons from the many salesmen who would throng the encampment, and with the bonds of brotherhood strengthened, the company would return separately to the Rockies, better able to withstand the rigors of the coming winter.

The rendezvous promised to be exciting and pleasant. The civilized towns that had to be visited first would be drab, dull, and commonplace.

Only an incident that occurred as the trio emerged from the mountains and began to head across the plateau that led to the flatlands of eastern Colorado marred the serenity of the journey.

Just to vary the monotony of the trip, Lance had changed places with Ponca and was bringing up the rear. Occasionally he and Paul exchanged a few words, but in the main Lance was silent. It was odd, he thought, but even now he was counting the weeks until he returned to the mountains.

Bantu was the first to know that something was amiss. The great stallion raised his head high, then snorted and pawed the ground.

Lance was alert, and imitating the howl of a coyote, softly signaled a warning to his comrades that danger was near.

An instant later a party of Apache burst out of the evergreen forest that lay ahead. These warriors were members of the tribe that Lance had humiliated when he and Ponca had first gone to the Rockies. Inhibited by the awesome reputation that the great Lion had acquired, the Apache had waited for what they regarded as the appropriate time to obtain revenge.

This, they had decided, was the best of all possible times. The Lion and his associates were spread out over a

long line of march, and the presence of their pack mules
laden with valuable furs destroyed their mobility.

What the Indians had failed to take into account in
their calculations, however, was the extraordinary degree
of teamwork that had become second nature to the trio.

Ponca began to fire immediately at the approaching
warriors, reloading with the agility and speed he'd acquired under Lance's tutelage. He was joined within moments by Paul, whose rifle began to speak, too.

Lance held his place at the rear of the column, realizing
that if he left his anchor spot, the braves, out of sheer
malice, would try to scatter the mules and deprive their
owners of the valuable furs. He stood in his saddle, and
his long rifle took the first toll, sending the lead warrior
sprawling.

The Apache were no less courageous than they had ever
been, but they were no match for marksmen whose
renown was deserved. Three more braves fell, and the rest
lost their appetite for vengeance and vanished.

Lance and Paul had become true mountain men, and
joined Ponca in scalping the four dead Apache, with
Lance keeping only the scalp of the senior brave.

The practice of taking scalps was second nature to
Ponca. His companions, who were products of a different
civilization, had no liking for the custom, but they had
good reason for engaging in it. After long discussions
around their campfire they had decided that a show of
scalps in their belts would act as a warning deterrent to
other mountain tribes that might otherwise have hostile intentions. So they conquered their own repugnance and
acted accordingly. Any belligerent warriors who failed to
recognize the Lion and his comrades nevertheless would
think twice before attacking a group whose prowess was
evident at a glance.

They resumed the journey, and Lance fingered his necklace of bear teeth. The brief flurry had been an omen, and
he couldn't decide whether it was a good sign or a bad
one. He was becoming as superstitious as all the others
who lived in the Rockies, he thought, but he didn't care.
The gates of Oakhurst Manor were closed to him, perhaps
for all time, so the mountains had become his only home.

Maintaining a steady pace, the three travelers reached

the plains of the Nebraska country without further incident. At last they came to the banks of the great Missouri River, resting there for several days until they were able to secure the services of a bargeman. They sold their mules to a company of homesteaders who intended to settle in Nebraska, then continued their journey on the barge.

When they came to Independence, Lance was tempted to call a halt so he could pay a visit to Lester and Dolores Howard. But he refrained because he didn't want to embarrass them. He was back in the United States now, and there was a price on his head. It was true that it would be difficult to recognize him. He wore a full beard, his hair was shaggy, and, heavily tanned, he carried a long scar on his face as a result of his encounter with the grizzly. He doubted that his own mother and father, Kai and Jeremy, would know him now. But he refused to jeopardize the safety and reputations of good friends who had already gone out of their way to help him.

The voyage by barge across the heart of the new state of Missouri was pleasant. They came to the Mississippi River just above St. Louis, and there the journey came to a temporary halt. They paid the bargeman and placed the furs in a warehouse until they could decide what to do next.

St. Louis was a brawling frontier town, a natural hub for men from north and south, east and west. Indians from a score of tribes came here to trade, and mingled with black freemen and slaves, as well as whites who spoke English or French or Spanish. There were settlers who knew no tongue but their native German, and other immigrants, heading toward the new settlements in the Minnesota country, who were at home only in their native Swedish.

The town, with a population of about three thousand, seemed to be a collection of warehouses, rooming houses, and saloons. Every man carried weapons at all times, and ladies did not go out after dark so they would not be mistaken for bordello inmates.

Lance and his companions found simple lodgings, then went out for something to eat. As they strolled down the dirt road that ran parallel to the broad Mississippi, passersby took care to give them a wide berth. The bronzed, bearded giant who was the leader of the group was too husky for comfort, and his lion-skin cloak, necklace of bear's teeth, and scalps at his belt spoke for themselves. No one wanted to tangle with such a group.

They had inquired where they would find fur traders and bargemen, halting first at a saloon frequented by the former. There Lance and Paul made separate discreet inquiries about fur prices, then compared notes.

"We won't do too badly here," Paul said, "but I'm disappointed. I thought we'd get much higher prices."

"So we will, farther down the river," Lance replied. "One fellow told me prices go up and up the closer you travel to New Orleans. He said we'd be paid double there."

"Maybe go to New Orleans," Ponca said.

"That depends on how much we'd have to pay to get there," Lance replied cautiously.

They went on to a tavern that was one of the bargemen's favorites, and there they were served enormous platters of steak, potatoes fried with onions, and slabs of freshly baked pie. Obviously the place catered to men accustomed to hard work in the outdoors.

Directly facing Lance and seated at the next table was a tall man in his late thirties. He had a booming voice and spoke in a French accent that called attention to him. The reason Lance noticed him, however, was his great size. The man was the only person he had ever seen whose height and breadth of shoulders were a match for his own.

The man became aware of him, too, and grinned at him, obviously feeling the same way.

Lance returned the grin, then devoted his attention to his blueberry pie.

The pleasant hum of conversation was broken by a man sitting near the door. "Heads up!" he called. "River toughs!"

A silence fell as a group of a dozen roughly clad men, all armed with clubs and barrel staves, filed into the tavern. Their intentions could not be determined, but the air of menace they brought with them was clearly felt.

The proprietor hurried toward them. "I'm afraid I have

no empty tables right now, gentlemen," he said. "You'll have to wait a few minutes."

"We don't like waitin'," the man at the head of the phalanx said. "Get rid of some of them scum."

"Please, gentlemen, we want no trouble here."

The leader laughed, then gestured to several of his companions.

They caught hold of a gray-haired man who was eating his dinner, and literally heaved him out of the place.

"Who's next?" the leader asked.

The giant with the French accent lumbered to his feet and sauntered toward the man. "You go now," he said.

"Who says?" the leader demanded.

His companions crowded forward.

On sudden impulse Lance joined the French-speaking giant and stood shoulder to shoulder with him. Unfairness always irked him, and he couldn't tolerate bullies. "You heard him," he said. "He told you to get out, and so do I."

The toughs eyed them in silence. Two men of their size couldn't be dealt with lightly.

Paul Beaufort and Ponca inched their way forward, too, and waited tensely.

"You know me," the man with the accent declared. "I'm Pierre Bateaux Gautier, and I say get out!"

"Nobody threatens us," the leader said. "You big ones have that much farther to fall." He raised his club, intending to strike Gautier with it.

Lance wrenched it from him and sent him sprawling with a single sharp punch.

That started the riot. All at once the entire band of toughs swarmed over him and the French-speaking giant.

Gautier laughed. "Now we'll fix them!" he roared, and catching two of the ruffians by their necks, smashed their heads together.

Lance's huge fist lashed out and crashed into the face of another river tough. He discovered he was enjoying himself immensely, and laughed.

"We're a good team," Gautier told him.

Paul and Ponca joined in the fray, too, but the damage they could inflict was limited because Lance and Gautier were the natural targets of the rivermen.

The pair gave infinitely better than they received. Lance

wrested a chair from the hands of a tough who intended to bring it down over his head, and using it as a shield, shoved it full into the man's face.

Gautier caught the unfortunate man as he went down and threw him into the midst of his companions.

"Looks like we have them on the run," Lance said as he moved forward.

"They started this, we'll finish," Gautier said, and plunged into the group with him.

Giant fists plowed into the toughs, and at close quarters their clubs proved useless. As one started to go down, Lance caught him by the heel, then flung him with such force that he sailed out of the door and landed in the dirt outside.

Gautier promptly matched the feat by picking up another, twirling him around, and sending him flying with a shove.

Within moments the brief encounter was at an end. Lance and Gautier solemnly shook hands.

The proprietor, still fearful, approached them. "Thank you for your help, gentlemen," he said. "Those river bastards enjoy creating a ruckus, but they won't come back here for a long spell. They don't seem to have done too much damage."

Gautier dusted his hands. "We broke some chairs and glasses," he said. "I'll buy you new ones."

The proprietor refused to accept his offer, and insisted on handing the victors a bottle of liquor as a gesture of his gratitude.

Lance presented his companions and introduced himself to the man at whose side he had fought with such stunning effect.

"I'm Pierre Gautier," his fellow giant said. "You call me Bateaux. All my friends call me that because for a very long time, when I was young, I was the best damn riverman in Canada."

They sat together over a celebratory drink, and Lance explained they had come from the mountains to sell the many bales of furs they had acquired in a year of hunting and trapping.

Gautier was delighted. To their surprise, he indicated that he owned the largest fleet of barges on the Mississippi

River. "In two days I sail to New Orleans," he said, "so I'll take you and your furs for no charge."

"That isn't right," Lance replied. "I appreciate your offer, but we've got to pay you."

The French Canadian pounded a huge fist on the bare table. "You're my friend! The friend of Bateaux pay nothing!"

It would have been ungracious to refuse, so Lance accepted the generous offer.

Gautier was not yet finished. New Orleans was the only place to sell the furs, he said, because the prices paid there would be so much higher than those offered in smaller river towns. Also, he declared, he knew every merchant of consequence in New Orleans, so he would arrange meetings with one or more of them in order to make certain that Lance and his associates obtained the best price for their merchandise. It was apparent that he could not do too much for people he liked.

Before they parted company, they agreed to meet the following afternoon, at which time they would take the furs on board a barge, where they would spend the night prior to a dawn departure. They shook hands warmly and went their separate ways.

The next morning at breakfast Paul had an announcement to make. "Lance," he said, "Ponca and I have decided we're not going down to New Orleans with you."

The Kiowa brave nodded gravely.

"Bateaux Gautier will help you get a good price for the furs, so you won't need us there. We've decided we'll head straight up the Mississippi to the Minnesota country instead, and we'll be waiting for you when you show up for the rendezvous."

"How come you don't want to come with me tomorrow?" Lance demanded.

Paul grinned. "That fight last night opened our eyes a mite. New Orleans is deep South, and Louisiana is a slave state. The three of us can hold our own in a battle, no doubt about that, but I'd rather avoid a brawl when I can. If I missed city life I'd go back to Boston, but I don't. And it strikes me that my skin may be the wrong color for a trip to New Orleans. We have plenty of money already, and you can bring our shares of what you get for the furs up to us at the rendezvous."

"No like white man's towns and white man's fights," Ponca added. "No like houses or eating places, either. Too hot, too crowded. We stay in outside air where we breathe easier."

Lance couldn't blame his colleagues for feeling as they did, and agreed with their plan. He was better qualified than either of his associates to handle the sale of the furs, and for that reason he would go to New Orleans, but he had no desire to linger there himself. For one thing, he was still a fugitive from justice, and although he anticipated no problems with the authorities, he had no desire to tempt fate. Even more important, he was afraid New Orleans might remind him of Charleston—and the life he had been forced to abandon. Just seeing young ladies in modish attire would make him miss Carrie all the more. For the moment he had achieved an emotional balance and could function without thinking of her incessantly, night and day. Eventually his defenses would break down again, as he well knew, but it was senseless to speed that process. Therefore he wanted to leave well enough alone.

The following afternoon Bateaux Gautier was on hand when the furs were loaded onto the largest of his barges, and he was impressed by the quality of the merchandise. "I bring many pelts to New Orleans," he said, "and these the best I see in long time. You take word of Bateaux, you going to be plenty damn rich!"

When he learned that Paul and Ponca were intending to travel up the Mississippi he insisted on providing accommodations for them in a convoy of his barges sailing to the headwaters of the great river, and they left before sundown that same day. They would await Lance at the rendezvous.

Much to Lance's astonishment, the quarters assigned to him in the superstructure built amidships on the barge were luxurious. He had a feather bed, an easy chair, and an oil lamp, with a rug on the floor, comforts he had almost forgotten during his long sojourn in the wilderness of the Rocky Mountains.

The bed was so soft, in fact, that he had difficulty in sleeping that night.

He was awake well before dawn, and joined Gautier in the even more handsomely appointed master cabin for breakfast. They ate grilled fish just taken from the river, large steaks with potatoes, a loaf of crusty bread, and, between them, a dozen eggs.

"You and me are big fellows," Gautier said with a booming laugh. "We eat big, do everything big. We make love big, too. You'll see when we get to New Orleans. Bateaux will take you where we find many pretty girls. You take your pick. Any girl except one. My girl."

Lance needed a woman and knew it, but his longing for Carrie was so intense he put the matter out of his mind. He would face the question when they reached the end of their voyage.

The journey down the Mississippi was a never-ending demonstration of the rapid growth of the United States. Prior to the Louisiana Purchase in 1803 the land on both sides of the river had been largely a wilderness. Now towns were springing up everywhere, and fields were cultivated as far as one could see. Just looking at the crops of corn and vegetables, tobacco and cotton, many ready for harvesting, made Lance homesick for Oakhurst Manor. He tried not to dwell on the thought, however, because he had no way of knowing whether he would ever be welcome there again.

Guided by expert boatmen, the great barge drifted silently down the broad river, and in the course of any given day they saw dozens of other barges and boats. The vast produce of the American West was being carried to New Orleans, and the Mississippi was the life-giving stream of an entire area. Lance could envision the day when the nation from which he was an exile would become a great power. Thanks to the mountain men, its territory was already expanding toward the Rockies, and it wasn't too much to believe that ultimately its domain might extend all the way to the Pacific. One day he would fight for his rights and make a concerted effort to clear his name.

He anticipated that the profits he would earn from the furs would enable him to hire an attorney who would begin that fight for him before he went up to the rendezvous and then returned to the mountains. It would be too dan-

gerous for him to remain in the United States while that
long legal battle took place, and he knew he would lose his
sanity if he had nothing to occupy his time. It would be
far better to return to the mountains with his colleagues.

Until he was cleared, he knew, he couldn't even write to
Mama and Uncle Scott, or Papa and Lisa. It would be unfair to them to ask them to carry the burden of knowledge
of his whereabouts. Only when he could return home with
his head held high would he be able to let them know he
was coming.

Each day at sundown the barge was anchored, and a
member of the crew went ashore to buy fresh produce.
Sometimes, when they saw deep woods, Gautier ordered a
halt so some of his sailors could go hunting. They had
poor luck, however, so one day he and Lance went ashore
for their own entertainment. Lance promptly found the
tracks of a wild boar, which he trailed and shot, and that
night they feasted.

The two men thoroughly enjoyed each other's company,
and the bonds of their friendship became strengthened.
They were the same type, direct and blunt, and not only
were there personality similarities, but their great size gave
them additional ties. Each seemed to understand the other.

At last they came to New Orleans, and Gautier proved
his worth anew in the bustling waterfront markets. He
directed his friend from the Rockies to a trader who
specialized in the buying and selling of furs, saying that
the man was honest.

Lance, who had no penchant for haggling, was offered a
price far higher than he had anticipated, the staggering
sum of nine thousand dollars. His share alone would enable him to hire the best attorney in the city to represent
him, and he would still be able to keep the better part. In
all he had now earned more than five thousand dollars as
a hunter and trapper, and had achieved a degree of financial independence denied to most men.

Nevertheless, he wanted nothing for himself. His buckskins kept him warm and dry, and he needed no new
weapons. Perhaps during his sojourn in the city he would
buy a gold locket and chain for Carrie and send it to her
anonymously. She would guess the source, he felt certain,

and at least would know he was well, thriving, and thinking of her.

The funds were deposited for him in a local bank, and when the negotiations were completed, he and Gautier brought their horses ashore.

"Now," the French Canadian said, "we'll go to the house of girls."

"I haven't even arranged for lodgings," Lance told him.

"We'll stay there," Gautier said, waving aside his protest.

Lance succumbed. He couldn't deny his purely physical need for a woman, and with his business transaction completed, there was no reason for him to hold back. The idea of staying at a bordello for a night or two didn't appeal to him, but he wouldn't argue with Bateaux. They would go to the house, and later in the day he would find other accommodations for himself.

Bantu had forgotten the intricacies of making his way through city traffic, and was skittish, but his master soon calmed him, and the stallion behaved like a gentleman, stepping smartly and picking his way through crowds of other horsemen and carriages.

As they slowed their pace, Gautier pointed. "We go there," he said. "You remember. Take any girl you want except my girl. She belong to Bateaux."

"Really?" The idea of an inmate of such a place "belonging" to any man amused Lance.

"You bet she my girl," the French Canadian assured him solemnly. "She plenty damn stubborn when I ask her to marry me, but someday she going to do it. You'll see."

It occurred to Lance that he wasn't suitably attired for such an elegant establishment, but it was too late to back off now. His purse was full of money, a great deal of it in gold coins, so he assumed he wouldn't be asked to leave.

A groom took their horses to a stable at the rear, and a majordomo led them to a handsomely appointed antechamber, where Lance again thought his soiled buckskins were inappropriate.

There Maria joined them, and Gautier greeted her with a hug. "This my friend. He come to see woman. Now . . . where my girl?"

"She's in the main parlor," Maria told him, smiling broadly.

Gautier immediately bolted out of the room.

Maria laughed and led Lance down a corridor.

They came to a much larger room, where several young women had been chatting. But all conversation had ceased because Gautier had lifted one of them into the air and was kissing her enthusiastically.

Lance caught only a glimpse of her, and saw that she had long blond hair and was wearing a revealing gown of scarlet satin.

Gautier set her on her feet again and gestured broadly. "This is my girl," he boomed. "This is my friend."

Lance Beaufort and Carolyn Emerson were stunned when they looked into each other's eyes. He was a bearded frontiersman, while she wore the heavy makeup and alluring dress of a courtesan, but they knew each other instantly.

For a long paralyzed moment neither could believe that they had actually come face to face. That they should meet at this place and under these circumstances shocked them to the marrow.

Lance was the first to react. Heartsick and horrified, the dream that had sustained him for so long suddenly twisted into a nightmare, he turned and raced out of the room, then dashed out of the house.

Gautier's roar of laughter shook the crystals in the ornate parlor chandelier. "My friend is shy," he said.

Suddenly he scooped Carrie into his arms and mounted the stairs to her suite.

She was still numb, but her mind was beginning to function again. She found it incredible that Lance should have come to the House on the Avenue and had found her here. How handsome and healthy he looked, with his clear eyes and glowing, tanned skin. His frame had filled out, too, and he more than fulfilled the image that had been locked within her for so long.

That he had discovered her in this place was worse than everything else that had happened to her since her troubles had started. Granted that she was the undisputed star in an establishment that had no equal anywhere in the United States. She was still a harlot.

How could she ever explain to him the bizarre sequence of events that had placed her in this position? How could she ever persuade him that she still loved him, that no one else had ever mattered to her, that it was their love and nothing else that had made her existence bearable?

Well, she would have no opportunity to explain anything. Lance had fled, and she would never see him again. She couldn't blame him for despising her.

Gautier, still chuckling, deposited her on her sitting-room floor.

Carrie regained her wits sufficiently to start asking questions about his friend.

The French Canadian thought she was amused, too, and replied willingly.

She drew him out with consummate skill, milking information from him.

Only once did he become suspicious. "Maybe you like my friend too much?" he demanded.

Carrie shrugged. "How could I, Pierre? I just saw him for an instant."

He was mollified, and by the time he finished his recital, he had told her everything he knew about the mountain man who had come to his help in a St. Louis waterfront tavern.

By now Carrie had learned enough to know that Lance was prospering in a way of life far different from that which he had led when he had lived at Oakhurst Manor and had been in charge of his father's shipping interests. He had not been caught and hanged for a vicious deed he had not committed. He was safe, and she had to content herself with what she had gleaned.

Even though her own life now had become unbearable.

"Pierre," she said, "take me away from here. Today. Right now. I don't care where we go, provided we leave immediately."

Gautier stared at her. "Will you marry me now?"

Her nerves were so ragged that her temper almost exploded. But she was fighting for her sanity, for her existence itself, and managed to keep a lid on her rage. "Don't rush me! No, I'm not ready to marry you. But I'm offering to go with you—anywhere—on condition that we go right now. And if that isn't good enough for you, I'll leave by myself!"

Gautier promptly backtracked. "I'll take you, Carrie," he said. "We'll go right away."

For hours Lance rode aimlessly, letting Bantu wander where he pleased. Not until sundown did he recover sufficiently to head back to the center of New Orleans, and there he engaged a room for himself and a stable for his mount at an inexpensive rooming house.

Still too upset to eat more than a token meal, he could not sleep and paced his room all night. Gradually the world began to right itself somewhat, and he was able to organize his thoughts.

It was a fact that Carrie, more beautiful than ever in spite of her gaudy makeup and flashy clothes, was a bordello inmate, available to any man who paid her price. Waves of jealousy still consumed him, but he forced himself to subdue them.

He had to concentrate on something else. Of paramount importance were the reasons that had led her into such a life. He knew nothing of these circumstances, so he had no right to condemn her. He himself had done many strange, unorthodox things since they had parted, so he had to assume that events beyond her control had forced her into an existence that seemed alien to her nature.

Above all, she had every right to believe he was dead. It was cruelly unfair to blame her for infidelity when she had heard nothing about him or from him. He had no right to sit in judgment on her.

Just the one brief glimpse of her had confirmed what he already knew: he still loved her with his whole heart and soul.

Soon after sunrise Lance wandered out-of-doors. His sense of direction unerring, he soon found himself standing across the street from the House on the Avenue. The place was tightly shuttered, and not even the groom at the door was on duty. Of course. It was far too early in the day.

At least he knew now what had to be done.

He walked to the waterfront, stopping for a hearty breakfast at a tavern that catered to dock workers and other laboring men. Then he engaged a cabin for himself and space for his horse on a barge that was leaving late in the day for the long voyage up the Mississippi to its headwaters. The sooner he rejoined Paul and Ponca for the forthcoming rendezvous, the better it would be for his sanity.

Then he returned to his lodgings and bathed, scrubbing himself with a stiff-bristled brush until his skin tingled. As soon as he dressed, he paid his bill, and for the next few hours he and Bantu killed time. He was so engrossed in thought that he didn't even realize people stared at him on the streets. He was tempted to buy some city attire for himself, but refrained. He had earned his buckskins, his lion cape, and his bear-tooth necklace; he was not ashamed of them.

Early in the afternoon Lance returned to the House on the Avenue. He intended to have a few words with Carrie. He wanted to apologize to her for bolting the previous day and above all to explain that she was under no obligation to him, that she was entitled to live as she pleased. Loving her still, he owed her that much.

A smiling Maria joined him in the anteroom. "I'm glad to see you changed your mind and decided to pay us a visit after all, sir," she said.

He was in no mood for small talk. "I want to see Carrie," he told her curtly.

"I'm afraid she isn't here right now." Maria seethed inwardly, furious that the establishment's biggest moneymaker had seen fit to depart so abruptly.

"When will she be coming back?"

The woman hesitated, unwilling to admit that she very much doubted they would ever see Carrie there again. Hoping to avoid trouble with this grim giant, she wanted to escape all responsibility in the matter. "I don't really know, but it may be that her best friend here can give you some information."

Lance had no choice, as he saw it, so he allowed her to conduct him to the main parlor, where she presented him to Melanie.

The redhead, who remembered him from his abortive visit of the previous day, greeted him with a dazzling smile. Unlike the middle-aged merchants and bankers who came to the place, here was a real man.

"I'd like to have a talk with you in private," Lance said.

"Of course." He really was shy, the girl thought as she led him up the stairs to her room, her walk seductive.

He quickly demonstrated that talk was actually what was on his mind. "I want to be fair," he said, "so I'll pay you for your time, ma'am."

The startled Melanie named her fee.

He paid her more than the sum she asked.

When he opened his purse, she saw that it was crammed with gold coins, and her interest in him was doubled. He might look like a crude frontiersman, but he was obviously rich.

"I want to ask you about Carrie," he said, "since I'm told you're her friend. Do you know where she's gone?"

"I have no idea," Melanie said. "She left with Pierre no more than a half-hour after you raced away yesterday."

"When will she return?"

"I don't think she's coming back. She took only a couple of clothing boxes with her, and she gave me all the rest of her things. She said to keep what I like and distribute the rest in any way I want. This was one of her dresses. Do you like it?"

Lance felt uneasy when the redhead moved closer to him. Her gown was flimsy, and she had a way of standing, a way of turning that made him very much aware of her breasts, buttocks, and legs.

"How do I look?" Melanie insisted.

"Very attractive." So Carrie was gone, perhaps because he had been such a boor. It was impossible to guess where she might have gone with Bateaux Gautier, and it would be difficult to trace her. Besides, she had not departed alone. He could not allow himself to forget that she had gone with a man who had repeatedly called her "my girl."

"Won't I do as a substitute for Carrie? You may as well get your money's worth." Giving him no chance to reply, Melanie sat on his lap, slid her arms around his neck and kissed him.

Lance's need for a woman was so great he couldn't help responding, and his deep frustration over Carrie's disappearance gave him added drive. Without quite realizing what he was doing, he began to caress the supple body that was being offered to him.

It became an easy matter for Melanie to lead him to the bed.

Soon Lance's lovemaking became violent, his demands insatiable.

Although Melanie had become an expert at the art of simulation, no client had really aroused her. But this giant was different, and soon her desire for erotic gratification was as great as his.

In their mounting mutual frenzy they fed each other's yearnings, and ultimately they found release together, with Melanie's sustained moan ringing in Lance's ears.

After a time the girl looked at him, her eyes shining. She had dreamed of just such a man before she had left her family's farm in Virginia, and now she had found him. The one mate who had ever given her the satisfaction she craved, he was remarkably gentle with her, his great strength carefully leashed. Obviously he was a frontier dweller, too, rather than a mundane professional or businessman, and this knowledge fulfilled her desire for the romantic. And as she had discovered when she had seen the contents of his purse, he had ample supplies of money.

Lance knew only that he was enjoying a moment of surfeit, even though Carrie had vanished.

Melanie began to ask him about himself.

He told her about his life in the Rocky Mountains with his partners, and in response to her subtle prodding he revealed that he had sold their furs for a large sum of money.

She made a shrewd guess. "You knew Carrie before she ever came here."

"Yes." He had no intention of discussing his past and Carrie's, any more than he would talk about his sudden decision, made just now, not to seek the help of an attorney in order to clear his name in South Carolina. With Carrie gone, it would be far simpler to put his entire past behind him. He would go with Paul and Ponca to the mountains, and perhaps he would spend the rest of his days there.

Almost inadvertently he glanced at the small clock over the mantel.

"Are you in a hurry?" Melanie asked, teasing him.

"Not really, but I'm leaving New Orleans later this afternoon." He explained further than he had booked passage on a barge that would take him to the Mississippi headwaters for the rendezvous.

The girl listened with interest when he told her about his surprise at finding large, well-appointed private cabins on river barges. Then she asked, "What's this rendezvous?"

"The mountain men meet for a jamboree. It's the only holiday we know, and we make good use of the time by buying supplies and weapons and traps and whatever else we need for the year ahead."

"It sounds glamorous," she said.

"Believe me, it isn't. Most mountain men are a rough, mean lot. They gamble heavily at the rendezvous, they drink too much, and the women they meet there are strumpets." He had the grace to flush. "I beg your pardon. They aren't like you. I mean, they aren't ladies."

"You think of Carrie as a lady, too, no doubt."

"Yes." Again he was curt.

"You're a mountain man, but I wouldn't call you mean or rough."

"Only when it's necessary. I had certain advantages of family background and education before I went out to the Rockies." He was saying too much, and fell silent.

Melanie realized her interrogation was making him uncomfortable, and knew how to distract him. "Love me again!" she commanded, her nude body pressing close to his.

Lance obeyed cheerfully.

Again their relations were harmonious, and afterward Melanie was thoughtful as they dressed.

He offered her additional compensation.

She refused, her indignation tempered by humor.

On sudden impulse he offered her the necklace of bear teeth he had been saving for Carrie. "They aren't very pretty and they don't look like much," he said, "but to me they're a symbol, because I fought that grizzly to a standoff. You might want to put this necklace away someplace and keep it as a souvenir."

"Souvenir!" Melanie exclaimed. "I'll wear it!" She slipped it over her head, then examined her reflection in the mirror. "I doubt if anyone else in the world has a necklace like this!"

"Maybe not." All Lance knew was that the gift was a success and she hadn't laughed at him. At least he would no longer be wearing it himself as a reminder of Carrie.

He watched Melanie as she sat before her dressing table repairing her makeup, and had to admit she was exceptionally attractive. She had eased his pain for a short time, and was grateful to her.

She accompanied him to the front door when he took his leave. "Just in case Carrie should come back here, which I doubt, I'll tell her you were asking for her. You never did mention your name."

"Lance Beaufort."

"I'll remember," she said, and kissed him lightly.

A groom fetched Bantu for him, and he was on his way again, the redhead receding from his mind.

He still had time to visit an attorney, but clung to the decision he had made. Perhaps he would write to Mama and Uncle Scott, Papa and Lisa, from the rendezvous, telling them he was alive and flourishing. On the other hand, he didn't want to hurt them, so perhaps he would wait for another year. He had no reason now to go back to South Carolina and engage in a long, dreary battle to clear his name. With Carrie gone from his life for all time, the mountains had truly become his home.

He paid a visit to a dry-goods store, where he bought gifts of cloth for Paul and Ponca. Then he made his way to the waterfront and boarded the barge that would be his home for several weeks.

The first order of business was making Bantu comfortable in the stable located just forward of the stern, and by the time he was done, the captain of the ungainly craft was ready to cast off. A cargo that included kegs of nails, tools, iron skillets, and bolts of cloth for settlers to the north had already been made secure beneath tarpaulins.

Instead of taking his saddlebags to his quarters, Lance stayed on the deck watching the barge slowly inch her way out into the broad Mississippi and start her slow voyage upstream. He stayed on deck for a long time, staring back at the lights of the South's largest city. In all probability Carrie was still there, living at an inn with Bateaux Gautier, and although the mere thought pained him, he realized he had to let her go.

Her life had changed as drastically as his had, and for reasons he couldn't fathom. He couldn't imagine what had led her into a career at a bordello, but that didn't matter, either. All that was important was that Gautier had a claim of some kind on her affections and wanted to marry her.

Certainly, after the wrench of her parting from Lance and their long separation, she had no cause to consider herself still betrothed to him. She was a woman now, not an innocent girl, and it was her right to live her life as she saw fit.

Lance tried to console himself with the thought that Gautier was a man of solid character, and he hoped Carrie would find happiness with him, even though he himself would never forget her.

New Orleans faded from sight, and when night came, the crew dropped anchor near the bank of the river. The captain and his sailors went ashore in a dinghy, intending to make a fire and cook a meal on dry land. But Lance still wasn't hungry, and instead of accompanying them, stayed behind with the skeleton crew.

He helped himself to some cold meat and bread, which he took with him, and went to his cabin for the first time. His saddlebags were no longer outside the door, so it was evident that someone had taken them in for him. He opened the door, then halted and gaped in astonishment.

Stretched out on the bed, attired in a filmy negligee, was Melanie.

Her smile was radiant.

Lance hastily kicked the door closed behind him, and as he locked it he saw his saddlebags resting beside two larger leather clothing boxes.

"I'm going to the rendezvous with you," Melanie announced.

"Like hell you are." Lance finally found his voice.

"It's taken me a long time to find you," she said complacently, "and I have no intention of losing you."

He began to sputter.

"You enjoyed yourself with me this afternoon, didn't you?" she demanded.

"Yes, but—"

"Well, that was just the beginning of what will be a steady diet. I promise you I won't be in the way when you're busy, I'll be loyal to you, and I'll never embarrass you." She rose from the bed, took the meat and bread from him, and after depositing them on a table, kissed him.

Lance was bewildered, but refused to give in. "See here, you've got to go ashore and head back to New Orleans."

"Oh, that's impossible," Melanie said cheerfully. "This is pirate country, and there are cutthroats everywhere. I wouldn't be safe, even with an escort, and I refuse to take the risk."

"But . . . but the rendezvous is no place for somebody as delicate as you!"

"I'm sure you'll protect me." She jangled the necklace of bear's teeth that she was wearing. "I'll have nothing to fear as long as I'm with you."

Again he tried to protest.

Melanie cut him short, and now there was an earnest note in her voice, her eyes serious. "I saw your expression yesterday when you suddenly recognized Carrie. You were in love with her, weren't you?"

Lance couldn't deny the obvious, and nodded.

"Well, Carrie's loss is my gain," Melanie said firmly. "I've been waiting all my life for you, and from now on I'm going to be your woman!"

12

Life in a wheelchair was confining, the Viennese physicians could offer no concrete assurances that the bullet from the French dueling pistol was working itself out, and Jeremy Beaufort was crotchety and restless. Ordinarily he had been even-tempered, but he hated his invalid's lot, which added to his sense of helplessness. And when he received a letter from Jerry assuring him that all was well at Oakhurst Manor and in the shipping business, his temper finally reached the boiling point.

"I no longer know what to believe," he said to Lisa as he brandished his son's letter. "Scott Emerson writes that funds at the shipping company are short. This letter from Jerry swears that the books balance to the penny. One of them must be mistaken!"

Lisa tried in vain to soothe him.

"There's only one certain way to find out. I've got to go home and look into this entire situation myself!"

"You can't, and you know it." Lisa spoke quietly.

"I must."

"Will you run the risk of being a cripple for the rest of your life?" she demanded.

Jeremy grimaced. "For all we know, and for all the doctors can tell us, I may be spending the rest of my life in a wheelchair in any event. They admit they have no way of knowing—or even guessing—whether the bullet is working its way out of my hipbone. It may stay there until I die, no matter how cautious I am, no matter if I do everything the doctors have prescribed."

"At the very least, there's always the chance the bullet will be dislodged if you obey the doctors' orders. If you don't, you know positively that you'll never be able to walk properly again."

"Then what am I going to do?" Jeremy asked miserably. "My business affairs at home are in a mess, and I can't even find out what's actually happening. There's no sign of Lance, who seems to have vanished from the face of the earth—"

"Do you think you could find him if you went home?"

"I could try! I might be able to locate Carrie, too!"

"How?" Lisa, as always, was practical.

"I don't really know, and I won't until I get there. Scott Emerson is a very able, conscientious man, but he's a lawyer, so he's conservative and cautious. Some of the methods I've used in the past have been unorthodox, as you well know, and they bring results. Sometimes."

"One result will be to guarantee that you'll remain confined to your wheelchair," Lisa said flatly.

"But something must be done."

"One thought has occurred to me," she said. "I could go home alone as your emissary—"

"No!"

Lisa ignored the interruption. "I'll grant you that I have no idea how to search for Lance and Carrie, and that I'd be as helpless as Scott and Kai have been. But I would be able to check into the affairs of the shipping company for you and make sure there are no problems at Oakhurst Manor. We'd be separated for about six to eight months, no more than that, and—"

"I won't hear of it!" Jeremy pounded a wheelchair arm. "I swore to you years ago, when I rescued you in the Caribbean and we were married, that I'd never be separated from you again. Whenever we've been apart, problems have developed, and I'm not going to take the chance again. That's final."

She was secretly relieved, but had felt compelled to make the offer.

"The shipping company could go bankrupt and Oakhurst Manor could fall apart before I'd allow anything unpleasant and dangerous to happen to you," Jeremy told her. "You mean more to me than anything and everything else."

Lisa went to him and put her arms around him.

For a long moment they clung to each other in silence.

Tears came to her eyes, and she averted her face so he wouldn't see them. Their secure world was disintegrating, and circumstances seemed to be making it impossible for them to fight against the tide. But they still had each other, so they could face Jeremy's continuing ailment, the collapse of his business interests, and even the inexplicable loss of his younger son. Their love would enable them to withstand any tragedy.

The barge moved up the Mississippi River at a leisurely pace, sailing by day and casting anchor near the shore each night. Lance paid for Melanie's passage because he felt he had no choice, and the captain and his crew soon adjusted to the presence of the unexpected passenger.

Lance's relations with the girl who had followed him on board became increasingly complex. They made love daily, sometimes morning and night, and their give-and-take was passionate, all-consuming. It was obvious that Melanie relished the experience, her demands almost insatiable, and Lance discovered that she fulfilled a deep need within him. He was able to accept her without reservation as his mistress, even though he soon realized that their affair obligated him to protect and look after her.

In spite of her background at the House on the Avenue, she was still very young, displaying attitudes that were romantic and sentimental. She appeared to be in love with him, but in his newfound cynicism that had come into being when he had stood face to face with Carrie, he found it difficult to determine whether Melanie's emotional state was genuine or whether she was playacting.

Not that it mattered. He was forced to accept full responsibility for her.

Certainly he was not in love with her, even remotely. He thoroughly enjoyed their sex relations, and he found that, little by little, he came to like her company. She might be naive and ingenuous, almost childlike in many ways, but her presence helped to fill the ever-present void that Carrie's abandonment of him had caused. He knew he still loved Carrie, that he could not put her out of his mind and heart, but by sleeping with Melanie every night and spending his days on deck with her, he necessarily could not think as much about Carrie or dwell on his loss.

It soon became evident that Melanie's wardrobe was too flamboyant for a voyage up the Mississippi in a company of men, and the very nature of the coming rendezvous of mountain men made it mandatory that her appearance there be somewhat more subdued. Her red hair, her figure, and her naturally ebullient nature could create enough problems, and there was no need to emphasize them.

Additional cargo was loaded onto the barge at Natchez and Memphis, necessitating prolonged stops at both towns, so Lance went ashore with Melanie and went about the business of buying new clothes for her. She plunged into the task with the zest she displayed for everything she liked, but he retained a veto power, rejecting attire that might cause troubles.

Thereafter Melanie dressed with greater modesty in public. She kept her more provocative gowns, however, and delighted in wearing them in private for him behind the closed door of their cabin.

Lance found her attitudes bewildering. In bed she was a woman, wise in the ways of sex, who used infinite techniques to arouse his appetites. At other times, however, she behaved like an adolescent, forcing him to realize that he was making life more difficult for himself.

On several occasions she tried to discuss Carrie with him, making it plain that she admired the older girl who had befriended her. At such times Lance withdrew into a shell, however, becoming curt and uncommunicative, so she gave up these efforts. She knew he still thought about Carrie and that his memories were painful, but she was

confident of her own ability to make him forget all other
women.

As the barge traveled northward, the weather gradually
became cooler. When they reached the rich prairie country, where the river formed the dividing line between Illi-
nois and Iowa, they anchored for two days. Melanie
remained behind while Lance went hunting with the captain and two members of the crew.

The party returned thirty-six hours later heavily laden.
Lance had shot a deer and also had brought down a buffalo. Both carcasses were dragged on an improvised sled,
and that night the whole crew feasted on fresh roasted
meat. Lance made frames on which he stretched the skins,
and told Melanie that when they were cured he would
fashion a cloak for her from the buffalo hide.

"If you're clever with a needle," he added, "you can
make a dress for yourself out of the deerskin."

The girl was delighted. "I'll really look as though I belong at your rendezvous," she said.

He couldn't help smiling. She was like a small child who
took pleasure in make-believe. "Think of the sensation
you'll create when you go back to New Orleans with your
new cloak," he told her.

Melanie looked blank. "New Orleans?"

"When you return there after the rendezvous."

"I never want to see New Orleans again," she said with
obvious sincerity.

Lance had taken it for granted that she intended to go
back to the House on the Avenue. "Then you'll go back to
your family in Virginia, I suppose."

"Hardly. I'd die of boredom."

He assumed he'd be obliged to send her anywhere she
wanted to go. It was the least he could do for her, even
though it had been she who had pursued him.

"I've decided," Melanie said, fluffing her hair and leaning against him as they stood on the deck, "that I'm going
out to the mountains with you."

He was so startled he could only stare at her.

Melanie smiled up at him, confident that she would
have her way.

"You can't mean it," Lance told her. "Life out there is

too rough for any woman except the squaws who have never known any other existence."

"I'll have you to look after me," she murmured, linking her arm through his. "I've always loved doing wild things. That's why I went to New Orleans. Now I won't be satisfied until you build me a cabin in the mountains and we live there."

She was too romantic for her own good, Lance thought. The hardships of mountain living were beyond the capacities of this luxury-loving girl, and at the appropriate time he would disabuse her of her impractical notion.

Melanie quietly led him to their cabin. She had expected him to be shocked by her idea, then opposed to it, but she was determined to have her own way. Now that he was exposed to her plan, she would win his acceptance bit by bit, and the best place to accomplish that goal was in bed. There, although he didn't quite realize it, she alone was in command.

Fort Snelling, a sturdy log house, stood high on a bluff overlooking the confluence of the Minnesota and Mississippi rivers, and there a company of United States infantry stood guard duty at the westernmost military outpost maintained by the United States government. Nearby were the St. Anthony Falls, named by French missionaries in the seventeenth century, and the power provided by the cascading water was utilized in a tiny mill that provided coarse-ground flour for the troops. Here were the navigable headwaters of the Mississippi, and here, in the next quarter of a century, settlers would come by the hundreds and thousands to found the Twin Cities of Minneapolis and St. Paul.

Off to the west, the plains stretched toward the horizon, and about a mile from the falls the temporary camp was established. Long rows of tents were erected, some of canvas and others of animal skins; there were lean-to shelters, and a few of the more ambitious visitors built real cabins, which they later would vacate and leave for the settlers who would follow in years to come.

This was the rendezvous, an annual event, held in a different place each year. Until recently, explorers, hunters, and trappers who spent years in the American and Canadian Rockies had been gathering quietly, without fanfare. Now, however, the rendezvous attracted scores of other visitors, too.

The mountain men, more than three hundred strong, provided the core. Lean and hard-bitten, they were the adventurers who preferred the solitude of their vast wilderness domain to life in cities or on farms. With them came some of their Indian friends and colleagues, men of the same stamp. The mountain men, some American, some English, some Scots, and some French Canadians, knew no nationalities or borders. In spite of the feuds and differences that sometimes caused bad blood between individuals and groups, they formed a band of brothers. Only those who had climbed to the top of a snow-capped peak, who had sighted an elk and brought him down, who knew the thrill of the chase and the loneliness of Rocky Mountain winters, could feel as one.

Prominent among the others at the camp were the representatives of the fur-trading companies, ranging from the great corporation created by John Jacob Astor to fledgling newcomers. Offering cash on the spot for pelts which they bought for prices far lower than those offered in the cities, the traders always had large supplies of whiskey and food on hand, and were lavish in their hospitality.

Almost as generous were the merchants who sold flour, sugar, coffee, and other staples, the vendors of pots and skillets, the representatives of gun manufacturers who offered for sale the most accurate rifles and pistols yet made.

On the outer fringe were those who preyed not only on the mountain men but also on those who dealt legitimately with them. Gaming sharks came from as far as the metropolitan centers of the Eastern Seaboard, hoping to win valuable pelts, lumps of unrefined gold and silver, and even the occasional gems that the mountain men sometimes carried in their worn rawhide purses. With these leeches traveled painted women of the same breed, prostitutes who did not hesitate to cheat and steal as they separated the mountain men from the wealth they had accumulated in the wilderness.

There were no formal meetings at the rendezvous, no one delivered speeches, and no activities were organized.

The mountain men gathered in small groups, telling their colleagues about passes they had found, the hazards of various glaciers and hidden valleys they had discovered. They talked about the attitudes of the Indian tribes that made their homes in the area, the regions where game abounded, and the problems of finding adequate firewood in certain locales. Their lives depended on the information they freely exchanged, and everything else that took place was peripheral. This was the essence of the rendezvous.

It did not matter that some ate heartily, gorging themselves on such treats as freshly baked bread. It was unimportant that others drank to excess, making themselves ill, or that a number spent all their money on the gaudy trollops from the East. What counted were facts that made it possible for man to survive in a hostile atmosphere. The few maps of the Rocky Mountains that had been drawn were notoriously inaccurate, so word of mouth was the mountain man's lifeline.

Fights seldom erupted between these rugged individualists, because it was universally accepted that in every violent physical disagreement someone would die. Lesser beings were fair game, but even when in their cups, mountain men took care to avoid disputes with each other.

Displays of strength, demonstrations of stamina, and acts of heroism were taken for granted. Mountain men rarely boasted of their exploits, being laconic by nature, and it was left to later generations to exaggerate and romanticize their lives. Any man who lived in the "high country," as it was called, accepted certain traits of character in his colleagues as natural and normal. As a consequence, mountain men rarely looked up to each other.

There were exceptions, to be sure. The grizzled Jim Bridger was regarded with awe, and so was the lean Kit Carson, who spoke in monosyllables and seldom smiled.

A similar accolade was accorded the mountain man known simply as the Lion. When Lance Beaufort made his way through the encampment, a lovely red-haired girl in a buffalo-skin cape at his side, the fur-company buyers, merchants, and gamblers watched him in silence. The fact that the girl wore his necklace of bear's teeth meant she was his woman, so the outsiders took care not to gape at her

openly for fear of offending him, and looked at her sur-
reptitiously.

Fellow mountain men came forward to greet him, and
he shook hands with all of them, obviously pleased to see
them. Those he regarded as friends were presented to Melanie, but those whom he knew less well were not given
that honor.

He was alert and solemn, conscious of the place he held
in the councils of his peers, and Melanie was thrilled.
More than ever she was convinced that she had chosen the
right man as her protector.

Asking no directions of anyone, Lance seemed to be
guided by instinct as he located the place where Paul and
Ponca had pitched their tents and left a space for his.
Lance's manner changed when he was reunited with his
partners, and he pounded them on the back with the same
exuberance they displayed in greeting him. If they were
surprised by the presence of Melanie, they did not comment. Under the code of the mountain men, an individual
was free to live as he pleased.

Lance gave Paul the bankbook made out in his name.
But Ponca, unaccustomed to the white man's civilization,
received his share of the profits from the sale of furs in
cash. Paul immediately confiscated the money.

"I'll give it to you after the rendezvous," he told Ponca.
"Meantime you won't be able to throw it away on booze
and whores."

Melanie was sensitive to anything that touched Lance,
so she realized his comrades were important to him.
Therefore she went out of her way to win their favor, flat-
tering them and playing up to them, yet taking great care
not to flirt with them. She sensed that her future with
Lance depended, at least in part, on his partners' attitude
toward her.

That evening she endeared herself to them. Offering to
cook the buffalo steak they intended to eat, she almost
burned the meat, and had to surrender the task to a grinning Ponca. She joined in the laughter caused by her inep-
titude, and both Paul and Ponca became her friends.
From that time they regarded her as a pretty mascot, and
when Lance went elsewhere they appointed themselves as
her guardians, making certain that no harm came to her.

The rendezvous was not what Melanie had expected. Her first discovery was that she didn't in the least mind the physical discomforts about which Lance had warned her. She enjoyed sleeping with him in the confined quarters of a cramped tent and eating in the open; in fact, under Ponca's tutelage she began to take lessons in the art of cooking over an open pit.

She couldn't help feeling superior to most of the people she saw. The shrill, unlettered harlots belonged to a different class, and none would have been employed at the House on the Avenue. Most of the men were lesser beings, too, and she recognized them as greedy and venal.

The mountain men stood apart and fascinated her, but she was careful not to show any strong interest in any of them. Without exception they appeared to be self-confident, at home wherever they found themselves. All seemed to share one quality above all: they had lived with dangers and hardships, and were at peace within themselves.

Melanie couldn't help congratulating herself on the wisdom she had shown. Lance Beaufort stood head and shoulders above all the rest in the company of the elite. Not only was he taller and more rugged, exuding an aura of animal magnetism that she found unique, but he was a natural leader who had won the respect of his peers.

His other assets meant a great deal, too. Although he refused to discuss his earlier life with her, his language and manners told her he had breeding and had been well-educated. And she knew from the gold in his purse and from the bankbook at which she had looked one night when he had been asleep that, unlike the majority of mountain men, he was a person of means.

In spite of her youth, Melanie was devoting a great deal of thought to her future. She didn't regret the impulse that had led her to run away from Virginia, but at seventeen she had to plan for what lay ahead. She had been popular enough at the House on the Avenue, but only Carrie had been able to earn truly large sums there, and Melanie had gained enough experience to realize that a career in such a place was limited. She would age rapidly, so she was smart to have left the profession.

Nowhere could she find a better protector than Lance, and Carrie had been foolish, for whatever her reasons, to break relations with him. Now that Melanie had established her own liaison with him, she fully intended to hang on to him.

Few young men were in a position to think of marriage, but Lance was relatively wealthy and independent, able to do whatever he pleased. Certainly he had enough money to buy a large tract of land or invest in a business somewhere. What was more, he was the type who would be loyal and hardworking as long as he lived.

Melanie knew she had to play her cards with care. But she had already made her plans. Somehow she would persuade and cajole Lance into taking her with him to the mountains. She didn't particularly look forward to a long sojourn in the high country, where comforts didn't exist, but she knew of no better way to convince him that her interest in him was serious and abiding. Perhaps after six months to a year of such living, she could lead him into marriage. Until then, he offered her complete protection and sexual gratification, both of which had been sorely missing in her life.

On the second morning of the rendezvous Melanie bathed and swam in a small lake only a short distance from the camp, with Paul standing guard behind a clump of trees. She returned in time to help Ponca prepare breakfast, and after they had eaten she insisted that she alone would clean the skillet and pot. The men willingly surrendered the task to her, and she knew from Lance's expression that he was impressed by her willingness to pitch in and do work that was alien to her.

"I've heard there's a salesman from Connecticut down the line who has a rifle with a new type of sight," he told her. "We want to look at it and maybe try it, if you don't mind."

"Go ahead," Melanie said. "I'll be finished sanding the pot and skillet by the time you come back."

Lance hesitated. "You're sure you'll be all right?"

Melanie laughed, and couldn't resist showing off some of the knowledge she had gleaned since their arrival. "If the Lion's woman isn't safe at the rendezvous, no one is safe anywhere!"

He was reassured, but nevertheless left his loaded pistols in the tent for her.

She thanked him, but couldn't imagine using them. Never had she fired a weapon of any kind.

After Lance and his partners sauntered off, she went to work with a vengeance, displaying far more dexterity than she had shown in their presence. Farm life hadn't been easy during her childhood, even though she had been taught to behave like a lady, and she was no stranger to pots and pans. Eager to please Lance, she began to scour with vigor.

It was odd, she thought, that she was enjoying herself. She had left her family's home because she had hated chores, yet here she was in the Minnesota country, on the edge of the wilderness, cleaning iron utensils as though her life depended on the results. She was modestly attired in a high-necked dress with long sleeves that she had bought in Memphis, she was wearing no cosmetics as yet today, and neither her activities nor surroundings were even remotely glamorous.

Yet she was happier than she had ever been.

Melanie glanced at Bantu and the other horses grazing in the field behind the tents and shook her head. Was it possible that she was actually falling in love with Lance? She didn't know, and only time would tell.

Leaving the pot and skillet to dry in the sun, Melanie took a small drawstring bag of silk from the tent, and sitting cross-legged on the ground in front of it, began to apply her makeup with the aid of a square of burnished steel. For Lance's sake she wanted to look her best.

All at once she realized someone was watching her, and looked up to see a short, totally bald man who was enormously heavy watching her from a distance of a few feet.

"Good morning," he said.

Melanie didn't like his tight smile, and nodded stiffly. The man looked vaguely familiar, but for the moment she couldn't place him.

"Don't tell me your friends have deserted you," he said.

"No, they're nearby."

"I saw them go off," he said, and smiled again. "I'm surprised to see you at the rendezvous. I thought your kind likes being pampered."

He made her uneasy, so she offered no reply.

"You don't remember me," Oscar Griffin said.

"No." Melanie's instinct warned her to beware, and she wondered whether she should leave immediately and go in search of Lance. But her pride compelled her to stay; she didn't want the fat man to know she was afraid of him.

"I met you and your grand friend in New Orleans," he said. "Not only did both of you reject me, but the great lady had me thrown out of the place."

"Now I remember," Melanie said, and peered past him in the direction that Lance and his partners had gone.

"Your friend has gone off to the fields to try out a new rifle," Oscar said. "I waited until I made sure he was nowhere around."

"What do you want?" Melanie demanded.

"You," he said, and smiled again.

She felt as though an icy blast of air had struck her.

"Don't stand on ceremony with me, wench," he said. "I own a house of my own and I know your kind. I'll give you a choice. Come with me to my tent, and I'll give you half of what I would have paid you in New Orleans. Refuse, and I'll take you right here—without paying you a penny. Which will it be?"

Not only did the man revolt Melanie, but she knew Lance would have no more to do with her if he found her engaging in sex with someone else. "Go away," she said.

"I haven't forgotten that day in New Orleans," Oscar Griffin said. "The memory of it has bothered me for a long time. I never expected I'd have the chance to even the score at the rendezvous, but I'm not one to miss an opportunity. So which shall it be—my tent or right here?"

The girl remembered the pistols Lance had left inside the tent, and jumping to her feet, tried to make her way there.

Moving with surprising speed and dexterity for a man of his bulk, Oscar Griffin cut her off and caught hold of her wrist. "No, you don't," he said. "I don't want to hurt you, wench, but you'll be sorry if you play tricks on me."

Melanie struggled in an attempt to free herself. "Let me go, damn you!"

"Keep a polite tongue in your head when you speak to me!" His free hand lashed out and slapped her hard across the face.

Tears came to the girl's eyes. Lance and his partners

had elected to pitch their tents in an isolated spot, so no one else was in the vicinity, and she was afraid this man would do her serious harm if she called for help.

Again she tried to wrench herself free.

His grip was firm, and he laughed at her.

Suddenly Bantu's trumpetlike bray sounded loud and clear as it echoed across the plain.

"You've made your choice," Oscar said.

Twisting her arm behind her back so she was helpless, he slowly and deliberately pinched her breasts.

The pain was excruciating, and tears came to Melanie's eyes.

"You're going to dance naked for me," Oscar said, "and then I'm going to teach you all kinds of tricks before I take you." He began to tug at her dress.

"Please don't tear my clothes," Melanie begged, thoroughly frightened by now.

Oscar released her but remained alert, ready to reach for her again if she tried to break away. "Then take them off," he directed.

She was desperate, and tried to play for time. "I . . . I've changed my mind," she said. "I'll go to your tent with you. For a fee."

He was enjoying himself now, and his small eyes glittered. "What makes you think that would satisfy me? I prefer it here."

"I know some tricks of my own," Melanie said. "Take me there and I'll show them to you."

"You lie!" he shouted, and began to shake her. "You and that other bitch humiliated me, and now you're going to pay for it. You're going to crawl to me. Naked. On your hands and knees. And beg for mercy."

He grappled with her, and his strength was so great there was no escape.

All at once a huge hand landed on Oscar's shoulder and twisted him around.

"The lady," Lance said, "doesn't care for your attentions."

Behind him Paul and Ponca approached at a run.

"There's been no harm done," Oscar said.

Lance continued to hold him in a viselike grip. "Nobody makes advances to my woman," he said.

Melanie couldn't control the sobs that welled up in her.

"To hell with you and your woman!" Oscar Griffin said, a knife materializing in his hand.

He had no opportunity to use the blade. He was quick, but Lance was quicker. The knife was wrenched from his hand, and flew off into the grass.

At the same moment, a heavy fist smashed into Oscar's face, instantly drawing blood.

Before he could recover from the blow, Lance struck him again, then yet again, pummeling him without mercy. The assault on Melanie had been bad enough; the attempt to use a knife had been equally unfortunate, and the Lion demanded retribution.

Paul made no attempt to interfere, and Ponca stood quietly aside, too. Their one desire was to ensure that there was fair play on both sides.

Oscar tried to strike back, but his blows were ineffectual. One of his eyes was already swollen shut, and his strength was no match for that of the lean giant who continued to lash out at him.

Bone crunched against bone.

Melanie, still weeping, covered her face with her hands.

Oscar tolerated the beating longer than most men could have done, perhaps because of his great weight, but all at once he sagged, then sprawled on the ground.

Lance went to Melanie and put an arm around her. "You'll be all right now," he said. "I heard Bantu's call, so I knew something was happening, but I got here before this pig could hurt you."

His embrace was gentle, and gradually the girl became calmer. Later, perhaps, she might tell him this man was no stranger, but had sought revenge for an incident in which she and Carrie had been involved.

Paul dropped to one knee and examined the man lying on the ground. "He appears to have had a heart attack," he said. "He's dead."

Lance was not unduly moved by the news. Under the code of the mountains, a man who assaulted another's woman deserved death.

What he had no way of knowing was that his vengeance had been greater and more just than he realized. Oscar Griffin had played a major role in the events that had led to Lance's flight from Oakhurst Manor and Carrie Emerson's subsequent panicky departure. Now, a half-continent removed from that scene, the Charleston gambler-criminal had paid for his perfidy with his own life.

At dawn on the third day of the rendezvous a small group of mountain men went out into the plains on a buffalo hunt, and returned a few hours later with two bulls and a calf. Other members of the group dug a large pit, still others felled several dead trees, and a huge fire was started.

While the meat cooked and three of the mountain men prepared a sauce of herbs gathered from the plain, all members of the clan were invited to the celebration. This was the first true gathering of the band of brothers since the rendezvous had started, and the mountain men responded enthusiastically to the invitation, many of them bringing crocks of whiskey, others carrying jugs of wine.

Only a handful of the outsiders were invited to the festivities, among them two of the weapons salesmen and a fur buyer who had himself spent a number of years in the mountains. This was a spontaneous gathering, and the participants would remember it in the autumn and winter that lay ahead.

A number of the men were accompanied by trollops with whom they had been associating at the encampment, but Melanie had almost nothing in common with these women and felt out of place.

Lance managed to put her at ease, however, by guiding her to the far side of the fire from most of the roisterers. There he sat on the ground beside her, with an arm around her shoulders. She was flanked on the other side by Paul and Ponca, and gradually she began to enjoy herself.

Cups and gourds were filled and passed around, and the first of innumerable toasts was offered. "To the mountains!"

That was just the beginning. They drank to the snow fields and glaciers, pine forests and passes.

Lance was embarrassed when he became the first person present to be honored. "To the Lion!" someone shouted, and the entire company drank.

Ordinarily abstemious, he entered into the spirit of the

occasion, joined by Melanie and Paul. Only Ponca abstained, because liquor made him deathly ill.

The smoke from the fire rose higher, the odors of barbecuing meat drifted across the plain, and some of the mountain men began to sing. Others told stories of their experiences in the past year, and the level of conversation rose to a roar.

Lance, still sitting with his arm around Melanie, was enjoying himself, his cares put aside. This was an hour to be treasured, and he made the most of it.

Melanie couldn't recall a happier moment. She had thrust her nightmare of the previous day out of her mind, Lance's strong arm was reassuring, and this scene was what she had imagined the rendezvous would be, a rollicking reunion of adventurers.

Two newcomers appeared at the far side of the fire, a man and a woman. The man was recognized by a number of the celebrants, and cups were thrust at him and his companion.

Ultimately they made their way around the fire, and Lance froze when he recognized Carolyn Emerson and Pierre Bateaux Gautier.

Carrie saw him at the same moment, and her face went blank.

Then Lance felt Melanie stiffen as she and Carrie exchanged quick, embarrassed glances.

Gautier saw Lance and pounded him enthusiastically, whooping with glee. "Hey, you here! Now Bateaux and his friend have damn fine time together!"

Meantime Paul Beaufort was looking hard at Carrie, uncertainty and incredulity in his face. "Carrie? You are Carrie, aren't you?"

All at once she knew him, and they embraced. "Paul!" she cried. "The last person on earth I expected to meet!"

A beaming Paul turned to Lance. "Look who's here!"

"I see her," Lance said, and averted his gaze.

She was unable to face him, either.

Gautier insisted on passing around a stoneware jug of brandywine after helping himself liberally to its contents.

Carrie raised the jug to her lips but did not drink.

Lance followed her example, and the glow he had felt previously was dissipated. Carrie looked lovelier and more desirable than ever, but it was obvious that she shared his misery.

Melanie was apprehensive, so she drank to excess in an attempt to calm herself.

The jug made the rounds again and again. Bateaux Gautier, his bull-like voice increasingly loud, launched into a long, complicated tale that he told Paul and Ponca, and he became lost in his own dramatic recital.

Melanie dozed on Lance's shoulder.

Through the haze of smoke from the fire Carrie and Lance couldn't help looking at each other, their eyes drawn by powerful, invisible magnets. Both were somber and unsmiling.

Suddenly the spark they had generated for so long was ignited anew. Melanie had become Lance's woman and Carrie was traveling with Gautier, but both felt compelled to explain their situations, and they began to speak at the same moment.

Never had there been a stranger or more constrained meeting. Both were thousands of miles from home, their heritage gone. Both were living beyond the pale of the civilization that had nurtured them, and were engaged in careers that had been farthest from their thoughts when they had last met and had planned to marry.

The smoke of the cooking meat continued to rise from the fire; the laughter of raucous mountain men formed a background, as did the voice of Gautier. Here, on the fringe of the great wilderness of the West, their destinies merged again, if only for a moment.

Sparing herself nothing, Carrie told him succinctly about the attack in her bedroom at Trelawney, her panicky flight and subsequent seduction by Emile Duchamp. "After that," she said, "I knew I was doomed, so I just drifted with the tide. It didn't matter what became of me."

It mattered to him, but he couldn't tell her as much, knowing she was Gautier's woman. Instead he launched into his own recital, and in an attempt to ease her tension, casually mentioned his own affair with the farm woman in Tennessee so she would realize that he, too, had strayed.

Such incidents, Carrie's expression indicated, had no real significance.

One thought burned in Lance's mind. "Do you have any

idea who the masked man was who assaulted you at Trelawney?"

Carrie hesitated. "Well, he had a way of raising his
hand to his face that makes me feel certain I'd know him
if I ever saw him again."

"But you do have a suspicion," he persisted.

"It isn't fair to make accusations I can't prove."

"I'd like to know," Lance said simply.

She shrugged, but refused to speak, in part because she
didn't want to come between brothers.

"I have thoughts of my own," Lance said, "and someday I'll be in a position to make certain."

Carrie saw the bleak, hard look in his eyes and shivered.
Here was a man who had become intimate with death,
and it held no terrors for him.

His expression softened and became wistful. "I suppose," he said, wording his thought with great care, "that
it's too late now for you and me."

"I don't know how you could even think in such terms,"
Carrie replied. "After what I've become."

"As if that mattered," Lance said.

She had thought she was impervious to tears, but they
came to her eyes. "This fire is so smoky," she murmured.

"You're obligated to Bateaux, I'm sure."

"Yes," she said. "He took me away from New Orleans,
and he's been wonderfully loyal to me for a long time."

"He's a good man." Lance swallowed hard. "If I can't
have you, I'd rather see you with him than anyone else.
This is none of my business, but do you intend to marry
him?"

"I haven't let myself think about it," Carrie said. "When
the time is right, I'll know, one way or the other."

"I see."

"Besides," she said, "you aren't really free yourself."
She looked at the sleeping Melanie.

"I'm not in her debt," Lance said.

"Maybe not, but she needs you. I tried so hard to persuade her to leave the place in New Orleans. She's young.
And she's defenseless. She isn't like you and me. You've
always been able to look after yourself, ever since you
were little. It took circumstances to make me strong and

tough, but that's what I am now. Melanie isn't that way. She needs someone to take care of her and protect her."

Lance smiled wryly and told her how Melanie had followed him onto the barge that had brought them to the rendezvous.

Carrie couldn't help laughing. "That's exactly what I mean. She's impulsive. And so trusting it didn't ever occur to her that you might send her away."

"I couldn't," he said, "simply because it was plain that she was depending on me."

"You'll save her from herself," Carrie said.

He appeared to be trapped.

She changed the subject abruptly and began to speak of Scott and Kai, Jeremy and Lisa. "I don't suppose you've written to them."

"How could I? There's still a big price on my head, and it wouldn't be fair to compromise them."

She thought it remarkable that he could still think in terms of fairness. "I haven't written either, because I haven't wanted to hurt any of them. I know they'd be heartbroken if they ever find out what I've become."

"Maybe, maybe not. I'm sure they still love you, just as they love me. I'd get in touch with them if I could."

"I'll have to think about that," Carrie said. "Someday, perhaps, I'll gain the courage to go home, at least for a short visit. If I do, I'll tell them I saw you. Your mother will be so relieved, and Papa Beaufort will be pleased to hear that you've become the Lion of the Rocky Mountains."

Lance flushed beneath his tan. "Stories about people become exaggerated," he muttered. Then, recovering from his embarrassment, he added, "I hope you do see them. It would give me peace of mind if they know I'm still alive and doing well."

Carrie made up her mind to return to South Carolina to see their families. She owed Lance that much, and a great deal more. She was still afraid to make such a journey, but for his sake she hoped she would gain the strength.

She reached out her hand to him.

He responded, and for a moment their fingers touched.

But his movement disturbed Melanie, who stirred, then awakened. She looked up at Lance, smiled at him, and pulled down his head. Her kiss was long and lingering, and only by creating a scene could he have removed her. It was better, perhaps, to accept the situation.

At last Melanie sighed, and, her arms curled around his neck, she continued to cling to him.

When Lance was able to look over his shoulder, Carrie was gone. She had retreated to the far side of the fire, dragging Gautier with her. Paul followed, and she reminisced with him until the meal was ready.

Lance had little appetite, but could not spoil the festivities by refusing to eat. And when someone passed him a jug of whiskey, he took a large swallow.

Night came, and the party grew increasingly boisterous. Some of the mountain men, their inhibitions loosened by liquor, began to look at Melanie with covetous eyes.

She could feel Lance's tensions, and was afraid there would be serious trouble if someone made untoward advances to her. When the Lion was spoiling for a fight, it was best that ordinary mortals beware.

"Take me back to the tent," Melanie murmured.

He quickly accepted the opportunity to escape from the fire. And his frustrations were so great that after he and Melanie reached their tent, his lovemaking was so violent and intense that he exhausted her.

Lance did not see Carrie again. The following morning Paul told him that she and Gautier had gone, departing on the barge that had brought them to the rendezvous. For the second time she had disappeared from his life.

13

The last furs were sold to the traders, the last supplies and weapons were purchased, and the mountain men who gambled lost the last of their money at cards. Early on the final day of the rendezvous the fires were started at dawn for what promised to be an orgy of eating and drinking.

But Lance had other ideas. "There's a feel of autumn in the air this morning," he said at breakfast, "so I reckon we'll pull up stakes today and be on our way."

Paul was agreeable, and so was Ponca.

As Lance had anticipated, Melanie was enthusiastic. "I'll be ready as soon as I clean the skillet. There will be just time for you to buy me that mare I saw and liked yesterday."

"Can you ride well enough to spend all day, every day in the saddle?" he demanded.

"You forget that I grew up on a farm!" the girl promptly retorted.

Paul grinned.

"The mountains are no place for a delicate creature like you, especially in winter."

"I'm stronger than you think," Melanie said complacently, and silently appealed to his partners.

Paul nodded vehemently. "Maybe I'm getting soft," he said, "but I like the notion of a lady keeping house for us in a snug cabin. If there's one thing I don't like about mountain living, it's making do in a lean-to shelter when the snow is eight and ten feet deep and the wind comes roaring down from the peaks."

Ponca laughed, pretended to shiver, and blew on his hands.

Lance immediately realized that Melanie had gone to them privately and enlisted their support. He was annoyed, but at the same time he had to admire her. She was a determined female who knew what she wanted and managed in her own way to get it.

In one sense his comrades were right. Winter living in the mountains, at best an experience that no man relished, would be far more pleasant and comfortable with a housekeeper in charge.

His real reason for wavering was far more intimate. He was shaken to the marrow after seeing Carrie again and at least suspecting that his still-active love for her was reciprocated. Men of strength and stamina and courage had been known to take leave of their senses during the long Rocky Mountain winters, and he had more reason than most to lose his balance.

When he and Melanie made love, he was able, for that time, to put Carrie out of his mind. Perhaps it was wrong to use this girl's erotic appeal and desire to be his woman for purposes unconnected with their own relationship. But he was in the grip of emotions far more persistent and ferocious than the grasp of the grizzly bear that had almost destroyed him, and he needed every weapon he could command in order to survive. Although he was no expert on the subject of romance, he doubted that Melanie loved him, any more than he loved her. He had a hunch she had attached herself to him for the sake of excitement, perhaps simply because she had tired of her life in New Orleans and wanted something different and new.

Whatever her motives, a key element was lacking in the feelings she demonstrated toward him. Of that much he was certain.

So it wasn't really wrong if he used her, just as she was using him.

"I'll agree," he said gruffly, not glancing at the girl and directing his remarks to his partners, "provided you lads build the cabin. Just remember you'll have to get started as soon as we find the right place, because it'll be winter almost before we know it."

Melanie clasped her hands together in silent joy. She had been sure of victory, and now she had won it.

"I know just the spot," Paul said. "Beside the lake under the twin peaks. What we've called Secret Valley."

"Is good!" Ponca chimed in.

Let them celebrate and think him weak. Lance rose abruptly and hurried off to buy Melanie the mare they had seen for sale the previous day. Even though she would cushion his own deep sense of hurt, it was a mistake to take a woman to the mountains in winter, and he was afraid he would regret his decision.

An hour later their gear was packed and farewells were exchanged with various mountain men, who could not conceal their surprise when they learned that the girl would accompany the party into the wilderness.

The pack mules that Ponca had acquired earlier in the week were led into line, and it irritated Lance that one of them was laden exclusively with Melanie's wardrobe, most of it consisting of attire she would be unable to wear in the mountains. He placed the girl directly ahead of the Kiowa at the rear of the caravan, then rode to his own place in front, and, not speaking, raised his hand as a signal. All four were silent as they left the rendezvous.

For several days Lance deliberately maintained a blistering pace, even though he knew he was just giving in to his own bad temper. But Melanie surprised him by making no complaints, keeping up with the men, and although obviously weary at night, doing her share of gathering firewood, cooking, and cleaning. Lance had to admit she was earning her right to full membership in the group, and thereafter their travel became more leisurely.

Late every afternoon when they halted and made camp for the night, Lance gave Melanie lessons in handling and shooting a pistol. "You need to be able to take care of yourself," he told her.

At first she was clumsy and afraid of firearms, but familiarity with weapons gave her greater confidence, and ultimately she became a reasonably good shot. Ponca, not to be outdone, taught her to use a lasso, and to the astonishment of all three partners, she became proficient at the art, wielding a rope or a Kiowa line of twisted vines with dexterity.

Paul, who felt left out, told her first-aid techniques useful in the mountains as they made their way westward. She was a conscientious pupil, listening carefully to the physician's instructions and repeating them to ensure that she understood. After two weeks on the trail she seemed well-prepared for the trials that lay ahead.

They rode toward the southwest, taking care to avoid the badlands, where roaming bands of Dakota and Sioux warriors fiercely resented the intrusion of outsiders. The braves of these nations were notorious scalp hunters, and not even the magic firestick of the Lion would save the group if they met a large party bent on destruction.

They swam their mounts across the mighty Missouri, its waters swollen by autumn rains, with Ponca and Paul leading the struggling mules. Lance was prepared to assist Melanie if it became necessary, but again she surprised him, demonstrating skill and determination. She was proving to be far less delicate than he had surmised.

The changes in the girl were remarkable. Some days she wore her deerskin dress, varying it with a man's shirt of linsey-woolsey and trousers of buffalo hide that Ponca had fashioned for her. Her cosmetics were forgotten now, but there was color in her cheeks, and her clear skin was radiant with her vibrant health. She proved sensitive to the moods of all three men, chatting when they felt like talking, remaining silent when they fell under the spell of the endless plains. Gradually she assumed the chore of cooking both breakfast and supper, and would allow no one else to clean the utensils.

Lance was forced to concede he had misjudged her. She bore virtually no resemblance to the provocative and flirtatious courtesan he had first encountered at the House on the Avenue. Even their intimacies were open and honest now, with Melanie enjoying their lusty encounters for their own sake and seldom using the bedroom tricks that had been her stock in trade.

They followed the Missouri toward the south for several days, and when they turned toward the west early one afternoon, Lance called a halt. "Warriors ahead and riding this way."

He and his companions immediately checked and loaded their rifles, and a suddenly apprehensive Melanie made certain the pistols she carried were ready for use. Firearms play was no longer a game.

The Indians approached in a body, riding their small plains ponies at a slow gallop, and even at a distance it was evident that they were armed, some carrying bows and arrows, others spears, and a few holding ancient flint-locks.

Lance studied the paint smeared on their faces and torsos, then smiled. "They're Omaha," he said, but offered no further explanation.

Melanie was still nervous.

"They're friendly enough if they're not crossed or cheated," Paul told her, "and sometimes they trade with us."

The braves came still closer, and Melanie counted at least fifty of them. It was remarkable, she thought, that her companions showed no fear.

The column drew to a halt. Two warriors who rode in the vanguard, a middle-aged man with an elaborate headdress and a husky warrior with three bright feathers protruding from his scalp lock, raised their right hands in salute.

An otherwise immobile Lance gravely returned the gesture.

It occurred to Melanie that virtually all of the Indians were staring at her, and her discomfort increased. Then the senior warrior who sat with the sachem moved forward on his pony and rode in a slow circle around her, inspecting her with keen interest.

Paul chuckled, Ponca suppressed a grin, and only Lance remained solemn.

The warrior returned to his place opposite the Lion and made a long statement in the language of the Sioux.

Lance replied at almost equal length in the same tongue.

The girl couldn't understand a word but knew they were talking about her.

The warrior made another speech, and this time his gaze met Melanie's.

She knew the expression. This savage wanted her, and she had to use all of her willpower to prevent herself from cringing.

Lance's reply was courteous, but his comments were brief.

The Omaha reached behind him and produced a large square of soft doeskin, one side covered with beads that made a colorful design.

Lance accepted the square from him.

Melanie felt a surge of alarm. Perhaps she had gone too far by insisting on accompanying Lance. It was possible that he was accepting the beaded doeskin in exchange for her.

Her panic subsided, however, when Lance took a loaf of pressed tobacco from a saddlebag and presented it to the warrior.

Again salutes were exchanged, and the parties went their separate ways.

Melanie, sitting erect in her saddle, pretended not to know that the braves were still ogling her.

When the Indians were no longer within earshot, all three of her companions laughed loudly and heartily.

"Will someone share the joke with me?" she asked indignantly.

Lance continued to laugh. "You're the first white squaw the Omaha have ever seen," he said, "and the sachem's son offered two flintlocks and a pony for you. He wanted to make you third among his wives."

"I'm afraid I don't share your sense of humor," Melanie said, then added, "I thought he was offering that piece of beaded doeskin for me."

"No, that was a peace offering, a gesture of goodwill. A square of beaded leather that intricate is worth at least twenty dollars in the Independence markets."

"I think I earned it," Melanie declared.

The doeskin would have been useful in trade with

mountain Indians for furs, but Lance handed it to the girl without comment.

"It will make a handsome skirt," Melanie said.

Not until much later in the day did it occur to him or his partners that in spite of their amusement, she alone had benefited from the encounter.

A few days later they came to the Missouri's great tributary, the Platte. "We'll be home before too long," Lance said. "We'll follow this river until it divides into two forks, and then we'll use the South Platte as our guide into Colorado."

Melanie was growing weary of the long journey, but knew better than to express her feelings. By now she could have been comfortably ensconced in a city, and could blame no one but herself for her presence in the wilderness.

One morning as the girl was boiling river water to mix with cornmeal to make a porridge and the men were breaking camp, the ground beneath their feet seemed to shake. The sky was cloudless, but Melanie nevertheless heard the sound of thunder and was bewildered.

Her companions wasted no time. Lance and Ponca hastily saddled their mounts and piled their packs on the broad backs of the mules. Paul dumped the contents of the iron pot onto the ground, expressing relief that the water wasn't yet hot. He stuffed the saddlebags, then lifted the confused Melanie into the air and placed her on her mare.

The mules were huddled together, with the four riders shielding them. The men arranged themselves in a V-shaped formation, with Lance at the point. Each drew a pistol, and Paul caught hold of Melanie's reins with his free hand.

"No matter what happens," Lance told the girl, his voice terse, "don't lose your seat. Stay glued to your saddle."

"And don't panic," Paul added. "Keep your head and you'll be safe enough."

For the first time she noticed a dust cloud on the horizon, which became larger and grew closer by the moment. The thunder roared now, and her mare neighed. The mules became restless, and the horses began to paw the ground.

Only Bantu stood motionless, his ears erect.

Gradually Melanie became aware of the most incredible and frightening sight she had ever seen. Many hundreds of mammoth shaggy beasts, those in the front ranks horned, were bearing down on them at breakneck speed. Surely the whole party would be trampled and crushed in the wild stampede.

The mare whinnied in fright.

"Steady," Lance called, not turning, and continuing to watch the rapidly approaching herd of buffalo.

Melanie leaned forward to pat and soothe her mare, but she shared the horse's fear. No human beings could withstand this fierce onslaught, and for the first time she was sorry she was making this journey. Boredom at the House on the Avenue or elsewhere was far preferable to the terrible death that awaited her, that was racing toward her with the demonic fury of a tornado.

Now Melanie could see the small red eyes of the bulls that were leading the charge, and she thought the animals were demented. They paid no attention to the people, horses, and mules directly ahead of them, and appeared intent on sweeping everything from their path.

The dust, carried by the wind ahead of the herd, became suffocating, and Melanie choked, her eyes watering.

The mare was finding it difficult to breathe, too, and tried to rear.

Paul tightened his hold on the reins.

Lance appeared to have eyes at the back of his head. "Damn you, girl," he shouted above the tumult. "Hold your seat!"

Melanie clung to the mare for dear life.

It wasn't easy for Paul and Ponca to control their own mounts now.

But Bantu stayed as motionless as a statue, challenging the onrushing bulls.

His master remained still in the saddle, his eyes fixed on the leaders of the herd.

In a few moments, Melanie told herself, they would be dead. If she was fortunate, she would lose consciousness before she quite knew what had happened to her.

Suddenly, when the front rank of the buffalo were only a few yards away, Lance's triumphant laugh pealed out, audible above the roar. He aimed his pistol over the head of a mammoth bull bearing down on him and fired.

The astonished Melanie watched the solid ranks of the creatures break, and before she quite knew how it happened, the shaggy animals were sweeping past in two ranks. The nearest of them was so close she could have reached out and touched them.

Paul was ready to fire, too, if it became necessary, and so was Ponca, but Lance had attended to the problem. Cows and calves followed the bulls blindly, leaving humans and horses and mules unharmed.

The girl's relief was so great that she wept.

But Lance wasn't yet finished, and his calm was so great it had to be seen to be believed. Placing his pistol in his belt, he drew his rifle and waited until the herd began to grow thinner. The clouds of dust were blinding now, even obliterating the sun, but he had no trouble seeing what he wanted to see.

At last he caught sight of a young calf that suited his purposes. Taking slow, deliberate aim, he placed a bullet between the creature's eyes. The calf stopped short, as though it had struck a thick stone wall, and then fell to the ground.

The bulls that formed the rear guard swerved so they wouldn't stumble over the calf's body.

Working quickly and methodically, Lance reloaded his rifle before replacing it in its sling.

The buffalo were gone now. The air began to clear, and the thunder of pounding hooves slowly receded.

Lance dismounted, went to the calf, and began to skin it, his air that of a man engaging in a common occurrence.

Melanie was so relieved she felt weak as she watched him.

Suddenly Lance looked at her and grinned. "I figured," he said, "that you needed a soft new shirt and boots to wear with your beaded doeskin skirt."

The girl continued to stare at him, uncertain whether to weep again or laugh. The only rational thought that came

to her mind was that this extraordinary man's notion of a
"shopping" trip was unlike that of the admirers she had
known in New Orleans.

A few days after they reached the flatlands of eastern
Colorado, a cold wind swept down from the mountains. It
persisted for two days, making it necessary for Melanie to
wear her heavy buffalo-hide cloak. That night Paul built a
larger fire than usual, and the girl inched close to it.

"Winter come early to mountains this year," Ponca said,
and there was a hint of concern in his voice.

Lance nodded without commenting, but the following
day he stepped up their pace, and thereafter maintained it.

Once again Melanie felt misgivings and wondered if any
man was worth following into this bleak wilderness.

Soon thereafter, as they climbed steadily onto higher
ground, they caught their first glimpse of the glistening
white peaks of the Rocky Mountains that lay to the west.
The first snows of the autumn had already fallen, and the
slopes were a dazzling white in the clear sunlight, too.

Melanie was desolate. The area ahead was so vast, so
lonely, that it staggered her imagination.

But Lance came to life. A smile lit his face, his eyes
shone, and he spread his arms wide as he looked toward
the towering heights. "We've come home at last," he said,
his voice as soft as a caress.

When they moved up through the passes, Melanie was
amazed to discover that the sun was so hot she had to
shield her delicate skin from its rays. But the nights were
so chilly that she huddled close to Lance when they slept,
and even his warmth did not prevent her from shivering
at dawn. He refrained from remarking that he had warned
her against coming to the mountains, and instead promised
to make her a sleeping bag of stout elk hide which he
would try to obtain the first time he went hunting.

The alien atmosphere frightened Melanie, too. On the
plains she had been able to see for great distances, but
here the deep forests closed her in, and on the heights,
where the terrain was uneven and gigantic boulders frequently obstructed the view, she conceived the notion that
enemies might be lurking anywhere.

To an extent she was right. One morning the horses

demonstrated great nervousness, with even Bantu becoming difficult to control. Lance immediately diagnosed the problem, and with the aid of Ponca he disposed of two rattlesnakes. The girl had to avert her gaze when he milked the venom from the reptiles' sacs to smear on the tips of his short spears, and she hastily refused his offer to make hairbands or belts for her from the skins.

At night, even with Lance's strong arms holding her close, she could not sleep when she heard coyotes howl, the mournful sounds echoing across the limitless canyons. She was reminded of the cries made by wounded dogs, but coyotes were wild beasts, capable of killing, and she wasn't reassured when Lance tried to soothe her by telling her that the creatures were more afraid of her than she was of them.

They made their way through two passes, frequently traveling above the timberline, and frequently the horses had to pick their way through snow fields. One part of this desolate wilderness looked like another to Melanie, but Lance seemed to recognize every foot of the terrain and knew where he was leading them.

After a journey that seemed endless they saw two great peaks ahead, their upper portions covered with snow. They appeared to be so close together they looked like a single mountain that had been split in two. But Melanie was learning that distances were difficult to judge in the Rockies, and after they made their way through a narrow pass they suddenly came upon a gorgelike valley that nestled between the twin peaks.

Even the girl could understand why her companions had elected to make their winter home here. Secret Valley provided everything that human beings needed for survival. In the center of the area was a lake fed by several rivers that came down from the twin mountains, and in these waters, Ponca said, there were fish that could be caught even in the dead of winter.

Beyond the lake stretched a thickly foliated, deep forest that extended for several miles. Here was timber for a house and for a barn to provide shelter for the animals, and the supply of firewood was inexhaustible. Game was plentiful in these woods, and here the temperature remained relatively warm because the twin peaks cut off the winds. As Melanie soon discovered, juicy berries were growing on bushes everywhere in the forest.

On the near side of the lake were large fields of grass, much of it still green, that would provide fodder for the horses and mules. Other plants grew there, too, and Paul said he would show Melanie several varieties of edible roots. Among them were sweet wild beets and tart onions.

The men went to work with a vengeance, Lance and Paul constructing a large cabin while Ponca devoted himself to making a crude barn behind it. Melanie, who had nothing better to occupy most of her time, made herself useful by gathering large quantities of berries and digging up roots.

The partners unearthed heavy rocks, which they used to line the enormous fireplace that would occupy the better portion of one entire cabin wall. Then they took a day off from their labors to obtain provisions. At first Paul's luck was mediocre, and he brought down only a brace of rabbits, but he persisted, and late in the afternoon he shot a wild boar. Ponca spent his day at the lake and caught a large mess of silvery fish with firm white flesh.

Lance went off alone and on foot to higher ground, and returned with a bag of birds that provided a welcome change of fare. He was heartened, too, because he had found elk tracks. Saying he would hunt again the following day, he felt reasonably certain that supplies would be plentiful throughout the winter.

Ponca next taught Melanie how to scoop up quantities of clay from the banks of the lake and deposit it in some of their cooking utensils. With her sleeves rolled up above her elbows, she worked on her hands and knees, her hands and arms filthy and her clothes soon streaked with sticky clay. This life was a far cry from the pampered existence she had led at the House on the Avenue, but she had enough of a sense of humor to laugh at herself.

She soon discovered the importance of the clay. Paul and Ponca used it to chink the cabin, packing it into spaces between logs and making the dwelling airtight. There were four windows in the cabin for the purpose of admitting light, and these were covered with heavy paper coated with boar grease to make it water-repellent.

Lance had gone hunting at dawn, this time mounted on

Bantu. Man and stallion did not return until dusk, dragging behind them a buck elk. Here was enough meat to assure them of food for weeks, and as refrigeration would not be adequate until heavy snows came to the valley and stayed there, Ponca immediately built up their lakeside fire to smoke the meat.

The skin was cured in the sun, and a portion of it was utilized for clothing. Lance kept his word, and fashioned a sleeping bag for Melanie out of the backside.

The girl's earlier fears were dissipating, and little by little she found that she was feeling more at home in Secret Valley. She was busy from sunrise to dusk, cooking meals and cleaning utensils, gathering more clay, and cutting the high grass to store for fodder. For this purpose she used an old sword that Paul had bought at the rendezvous and then had sharpened, and she actually felt the pride of accomplishment when she became adept at the chore.

It occurred to her that she was expending even more energy than she had done at her parents' farm, but here she had no choice. Those who wanted to survive the coming winter had to work. Besides, she had elected of her own free will to live with Lance, so she couldn't complain. He was still a satisfying lover, gentle and considerate, and she had never known anyone as even-tempered. He did the work of two men, yet always remained cheerful. He devoted a portion of each day to helping his partners build the cabin and barn, but now he went hunting regularly, too, and soon the pelts of beaver, the skins of fox and lynx began to mount in a temporary shed. Here were the furs that would earn large sums the following year.

Just looking at them convinced Melanie she had made the right choice. She never forgot that Lance had already gained considerable sums of money, and now he would earn a great deal more. Ultimately she would persuade him to settle elsewhere, either buying a substantial property with slaves to man it, or, her secret dream, purchase a dwelling in one of America's larger cities. Certainly she had not given up farm life in order to spend the rest of her days in an even more strenuous existence in the wilderness.

In spite of the improvement in her lot, however, Melanie was troubled. Ordinarily she was confident of her ability to charm any man and bind him to her, but she realized her hold on Lance was tenuous. He was attentive and a marvelous lover, but she frequently had the feeling that his mind drifted elsewhere.

Sundown seemed to be a difficult time for him. Invariably he went alone either to the edge of the lake or the boulders that stood on the heights behind the camp. Invariably he stood very still for a long time, his gaze fixed on some invisible object in space. At this hour he seemed remote, untouchable.

One day she asked Paul about this strange habit. "Why does he go off alone that way?" she demanded.

Paul replied with a noncommittal shrug.

"What is he thinking?"

"He's never said." Paul's voice was chiding. "I've never inquired. Every man is entitled to his own measure of privacy, you know."

One night, soon after Melanie and Lance began to use the new sleeping bag, she gleaned her first clue. He was holding her so tightly that she awakened, but discovered that he was still sound asleep.

She moved slightly in order to loosen his hold.

Lance smiled in his sleep and spoke distinctly. "Carrie," he said.

From that moment Melanie knew she had a rival. She couldn't blame him—or any man—for dreaming of Carrie, whom she herself had admired for so long. But it seemed unfair that he should be thinking of another, even Carrie, when she herself was here beside him, making love with him, doing her share of the hard work necessary to create a snug winter refuge in the mountain wilderness.

There was no way she could fight back. There was no way she could give herself to him more freely or with greater gusto, no way she could work any harder. Her rival was a ghost, an apparition from the past who existed now only in his mind. The flesh-and-blood Carrie, she felt certain, was living a life of luxury somewhere with Bateaux Gautier, reveling in the hot baths her maids drew for her, enjoying the rich silks and satins in which Bateaux swathed her.

Melanie tried to conquer her sense of frustration, but

the task wasn't easy. Sometimes she sulked and occasionally her temper flared for no apparent reason. Lance always remained so calm that she soon felt ashamed of her outbursts, but she couldn't help wondering, too, if his tranquillity was caused by a deep-rooted indifference to her. That thought contributed nothing to her peace of mind.

Actually Lance was aware of more than he revealed to her. In some way he couldn't fathom, he believed, she had divined his inner state of mind and knew he still loved Carrie. Not that he felt apologetic about that love; it was a part of him, and would remain with him as long as he lived. He had tried to stop loving Carrie and had failed miserably, so he knew better than to compound his misery by making a further effort.

He couldn't quite feel sorry for Melanie, either. Occasionally he saw her looking at him with a calculating expression in her eyes, and he felt reasonably certain she didn't love him. He was useful to her, she was enjoying living with him, and that was that. He felt certain she wouldn't weep when the time came for them to part.

Nevertheless he hoped her equanimity soon would be restored. People lived at close quarters during Rocky Mountain winters, and unpleasant moods could create serious problems.

At the end of three weeks the house was finished except for the overhead covering, and all of the partners went to work on the roof. It was sloping, to provide for runoffs, and they crisscrossed logs, packed together tightly to withstand the weight of many feet of snow. Over this base they built a second layer of smaller branches, then added a third at the top, fashioned of interwoven twigs. They gathered reeds from the end of the lake, which they plaited with strong vines from the forest and heavy strands of grass, and this last layer, in effect, formed something that resembled a thatched roof.

They moved into the cabin the day the roof was completed, and lighted the fire in the hearth that would burn day and night. "All right now for winter to come," Ponca announced with satisfaction.

Twenty four hours later the first heavy snow fell, leaving a deposit of more than eight inches. But the roof proved effective and the interior remained dry.

The only furniture consisted of empty kegs, which were utilized as chairs and as tables. At first, hard-packed earth served as the floor, but Melanie quickly discovered it was too chilly. She proved to the men that dried reeds served as insulation that warded off the chill, and thereafter they kept the ground covered with a thick blanket of rushes.

By day there was one room. At night an improvised wall of animal skins sewn together was lowered to provide Lance and Melanie a corner of their own. At Melanie's insistence this cubicle opened onto a portion of the fireplace.

Snow fell daily for a week, and at the end of that time Paul estimated the covering at more than twenty inches. Melanie soon learned the snow provided insulation that helped keep the interior warm.

The arrival of winter did not mean anyone worked less hard. Every day there were trees to be felled and firewood to be cut in order to meet the insatiable demands of the hearth. Every day there was small game to be found in the nearby forest, and Melanie was astonished to see that berries continued to grow. Snow and ice had to be melted in kettles for drinking, bathing, and the washing of clothes; the floor had to be swept with a broom of boar bristles; and the preparation of meals was a never-ending responsibility. Sometimes Melanie varied the monotony of her chores by going fishing, Ponca cutting a hole in the ice that covered the lake so she could lower her line.

Lance was even more active than he had been. This was the best season for the acquisition of furs, he told the girl, and he roamed through the mountains every day, always returning with booty. Sometimes he was accompanied by one or the other of his partners, particularly when they suspected that a pack of wolves or a band of lynx might be in the vicinity. The temporary shed was replaced by a more substantial warehouse, and the piles of furs steadily grew higher.

"This is our best season, the best we've known," Paul said.

Melanie rejoiced privately. The more Lance earned, the more there would be for her to spend when they returned to civilization.

The conviction grew within her that she deserved everything he would buy for her. Her hands became rough and callused, her few frontier clothes were shabby, and she bore scant resemblance to the glamorous young courtesan who had achieved popularity at the House on the Avenue.

Melanie was not only bored but felt like a drudge. Even though Lance still made love to her regularly, they had little to discuss other than his hunting exploits of the day. Paul had even less to say, and at best it was difficult to converse with Ponca. Melanie couldn't help wondering whether she was losing her feminine appeal.

The arrival of an unexpected visitor gave new zest and excitement to Secret Valley life. As it happened, Lance and Paul had been absent for more than two days on a hunting expedition high in the mountains, and Ponca was cutting down a dead tree in the forest at the time the newcomer arrived.

He was a tall, lean mountain man in his twenties, fully bearded and wearing soiled buckskins, and it didn't matter that his appearance was undistinguished or that he rode a weary gelding. His name was Randy, he said, and he had been attracted to the valley by the smoke rising from the hearth.

Recovering from his initial astonishment at finding a young, pretty girl in this remote dwelling, Randy nevertheless continued to stare at Melanie.

His obvious interest delighted her, and soon she began to feel she hadn't lost her allure after all. Lance took her for granted, while Paul and Ponca treated her like a junior colleague, but the visitor was conscious of her only as a woman. When she moved around the cabin, throwing wood on the fire or attending to other chores, she was conscious of the man's steady scrutiny. Once, when she turned quickly, she knew he wanted her.

When he wasn't watching her, Randy noted every detail of the cabin, and when he went off to stable his gelding, he took advantage of the opportunity to inspect the fur warehouse and the new pantry where frozen meat and fish were stored. This place represented a dream come true, principally because of the redhead's presence but also because of the food and furs that had been accumulated.

When Ponca returned from the forest, he took an instant dislike to the visitor, and when Randy asked for some whiskey, the Kiowa reacted with uncharacteristic rudeness. "No whiskey here," he said curtly. "Only have little brandywine. Save for time when need."

A short time later the hunters returned, their packhorses heavily laden with beaver and fox, and it quickly became evident that the stranger made no favorable impression on them, either.

The rules of hospitality in the wilderness were inviolate, however, and Lance invited the man to stay for supper and the night.

Randy accepted.

In spite of the reaction of Lance and his partners, Melanie was exhilarated. The presence of the outsider not only provided a break in the drab routine into which she had settled, but there was no doubt that Randy was very much aware of her as a female. She happily accepted his offer of help when she started to prepare supper, and she repeatedly saw him studying her breasts, waist, and hips, even though she was wearing bulky clothing of animal skins.

The temptation to flirt with Randy was too great for the girl to resist. Partly because of the sheer pleasure she derived from seeing him respond. It wouldn't hurt Lance to realize that someone else was interested in her, and a jolt of active jealousy might arouse him from his lethargy.

The partners spoke infrequently during the meal. Paul and Lance, tired after their strenuous expedition, yawned frequently.

But Melanie more than compensated for their silence. She chatted merrily with Randy, smiling at him, fluttering her eyelashes, and occasionally touching his arm as she emphasized a point.

Even though Lance was sleepy, he missed no nuance, and Melanie was privately elated. Active jealousy was known to have an invigorating effect on a man.

After they finished supper, Melanie cleaned up. Only Randy complimented her on the new candles she had made a few days earlier.

Soon they retired. Lance lowered the curtain that separated the cubicle from the rest of the cabin, then Melanie climbed into the sleeping bag beside him and blew out the candle. She was both surprised and hurt when he promptly fell asleep.

Not until Randy left after an early breakfast the next morning did Lance mention the subject. Waiting until Paul went off to chop firewood and Ponca walked down to the lake to fish, he cleared his throat, then said, "I reckon you know you made a mistake last night."

The girl was wide-eyed, pretending ignorance.

Lance had no intention of sparring. "You weren't a guest at a cotillion or assembly," he said, "and mountain men aren't the Virginia gentry. You were wrong to pay so much attention to Randy."

Melanie had a point of her own to make. "You're jealous!"

He shook his head. "That's not so. Anytime you want to leave me for someone else, you're free to go. I'd never fight to keep any woman. But I don't believe you're particularly anxious to ride off into the mountains with that fellow."

She was shaken and angry. "Certainly not!"

"I'm not criticizing you." Lance spoke quietly. "I'm just trying to make you understand that wilderness rules aren't like any you've ever known elsewhere. In the past few years at least two mountain men have been murdered by visitors who hankered after their Indian squaws. You're a damn sight prettier than any squaw, and a fellow can get strange ideas in his head when he's gone without a woman for a long spell."

At least he conceded that she was still pretty!

"If Randy hadn't been outnumbered three to one, he might have tried some trickery, after the way you were encouraging him. Maybe you were just being friendly by Virginia standards, or polite by New Orleans ways, but it's different out here. A woman hardly speaks to a man unless she wants him to bed her."

"I've never heard anything so ridiculous," the girl replied, her temper flaring. "Randy knew I lived with you, and I can't imagine anybody in his right mind trying to harm the Lion."

Lance shrugged. "A bullet can kill me as quick and easy as it can someone else. Besides, we've heard things about this Randy from time to time, and his reputation isn't all that good." He pulled his buffalo cloak over his shoulders, then patted her. "There's no harm done," he said, picking up his rifle and starting toward the door, "but I thought you'd want to know for your own benefit."

Not until long after he had gone did Melanie become calmer. He wasn't jealous. He really wouldn't care all that much if she found another man and went off with him. But "for her own good" it was dangerous to engage in an innocent flirtation with a visitor.

She began to count the months until the warm weather came and she could persuade Lance to take her back to civilization.

14

────••═══●═══••────

The miracle occurred so suddenly, so unexpectedly, that it caught Jeremy Beaufort completely by surprise. He was moving from his bed in the Vienna town house to his wheelchair, as he did every morning, as always insisting that he perform the feat unassisted, when he felt a sharp and persistent twinge in his hip.

Instinctively he clapped his hand to the spot, and then began to laugh in wonder.

Lisa heard him from her adjoining dressing room and hurried into the bedchamber.

"Look!" In the palm of his hand was the lead pellet that had crippled him.

She stared at him in astonishment.

"I wouldn't have believed this," Jeremy said, "if the same thing hadn't happened to President Jackson. He told me about it himself. Years ago a bullet lodged in his body, and the doctors were afraid to dig it out. Well, little by little it worked its way to the surface, and one day, when he was at work in the White House, it fell onto his desk. That's what happened to me, apparently, but it took less time than Andy Jackson's bullet. Aside from a break in the skin that must have been caused when I changed positions without realizing it, I'm perfectly fine again."

Lisa examined the place on his hip that was bleeding slightly, then looked again at the bullet and marveled. Her prayers had been answered and she was so overjoyed that she wept, but she took the precaution of insisting that he stay in his wheelchair until he underwent a medical examination.

Dr. Hummellmann was summoned, and arrived a short time later with an associate. They examined Jeremy at length, and both were smiling.

"I suppose I can do anything now," the exuberant United States minister to the Austrian Empire declared.

"Not yet," the physician told him. "You've been fortunate, Mr. Beaufort, but don't spoil your luck. If I were you I wouldn't try dancing a waltz just yet." Knowing what was in his patient's mind, he added, "And it would be wrong to travel."

Jeremy's face fell. "I don't understand."

"It's really quite simple," Dr. Hummellmann explained. "Your hip has been immobile for a long time. Now the cause of that stiffness has disappeared, but your joints are still stiff. Suppose you had two pieces of metal that worked together in a cog, and one was rusty. It would be necessary to remove the rust before the cog would begin to function efficiently."

"That makes sense," Lisa said.

Jeremy was impatient. "Hold on. How long—?"

"I'm going to prescribe a program of exercise for you, Mr. Beaufort," the physician told him. "It will be mild at the start, and if you respond to it properly—as you should—we'll increase it gradually. In that way you'll ultimately recover the full use of your hip, and you won't even walk with a limp."

"Splendid, Doctor." Jeremy persisted, "But how soon will I be able to make the journey back to the United States?"

"I don't like to set specific dates, because the human body is unpredictable, and I hate to disappoint patients. But if all goes as it should, I see no reason why you can't make the trip by the time the warm weather arrives."

After the physicians had departed, Jeremy and Lisa sat

grinning at each other, their forgotten breakfast growing cold on a tray beside them.

"By next week," he said, "I'll be able to walk a block or two. The first thing I'm going to do is take this bullet to the court jeweler down the street. I'm going to have him set it in a bed of diamonds and make it into a necklace for you."

Lisa tried to protest.

"My mind is made up," he said.

She knew better than to argue. "Very well, then. In return I'm going to get you a gift, too, one that's far less expensive. I'm going to buy you a calendar, and you can start marking off the days until we can go back to Oakhurst Manor."

"That," Jeremy said, "is the most wonderful present that anybody could buy for me."

The winter offered the best hunting the mountain men had known in many years, and the warehouse behind the log cabin was filled with furs. The profits, Lance and Paul estimated, would be even greater than they had earned the previous year.

The hunting season was still far from ended, however. Spring came late to the mountains, so the animals were slow to change their coats, and the hunting remained well above average long after the snows began to melt and grass started to sprout.

"This year we won't wait until the rendezvous to sell our catch," Lance told his partners as all three set out for the heights, leaving Melanie behind them at the cabin. "We can leave as soon as the really warm season arrives."

"I don't think we'll have much choice," Paul replied. "If we wait too long, we won't have any place to store our furs."

They headed above the timberline, and Lance broke the silence. "It's just as well we'll be leaving," he said.

Paul exchanged a quick glance with Ponca, then deliberately pretended to misunderstand. "You're right. I've had the greatest experience of my life out here, and after we sell these furs I'll be able to buy the biggest house in Boston. But I've had my pleasure now, and by summer I should get back to my practice."

"I know how you feel," Lance said. "But that isn't what I meant. I was thinking of Melanie."

His companions made no reply, but none was necessary. As the winter had progressed, Melanie had suffered from a version of what mountain men sometimes called "cabin fever." She had been out of sorts and increasingly morose, frequently giving in to fits of temper and then sulking for days. There was no romance in mountain living for her now, and it was obvious that she was eager to return to the civilized world she had left behind the previous autumn.

"Not that this is any of my business," Paul said at last, "but I can't help wondering about your plans and how they may include Melanie. We know I'm returning to Boston, and Ponca says he's had enough of the mountains, too."

"I go back to Kiowa people," the Indian said. "Be so rich they make me sachem."

Lance chuckled, then sobered. "I'll never have enough of all this," he said, gesturing in the direction of the snow-covered heights. "The mountains are in my blood for the rest of my days. But there are other things I must do this summer."

They respected his privacy and asked no questions. If and when he chose, he would offer them a fuller explanation.

"As for Melanie," he said, "I'm not yet sure what to do. I was opposed to having her come out here, and I'm afraid I was right, even though she's taken the physical hardships in her stride. I intend to see that she doesn't suffer financially, of course, but beyond that I haven't made up my mind."

Paul's smile was thin. "She may have made her own decision, you know," he said. "And if she intends to stay with you . . . well, you'll have hell's own time getting rid of her."

Lance nodded unhappily. What to do about Melanie loomed as a major problem, but he had others that were even more important.

He had spent the whole winter and spring pondering, weighing his future, and at last he knew what had to be done.

Carrie didn't figure in his plans. He still loved her, but she had moved out of his life, never to return, so she would remain locked in his memory and in his heart. But he doubted that he would ever see her again.

There was one problem on which he could and would act decisively. The claim that he had assaulted Carrie at Trelawney was as false as it was absurd. By now the passions of those who had wanted to hang him had cooled, so he was ready to go home and fight the charge. It was true he had killed two members of the posse, but he believed he could demonstrate that he had acted in self-defense. As he would tell any judge and jury, he had faced the dilemma of killing or being killed. There was a chance— perhaps a good chance—that he would be exonerated.

One of the problems from the start had been that he couldn't ask Uncle Scott to act as his lawyer, because as Carrie's guardian he would have been placed in an untenable position. With what Lance had already earned, however, combined with the prices the new furs would command, he would be in a position to hire the best attorneys in the United States. If necessary he would fight his case all the way to the Supreme Court. He was tired of being a fugitive from justice, and had lived long enough in the shadows.

He had grieved long enough, too, because of the hurt he had been inflicting on his parents. Kai Emerson was not only a mother who loved him, but was a sensitive woman who, he knew, had been deeply worried by his absence and silence. He wanted to comfort her, to assure her that he was in robust health. As for Papa, Lance knew how proud Jeremy was of the Beaufort name. Undoubtedly it had decimated him to have a son living under a cloud. The day was at hand when Lance wanted to grasp his father's hand and say, "I'm innocent, and I intend to prove it."

Even if everything worked out for the best, it would be strange to be living at Oakhurst Manor again without Carrie, but that was a permanent reality he had to face. He was strong in every other way, and he would have to gain the strength to go on without her.

Inevitably his thoughts turned to his half brother, too. The long separation had convinced Lance that he had no real affection for Jerry, whom he didn't trust. Carrie had hinted that she suspected it had been Jerry who had assaulted her. The truth might be difficult to unearth, but if it was possible to prove that Jerry had been responsible, Lance knew he would take justice into his own hands. No matter what the consequences.

He grasped the reins more tightly, his knuckles whitening. The Lord would have to forgive Jerry if he had soiled Carrie; Lance would show him no mercy.

Not until Ponca found the tracks of a wolf pack did Lance stop brooding and begin to concentrate on the day's work. Perhaps he, like his partners, had spent a long enough time in the mountains. The time was ripe for him to go home, to return to his roots. He had proved himself as a mountain man, and now it was time to clear his good name.

The day's hunting was fruitful, and by late afternoon the pack mules were laden with pelts. This single day's activity, Paul estimated, would earn them more than one thousand dollars.

They returned to Secret Valley in high spirits, and even Lance momentarily put his cares aside. The days were growing longer, so it was still daylight, and he thought that when he went East he would miss the Rocky Mountain sunsets. Granted, he was inclined to brood at dusk, but the beauty of the wilderness at that hour always would be a part of him.

When they reached the valley, they saw a strange horse tethered at the rear. Lance asked his companions to stable their mounts and attend to the mules while he investigated, so he dismounted a short distance from the cabin and instinctively walked silently toward the door.

He wasn't particularly concerned. Melanie could handle firearms, and after spending many months in the wilderness he knew she could look after herself. Also, various visitors had dropped in from time to time, and even the roughest of mountain men or the most cunning of renegade Indians would think long and hard before creating trouble at the home of the Lion. His reputation was his best protection. And Melanie's.

Lance entered the cabin, then stopped short.

Melanie stood in front of the hearth locked in an embrace with a man who was kissing her passionately.

Sensing the presence of someone else, the couple moved apart.

Melanie's partner, Lance saw, was Randy, the mountain man who had visited Secret Valley early in the winter.

The girl was so terrified she stood unmoving, a shaking hand raised to her mouth, her eyes wide.

Randy's face was expressionless.

Before Lance could speak, Paul and Ponca burst into the cabin. The former pointed a finger at the intruder. "That bastard's saddlebags were crammed to overflowing with our furs," he said.

"Who says they belonged to you?" Randy demanded.

"We say." The ordinarily imperturbable Ponca was furious. "We make our special mark on inside of every skin. Our mark on the skins in your bags."

Randy paled beneath his heavy tan, but looked defiant.

Lance flexed his fingers, which anyone who knew him recognized as a sign that he had been provoked beyond endurance.

Melanie saw the gesture and gasped.

"Randy," Lance said, "you've abused my hospitality. You stole my furs and you tried to steal my woman."

"You can claim you owned them furs, but that don't mean it's so," the man said. "And the woman is free to do what she wants."

Paul started to speak.

But Lance silenced him with a sharp gesture. "I'll take care of this," he said. The code of mountain men had been broken, his own honor was at stake because of Melanie's involvement, and he felt he had to assume sole responsibility.

Only a man of great courage or one who had no alternative dared to face the Lion, and Randy was cornered. There was no law in the Rockies other than those the mountain men themselves made and enforced. His accuser was his judge, and it was obvious that he was guilty.

He didn't know the Lion's intentions, but he wasn't going to wait long enough to learn them, and a double-edged knife with a curved handle suddenly appeared in his hand.

Melanie found her voice and screamed.

Lance paid no attention to her and advanced slowly, his sense of balance remarkably like that of a great puma.

"Be careful," Paul told him. "The fellow is armed."

Lance nodded but made no attempt to draw either a pistol or his own knife. No self-respecting mountain man used weapons under his own roof.

Randy lunged, his knife upraised, and tried to slash him in a sudden wicked thrust.

But Lance had anticipated the blow and sidestepped, moving no more than a few inches.

The hysterical Melanie began to weep.

Paul tried in vain to silence her.

Lance ignored the commotion, and concentrating his full attention on his foe, slowly circled the man.

Randy feinted, then drove at him again.

This time, as Lance dodged the blow without seeming effort, a huge hand shot out and grasped Randy's wrist.

The pressure applied by Lance's powerful fingers was so great that the man gasped, and the knife clattered to the floor.

Ponca darted forward and scooped it up. "Now fight going to be equal," he said.

The desperate intruder tried to bluff. "You call it equal when there's three of you and only one of me?" he demanded, his voice strident.

Lance replied softly. "My partners won't touch you," he said. "There's no need. Beat me fair and square, and they'll let you go free."

Randy's eyes darted around the room as he weighed his chance of escape. It was apparent that he thought of bolting toward the door, but Lance's bulk blocked him.

"You abused my hospitality." The calm statement was a final judgment, spoken in sorrow and seemingly without rancor.

Suddenly Lance's fist shot out, and although the blow traveled only a few inches, its impact was so great that it staggered the man.

Randy tried to return the blow, but his fate was already sealed. He was no match for the avenging Lion, and the panic in his eyes indicated that he knew it.

Lance displayed no emotion as he landed a second punch, then a third.

Randy dropped like a felled tree, the back of his head striking the stone flooring of the hearth. He lay still, making no sound.

Even as Paul hurried forward to examine him, the diagnosis was plain. "He's dead."

Melanie was too horrified to weep.

But Lance felt nothing and showed no reaction. The intruder had broken the fundamental laws of mountain living, unwritten rules that had been made to help ensure the survival of the adventurers who came to this wilderness. Now the transgressor had paid the supreme penalty, which he had deserved.

Melanie was too afraid for herself to feel any sorrow for her would-be lover.

Lance stood immobile.

His partners realized he had unfinished business to attend to, and hastily removed Randy's body, which they would bury in the forest, where it wouldn't be attacked by hyenas or buzzards.

As the door closed, Lance turned and looked at Melanie for the first time. His eyes betrayed no feelings.

The girl shrank from him.

"I'm not going to hurt you," he said quietly. "I don't hit women."

She began to gain her courage. "It was so awful," she murmured. "I don't know what I would have done—what I *could* have done—if you hadn't arrived when you did."

Lance made no reply, convinced that she would go on if he remained silent.

"Randy must have stolen the furs before he came in the house," she said. "The first thing I knew, he was standing inside the door staring at me. He . . . he drew his knife and threatened to kill me if I didn't do what he wanted. I knew he meant it so I . . . I was trying to humor him." She paused to suck in a deep breath.

"You lie," Lance said with a weary smile. "His knife was in his belt when he was kissing you, and you were returning his kiss."

"No," Melanie protested. "You don't understand. He must have put the knife away—"

"It doesn't matter, does it?" Lance spoke with gentle firmness. "All I know—and you know it, too—is that if

I'd walked in five minutes later you would have been coupling with him. Voluntarily."

For a long moment the girl stared at him, and then burst into tears. "I'm sorry," she sobbed. "I didn't do it deliberately, and Randy's visit wasn't planned."

Now, he thought, she was telling the truth.

"I was bored, that's all. I hardly knew him, and he didn't mean anything to me. But I was alone with him, and . . . and one thing just naturally led to another."

"I warned you long ago not to come with me to the mountains," Lance said. "There aren't many who can tolerate this life."

"Everything will be so much better between us—for both of us—after we go back East," Melanie said, recovering slightly and speaking very rapidly. "We'll buy ourselves a lovely house, and I'll make it up to you for this mistake. You'll see. I'll be the best wife any man ever had."

"I reckon you can be a good wife if you set your mind to it," Lance told her, "but it'll be in a marriage to someone else."

"Surely you aren't going to hold this against me!"

He shook his head. "No, I'm not. You've had ideas, maybe, but now that we're bringing everything out in the open, I've known all along that marriage has never been in the cards for you and me. I have obligations to fulfill, and what I do must be done alone."

Melanie couldn't accept his stand. "You're just rejecting me because you're jealous. Kissing Randy didn't mean anything to me!"

Her sights were so narrow, he wondered how he could convince her he meant what he had said.

"Carrie has been far worse!" she cried. "She's gone to bed with more men than I can count, but you love her!"

A searing flame enveloped Lance, and he took a single step forward, his face and voice bleak, his eyes suddenly granitelike. "Don't mention Carrie in my presence again!" he commanded. "Not ever!"

Melanie knew she had gone too far and that for the present her battle was lost. By attacking Carrie she had erected a new barrier between herself and Lance.

Very well, she wouldn't repeat the error, and in one way or another she would compensate for it.

Certainly she felt no pity for Randy, a casual stranger with whom she had amused herself for lack of anything else to do.

What mattered was that she couldn't afford to lose Lance, and had no intention of losing him. Under no circumstances would she return to New Orleans, and the life of a courtesan would be no better elsewhere.

This long, dreary winter had taught her what she wanted. Her one aim was to become Mrs. Lance Beaufort. He had told her more about himself, in bits and pieces, than he realized, and she knew there was at least the possibility that he would recover his heritage. How grand it would be to live the life of a lady on a great South Carolina plantation!

Even if his effort failed, however, he would have ample funds to establish a secure future for them elsewhere. Her beauty would be wasted on the Virginia farm of her parents, and it was unlikely that she would ever find another man who was Lance's equal. In her experience she had never met anyone as ambitious, as vigorous, or as fearless. Much less one who was as satisfying a lover.

So she would not give him up, even if his plans didn't include her. He wasn't all that difficult to fool. For instance, he had jumped to the conclusion that she and Randy had just started making love when he had walked in, when the truth of the matter was that they had spent the entire afternoon together and had been on the verge of parting. Luckily, dead men couldn't talk out of turn.

Confident of her own abilities, Melanie vowed that no matter what Lance intended, she would become his wife.

The new Astoria Inn, recently built by John Jacob Astor, the fur magnate who was one of America's first self-made millionaires, was the finest hostelry in New York, perhaps in the entire United States. A stunning six stories high, it was located in the most fashionable part of town, on the Broad Way near Wall Street. There were marble pillars in the lobby, where the floor was also made of marble; most suites and rooms boasted fireplaces of glazed brick; and as a penultimate touch of elegance, there were fur throws on all the beds.

The servants were dressed in livery, as they were in the great homes of the South, and guests who ate in the luxurious dining room, which featured a chandelier of genuine crystal, were requested to order their meals in advance so the chefs could prepare dishes for individual tastes.

America had never seen an inn like the Astoria, and the people who stayed there were so out of the ordinary that crowds sometimes gathered in front of the place to watch them come and go. An incandescent young English actress, Fanny Kemble, who had just made a great success in town, stayed there with her father, and such authors as Washington Irving and James Fenimore Cooper dined there frequently. Former President John Quincy Adams, who had returned to the House of Representatives, was a guest whenever he was in town, and so was Senator Daniel Webster.

No one created a greater stir than the willowy blond with long hair. Always handsomely dressed, she went out every morning for a carriage ride in her own coach, and every afternoon she went shopping, always alone. Sometimes she was seen in the evenings with a great bear of a man whose state of overdress indicated a lack of breeding.

None of the people who gaped at Carolyn Emerson would have guessed that she was lonely, upset, and increasingly determined to make drastic changes in her way of life. She had spent the entire autumn, winter, and spring traveling through the United States with Pierre Gautier, and she had to admit she didn't regret the experience.

She had seen a great deal of the country. Following Pierre's advice, she had invested in various commercial enterprises, doubling her money and then doubling it again, so that by now she was comfortably situated. Never again would she have to worry about the financial security that had been so important to her in the past.

Carrie had enjoyed New York when she and Pierre had first come here, and it had been exciting to attend all four of the city's theaters, go to lectures, and dine every evening in a different place. But now, six weeks later, the city had palled and she felt as though she were drifting.

One of the principal reasons was the change in her relationship with Pierre. He was still gentle, considerate, and generous, to be sure, because that was his nature. But her interests bored him, and recently he had been drinking harder than ever. Also, although he hadn't admitted it, he had reverted to his old habits and sometimes slipped away to visit the city's bordellos. He was one of those men, Carrie had concluded, who was incapable of fidelity.

What he needed was a return to hard work in familiar surroundings. He needed to go back to a world where he was known, respected, and useful; he needed to travel up and down the Mississippi River on his fleet of barges, which were contributing so much to American prosperity.

Her own requirements were equally clear in her mind. Fate had forced her to lead a life of which she was secretly ashamed, even though she had prospered. Now, with the incidents that had caused her to flee from South Carolina buried in her past, and her future assured, she had to reestablish her priorities.

It was essential that she go back to Trelawney, at least for a visit, to see Uncle Scott and Mama Emerson, whom she loved and who loved her. To see Lisa and Papa Beaufort, for whom she felt equally great affection and to whom she would always be indebted. Although her reasons for not getting in touch with them had been valid enough for a long time, she no longer had an excuse to absent herself from them, to keep them in the dark regarding her whereabouts.

As Carrie well knew and could never forget, one person stood at the core of her existence. She had refrained from going home because she had been afraid her memories of Lance Beaufort would overwhelm her. But she was a woman, not an adolescent, and her duty made it mandatory that she go back to Trelawney.

She should have put Lance out of her life after she had seen him early last autumn at the rendezvous of mountain men. But that brief chance encounter had created the opposite effect. How much time had they spent together? A half-hour, perhaps. No more. But it had been such an overpowering experience that she had insisted Pierre take her elsewhere the following morning.

She hadn't needed that meeting to know that she still

loved Lance. Now, however, she pictured him in her mind as he was, a rugged, bearded frontiersman, fearless and strong, who was respected above all others in the world in which he lived. What a far cry from the debonair young South Carolinian who had never known suffering.

For an instant at the rendezvous campfire, when her hand and Lance's had touched, Carrie had thought her heart would stop beating. She had gone to bed with many men, none of whom had meant anything to her, but cold chills still moved up and down her spine when she recalled the warmth of Lance's hand.

Their conversation had been factual, almost mundane, as they had brought each other up-to-date on their varied experiences. She could remember few of the words they had exchanged.

But his eyes had told her a different story, and Carrie realized beyond all doubt that Lance still loved her, just as she loved him.

Why, then, had she urged him to take Melanie out to the mountains with him? Melanie, who was young and pretty, seductive and lively. Melanie, who in spite of her youth was no novice in the art of enchanting men.

The only reason Carrie could give herself was that she had felt guilty about her association with Pierre, a tie that it would have been unfair and embarrassing to break. Because she was involved, she had wanted Lance similarly distracted by someone else. How foolish she had been. By now it was possible that Lance and Melanie were married. Even if they weren't, she knew Melanie well enough to realize that his involvement was great and complicated.

Sometimes she thought she actually hated Lance because of her inability to thrust him out of her heart. But that was stupid, too. She had learned to live with emptiness that would remain with her until she died. So be it.

But she couldn't afford to think in long-range terms because she had immediate problems that demanded practical solutions, and she couldn't afford to allow sentiment to interfere with the decisions she was required to make.

That realization was brought home to her forcibly when Pierre staggered into their Astoria suite at midnight, mumbling incoherently and reeking of whiskey. It was surprising that he had been able to function sufficiently well to find his way there.

Carrie felt sorry for him and put him to bed. She couldn't help noting that there were smudges of lip rouge on the front of his shirt, but she felt neither rancor nor jealousy, and that knowledge alone helped make it possible for her to clear her mind.

Nevertheless she spent a restless night, and was dressed for the day by the time Pierre awakened. She had breakfast sent to their suite, but took care not to discuss anything of importance until he began to recover, a process aided by a mug of ale she had thoughtfully ordered for him.

"It appears that you're trying to drink New York out of whiskey," she said with a smile.

Gautier's smile was rueful. "I try," he said, "but there is always more whiskey. Are you angry with me, Carrie?"

"No," she replied, shaking her head. "But we're foolish to be living this way. You're at a loss because you aren't doing anything useful, and I'm not very happy, either."

"Bateaux don't mean to be bad," he said. "But many bad things happen."

"I know. You become involved without realizing it. Even when you spend time with local women."

He flushed and looked abashed, but was too honest a man to deny the truth. "Bateaux is one damn idiot," he said. "You're the most beautiful girl in the world, so why do I need other women? I go to them, then I feel stupid."

Carrie's own experience made it possible for her to understand the problem. "There are some men who aren't satisfied with one woman, no matter who she might be. They've got to keep searching." She refrained from adding that the search almost inevitably was fruitless and that the seeker rarely found true gratification.

"You're too good for me," he said with a lugubrious sigh.

"That's not so, but we've been frittering away our lives. You're restless and I'm bored. I'm relieved that we haven't married, because it wouldn't have worked out well for either of us."

Gautier began to catch the drift of her conversation, and squared his shoulders. "What do you want us to do?"

"I know what you need to do, Pierre. Go back to work. Start leading convoys of your barges up and down the Mississippi again. You've spent most of your life out-of-doors, and cities stifle you. I'm sure you'll drink far less."

"That's true," he admitted. "When Bateaux is working, I don't want any damn whiskey. I belong on the river, so I'll go back there!"

She was relieved and pleased that he was demonstrating so much common sense.

"Will you go back to New Orleans, Carrie?"

"Never," she said firmly. "I've put that life behind me forever."

Gautier was dismayed. "Then what will you do?"

"First, I intend to visit my family, the relatives who brought me up. I've neglected them far too long, and I must live up to my obligations to them."

"Then where will you go?" he persisted.

"I . . . I don't know." A note of uncertainty crept into her voice.

"Maybe you'll stay at home and marry somebody else."

She had lost Lance, the one man she would marry, but there were other obstacles, too. "Even if I were interested or could become interested in someone—which won't happen—no South Carolina gentleman would want me. You think of me as a lady, but they wouldn't agree. My background is a little too rich and colorful for them. There's one thing I won't do, Pierre. I won't live with any man as we've lived together. I'm finished with the life of a courtesan."

"Do you suppose you and me will see each other again?"

"Stranger things have happened. I've given up trying to predict the future."

He was a realist and accepted her decision. "We'll do what you want," he said, "but before we say good-bye, I want to give you a special present."

"I'd rather you didn't," Carrie said. "It's a matter of principle. I've already accepted far too much from you, and thanks in part to your help, I've achieved financial independence. So I'd like to start my new life by not taking gifts from anyone."

Gautier's eyes became misty, and he blinked rapidly.

"There's nobody in the whole world like you, Carrie. Anytime you need a friend, anytime you want help, I'll give you anything you wish!"

She knew he meant the offer literally, and was grateful for it.

"How soon do you want to leave?"

"The sooner you get back to the Mississippi, the sooner you'll stop drinking, Pierre. And now that I've actually made up my mind to go, I'm anxious to start. Immediately."

He was dismayed. "So soon?"

"The longer we wait," Carrie said, "the more painful it will be for both of us."

"We'll go tomorrow," he said, and quickly planned a final surprise. Even though she wanted no gift, he would buy her a handsome carriage and a team of matched horses to pull it. Then, attended by her own servants, she could make the journey to South Carolina in style. Her homecoming had to be an event that people would remember, and he had no intention of allowing her to detract from its drama by traveling via commercial stagecoach. Carrie was unique, and Gautier was determined that everyone from her past realize it.

15

President Jackson reluctantly accepted the resignation of Jeremy Beaufort as United States minister to the Austrian Empire, but expressed his deep gratitude for service rendered under the most difficult of personal circumstances. Tom Beaufort was appointed acting minister in his brother's stead.

Jeremy, walking without a limp, his hip completely recovered, traveled with Lisa by way of Switzerland, and after they crossed into France they spent several days in Paris before going on to Brest. There they engaged passage on a ship that would take them directly to Baltimore, which would enable Jeremy to report in person to the president and the State Department in Washington City before they returned home.

Their quarters on the merchantman were spacious, and they stood together on the deck as the vessel, her sails filling, cleared the port and headed into the open Atlantic. If the weather remained fair, they would arrive in the United States in less than a month.

"It's hard to believe we're really going home," Lisa said

with a smile as she held her husband's arm. "I don't know when I've looked forward so much to anything."

"I wish I shared that feeling," Jeremy replied. "I'm just hoping we don't have too much unpleasantness in store for us."

"Well, you know Lance won't be there, but at least you can take direct action yourself trying to trace him."

"Indeed I shall, but that isn't what I meant."

"I know," she said, and squeezed his arm sympathetically.

She hadn't necessarily approved when he had insisted that they notify no one of their impending arrival. He wanted to surprise Jerry, and under the circumstances had felt it wouldn't be fair to tell Scott and Kai Emerson that they were homeward bound.

Jeremy knew what Lisa was thinking. "After we leave Washington City," he said, "we'll travel straight to Charleston, and instead of going right on to Oakhurst Manor, we'll stay in the city for a few days. I shouldn't need more time than that to look into the affairs of the shipping company and find out for myself what's wrong. Scott has done his best to help, I realize, but nobody can read and interpret those ledgers as I can."

She hoped he was prepared for a major disappointment in Jerry, but was reluctant to say too much. Scott Emerson had hinted in his letters that Jerry was guilty of chicanery, but even he had hesitated to make a direct accusation in so many words. By reading between the lines Lisa had become convinced that Jerry was stealing from his father's company, and she was afraid that factual confirmation might be a shock too great for Jeremy to bear.

He had made excuses for his elder son over so many years that he might react too strongly when he was forced to face the truth. He was the most controlled person Lisa had ever known, and almost always managed to keep his temper in check. But there was an undercurrent of violence in his nature that he himself rarely recognized, and she was afraid of what he might do when he knew for certain that Jerry had deliberately cheated him out of thousands of dollars.

Not that she felt sympathy of any kind for Jerry. It was her husband's peace of mind that was her greatest concern, and she was afraid that if he gave in to rage and laid hands on Jerry, he might never forgive himself.

But her own powers were limited. It would be wrong if she tried to intervene, and in a situation of this sort she realized that Jeremy would pay little heed to any advice she might offer him. As the head of his family, he had to make his own judgments and act accordingly, and it would be her place to support his decisions and actions.

Once again their rare ability to communicate their thoughts without speaking them aloud asserted itself, and Jeremy patted Lisa's hand. "No matter what we find, I just want to locate Lance, have the charges against him withdrawn, and straighten out our financial affairs. Even if Jerry has misbehaved, I don't intend to let myself forget that he's still my son. And I can't help but be convinced that—no matter what he may have done—there must be some logical explanation for it."

Lisa made no reply, her fears increasing. He was so clearheaded in most of his dealings, but he still had a blind spot in his view of Jerry, and her instinct told her that grave troubles loomed ahead. Their homecoming promised to be as grim as the thick banks of gray clouds overhead that threatened a stormy voyage.

Relations between Lance and Melanie changed drastically after he found her in Randy's embrace. She thought she had fooled him and believed there was no way for him to know about her affair with the mountain man who had paid for his transgressions with his life, and to an extent she was right. But Lance hadn't accepted her story that Randy had threatened to kill her if she refused his lovemaking. So his whole attitude toward her was altered.

Quietly, without creating an issue, he avoided sleeping with her. Melanie knew she was losing her hold over him, which had always been tenuous at best, so she did her utmost to charm him. She began to wear makeup again, and as the weather grew warmer, she dipped into her wardrobe for clothes that were inappropriate for daily life in a mountain cabin.

Nothing she did had any effect. Lance was pleasant to her and treated her with consideration, but he nevertheless made it plain that he did not intend to become intimate with her again.

He and his partners prepared their bales of furs for the long journey that lay ahead, and the death of Randy having changed the atmosphere, they advanced their planned date of departure. They had already accumulated so many pelts that a few more animal skins wouldn't increase their income appreciably.

Lance knew he had reached a major turning point in his life. He was completely at home in the Rocky Mountains, well able to survive and cope with any situation that might arise. But he had no idea whether he would ever see this part of the world again. Once he returned to South Carolina, he might be arrested and imprisoned, and there was even a chance he might be sentenced to death, although he believed that the attorneys he would hire would render that possibility remote.

There were too many clouds hanging over his head to enable him to remain at home. Since there was no way he could be reunited with Carrie, he had no desire to stay there. It would be too painful to live there and spend years thinking of what might have been.

Therefore he had no intention of bidding a permanent farewell to the Rockies. Circumstances, combined with a little luck, might enable him to return.

If he came, he would travel alone. Paul had indulged his desire for adventure, but his career as a physician made it necessary for him to return to Boston. Circumstances had separated Ponca from his tribe, but he wanted to return to his own people, and that desire had to be respected. A successful partnership was coming to an end.

As for Melanie, Lance was through with her. He had stumbled into a relationship with her because he had been shocked when he had encountered Carrie at the House on the Avenue in New Orleans. Thereafter Melanie had pursued him, taking every initiative, and he had given in to her desires, living with her because she had provided him with insulation from his own feelings.

Now, however, he was prepared to face ultimate realities. Never would he be reunited with Carrie, and he couldn't allow himself to go through life as an emotional cripple. He had to admit that no other woman could substitute for Carrie, no other woman could take her place.

Certainly he had used Melanie, but she had taken advantage of him, too, and by now they owed each other nothing. He was well aware of her desire to solidify their relationship and make it permanent, but he could not contemplate marriage to a girl who cheated on him. Marriage had to be based on total trust.

What was more, he was in no position to marry anyone. His future was too uncertain. And as he couldn't have Carrie, he wanted no one else.

Nevertheless, he still felt a sense of obligation to Melanie. In spite of her infidelity, he had lived with her, and he didn't want to be responsible for driving her back into the life of a courtesan. Therefore he intended to make her a cash gift that would enable her to reestablish her priorities and make a new life for herself.

What Lance failed to realize was that Melanie had no intention of falling in with his plans. She wanted him and she refused to relinquish him. Not only was he financially comfortable, but she felt confident he would overcome his difficulties and resume his place in the South Carolina aristocracy. Only a girl who had grown up on a small Virginia farm could appreciate what it would mean to marry Lance and live at the very top of the social and financial ladder.

On top of everything else, he was the only lover who had ever given her physical satisfaction. She would never find another man like him, and would be stupid to let him escape from her grasp.

Melanie bided her time until the plans to leave Secret Valley were far advanced. Then one day she saw her chance. Ponca was fishing in the lake, Paul had gone off into the forest to chop a last load of firewood, and when Lance returned to the cabin from the stable, where he had been arranging furs in bales, the girl was alone with him.

Seizing her opportunity, Melanie went to him, embraced him, and pressing close, kissed him.

Lance gently disengaged himself.

She looked up at him and pouted. "You just don't like me anymore."

"I do," he replied. "But we're heading in different directions."

"We could go in the same direction."

"I think we've already proved that wouldn't work out," he said.

"You're still upset because of the day you saw me with Randy." When she wished, Melanie could make herself look pathetically helpless. "I told you at the time—"

"I know what you told me, but that doesn't matter. And I wasn't jealous of Randy. I had to fight him when I caught him stealing, and he drew a knife. Even if Randy had never existed, the results would be the same. There are difficult days ahead for me, and the time is approaching when you and I must part."

"But why?" She sounded plaintive.

"The best reason, I reckon, is that we don't love each other," Lance said.

"Speak for yourself."

He shook his head. "You don't love me, either."

"How can you say that?"

"Because there was a girl who loved me, a long time ago, and I know the difference."

Melanie realized he meant Carrie, who was coming between them again, and never had she hated another woman so much.

Lance was conscious only of her stricken expression. "I'm not abandoning you," he said. "When we sell our furs I'm going to give you a fair share of what we make. That'll give you a nest egg so you can start a new life."

"Doing what?" she demanded.

He was nonplussed. "Anything you want. You could start a school, or buy property, or do any one of a hundred things."

"I could even open a bordello of my very own," she said bitterly.

Lance saw she was being sarcastic and didn't mean it, so he was relieved. Certainly he didn't want his conscience troubled by her return to the House on the Avenue or some other place like it, even though he realized he would have no control over her after they parted and that she would be free to do as she wished.

"I want no harm to come to you," he said. "Not in the wilderness or anywhere else. Even after we get back to civilization, it wouldn't be right for a girl as pretty as you

to travel alone. So I'm going to escort you all the way to
your family's home."

"I hate Virginia," Melanie cried, stamping her foot,
"and I loathe my family's farm. With a half-dozen of my
brothers and sisters still at home to do the chores, I doubt
if Ma and Pa even know that I'm gone!"

He saw she wasn't joking. "Then maybe I can help buy
you a business in Alexandria, say, or in Richmond. A nice
little inn, for instance, or a tavern."

Melanie began to weep.

The sight horrified him, and he felt paralyzed.

She saw through her tears that she was creating an effect at last, and she cried harder.

"I've told you every thought that comes to mind," he
said in exasperation. "What the devil do you want?"

"You!" Melanie threw herself at him.

Lance took her in his arms clumsily, hoping he could
calm her.

Her ruse was so effective it was easy for her to give in
to seeming hysteria.

The Lion of the Rockies had killed a puma, fought a
grizzly bear on equal terms, and won fight after fight with
fierce Indian warriors whom no other frontiersman had
been able to vanquish. But he was incapable of handling
this red-haired girl who weighed less than one hundred
and fifteen pounds.

She clung to him, her tears still flowing freely.

He patted her shoulder but was at a loss for words. He
suspected she was taking advantage of him, but that didn't
make his task any easier.

Melanie caught him slightly off balance and dragged
him with her down to the mat that she had woven in front
of the hearth. Again she pressed close to him, and her
tear-streaked face was close to his.

Before Lance quite realized what was happening, he
found himself kissing her.

The girl's arms tightened around his neck, and she
began to rub her supple body against his.

Now, reacting with the instincts of a vigorous male animal, he began to make love to her. Not until later would
he worry about the consequences.

Melanie responded instantly, and was so subtle, so

clever, that it didn't occur to Lance that she was actually
the aggressor.

She was no longer weeping, and in his confusion he was
grateful for that much.

She had won, Melanie told herself, and silently exulted.
As long as he still wanted her, she was able to control
him, and there was no way he was going to leave her.

Scott Emerson expected to return to Trelawney at noon
after spending several days in Charleston, but it was late
afternoon before he appeared.

Kai saw he was weary when he joined her in the
ground-floor parlor they used as their private sitting room,
but she merely poured him a small glass of sack and asked
no questions. If he wanted to discuss the problems he had
encountered in town, he would talk whenever he was
ready.

She didn't have long to wait. He sipped his drink, closed
his eyes for a moment as he leaned back in his easy chair,
and then sighed. "There's real hell to pay at Oakhurst
Manor," he said.

Kai was not surprised. "Now what?"

"Things are snowballing there. The sheriff came to me
with a letter from a Boston school inquiring about the
whereabouts of Cleo Beaufort. You remember the supposed slave girl Jerry had put to death for trying to kill
him? I suspect that may have been Cleo, although it will
be hard to prove."

His wife gasped. "How awful! Cleo was such a lovely
girl."

"That's just the beginning. Yesterday afternoon I was
called over to the bank. They know I represent Jeremy, of
course, and they wanted me to see some preliminary figures they're working up. They'll be sending him a full report when they pull everything together. To simplify as
much as I can, Oakhurst Manor is in serious financial
trouble."

"How could that happen?" Kai was bewildered.

"All too easily, I'm afraid." Scott's smile was thin.
"Jerry appears to have squandered the income that the
plantation has earned from the sale of cotton and tobacco.
Substantial sums came in, but they went out again. That

fellow Griffin appears to have died out West somewhere last year, so his gaming house in Charleston is closed down, but there are others in Savannah, and Jerry has been making quite a few trips there of late."

"He's losing the plantation's income at cards?" It was difficult for her to comprehend such folly.

"That's only the beginning. He's treated his slaves so badly that a number of them died, so he bought twenty-five new field hands at the Charleston market. But he hasn't paid for them, and even though he's a Beaufort, the slave dealers are planning to sue. He also bought several teams of horses and a dozen new wagons, but he owes for them, too. Among other things. The list of his debts is as long as my arm."

"But he must pay his debts!"

"After my last talk with him," Scott said, "I know only too well that he won't listen to me. Only one person can handle this situation. Jeremy. If it isn't too late."

"What do you mean?" Kai asked.

"Even Jeremy isn't made of money. I don't know what balances he keeps in his private accounts, but with Oakhurst Manor badly in debt and the finances of the shipping company in shambles, he'll need a fortune to straighten out his affairs. I'm not saying he'll go bankrupt, but he'll need a substantial loan. Or else he'll have to sell part of Oakhurst Manor."

Kai shook her head. "You know he'll never part with one square yard of that plantation!"

"He may not have any choice. The bank will write to him when the report is ready, and I'll attach a letter of my own."

"Shouldn't you write him immediately, dear?"

"No, he should see the whole picture, and another week or ten days won't make that much difference." Scott rose and went to the sideboard for more sack. "I feel so badly about all this, but I'm helpless. Jerry insists on doing things his own way, and he's ruining his father's properties. Not to mention destroying his own inheritance. And Lance's."

Before Kai could reply, a servant burst into the room. "Missy, come!" he shouted.

Scott's hand trembled so violently that he spilled sack on the rug.

Kai picked up her skirts and raced out to the portico, with her husband close behind her.

They stood together, scarcely breathing, and saw a large brass-studded carriage moving slowly up the driveway. Two men in livery were on the box, and several large leather clothes boxes were lashed to the roof.

Riding alone inside the carriage was an impeccably groomed young woman whose expert use of cosmetics indicated her worldliness. It was evident, even at a glance, that her attire was expensive, although her style was far more theatrical than that of the quiet plantation country.

Carolyn Emerson emerged from the carriage, and uncertain of her reception, stood for a long moment.

A weeping Kai extended her arms.

Carrie's facade was swept aside, and she cried, too, as she ran up the stairs and they kissed.

There were tears in Scott's eyes as he embraced the niece he regarded as a daughter. "Well . . ." was all he could say. "Well . . ."

Suddenly all three were talking at once, and not until they went inside to the little parlor did they begin to make sense.

"You didn't even let us know you were coming!" Kai said.

"I wasn't sure you'd want me," Carrie replied quietly.

"I can't imagine why we wouldn't," Scott said.

"Because you won't approve of the way I've lived." Carrie had no intention of discussing details, but she refused to dissemble.

"This has been your home since you were a baby," Kai said fiercely, "and it will be your home until you die!"

"Thank you, Mama Emerson." Carrie felt like weeping again.

Scott took in every detail of her sophisticated appearance. "You're married?"

"No, Uncle Scott. The only man in my life I could have or would have married, ever, was Lance." Later she would reveal that she had achieved financial independence. There were more important things to tell them first. "I saw

Lance early last autumn, by accident. We met out in the Minnesota country."

This was the first Kai had heard of her missing son, and for a moment she was on the verge of fainting.

"He's well, Mama, and he's made a wonderful new life for himself." Carrie went on to explain that Lance had become a hunter and trapper, and was known in the Rockies as the Lion. "He misses both of you. Very, very much. The only reason he hasn't been in touch with you is those insane charges against him. He refuses to compromise you."

Kai was so ecstatic, just knowing her son was alive and well, that she couldn't speak.

"Long ago," Scott said, "the charge that he assaulted you was rescinded. At my instigation."

"Thank God, because he didn't do it," Carrie replied fervently.

"Also," he went on, "there's evidence to suggest there was a conspiracy against him. The prosecutor in Charleston is working on it, and I've been helping him. We don't yet have conclusive proof, but we might be able to get confessions from some of the men involved if Lance could confront them in person. Do you know how to reach him, Carrie?"

"Not directly," she said, and thought of Pierre Gautier. "But I have a . . . a friend who sometimes makes his headquarters in New Orleans. I can write him to pass the word up and down the Mississippi, and one of these months, when Lance comes that far to sell his furs, he'll be given the message."

"Good. We'll try to be patient." Scott continued to study her, and the thought occurred to him that she bore a remarkable resemblance to her mother. Alicia had been sophisticated and svelte, too, when she had returned to South Carolina, bringing her baby with her.

There were other matters on Kai's mind. "You sound as though you still love Lance."

"I do, Mama," Carrie said.

"But he doesn't love you anymore?"

"He didn't say when we met. But I . . . I think he does."

"Then why didn't you get together and marry when you

saw each other out there in the wilderness?" Kai had the faculty of cutting to the heart of a matter.

"There were . . . complications," Carrie said, and realized she would have to explain further. "I wasn't traveling alone."

Kai tried not to show her feelings, but inadvertently stiffened.

Scott frowned, and continued to think how much Carrie resembled her mother. Alicia had been equally cosmopolitan, her eyes knowing, when she had returned from her travels at approximately the same age, and the mere possibility that history might be repeating itself gave him an eerie feeling. But there were serious differences, too, and he seized on them. Alicia had been withdrawn and surly, refusing to mention her affair with Emile Duchamp. Carrie, on the other hand, was being candid, making no secret of what obviously had been a hectic past.

"There was another reason, too," Carrie said. "Even if I had been alone, Lance wasn't. He had a girl with him. A very attractive girl whom I'd known in New Orleans."

"I can't imagine him preferring anyone to you, Carrie!" Kai exclaimed. "I don't care how attractive she is!"

Mama Emerson's loyalty was heartening, but Carrie didn't know how to explain that Melanie, having found the protector she wanted in Lance, wouldn't give him up without a struggle. Melanie's surface softness and ingenuousness appealed to men, but in spite of her youth she was tenacious and clever.

"Maybe I should have fought for him, and perhaps he felt the same way about me. But I had too much pride. False pride, I suppose. And I can't tell you how Lance may have felt, because we just talked for a short time and we didn't get that personal."

"Is he married to this girl?" Kai wanted to know.

Carrie shrugged. "He wasn't at the time I saw him, but that was many months ago."

"If we can ever get him home," Scott said, "perhaps you and Lance might patch up your differences."

The girl shook her head. "When an opportunity has been missed, it can't be recovered. There's no way to recapture the past."

"I don't agree!" Scott was emphatic.

"You don't understand, Uncle Scott. Lance is no longer a boy just starting out in life. He's done remarkable things in the mountains, and everyone in the West knows and respects the Lion. He's no ordinary person."

"Do you think of yourself as ordinary, dear?" Kai asked.

"Unfortunately, I'm not." A note of unconscious bitterness crept into Carrie's voice. "I'm not going to hurt you by dwelling on details, but I haven't lived the life of an angel since I left Trelawney. Let's just say that Lance wouldn't want to marry me, and neither would any other honorable man."

"You run yourself down too much," Scott said.

"No, Uncle Scott, I'm being practical. I've made my own way in the world, and I can live comfortably, without asking help from anyone."

His gaze was searching. "What do you want for yourself?"

"I don't know. I simply can't look ahead. More than anything I wanted to come home for a visit, and now I'm here. That's enough for the present. Eventually I'll have to make plans, but right now I can't even think of the future."

Scott had no intention of allowing her to drift, knowing she would return to the unsavory existence she had been leading. But it was premature to create an issue. He would give her time to relax, to settle into the routines of gracious ways that characterized life at Trelawney. Only then would he insist they have a blunt discussion of the future.

One thing was certain in his mind: under no circumstances would they lose her again or permit her to destroy herself. They loved her too much for that.

He and Kai accompanied her when Carrie went up to her old room to unpack her belongings, and neither commented when they saw the flamboyant clothes in her wardrobe. That attire told them more about her past than anything she might have said to them.

From the moment they had greeted her, Scott had been puzzled by a brooch she was wearing at the neckline of her low-cut gown. It was elliptical, an unusual shape, and one large diamond in the center was surrounded by a number of smaller diamonds. All at once he recognized it: his mother had owned an identical brooch, and had given it to Alicia on her eighteenth birthday. Surely there couldn't be two such brooches!

Trying to speak casually, he said, "You mentioned spending some time in New Orleans. The last we knew of your mother, she was living there. That was a number of years ago, to be sure. I wonder if you happened to meet her."

"I wasn't traveling in circles where I met ladies, Uncle Scott," Carrie replied.

A servant came to the door to announce that supper was ready, so he let the matter drop for the moment.

After the meal they adjourned to the parlor, and Kai referred for the first time to the incident that had sparked the girl's disappearance. "It just occurs to me that I should have put you in another room, Carrie," she said. "I don't want you to be upset—"

"I won't be, Mama Emerson. The memories of all the years I spent in that room more than make up for what I remember of one ghastly night."

"It may not be too late for the cause of justice to be served," Scott said. "Do you know who assaulted you?"

Carrie shook her head. "He was masked."

"So you said in your original testimony, and I assure you I've memorized every word of it. But if you have any idea who did it, I'll prosecute him if I have to follow him to hell."

"I've thought about it a great deal," Carrie said, "and the one definite conclusion I've reached is that he couldn't have been a stranger. He not only knew me, but he knew this house. He was thoroughly familiar with the fact that my bedroom windows opened onto the portico roof."

"That same thought has occurred to me," Scott replied. "Many times."

"I hate to say this," Carrie said, "because I have no proof. But I've often wondered if it was Jerry Beaufort."

Kai sighed and exchanged a significant glance with her husband. "Jerry again."

"I'll know when I see him," Carrie said, "because he had certain mannerisms that I haven't forgotten."

"Don't go over to Oakhurst Manor," Scott told her, and

explained in detail how the neighboring plantation had deteriorated during the absence of Jeremy and Lisa. "And there are unending new developments that make me uneasy. The latest is a request from the Boston police about the whereabouts of Cleo Beaufort, who supposedly was coming down here for a visit."

Carrie interjected that she had seen Paul at the rendezvous, and that he was now Lance's partner.

They pressed her for details, and then Scott told her what little he had gleaned about the slave girl who had been hanged at Oakhurst Manor. "I have the feeling, no more than a hunch, that the girl might have been Cleo. Who was no slave. But like everything else that involves Jerry, I can't verify my suspicions."

"The one important thing for you, Carrie," Kai said, "is that you stay away from Oakhurst Manor. The atmosphere there is unsavory at best these days. And if it was Jerry who assaulted you, a visit there could be dangerous for you."

"With Papa Beaufort and Lisa not there, and with Lance thousands of miles away," Carrie said firmly, "I wouldn't dream of going to Oakhurst Manor."

Scott was relieved by her decision to avoid Oakhurst Manor. In fact, although he had no intention of mentioning his arrangements to her or to Kai, he had already given arms to several of his most trusted servants and had instructed them to maintain a discreet guard over Carrie. When the news of her arrival at Trelawney spread, and perhaps the man who had attacked her learned she had come home, he might try to pay her another visit. It was best to be prepared for any eventuality.

For the moment he was still fascinated by the ellipticalshaped bar she was wearing on the front of her dress. "That's a lovely brooch," he said.

"Isn't it?" Carrie smiled.

"May I ask where you got it?"

"An admirer gave it to me."

Scott had no way of knowing that Carrie was telling him the literal truth, that she wasn't being reticent. She had never learned the identity of her "admirer."

He decided it was best not to mention that her grandmother and then her mother had owned that very brooch.

It would serve no useful purpose to rake up the painful past, and at least he was grateful that fate had intervened on her behalf and that a prized family heirloom was in her possession.

Carrie saw her uncle's expression, and almost blurted out the story of the box of jewelry she had received via a messenger. The fact that she had never found out the identity of the donor continued to pique her curiosity, but Uncle Scott and Mama Emerson wouldn't appreciate the strange tale, and she saw no reason to hurt them.

It was enough that she had acquired a fortune in gems and loved all of them. As she so often reminded herself, it did no good to dwell on the past.

16

---—••—◆▶▶—••—---

The Platte Valley of the Nebraska country was a vast
expanse of flatlands that extended along the route used by
hunters and trappers going to and from the Rocky Mountains. Waist-high grass extended toward the horizon in every direction, and the fur traders who occasionally visited
the few outposts in the region told a standing joke to the
effect that there were more buffalo than people in the area.
They were not exaggerating, and even the warriors of the
Omaha nation seldom ventured this far from their villages
on the banks of the Missouri River.

The trail across the flatlands was well-defined, however,
mountain men having been using it since 1824, and travelers from the West ultimately came to a tiny fort and trad-
ing post on the bank of the Missouri. First established by
the French in 1795, it had been fortified and somewhat
expanded during the War of 1812 by Manuel Lisa, the ex-
plorer. But its days were numbered, and not until the second half of the century would the city of Omaha be
founded a short distance to the south.

So few white men ventured into the Nebraska country
that the Indian tribes of the area regarded them as curiosi-
ties rather than threats, and the fort was rarely molested

by raiders or thieves. No sentry stood duty at the heavy wooden gate, and the inhabitants of the fort, most of them transients, lived there without fear. The only permanent residents were the co-owners of a small general store, one American and the other French, and two young couples who were carving farms out of the wilderness nearby.

During the summer and autumn a representative of John Jacob Astor's fur company spent most of his time at the fort, and he alone was interested in the little caravan that approached one day shortly before sundown. He had never met the Lion, but immediately guessed the identity of the blond, bearded giant wearing a puma-skin cape who rode in the lead. He confirmed his surmise when he saw the red-haired girl; everyone who dealt with mountain men knew that the Lion had broken tradition by taking a woman to the Rockies with him.

Only because Lance Beaufort was eager to move on to South Carolina and didn't want to take the extra time to go to New Orleans for the purpose of selling his furs was he willing to make a deal for the bales of skins that his pack mules were carrying.

As Astor's agent soon discovered, however, the Lion was a far more astute businessman than most hunters and trappers, and insisted on being paid a price only slightly lower than his merchandise would command in the New Orleans markets.

They spent an entire evening haggling, then resumed their talk the following morning. Lance held firm, and the agent, who wanted the prime furs, finally agreed to his price, taking the mules in the bargain. Lance took payment in cash, then rejoined his comrades, who were killing time outside the log fort.

"Here," he said, and spread out nine thousand dollars.

Melanie's eyes gleamed when she saw the money.

Lance and Paul pocketed their shares, both of them relieved that the transaction had been completed.

Ponca surprised them by rejecting his portion. "No need money," he said. "No want money. No use in land of Kiowa."

They tried to persuade him to change his mind, but he held firm. His nation's hunting grounds were located on the far side of the Missouri, and he intended to rejoin his people without delay. He had a rifle and ample ammunition, two wool blankets, a kettle, and a horse superior to that owned by any other Kiowa brave. By his own standards he was already wealthy, and he had no use for the white man's money.

"You my brothers," he said as he embraced Lance and Paul in turn. "Someday we meet again." Giving them no chance to protest further, he went off alone.

They watched him in silence as he swam his mount across the Missouri.

When he reached the far bank he raised an arm in farewell, then rode off at a canter.

Lance felt a sense of great loss.

Melanie shattered his mood when she said, "Imagine anyone refusing three thousand dollars."

Lance counted out half of the money that Ponca had left and thrust it into the girl's hand. "Here," he said, "take my part. I have enough for my own needs."

"So have I," Paul said, and insisted that the girl take the additional fifteen hundred dollars he had just received. "If I'm too rich I'll never get back to my medical practice. It's going to be hard enough as it is."

Melanie was overwhelmed. Never in her life had she handled more than a few hundred dollars at a time. Now, suddenly, she had been given a small fortune, a sum equal to what her father earned in five years on his farm.

Thanks to Ponca's generosity, the girl would have no financial problems for a long time to come, and Lance was secretly relieved. He would add to the sum before he parted company with her, but now it would be far easier for him to insist that they go their separate ways. Any debts he might owe her, moral or personal, were canceled, and there was no way she could insist on accompanying him when he went to South Carolina to initiate the fight to clear his name.

He had to admit that Melanie bewildered him. Only once had he been intimate with her since the day he found her with Randy, but in their day-to-day existence she continued to behave as though their relations were normal. Obviously he had underestimated her tenacity, but now the end was in sight.

They resumed their journey the following day, taking

passage on a barge that carried them across Missouri to St. Louis, which had doubled its population in a year. There, during a brief pause, they arranged to go by boat to Cincinnati.

Melanie insisted on sharing a cabin with Lance, and as soon as they went on board she transformed herself from a frontier dweller into a city girl. Other passengers gaped at her when she appeared in the little dining salon in full makeup and wearing one of her sophisticated New Orleans gowns. She took care, however, not to flirt with any of the merchants and traders who made up the company. Instead she played the role of the devoted wife to perfection; she was gambling for high stakes and would do nothing that might interfere with the achievement of her goal.

Cincinnati was the fastest-growing town on the Ohio River, and boasted a number of universities, hospitals, and concert halls as well as inns of a quality found only on the Atlantic seaboard. It was the gateway to the South, however, with slavery practiced across the Ohio in Kentucky, so Paul had no intention of tarrying any longer than necessary.

After an overnight stay at an inn, he bought a place on a stagecoach that would take him to New York, en route to Boston, and then he said good-bye to his companions. "I wish you the best of luck in whatever you undertake," he told Melanie. "I'm sure you'll succeed in whatever you do because you have the will."

Lance wrung his hand, and was speechless.

"You and I will keep in touch with each other," Paul said. "Our experience together has been the greatest of my life, and I can practice my own profession now with a clear mind. Thanks in good part to you. I'm not going to South Carolina—for obvious reasons—but after you've cleared up your problems there, I hope you'll visit me in Boston."

"I will," Lance said. "I hope your sister is well. Give her my love."

Both mountain men became emotional, their voices growing husky, so they did not prolong their farewells. The years they had spent together in the Rockies, sharing dangers and hardships, had forged indissoluble bonds between them. And when they parted, Lance thought that Paul, far more than Jerry, was truly his brother.

The next day Lance and Melanie resumed their own journey on horseback, with the girl's belongings loaded on a pack mule that Lance bought for her in Cincinnati. They rode southeast through Kentucky toward the Cumberland Mountains, which they would cross into Virginia, and the girl appeared to have given in to Lance's plans for her.

He learned otherwise, however, when they stopped for a night in the town of Lexington, in the bluegrass country. Their mounts had been stabled for the night, and after they ate supper in a tavern adjacent to their inn they retired to their quarters for the night. It was then that Melanie opened her barrage.

"We should stay here for an extra day," she said, "so you can buy some new clothes for yourself."

Lance looked at her blankly.

"You seem to have forgotten that we're back in the civilized world again. I try to look the part, but people stare at you in those buckskins."

"I'm a mountain man," he said gruffly.

"You were," Melanie replied, "but you're about to resume your place as a South Carolina gentleman."

"That remains to be seen."

"I think both of us should look our best when we reach Oakhurst Manor," she said, speaking casually.

Now he understood, and shook his head. "I'm dropping you off at your father's farm," he told her.

"You can't get rid of me that easily." Melanie faced him defiantly.

"We have no real future together. Surely you know it as well as I do."

"I don't know any such thing."

"I don't know what may happen when I get home," Lance said. "I may be thrown into jail in Charleston. Or I might even be hanged by a posse."

"Never," Melanie said, and smiled. "You're indestructible. I'm sure you'll win every battle against your enemies, and I'm going to celebrate your victory with you."

"I don't want to hurt your feelings," Lance said, "but you and I are coming to the end of our road together.

You joined me—without my advance knowledge—when I sailed from New Orleans up to the rendezvous. Then you insisted on coming out to the mountains with me. I won't deny that I was attracted to you. Any man would be because you're an exceptionally pretty girl. But the winter we spent together in the Rockies should have proved to you, as it proved to me, that we have no real future together."

"I say we do!"

"I bore you, Melanie, even though you won't admit it to yourself. Eventually you'll find someone else who interests you more than I do, and you'll go off with him."

"That's just a guess. You don't know it will happen."

"Let's say I don't want to take that chance. We've lived together for almost a year, and we enjoyed ourselves most of that time. Now you have enough money to be independent, so let's part as friends, with good grace and good feeling on both sides."

"For a long time now," Melanie said, "I've planned to become Mrs. Lance Beaufort. Nothing is going to change my plan."

She had backed him into a corner, so he had to be blunt. "I'm sorry," he said, "but I have no intention of marrying you. Or anyone else. And that's final."

She couldn't help taunting him. "You'd marry Carrie in a minute, if you could!"

Lance refused to rise to the bait, and kept his tongue under control. "My relationship with Carrie ended permanently long before you came into my life. I reckon she's traipsing around the country somewhere with Bateaux Gautier, and may even be married to him by now. But even if she isn't, there's no way she and I could ever get together again. What she and I had is dead, and was killed by both of us. So our problem has no connection with her."

Melanie's expression indicated that she didn't believe a word of what he was telling her.

"You have enough money now to bring a handsome dowry into a good marriage. Take advantage of your situation to settle down with a solid man and raise a family. Live up to your potential, which is enormous."

"Only with you," she said, and went to him.

Lance was embarrassed and backed away from her.

Smiling steadily, her eyes provocative and her mouth enticing, she slid her arms around his neck.

Lance was well aware of the trap she was trying to set for him. In the past she had used her sex appeal to snare him, and now she was using the same tactics. If he succumbed to his male desires, there would be no escape from her.

He caught hold of her wrists and forced her arms to her sides. "Enough!" he commanded. "If I must, I'll engage separate rooms for us from now on. Or else I'll leave you here and let you make your way back to Virginia by yourself. Just get it into your head that you and I are finished, and there's no way we're going on together. I've felt obligated to see you to your family's home, but I'll expect you to behave yourself for the rest of the journey."

Melanie subsided, her surface attitude one of meek submission to his will that she was far from feeling. She had just lost a battle, but a long campaign still stretched ahead, and she intended to win it. Knowing him as she did, she was sure he would settle his troubles in South Carolina, and she had every intention of becoming the legal mistress of a vast and wealthy plantation.

It was true enough that she had sufficient funds to provide her with an attractive dowry, but she didn't intend to hand that money over to some Virginia farmer. Once she was Lance's wife and took her place among the Beauforts of Oakhurst Manor, she would be able to spend every penny on herself. Along with far greater amounts that her husband would give her.

"I'll do what you say," she murmured, "because you give me no choice."

Lance was satisfied, but it was fortunate he didn't see the determined, calculating expression in the girl's seemingly innocent green eyes.

Jeremy and Lisa Beaufort traveled to South Carolina without delay after spending several days in Washington City. There Jeremy had turned over the business of the American legation in Vienna to Secretary of State Van Buren, and had been gratified to learn that his brother would succeed him as minister. President Jackson had thanked Jeremy for the services he had rendered under trying circumstances, and had expressed the hope that the day might come when he could reciprocate.

So Jeremy was in high spirits on the journey in spite of his apprehensions. Perhaps his affairs weren't as muddled as Scott Emerson had indicated, and he clung to the thought that there would be a simple explanation for Jerry's activities, which Scott's reports so sharply contradicted.

Riding in a hired carriage, they traveled at a steady pace without exhausting themselves, and when they reached Charleston they drove straight to their town house. There the first shocks awaited them.

None of the servants they had left at the house were on duty there any longer, and had been replaced by slovenly newcomers who took no pride in their work. Even more disturbing, however, was the appearance of several rooms. Major items of furniture had been removed, as had valuable bric-a-brac, silver, and a set of exquisite dishes that had belonged to Jeremy's grandmother. Members of the household staff could offer no explanation for their disappearance. Mr. Jerry did what he pleased with the property, they said, and it was apparent that no one dared to question him.

Leaving Lisa to restore some semblance of order at the house, Jeremy went to the offices of his shipping company, and after he had spent several hours with his senior employees a number of facts were plain. Close to twenty thousand dollars was missing. The flagship of the Beaufort fleet, the merchantman *Elizabeth*, which had been Jeremy's pride, had been sold to a New England company, but Jerry had kept the money and had not deposited it in the shipping corporation's accounts.

Overall, the Beaufort shipping company was having a hard time making ends meet, and a firm hand was needed at the helm to restore it to its former place.

Heartsick and worried, Jeremy went to Scott Emerson's office.

His surprised friend was delighted to see him, but made no attempt to hide his own concern. They went together to the bank that had handled the major Beaufort accounts for two generations, and there Jeremy discovered that

Oakhurst Manor was in trouble, too. The plantation's income had dropped alarmingly, and a number of large bills had remained unpaid. It was obvious that Jeremy would have a long, difficult struggle ahead to straighten out his affairs.

Scott accompanied him to the town house for supper, and with Lisa participating in the discussion they talked far into the night. The only good news was that Carrie had come home, at least for a visit, and had revealed that Lance was alive and well in the West.

"I haven't yet been able to have the murder charges against him dropped," Scott said. "We'll need his own testimony for that, and maybe we can prove there was an active conspiracy against him. The state is sympathetic, and Lance certainly won't be prosecuted until he has a chance to tell his own story."

"I'll write to him," Jeremy said, "and then I'll make several copies of the letter. I'll hire messengers who can go out to the mountains to search for him, and if one of them can find him, I hope he'll come home."

Lisa agreed the idea made sense.

"Before I do anything else," Jeremy said grimly, "I've got to have a session with Jerry and find out what the devil he's been doing. And why."

"I have reason to believe he's lost large amounts of money at cards. First at a place here that closed after the owner died rather mysteriously on a trip out West, and more recently in Savannah."

"I wish you'd come with me when I drive straight to Oakhurst Manor tomorrow morning to confront him, Scott. I want to place on the table every fact that both of us can muster."

"Let's not be premature," the lawyer replied. "Come first to Trelawney, where we can organize our figures."

"I like that idea better," Lisa said. "Besides, we'll have the chance to see Carrie before we subject ourselves to the unpleasantness of a confrontation with Jerry."

After they discussed the matter at length, Jeremy was persuaded it was wiser to marshal his facts before facing his elder son.

Neither he nor Lisa slept well, and they left with Scott soon after sunrise, arriving at Trelawney in time for a breakfast reunion with Kai and Carrie. Ultimately, after the initial euphoria wore off, Carrie was persuaded to repeat her belief that it had been Jerry who had assaulted her.

Lisa was not surprised, but withheld comment.

Jeremy was white-lipped. "It appears that Jerry has a great deal to explain," he said.

"There's still more," Scott told him reluctantly, and repeated all he had heard about the slave girl who had been hanged at Oakhurst Manor.

Lisa was horrified. "Do you really think it could have been Cleo? She wasn't a slave!"

"If Jerry held her captive—and there's no doubt that some black girl was his prisoner—no one would have been in a position to deny that she was a slave," the lawyer explained.

"If all these charges are true," Jeremy said, "and I must admit that the financial mess he created is real enough, Jerry has lost his senses."

"I don't want to hurt you, Papa Beaufort," Carrie said bluntly, "but I don't think you've ever seen Jerry as he is."

Lisa nodded in agreement.

"He can be dangerous when he's crossed," she continued. "He was always afraid of you, and after we grew up he minded his manners in front of Lance, too. But nobody else could handle him."

"Well, he'll have his wings clipped today," Jeremy said.

"Not until we have a full and accurate list of figures to show him," Scott said, and took his friend off to his study to prepare the specific financial charges.

The women remained at the table, but Kai soon excused herself so she could organize her household staff for the day.

Carrie poured more coffee for Lisa and herself.

The older woman studied her intently. "Scott indicated to us last night that you aren't planning to stay here permanently."

"It wouldn't be right."

"Where will you go, Carrie?"

"I haven't decided."

"Suppose Lance comes home—without this girl who has

been living with him in the mountains. Would you marry him?"

Carrie flushed. "That would be impossible!"

"Even if he wanted to marry you?"

"He wouldn't!"

Lisa smiled faintly, her tone compassionate as she said, "You don't think you could be any man's wife."

"What makes you say that?" The girl was defensive.

"I gather you've been discreet in discussing your past with Scott and Kai," Lisa said, speaking quietly, "and I approve. It accomplishes nothing to hurt people who would find it difficult to understand. But that doesn't alter the fact that you spent several years living as a courtesan."

Carrie was too proud to deny the truth, and merely shrugged.

"In a world that's controlled by men," Lisa said, "an attractive woman does what she must in order to survive."

The girl's eyes widened.

"You take money in return for what they demand from you—and take from you by force when you won't give it to them voluntarily."

It was astonishing that a great lady could grasp the principles so completely. "How could you tell about me?" Carrie asked.

"Because, my dear, I was a courtesan myself when I was your age." Lisa spoke matter-of-factly.

"You?"

"I met Jeremy at the house where I worked in the West Indies. Before he married Sarah, and long before I became the wife of a British nobleman."

Carrie was so surprised she was speechless.

"We fell in love at first sight, and neither of us ever recovered," Lisa said. "Sarah knew long before she died, and forgave us. My first husband—who realized that I never loved him—guessed it, too. I was miserable for years, and so was Jeremy."

"Why are you telling me all this?" the girl demanded. "I never guessed any of it in all the years I was growing up."

Lisa chose to reply indirectly. "It was a miracle that brought Jeremy and me together, and we've been happy—as we knew we'd be—from that day to this. But miracles don't occur very often."

The clear green eyes that bored into Carrie made her uncomfortable, and she averted her gaze. "There have been no miracles in my life," she said, "and I don't expect any."

"Precisely. What I'm trying to tell you, my dear, is that you must create your own."

The girl's laugh was bitter.

"You feel unclean," Lisa said, "unworthy of marriage because men have bought your body I know the feeling well. I lived with it myself for a long time."

Carrie surprised herself by wanting to weep.

"What you forget is that nobody has bought your spirit. Nobody has bought your mind. Nobody has bought your soul. You've gained sexual experience, but that doesn't mean you've built a fence around yourself. It doesn't exclude you from the right to happiness in marriage to the right man."

"Why are you torturing me, Aunt Lisa?"

"You still love Lance, and I defy you to deny it!" Lisa's challenge was deliberate.

"If I do," Carrie replied slowly, "then I'm stupid, and I deserve to be miserable."

"I knew Lance loved you long before he realized it himself. Lance is like his father, Carrie, and I know Jeremy far better than he knows himself. Lance gave his heart to one woman, and his feelings will never change. He'll love you—and only you—as long as he lives."

The tears came suddenly, in a rush.

Lisa gave her a handkerchief and remained silent, giving the girl time to compose herself.

Carrie dabbed at her eyes. "You understand my private hell," she murmured.

"You make your own hell," Lisa said, her attitude no longer sympathetic.

Carrie was startled.

"You feel it would be unfair to Lance to become his wife and bear his children. Just because you've known other men. Have you ever yearned for even one of those men? No. Has one of them caused you a sleepless night? No. Have you ever said to yourself that you'd be proud and happy to be married to this one or that one? No."

Carrie listened because her only alternative was that of

leaping from the table and running out of the room, and she couldn't be that discourteous to Aunt Lisa.

"Your mistake, my dear," the older woman went on, "is that you're indulging in the one luxury a girl in your position can't afford. You're wallowing in self-pity, telling yourself you're no longer good enough for Lance."

"That's true."

"It's rubbish. Jeremy and I have rarely been happier than we were on the day you and Lance told us you wanted to be married. Nothing you've done from that day to this changes our opinions of you."

Carrie tried to interrupt.

But Lisa silenced her with a curt gesture. "I know what you're going to say. That what we think or want doesn't matter. That only Lance's desires are important."

"Exactly!" Carrie knew she had been goaded, but nevertheless rose to the bait. "Because of your background, you and Papa Beaufort may be more generous and liberal than most parents. But that doesn't mean Lance would want to marry a whore!"

"I suggest you exercise patience until Lance comes home," Lisa said, "and then let him make that decision for himself."

They rode in silence down the narrow dirt lane that seemed to meander aimlessly through the hills of Virginia. On both sides of the road were fields of tobacco and vegetables, and occasionally they passed a neat farmhouse of red brick, its outbuildings invariably including a small smokehouse. This was the land that had produced four of America's seven Presidents: George Washington, Thomas Jefferson, James Madison, and James Monroe. There were large plantations here, to be sure, but most of the state's citizens were small sturdy farmers, proud of their freedom and ability to wrest a living from the soil, devoted to the principles that had produced the Declaration of Independence and the Constitution of the United States from that same soil.

Melanie, riding her mare sidesaddle, was in the lead, elegant and chic, looking as though she had come from another world. But she knew which way to turn at every crossroad, and was so familiar with her surroundings that she took them for granted and ignored them. Her air was disdainful, indicating a belief that she no longer belonged here, and it was true that she bore little or no resemblance to the women in calico they saw feeding pigs and chickens or working in gardens. This had been her world, but she had severed her roots.

After riding for several hours, they came to an unmarked crossroad similar to several others they had passed, and Melanie drew to a halt, then dismounted.

Lance jumped to the ground and joined her, while Bantu happily munched on a patch of clover.

"I don't want you to come any farther," Melanie said. "Ma and Pa live only a half-mile from here, so I'm safe enough now."

"You don't want me to meet your family?"

Her red curls danced as she shook her head. "Ma would pester me with questions for a month, and Pa would get even nastier than usual. You wouldn't think much of them, either, so it's best to leave well enough alone."

Lance was forced to submit to her wishes.

"This is your last chance to change your mind and take me with you," Melanie said.

"It's best for both of us that we part," he told her, and handed her a leather pouch. "Here's an extra thousand dollars you can add to Ponca's share of the fur money."

She was quick to take the purse, and smiled when she found it gratifyingly heavy. Only then did she say, "You can't buy me off, Lance."

"It didn't cross my mind that I could," he replied. "I've just tried to help provide for your future, and I wish you well."

"Not here." Melanie's distaste was plain as she glanced at the fields beyond the four corners of the crossroad. "Even the weeds haven't changed since I last saw them. Life here is the same as it was in my grandfather's time."

"That sounds pretty good to me." Lance refrained from saying that Melanie needed a stabilizing influence in her life and that the land of her birth could provide it.

"I'm not saying good-bye to you," she told him, "because you and I are going to see a great deal of each other in the future."

He tried to be polite. "It may be that our paths will cross again." He had been generous and considerate in his relations with this girl who had thrown herself at him, and he owed her nothing, but he was making an effort to observe the amenities.

"Oh, we'll meet," Melanie said. "You can depend on it."

She reached up to him and kissed him, clinging to him for a long moment. Then she turned away abruptly, and not looking at him again, mounted her mare and rode off, holding on to the reins of her heavily laden pack mule.

Lance watched her as she moved down the road, a cloud of dust eventually hiding her from sight.

Then he returned to his stallion, and Bantu needed no urging as they started off toward the south.

A chapter in Lance's life had come to an end, and he was not sorry to see the last of Melanie. He couldn't and didn't blame her for tricking him into allowing her to accompany him all through these past months. He was a man, responsible for his own destiny, and his physical appetites had caused him to give in to her. But he had more than repaid any obligation he might have owed her, and he was relieved to put their relationship behind him. How she worked out her life was not his concern or responsibility.

Now he had his own future to fulfill in South Carolina. He would see his mother and his father, and would stay long enough to clear his name. Then, with his honor restored, he would be free to do as he pleased.

Papa well might want him to stay, perhaps to return to the family shipping business in which he had made such a promising start. Well, he couldn't do it, any more than he could take up permanent residence again at Oakhurst Manor. Sometimes he still dreamed of the place, but it was no longer his home.

Facing reality, that he had no home other than the vast reaches of the Rockies, he had made a new career for himself, a new life: he was a mountain man who would roam for the rest of his days through an endless rugged wilderness.

Life would have been different, perhaps, had it been

possible for him to get together with Carrie. But circumstances had forced them apart, then kept them apart, and as a pragmatist he knew better than to wish away his life yearning for what could not be.

17

---••—◆—••---

"If you don't mind postponing dinner for an hour or two, Kai," Jeremy said, "I'd rather wait until Scott and I have seen Jerry and heard what he has to offer in the way of excuses."

"Of course." Kai Emerson knew he had no appetite.

Jeremy was pale, obviously shaken, and dreading his confrontation with his elder son, and Lisa wanted to cradle him in her arms and comfort him. But he had a man's duty to perform, so she kissed him briefly and smiled at him as he and Scott left Trelawney.

The two old friends cantered across the fields and soon reached Oakhurst Manor, their arrival unannounced.

This was Jeremy's home, the plantation he had inherited from his own hardworking father, a property he loved almost as much as he loved his wife, and his heart pounded as he caught his first glimpse of the familiar, handsome manor house. He had been born here, as had his father before him, and he felt a sudden surge of pride.

On the surface, at least, little was changed. Oh, the portico and Greek columns were a trifle shabby and could use a coat of white paint, just as the brick front needed point-

ing, the thick coat of grass that covered the front lawn
was too long, and Lisa's flowerbeds that had surrounded
the house were choked with weeds. But these were minor
faults, easily remedied. Oakhurst Manor itself was a sturdy
rock and stood intact.

A groom Jeremy had never seen took their horses.

The master of the plantation had no intention of having
himself announced, and opened the front door, acting as
though he had never been away.

As he and Scott walked together into the reception hall,
the majordomo appeared, his swollen face indicating he
had recently suffered a beating. The man had been a minor functionary on the household staff before Jeremy had
gone off to Europe.

Recognizing him immediately, Jeremy extended a hand.
"How are you, Simon?" he asked pleasantly.

The majordomo, obviously terrified, shrank from him.

An investigation of his strange conduct could wait until
later. "Where's Mr. Jerry?"

The man pointed toward the second floor, then hastily
fled toward the rear of the house.

Jeremy exchanged a glance with Scott Emerson,
shrugged, and started toward the broad staircase.

They mounted it together in silence, and with one accord headed toward the master suite. The sitting-room
door was open, and Jeremy did not bother to knock.

Jerry, in need of a shave and his collar undone, was
sprawled in an easy chair, a glass in his hand.

Two other men, both fairly young and hard-faced, were
with him, and they, too, were drinking.

"I hope I'm not interrupting you, gentlemen," Jeremy
said, and turned to his son.

Jerry leaped to his feet. "Papa! I didn't know you were
home. I thought you were still in Vienna!"

"Lisa and I have just arrived." Jeremy extended his
hand.

His son neither shook his hand nor embraced him, but
instead stared first at him, then at Scott. "Why is Uncle
Scott here with you?"

"I don't know any reason my oldest friend and my attorney shouldn't come to my own house with me." Jeremy
managed to speak calmly, as he always did when situa-

tions became unpleasant. "Aren't you going to present your friends?"

"They're from Savannah," Jerry muttered, and waved the pair into the corridor. "Wait out there," he told them.

"You don't seem very happy to see me," Jeremy said as he and Scott seated themselves.

His son took a long swallow of his drink, then rubbed the stubble on his chin. "I . . . I'm surprised. It never occurred to me you'd show up out of the blue like this instead of writing that you were coming home, Papa."

"I preferred to arrive unannounced," Jeremy said. "For the simple reason that affairs here seem to be chaotic."

"Don't believe everything Uncle Scott tells you. He's after my scalp these days. For whatever his reasons." Jerry's eyes darted from one to the other.

"Perhaps he has good reason," his father said. "And rather than take any one person's word—for anything—I always make my own investigations. Which I've now done. I spent the better part of yesterday in Charleston. At the shipping company, and then at the bank."

"Are you trying to trick me, too?" Jerry's voice rose.

"Certainly not, but I hope I haven't been tricked and swindled," Jeremy said. "I hope you'll be able to explain why the shipping company is short almost twenty thousand dollars, and not only why the *Elizabeth* was sold without my permission, but also why the proceeds of that sale have disappeared. And why Oakhurst Manor, one of the most profitable plantations in the state, should be in financial difficulty."

"I've been in charge, and I've handled affairs as I've seen fit." Jerry was becoming surly.

Jeremy nodded to his friend.

Scott produced several sheets of paper from a pocket of his swallow-tailed coat. "It will save time and be less wearing on everyone if we deal in specifics," he said. "I suggest you look at this list, Jerry, so you can go over it item by item with your father."

To their astonishment, Jerry leaped to his feet and knocked the papers to the floor, scattering them. "I refuse to be badgered by anybody!" he shouted. "Maybe you think you're clever, conspiring against me and trying to back me into a corner, but it won't work!"

Staring at him, Jeremy knew his worst fears were realized: his elder son and heir was insane. "Sit down, Jerry," he said. "Making a scene accomplishes nothing constructive. I must find out what has happened to a very large sum of money that belongs to me."

Jerry hurried to a small table that stood in the far corner, opened a drawer, and then turned suddenly. He held a pistol in each hand, and cocked them grimly. "You've interfered with me for the last time!" he screamed. "You should have died in the fire in this very suite, but that damn Lance interfered, and I had to take care of him, too! This time there won't be any mistakes!"

Jeremy's blood ran cold. He had faced danger many times in an active life, and ordinarily would have tried to knock the pistols from his son's hands. But the knowledge that Jerry deliberately had tried to murder him and Lisa, and in some way was responsible for Lance's difficulties, too, momentarily paralyzed him.

Jerry called to his friends from Savannah.

They came into the room at once, each holding a double-edged knife. "You want us to fix them?" one of them asked.

"Not yet," Jerry said. "Their women will start asking too many questions, and that could cause complications. They must be over at Trelawney, so we'll get them over here, too, and dispose of all of them at once. Tie up these two and lock them in the bedroom yonder."

"My God," Jeremy whispered.

Scott was equally horrified.

Neither could offer resistance as they were bound, carried into the master bedroom, and thrown onto the floor.

"He's insane," Scott said as the door was closed and locked. "He's not only going to murder us, but he's going to trick Kai and Lisa into coming here so he can kill them, too. He was responsible for the fire. In some way he was responsible for Lance's troubles. And I'm certain now it was he who attacked Carrie—and had poor little Cleo hanged. The truth is worse than my suspicions about him."

Jeremy tried to concentrate on their immediate situation. "Those young thugs know how to handle ropes," he said. "It will take hours to loosen these bonds, and by then it will be too late."

"We're outnumbered, and they have all the weapons."
Scott laughed savagely, helplessly. "To think we were stupid enough to come here unarmed."

"A man doesn't think he's going to be made a prisoner in his own home by his own son." Jeremy was trying in vain to free himself from the ropes that bound his wrists behind his back.

"We can't let him trick Kai and Lisa into coming over here," Scott said. "There must be some way to stop him."

"Do you have any practical suggestions?" Jeremy's smile was wry.

"No, damn it." Scott was silent for a moment, then lowered his voice. "I doubt if he's learned that Carrie has come home, so she may be safe. But God help her if she falls into his hands, too."

Jeremy continued to work patiently as he attempted to loosen his bonds.

"Perhaps we can bargain with him," Scott said.

"No!" Jeremy was adamant. "I wouldn't trust him to keep any agreement he might make."

"Then he'll murder all of us. You saw his eyes. I'm sure he intends to go through with this insanity."

"We're not dead yet," Jeremy told him. "So don't panic, Scott. If we keep our heads, we may be able to find some way out."

"You're the man of action. What can we possibly do?"

"I have no idea. Yet."

Scott's groan was one of angry frustration rather than fear.

"If necessary," Jeremy said, "we can die with dignity. I was born in this room. Jerry was born in this room. So I suppose it's a fitting irony that I die here—at his hand."

Bantu seemed to sense that the long journey was coming to an end and moved steadily at a slow canter, never tiring, his hooves beating rhythmically on the dirt roads that led to Oakhurst Manor. Lance gave the great stallion his head, and together they shared a sense of growing excitement. This was the land they had known and loved all of their lives. This was home.

Even the problems that Lance knew he faced in the immediate future were less important, at least for the moment. He had problems with the law, but somehow he would overcome them. His mother would be hurt by his long silence, and he had no clear idea how his father would react when they met, but he hoped he could persuade them he had been given no choice, and that for their sakes he had refused to compromise them.

Only the emptiness that was always a part of him remained, and for that there was no cure. He had dreaded a return to South Carolina because everything he saw would remind him of Carrie. So it did. There was the plantation to which he had escorted her when they had attended their first formal ball. There was the pond that had been one of their favorite picnic sites. And ahead, only a few miles down the road, was the church where they would have worshiped together for the rest of their lives had not fate interfered and decreed that they follow separate, strange destinies.

Suddenly Bantu threw back his head for a moment, then lowered it again and broke into a full gallop. Lance patted him, leaned forward in the saddle, and allowed the stallion to set his own pace. The horse knew only that he was going home, and the man allowed himself to share that sense of exuberance. In spite of his troubles, the Lion of the Rocky Mountains rejoiced.

When two hours had passed and Jeremy and Scott had not yet returned to Trelawney, Kai began to fret. "Their meeting shouldn't be taking this long," she said.

Lisa, her faith in Jeremy unbounded, tried to soothe her. "Jerry has a great deal of explaining to do, and you can be sure his father is tolerating no nonsense from him. Not anymore."

They were interrupted by Carrie, who came into the parlor carrying a folded square of sealed parchment. "A messenger just brought this from Oakhurst Manor," she said, a puzzled expression on her face.

On the outside, in Jerry's scrawled hand, was written: "To the ladies of Trelawney."

"Open it, dear," Kai told her.

Carrie broke the seal, and they read the brief communication: *"Our discussions have reached a stage that makes it necessary for you to join us. Please come at once. Jerry Beaufort.*"

Lisa stood, and Kai said, "I'll order the carriage."

"Wait," Carrie told them, and examined the note. "I don't like this."

The older women looked at her in surprise.

"This is odd," she continued. "I can't imagine why any of us would be needed at this meeting. And if we were wanted, it would be more natural if Papa Beaufort sent for us. Or Uncle Scott. Certainly not Jerry."

"I see what you mean," Lisa said. "I can't imagine what may lie behind all this, but you could be right."

Carrie weighed the matter for a moment, then made up her mind. "There's no call for all of us to go to Oakhurst Manor until we find out what this is all about. Let me go alone, and if you're really needed, I'll either come back here for you myself or I'll send you a note."

"But what could make all these precautions necessary?" Kai asked.

"I have no idea," Carrie told her, "but I don't trust Jerry—in anything."

"Neither do I," Lisa said.

Kai sighed. "I think this is all rather silly, but I'll do it your way. After all, we can always ride over there in a few minutes."

Carrie went upstairs to her room for her purse and a lightweight shawl. Then, acting on a sudden impulse that she made no attempt to analyze, she opened a dresser drawer and removed a tiny knife with an inlaid mother-of-pearl handle, its blade only two inches long. Bateaux Gautier had given it to her after their first meeting, and Carrie had regarded it as something of a souvenir. Now, however, her uneasiness over Jerry's possible motives caused her to feel she should be prepared for any contingency that might arise. Perhaps she was being foolish, but she felt somewhat better after she slipped the knife inside her neckline. At the very least it gave her a greater sense of security.

As she left the house she paused for a final word in the parlor. "Lock the doors, keep them locked, and don't let anyone in," she said. "And if I haven't returned in an hour, send word to the sheriff."

Kai was badly upset. "Things can't be as bad as you imagine," she said.

"I'm not imagining anything," Carrie said, "but I'm taking no chances, either."

One of the grooms brought a horse for her, and she rode the short distance to Oakhurst Manor, doing her best to remain calm. Her feeling of uneasiness persisted, in spite of her attempts to overcome it, and she told herself she was being ridiculous. Papa Beaufort was a former commodore in the United States Navy, well able to take care of himself after fighting in a score of battles. And Uncle Scott was a resourceful, vigorous man. Surely nothing untoward could have happened to them.

The sun was setting as she approached Oakhurst Manor, turning the white portico and columns a glowing shade of pink. For a moment Carrie couldn't help wishing the calendar could be turned back to the days when she and Lance had been young, innocent, and confident of their future together.

The majordomo admitted her, hurried up the stairs, and returned a moment later, beckoning.

Carrie felt a twinge of misgiving as she made her way to the master-bedroom suite. By rights the meeting should be taking place in the library or one of the parlors.

As she entered the sitting room she found herself staring into the muzzle of Jerry's pistol.

"Welcome home," he said with a broad grin as he ushered her into the bedroom.

Papa Beaufort and Uncle Scott were stretched out on the floor, their wrists and ankles bound. Standing guard over them were two flashily dressed men, both armed with knives, and they reminded Carrie of the cheap gamblers in New Orleans who had sometimes visited the House on the Avenue after enjoying a lucky evening at cards.

"I didn't even know you were back," Jerry said to her, "but I'm delighted you accepted my invitation. Where are the others?"

In spite of the sense of dread that filled Carrie, she recovered her aplomb sufficiently to remain silent.

"He's mad," Jeremy told her. "He intends to kill all of us."

"Not quite yet," Jerry said, and laughed. "First I want

your wives here to share in the festivities with you. I want no repercussions later from widows, so I prefer to dispose of the sluts at the same time I get rid of you."

If Scott had been able to break his bonds, he would have leaped at Jerry's throat.

Jeremy merely looked at his son, his expression compounded of disgust and sorrow.

Jerry raised a hand to his face, as though brushing away an insect.

That gesture was engraved on Carrie's mind, and she gasped. "He's the one who attacked me!" she cried.

Jerry's eyes glittered as he turned back to her. "You didn't know it all along? You disappoint me, just as you disappointed me that night. By now you must have more experience, though, so I'll bet you're livelier." He turned to the taller of the pair from Savannah. "You want her? Take her, and we'll all watch!"

The man jammed his knife in his belt and advanced slowly toward Carrie, flexing his hands.

"Stay away from me!" she cried, and screamed at the top of her voice.

The long driveway, lined with graceful trees, looked just as it had in Lance's dreams, and he slowed the prancing Bantu to a walk so he could savor this moment. It was dusk, and the ground floor of the lovely Oakhurst Manor mansion was in darkness, with lights burning only in the master-bedroom suite on the second floor. The breeze was soft, the scent of flowers was in the air, and until this moment he hadn't realized how much he had missed this place.

"Stay away from me!" a young woman cried, and screamed.

Lance recognized Carrie's voice and reacted instantly. Snatching his rifle, with his quiver of short spears still slung over his shoulder, he leaped to the ground and bolted into the house.

Several servants were huddled together at the foot of the stairs, but they scattered when Lance raced toward them, then mounted the steps three at a time.

The Lion had come home.

Bursting into the master-bedroom suite, he took in the

situation at a glance. Papa and Uncle Scott were trussed and lying on the floor. Jerry stood with a pistol in each hand, enjoying himself hugely as he watched a slimy man advancing toward a terrified Carrie backed into a corner, while yet another man, armed with a knife, also watched.

"Stop!" Lance commanded, his voice sounding like the crack of a whip.

Everyone in the room stared at the intruder, a bearded, tanned giant in buckskins who wore a puma-skin cape over his shoulders.

Jerry, still gaping at him, was the first to recover. "Ah, so you're here, too," he said. "Boys, there's a thousand dollars' reward for his capture, dead or alive. I posted it myself. Get him!"

The man who had been moving toward Carrie halted and drew his knife again. He approached Lance from the right, while his companion inched forward from the left.

"I advise you to drop your arms," Lance told them as he held his ground.

They continued to advance, obviously intending to rush him when they drew still closer.

Lance acted so quickly that neither had a chance to escape. He drew a short spear so quickly that his hand was a blur, and threw it with deadly accuracy. Then he repeated the gesture.

Both of his would-be attackers were crumpled on the floor, writhing in pain. The rattlesnake poison in which the spear tips had been dipped was taking effect, and within moments they would die.

But Lance felt less compassion for them than he did for a reptile, and paying no further attention to the pair, he concentrated on his half brother. "Jerry," he said, "it looks like you've got to answer for a lot of wrongs."

"Not to you!" Jerry's voice soared. "I've waited a long time for this, and I'll get rid of you myself!"

Lance stood still, carefully measuring the distance between them as Jerry raised his pistols.

Carrie had been virtually forgotten, but she had her own score to settle with the man who had caused her so much suffering. She crept toward him, then slashed wildly with the tiny knife she drew from inside her dress.

The blade cut the back of Jerry's right hand, and the pistol he held in it clattered to the floor.

Before he could fire the other pistol, Lance leaped forward and knocked it from his grasp.

Lance kicked both pistols under the four-poster bed. "Carrie," he said, "cut Papa loose. Uncle Scott, too."

She did as she was bidden.

Lance continued to keep a sharp watch on Jerry, who had backed away from him and stood near the windows. "I picked the right time to come home. What's this all about?"

"Jerry was going to kill all of us," Jeremy said. "Your mother and Lisa, too, as soon as he could trick them into coming over here from Trelawney."

Lance's slow smile was cold, menacing.

"He's the one who attacked me," Carrie said. "He blamed you and actually offered the reward for your capture."

"He enslaved Cleo and then hanged her," Scott said.

"And he's stolen so much money from us that our finances are in a shambles." Jeremy found it difficult to speak.

Lance continued to smile. "I reckon this moment has been a long time in coming for both of us, Jerry," he said. "Man to man, with our bare hands."

Jerry looked around the room wildly, and could find no escape. His father and Scott were standing in front of the door, blocking it. They were looking at him with contempt, waiting for him to be beaten senseless by this hulking brute, and so was Carrie.

He shrank from his half brother and stood with his back to the open window.

Lance, the avenger, moved toward him very slowly, still smiling.

Lithe and alert, dangerous beyond measure to an enemy, he reminded Carrie of a mountain lion about to spring.

In sudden unreasoning panic Jerry threw himself backward and toppled out of the window. He screamed, and then the sound stopped abruptly as he struck the ground.

The others hurried to the lawn, and found him there with his head twisted grotesquely. He had broken his neck, dying instantly as he had struck the ground, and his sightless eyes stared vacantly into space.

"The Lord's will was done," Jeremy said softly. "He did so much evil that he wreaked divine vengeance. May the Almighty have mercy on his soul."

For the first time he embraced his younger son.

A few moments later the sheriff and a party of his deputies arrived, summoned by Kai, and were told the full story of what had happened. Papers in the pockets of the pair from Savannah revealed that they had been employees of a gaming house there, an establishment notorious for cheating its customers.

All three bodies were removed, and then the sheriff shook Lance's hand. "The last formal charges against you will be removed from the record first thing in the morning," he said, "and your name will be clear. It's good to have you home, Mr. Beaufort."

The survivors of Jerry's intended murders went to Trelawney, where Kai had a tearful reunion with her son. Then it was Lisa's turn, and after hugging and kissing her, Lance lifted his stepmother high into the air.

Everyone talked at once as they adjourned to the parlor for glasses of sack, and they were so busy bringing one another up-to-date on all that had happened over the years that supper was almost forgotten. Ultimately cold meats, bread, and cheese were served.

Lance had little appetite, and Carrie wasn't hungry, either. In spite of all the excitement, they studiously avoided each other, rarely speaking directly or even exchanging glances. The barriers that had been created between them still stood.

At last Jeremy rose and placed an arm around Lisa's shoulders. "Tomorrow will be a long and busy day," he said, and turned to Lance. "I've lost one son, may God pity him, but I've regained another. Let's go home."

Lance found his own bed too soft and comfortable, and his mind was so active he could not sleep.

Early in the morning, soon after sunrise, Jeremy called a meeting of the entire staff, field hands and house servants alike. Lance, still clad in buckskins, stood beside him.

"There's going to be a new era here," the master of

Oakhurst Manor said. "For those of you who knew me in earlier years, it will be a return to the old ways. I've told the overseers to throw away their whips. Beatings aren't needed here. Work for me and with me, as so many of you did in the past, and I'll share my prosperity with you. You'll have the best food, clothing, and furniture I can get for you. We're going to reopen the schools for your children and the hospital for the sick."

There was a moment of silence, and then the entire staff cheered.

Lance accompanied his father into the house, where Lisa soon joined them at the breakfast table.

"There's so much to do to just start putting my business affairs in shape that I scarcely know where to begin."

"You'll manage," Lisa told him.

He turned to his son. "Lance, did I glean correctly from what you were saying to your mother and Scott last night that you're thinking of going back to the mountains?"

Lance nodded slowly. "The Rockies are in my blood. They offer a constant challenge. Maybe that's why."

"There are other challenges," Lisa said.

Jeremy hesitated. "You're a man now, not a boy, so I hate to bind you to me. But you're my only son now, and I need you. Will you stay here and help me?"

Instead of replying, Lance hurried out of the dining room, returning a few moments later with a large leather pouch. "As I understand it, Papa," he said as he resumed his seat, "you're offering me a junior partnership."

"No, a full partnership. If you'll take it, we'll stand together as equals."

Lance squared his shoulders, and put his life in his beloved Rocky Mountains behind him. Then he grinned. "All right, Papa, we're partners," he said, and extended his hand across the table.

Tears came to Jeremy's eyes as he gripped his son's hand.

Lisa realized that Lance had a surprise in store, but even she was startled when he opened the leather pouch and poured money in gold, silver, and specie onto the table.

"Partners share equally, Papa. I have about ten thousand dollars here that I won't be needing for my legal defense or anything else. We'll put every penny of it into Oakhurst Manor and the shipping company, which should get rid of the most pressing debts and help us get on our feet again."

"I . . . I can't accept this from you, son," Jeremy said.

"We've shaken hands on a partnership," Lance replied in a low, firm voice, "so you have no choice. You said yourself that we'll share as equals."

Lisa told herself she should have known he would do something like this, and going to him, she kissed him.

Jeremy was so overwhelmed that he was speechless.

"I reckon we have enough to do that we shouldn't waste time sitting around being sentimental," Lance said.

"You're right." Jeremy became brisk. "We'll both concentrate on the plantation for a few days, and then we'll see what we can do about reorganizing the shipping company. With these funds to pay our debts, I'm sure we can float a bank loan to buy a new flagship."

"You might want to think about moving into Mississippi River barges, too, Papa. There's a lot of money to be made in the fur trade and carrying the produce of the West to New Orleans."

Jeremy looked at him in admiration.

"There's no rush about this, of course. We can look into it in the weeks ahead as we decide how to distribute our weight."

"I thank the Almighty for my partner," Jeremy said to Lisa. Then, afraid he would be overcome by emotion again, he came brusque. "Boy, let's go to work!"

Both men stood, and Lance smiled. "I won't make a habit of this, naturally, but your new partner would like to attend to a personal errand before he buckles down."

"Oh?"

"I want to attend to some unfinished business." Lance tried to sound casual. "So I thought I'd ride over to Trelawney for a short visit."

A delighted Lisa laughed aloud.

"While I'm about it, of course, I'll tell my mother I'm going to stay here, which should please her very much."

"I hope she won't be the only one," Lisa said pointedly.

Lance left quickly so they wouldn't see that he was embarrassed. He went to the stable, where he saddled Bantu himself, and then, telling himself the stallion needed exercise, he galloped to Trelawney.

Kai and Scott were just finishing breakfast as he arrived, and insisted he join them for coffee.

He told them about his new arrangement with his father, deliberately refraining from mentioning that he had given Jeremy all of his own savings, and they were elated.

"There's a real place for you here," Scott said.

"A man does what's needed," Lance replied, and took a deep breath before he blurted, "Where's Carrie?"

"She hasn't come down yet," Kai said.

"I'd like a word with her."

His mother summoned a serving maid. "Tell Miss Carrie that Mr. Lance is here and wants to see her."

Much to the amusement of his mother and stepfather, Lance betrayed his nervousness by spilling his coffee.

Again they discussed all that had happened, including the events of the previous evening, until Scott announced that he had to leave for his Charleston office.

When Kai was alone with her son she said, "I don't know what's taking Carrie so long."

Lance shrugged.

"Are you going to be satisfied with life at Oakhurst Manor and in Charleston after your adventures in the mountains?" she wanted to know.

"I hope so, Mama," he said, choosing his words with care. "Papa really needs my help after the nasty mess that Jerry left. So I've got to stay. I couldn't live with myself if I deserted him."

"I realize that, and I admire you for your loyalty. But you haven't answered my question."

"I can't answer it yet, Mama. The answer . . . doesn't depend on me."

Before Kai could reply, the serving maid came to the door. "Miss Carrie says to tell you she's in the solarium, Mr. Lance."

Kai smiled at her son in an attempt to encourage him.

Lance walked stiff-legged to the solarium at the rear of the big house, wondering why his stomach was leaping. He would rather grapple another grizzly, he told himself, than face the scene ahead. He walked into the solarium, where potted plants and flowers were blooming everywhere, and stopped short.

Carrie stood at the far side of the long room, awaiting him, and her appearance was startling. She was clad in a snug-fitting dressing gown of black satin, the skirt cut high on one thigh, the neckline slashed almost to her waist. She was wearing heavy makeup, too, with a beauty patch on one cheek and another emphasizing the deep cleavage between her breasts.

Lance realized she had gone to considerable effort in a deliberate attempt to shock him, but he couldn't understand her reason.

"Good morning, Lion," she said.

"Lance to you," he replied, matching her cool tone.

"You're still in buckskins, so I suppose it's natural that I think of you in Western terms."

"Well, I won't be wearing them much longer. Only until I have some new clothes made. I'm staying home." He told her, briefly, that he intended to help restore the prosperity of Oakhurst Manor and the Beaufort shipping interests.

"I'm sure Papa Beaufort is pleased and that your mother is ecstatic," she said. "It's almost as though you'd never gone away, even though it may take a long time to undo the damage that Jerry created."

There would never be compensation for the years he had been separated from her, he thought, but she was being so remote at this moment that, rather than express himself freely, he merely nodded.

"Melanie will be happy, too. She'll enjoy Oakhurst Manor far more than mountain life."

"I've seen the last of Melanie," Lance said curtly. "I dropped her off in Virginia on my way home, and I said a final good-bye to her."

"You're an optimist." Carrie's laugh was brittle.

"I've seen to it that she has no financial worries, so she has no hold on me."

She raised a painted eyebrow. "I find it difficult to believe that she would voluntarily part company with you."

He had no desire to discuss Melanie, who was gone from his life. "What are your plans?"

"At the moment I have none."

"I've been wondering whether you've come back to Trelawney to stay," Lance said.

Carrie's smile was deliberately vague. "Oh, no. I've just come home for a visit."

"I see." He steeled himself. "You intend to rejoin Bateaux Gautier."

"No, I broke up with him when I left him in New York some weeks ago. He'll always be my friend, but he'll never again be more than that."

"This may be none of my business, but is there a new man in your life?"

"Not at present," Carrie replied, her manner indicating that it might not be long before she found a new protector.

He hesitated for a moment. "Where do you reckon you'll be going when you leave?"

"I haven't decided." She shrugged delicately. "Someplace where there's excitement and men are wealthy."

Somewhat to his own surprise, a low growl rose from deep within Lance. "To hell with that," he said as he started down the long room toward her. "You and I have wasted enough time. You're going to marry me."

Carrie let him draw closer before she raised a hand. "Stop right there!"

He halted reluctantly.

"Look at me," she said.

"That's precisely what I've been doing since I came into the solarium."

"I mean really look! No lady ever dresses this way. Certainly you realize that many men have seen me like this."

Lance began to lose patience. "What of it? The past doesn't matter. All I care about is our future. Together."

"We have none," Carrie said. "I'm a harlot."

"What you've done in the past has nothing to do with you and me," he said, his voice growing louder.

He was so persistent she almost weakened, but she managed to hold her ground. "What you don't understand is that I'm for hire," she said, her voice almost breaking.

"Very well." Lance became brutal. "Then I'm hiring you."

She was so startled she didn't know what to reply.

"I'm engaging your services on an exclusive basis," Lance said. "By the day, the week, the month, and the year. For as long as we live. And to make certain the contract is binding, you're going to church with me and become my wife. That's final."

Giving her no chance to protest, he stepped forward and kissed her.

Carrie melted in his arms.

"You know I love you," Lance said, still holding her.

All at once the tears came. "It's because I love you, too, that I tried to put you off. I don't want you to be burdened with a trollop."

"You're my woman," Lance told her, "and you're going to become my wife."

Carrie's tears badly smudged her makeup, but as he kissed her again, neither of them cared.

The Beaufort and Emerson families rejoiced when they learned that Carrie and Lance, putting the past behind them, intended to be married. Kai and Lisa wanted to invite all of their friends and neighbors to the wedding, but were forced to defer to Carrie's wishes.

"We've been in the limelight enough, and there's been too much talk about us as it is," she said. "I want the smallest possible wedding, and so does Lance. All that matters is that we'll be husband and wife. We aren't even going anywhere on a honeymoon. Both of us are too happy to be home, and he has so much work to do he can't possibly take the time to make a trip anywhere."

They spoke to the clergyman, and plans were made for the ceremony to be performed the following week.

In the meantime Lance plunged furiously into the task of helping his father restore Oakhurst Manor to a sound basis and reorganize the shipping company. He worked for several days at the plantation, then went into Charleston for a hectic forty-eight hours.

It was late at night when he returned to the country, too late for him to stop off at Trelawney to see Carrie. Instead he would join her for breakfast the next morning, he promised himself, and rode straight to Oakhurst Manor.

Jeremy and Lisa were about to retire when he arrived,

but stayed awake long enough for Lance to give his father a report on business developments in the city.

As he was about to go to his own room Lisa said, "I almost forgot. A letter came for you today. I left it for you on your dresser."

Lance made a detour to the kitchen for a roast-beef sandwich and a glass of milk, which he took upstairs with him.

He picked up the letter and looked at it curiously. It was addressed to him in an unfamiliar feminine hand, and the paper was perfumed. He broke the seal, opened the letter, and was so stunned he had to read it twice before the room stopped spinning and it made sense to him:

> My darling Lance,
> I've just learned that I'm carrying a baby. *Your* baby.
> I know you'll be as overjoyed as I am.
> I'm coming to Oakhurst Manor to join you, and by the time you receive this note, I'll be on my way.
>
> Your very own
> Melanie

Lance realized he had underestimated Melanie's cleverness and determination. She had placed him in an untenable position, and he had no idea how to handle the situation.

All he knew was that, regardless of the consequences, he had to show the letter to Carrie in the morning.

His dilemma was as unbearable as it was cruel. He and Carrie had gone through hell for years before being reunited, but now their entire future was being placed in jeopardy by an unscrupulous girl who was determined to have him for her own.

How would Carrie react when she saw the letter? Would she dismiss him permanently from her life, as she had every right to do?

And just how legitimate was Melanie's claim? He didn't want to do her an injustice, but he'd be merciless if she was just trying to trick him into marrying her.

His head spinning, Lance realized only that Carrie's happiness and his own were hanging in the balance. He himself was powerless, and the women in his life would determine the future.

SIGNET Books You'll Enjoy